DATE DUE			

Miss Leonora

AND FIFTEEN OTHER STORIES BY

NEW YORK

When Last Seen

PETER TAYLOR

IVAN OBOLENSKY, INC.

EDITOR'S NOTE

Since Peter Taylor's earlier volumes of short stories, THE WIDOWS OF THORNTON and A LONG FOURTH, have long been out of print, the editors felt that his best early stories should be republished in a collection which would include the new stories that had as yet never been anthologized. Thus we now make available a comprehensive volume demonstrating Peter Taylor's virtuosity as a writer. The short story form is perhaps the most demanding upon the writer and, in the countless reviews and comments that Mr. Taylor has had throughout his career, he has been declared one of the masters.

All of the stories in MISS LEONORA WHEN LAST SEEN AND 15 OTHER STORIES have appeared in magazines. Of the six stories in the volume that have hitherto been uncollected, RESERVATIONS, MISS LEONORA WHEN LAST SEEN, A STRANGE STORY and TWO PILGRIMS all appeared in *The New Yorker*. AN OVERWHELMING QUESTION appeared in *Encounter*. IN THE DRUGSTORE appeared in *The Sewanee Review*.

Table of Contents

———◦•◦———

MISS LEONORA WHEN LAST SEEN

and fifteen other stories

Reservations

A Love Story

———

It was arranged, of all things, that the bride and groom should make their escape from the country club through the little boys' locker room! But this was very reasonable, really. At nine o'clock on a night in January, the exit from the little boys' locker room to the swimming-pool terrace was the exit least likely to be congested. It was the exit also most likely to be overlooked by mischievous members of the wedding party. Every precaution had to be taken! No one was to be trusted!

In the lounge of the women's locker room, the bride got out of her gown in exactly thirty seconds. (She had taken an hour, more or less, to get into it.) She pushed the wedding dress into the hands of one of the club's maids and from the hands of another accepted the tweed travelling suit—puce-brown tweed trimmed with black velvet. Because it was imperative that no suspicion of her departure be roused among the guests, the bride was not attended by her mother or by her maid of honor. Her mother and all the bridal attendants remained upstairs at the party, where there was dancing, and where waiters moved about balancing trays of stemmed glasses. At two minutes to nine, the bride ran on tiptoe along a service passageway that connected most of the rooms on the ground floor. She was accompanied now by the elder of the two maids who had assisted in the change from white satin to tweed. This woman was one of the club's veteran maids, a large, rather middle-aged person who, though she dyed her hair a lemon yellow and rouged her cheeks excessively, was known for her stalwart character and her incorruptibility. In the passageway, the bride chattered nervously to this companion who had been assigned to her. She told how she had written her name in the club's bride's book as "Franny Crowell," having forgotten momentarily that she was now Mrs. Miles Miller. The maid was not a very responsive sort, and said nothing. But this didn't bother Franny; she went on to say, sometimes laughing while she spoke, that somehow she could not shake off the feeling that it was a pity and a shame to be slipping away from a party given in your own honor.

In one hand the maid held the key to a door down the passageway that would let the bride into the little boys' locker room. In the other hand she carried a pair of fur-trimmed galoshes. As they approached the locked door, the maid interrupted Franny's chatter.

"Your father said tell you your fur coat's in the car, with your corsage pinned to it. He said be careful you don't sit on it." Simultaneously the maid held out the galoshes, giving them a little shake that indicated Franny should take them.

"What are those?" Franny chirped. "They're not mine."

"No, they're not yours, Mrs. Miller," said the maid, still pressing them on her.

"Well, I don't believe I'll want them," Franny said politely.

"Yes, your mother said so. It's snowing outside now—a nasty, wet snow, Mrs. Miller."

"But they're not mine, and they're not Mother's either. . . ."

How long has it been snowing?" She hoped to change the subject.

"Two hours off and on, Mrs. Miller. Ever since you got here
from the church. It's not sticking, but there'll be slush under-
foot."

"Well, whose are they?"

"Your mother snitched them from one of the guests—out of
the cloakroom. She told me, 'Something borrowed.' "

Franny burst into laughter and took the galoshes. But she
resolved not to put on the ugly things until after Miles had
seen her and got the effect of her outfit.

While the maid fitted the key into the lock, Franny stood
with her eyes lifted to the low basement ceiling. She heard the
sound of the dancing overhead, and she speculated about
which of the dancers upstairs these boots might belong to and
thought of the pleasure it was sure to give some childhood
friend of hers, or possibly some aunt or some woman friend of
her parents, to learn that *she* had provided the bride with the
one item that had been overlooked—the something borrowed.

Presently the door before her stood open. But Franny's
eyes and thoughts were still directed toward the ceiling.
"There you are," said the maid, obviously provoked by the
bride's inattention.

Franny lowered her eyes. She looked at the woman beside
her with a startled expression. Then she glanced briefly into
the shadows of the unlighted locker room. And in the next
moment she was clutching frantically at the starched sleeve of
the maid's uniform. "But he is not here!" she exclaimed. Her
tone was accusing; she eyed the maid suspiciously. Then, as if
on further reflection, she spoke in a bewailing whisper: "He
isn't hee-er!" According to the plan, he was to have been admitted to the little boys' locker room through a door from the
adjoining men's locker room. But had he ever intended to be
there? *He was gone! Of course he was! How else would it be?*
Already Franny was thinking of what kind of poison she

would administer to herself, of how she would manage to obtain the poison, of how she would look when they found her.

"What do you mean 'not here'?" said the maid, jerking her sleeve free.

Franny smiled coolly. She knew how she must carry it off. "Maybe I'll stay on for the party, after all," she said.

"What do you mean 'not here'?" the maid repeated. "He's standing there before your eyes."

Franny looked again, and of course there her bridegroom stood. "I didn't see him, it's so dark," she stammered.

But, instead of going to the bridegroom, suddenly the bride threw her arms about the woman with the lemon-yellow hair who had delivered her to him. This trustworthy woman had been known to Franny during most of her young life, but she was by no means a favorite of Franny's. And almost certainly Franny had never been a favorite of the woman's, either. . . . But still it seemed the thing to do. Somehow it was like embracing the whole wedding party or even the whole club membership, or possibly just simply her own mother. And, no doubt, in that moment this woman forgave Franny many an old score—forgave a little girl's criticism of sandwiches served toasted when they had been ordered untoasted, complaints about a bathing suit's not having been hung out to dry, and many another complaint besides. At any rate, the woman responded and returned the warm embrace. Then for an instant the two of them smiled at each other through the general mist of tears.

"Goodbye, little Miss 'Franny Crowell,' " the woman said.

"Goodbye, Bernice," said Franny, "and thanks for everything." Yes, the woman's name was Bernice. What a bother it had always been, trying to remember it, but now it had come out without Franny's having to try to think of it even.

Bernice took several steps backward, as if quitting a royal presence. At a respectful distance she turned her back, and in her white gum-soled shoes she retreated silently down the long service passageway.

While waiting for the bride to come through the doorway to him, the bridegroom had literally stood dangling his little narrow-brimmed hat, shifting it from one hand to the other. He did not know what to make of that blank look she had given him at first, didn't know what to make of her saying "He is not here," didn't know what to make of her throwing herself into the arms of the hired help instead of into his own. . . . The embrace perhaps he understood better than the look. But anyway, she had come to him at last, which was what he wanted most in the world at the moment. Presently he had seated her on one of the rough wooden benches in the locker room and, on his knees before her, he was struggling to push her feet into the borrowed galoshes. Franny had held on to the galoshes through both her embraces, and as soon as she had handed them to Miles and was seated on the bench, she began to chatter again—about the galoshes now, about how her mother had positively stolen "the ugly things" from somebody upstairs.

It wasn't easy getting the galoshes on.-They were a near-perfect fit, but Franny seemed incapable of being any help. Her little ankles had gone limp, like an absent-minded child's. But finally Miles managed to force both galoshes on. He zipped them up neatly, and then lifted his face to Franny and smiled. Franny extended one of her tiny gloved hands to him, as if she were going to pull him to his feet. Miles seized it, but he remained on one knee before her, pressing the hand firmly between the two of his. While he knelt there, Franny made a vague gesture with her free hand, a gesture that indicated the whole of the dark locker room. "I've never been in here before, Miles," she said.

"Neither have I, you know," Miles said playfully.

"Oh," Franny breathed, thoughtfully. "No, you probably haven't, have you."

Now she felt she understood. . . . *That* was why she had not been able to see him there at first. She had never *imagined* him there. It was because Miles Miller was not one of the local boys she had grown up with, wasn't one of that familiar group from whose number she had always assumed she would someday accept a husband. He was better than any of *those,* of course; he was her own, beloved, blue-eyed, black-haired, fascinating Miles Miller, whom she had recognized the first moment she ever saw him as the best-looking man she had ever laid eyes on (or ever would), as the man she must have for *hers*—and the very same Miles, of course, that at least half a dozen other girls of her year had thought they must have for *theirs.* Moreover, he was the young man who doesn't turn up in *every*body's year: the young bachelor from out of town, brought in from a distant region by one of the big corporations to fill a place in its local office, a young man without any local history of teen-age romances to annoy and perhaps worry the bride. And in Miles' case the circumstances were enhanced still further. He was an only child, and his parents had died while he was still in college. For his bride there would be no parents or brothers and sisters to be visited and adjusted to, and, since he had lived always on the West Coast and gone to Stanford, no prep-school friends, not even—at such a distance—a college room-mate to be won over. Once they were married, Franny's family would be *their* family, her friends *their* friends. Besides all this, her Miles was at once the most modest and most self-assured human being imaginable. With one gentle look— gentle and yet reasonable and terribly penetrating—he could make her aware of the utter absurdity of something she said or did, and make her simultaneously aware of how little such absurdities mattered to someone who loved you.

Franny bent forward and kissed her husband gently on his smiling lips. He came up beside her on the bench, no longer smiling, and took Franny in his arms. For Franny it was as it had always been before—every time he had ever held her in his tender, confident way. It was as though she possessed at last, or was about to possess at last, what she had always wanted above everything else and had never dreamed she wanted—or, that is, never dreamed she wanted in quite the same way she wanted everything else. That was what seemed so incredible to her about it: *This* desire and *this* happiness differed only in degree from the other longings and other satisfactions one experienced. There was nothing at all unreal about it. And somehow the most miraculous part was that the man she was going to marry was not he man she had ever imagined herself marrying. On the contrary, he was the frightening stranger of her girlish daydreams—the dark, handsome man she was always going to meet on a train coming home from boarding school at Christmas or during the summer at Lake Michigan. In her daydreams she sometimes even bore that man a child, but there had always had to be a barrier to their marrying. The man was already married (perhaps to an invalid!), or he was a Jew, he was a Catholic—a French Canadian—or he was the foreign agent of a country committed to the destruction of her own country, or (when she was still younger) there was insanity or even a strain of Negro blood in his family! Yet the stranger had turned up after all—after she had almost forgotten him—and there was no barrier.

Still holding Franny close to him, Miles got to his feet and for a moment lifted his bride completely off the floor. "Franny, oh, 'little Miss Franny,' let's go!" he said. Franny laughed aloud. And to Miles she sounded for all the world like a delighted little girl of four or five. "Let's be on our way," he said, still holding her there. "Let's get out of here."

"Carry me to the car, Miles," she whispered.

"I will," he said. "You bet I will. Not this way, though. I'll set you down and get a good hold and then we'll dash."

But just as Franny's feet touched the floor, there came a great rattling sound from over toward the door to the terrace. Franny gave a little shriek that came out almost "Aha!" And then, in a quiet voice, in a tone of utter resignation, she said, "They've found us." She meant, of course, that the mischief-makers had found them. "We'll *never* get away."

"No, they haven't, darling," Miles said impatiently.

Franny turned away from him. At the far end of the room she saw a man's figure silhouetted against the glass door to the terrace. She realized at once that the man must be one of the club's waiters. It was he, she surmised, who had let Miles in from the men's locker room. He had been present all the while, and actually he was now holding the terrace door a little way open. The rattling noise had, plainly, come from the long Venetian blind on that door. But the source of the rattling no longer interested Franny; she was too angry with Miles for not having told her they weren't alone.

Suddenly her impulse was to turn back and deliver Miles a slap across the face. His inference that the waiter's presence hadn't mattered was insulting both to herself and to this man who had so faithfully performed the duties assigned him. But before she could turn or speak, Miles had seized her by the hand and the waiter had thrown open the door. Hand in hand, the bride and groom ran the length of the little boys' locker room. In the excitement of the moment, Miles had forgotten that he was going to carry Franny to the car. It was well for him that he had. Franny consented to let him hold her hand only in order to keep from embarrassing the waiter. Halfway to the door she made out just which of the club's waiters he was, and she could easily have called him by name. But instead she dropped her eyes, and she kept them lowered even when Miles paused in the doorway to slip a bill into the hand at the end of the white sleeve. In her pique with Miles, she wondered if the bill was of as large a denomination as it ought to be.

Outside, they ran along the edge of the gaping swimming pool and on in the direction of the tennis courts. Beyond the courts, Miles' new car was hidden. The wet snow was falling heavily, and it was beginning to stick now. It seemed to Franny that the snow might fill the empty swimming pool before the night was over. They went through the gate into the area of the tennis courts. From there Franny glanced back once at the lighted windows of the low, sprawling clubhouse. Through the snow it seemed miles away. They ran across the courts and through the white shrubbery. Neither of them spoke until they were in the car. By then their rendezvous in the locker room seemed like something that happened too long ago to mention. As Miles was helping her into her coat, and she was carefully protecting the big white orchid that she knew her father had pinned on the coat with his own hands, Franny said, "What are we going to do, Miles? I'm terrified. I hate snow. We can't get even as far as Bardstown tonight."

"Of course we can't, honey," he said. He had switched on the car lights and was starting the motor. "We'll have to stay here in town tonight. I telephoned the hotel a while ago. We'll have to stay there."

They had planned to spend the first night at Bardstown, which in good weather was only a few hours away, down in Kentucky, and where there was an attractive old inn. They had planned to make it to Natchez by the second night, and to be at the Gulf Coast by the third. Franny's father had urged them to fly down, or to take a train. But they were able to think only of what fun it would be to have their own car once they got to Biloxi. It had been silly of them, they acknowledged now, driving into town through the snow, but they did have the satisfaction of knowing that all planes would be grounded on such a night, anyway. And to both of them the idea of spending their wedding night in a Pullman berth seemed grotesque.

It took Miles three-quarters of an hour to get them through the snow and the traffic to the downtown hotel where he had managed to make reservations. Along the way, he apologized to Franny for putting them up at this particular hotel—the hotel, that is, where he had himself been living during the past year and a half. "As luck would have it," he explained, "there are two big conventions in town this week. I was lucky to find a room anywhere at all. I hope you don't mind too much."

"Why in the world should I mind?" Franny laughed. "We're a bona-fide married couple now."

Yet the moment she had passed through the revolving door into the marble-pillared lobby of the hotel, Franny rested a gloved hand on the sleeve of Miles' overcoat and said, "I *do* feel a little funny about it, after all."

"I was afraid you might feel funny about it," Miles said. They stood there a moment waiting for the boy with their luggage to follow them through the revolving door, and Miles began to apologize all over again. "The other hotels were all full up," he said. "It's only because I happen to hit it off so well with Bill Carlisle that I was able to get a room here. It wasn't easy for him even; he's just the assistant manager. Your father, or almost any of the guys in the wedding, might have found us something better. But it seemed worse, somehow, to have any of them—even your father—know exactly where we're spending the night, since we can't get out of town. I guessed you would feel the same way about it."

But Franny was not listening to Miles. She had become aware that she was the only woman in the lobby, and the mention of the assistant manager's name had further distracted her. Bill Carlisle had been invited to the wedding—she recalled addressing his invitation—but he had not been invited to the reception and supper dance. As for her own acquaintance with him, it was very slight. She had known him for a long time, however, and she knew that he knew just about everyone that she did. She interrupted Miles' apologies to say, "Do we have to see Bill Collier?"

"Who?" asked Miles.

"You know—the assistant manager."

"Of course we don't, darling," he said. "We don't even have to register. That's all set."

The boy with their luggage had joined them now. Another boy had appeared with their key and was beckoning them to follow him to the elevator. As they crossed the lobby, Franny began laughing to herself. Miles noticed, and asked what was funny.

"I was wondering," she said, "do you think he'll have put us in your room?"

"Will who have?"

"You know, your friend Bill—the assistant manager."

"At least it won't be that," said Miles. "There was someone waiting to take it over when I got the last of my possessions out this morning."

"What a shame," Franny whispered. "It would have been kind of interesting, and no one but Bill Cook need ever have known."

"Bill Carlisle's his name," Miles said rather petulantly. Then he added, "He's a pretty nice fellow, in case you don't know."

"Certainly he is," Franny said with a wink. "I've known him for years."

Franny stepped into the elevator, followed by Miles. Then the boy with the luggage got in, then the one with the key. Franny observed that both the boys were mature men, and the key boy was even bald-headed. They kept their heads bowed, very courteously, not even looking up when presently they had occasion to speak to each other.

"Where's Jack?" the luggage boy asked quietly.

"He's coming," said the key boy.

"Who's Jack?" Franny asked Miles.

Thinking the question directed to him, the luggage boy replied, "He's the elevator boy." As he spoke, he glanced up at Franny. Probably he thought it was demanded of him. Unlike the key boy, he had a heavy head of hair, as dark and thick as Miles' own, and the face he lifted was youthful, almost handsome even, with a broad jaw and black, rather cruel eyes that seemed brimming with energy. As soon as he looked up he realized his mistake and bent his head again. But he had reminded Franny of someone—someone she didn't like. Or *did* like. Which was it? She couldn't think who it was, and felt vaguely that she didn't want to. And what would Jack, the elevator operator, be like, she wondered, when he turned up? Somehow she was sure he would be a redhead. Presently he would come running; he would hop into the elevator, close the door, push the button, and there she would be, locked in the elevator with Miles and with the three men in their dark-green livery and with the heap of luggage, and the elevator would shoot them up to their floor and stop with a sickening little bounce. She wished Miles would *say* something!

"Jack seems to have gotten lost," Miles said. Franny burst out laughing.

Immediately, Jack appeared, as if from nowhere. He was a Negro boy, but with light skin and a reddish tint to his hair.

Franny was conscious of Jack's arrival, and conscious of the color of his hair, but at the same time her real attention had been caught by a figure out in the lobby. It was the figure of a woman, and she was moving swiftly across the lobby toward this elevator, making her way between the heavier figures of the conventioners in their tweed overcoats and gray fedoras. (Most of them, it seemed to Franny, were smoking cigars, the way conventioners were supposed to.) The woman was wearing a navy-blue topcoat and hat, and carried an oversize handbag. "Wait!" Franny said to the elevator boy.

"What do you mean, 'Wait'?" Miles asked.

"Don't you see who that is trying to catch us?" Franny said, rising on her toes.

"I see who it is, but you don't know her, and I can promise you I don't either."

One of the hotel boys snorted, but he cut it off so short Franny couldn't tell for sure which of them it was. She suspected the bald-headed one.

"It's Bernice! The maid from the club!" Franny tried to recall whether she had forgotten anything essential. No, the woman must have an urgent message for her. Her father or her mother had been taken ill, or there had been some disaster at the club—a fire perhaps. She remembered distinctly having left a cigarette burning in the women's lounge.

"It's no such thing," Miles was saying. "Let's go, Jack!"

The woman was close enough now for Franny to see it was not Bernice. The long stride and the yellow hair sticking out from under the hat had deceived her. But she should have known, shouldn't she, that Bernice could not have worn such heels.

The elevator door was closing right in the woman's face, and even if the woman wasn't Bernice, this was more than Franny could bear. "Stop it!" she commanded, utterly outraged by the ungallant behavior of these men. "There's room for another person, easily!"

The boys looked at Miles. "Let the lady in," Miles thundered.

Jack slid the door open. But the woman hesitated. With a swift glance she seemed to have taken in every aspect of the situation—that it was a bride and groom she was intruding upon, that the bride had insisted upon holding the car for her, that the groom had protested. She now signalled Jack to go on without her, but with Miles' thundering command still in his ears Jack made no move to do so. Miles kept silent. And so did Franny, who in a last-minute glance as swift as the woman's had taken in *her* total situation—that she was a middle-aged prostitute late for an engagement. There was but one solution to the awful silence and to the irresolution of the elevator boy. The woman stepped into the elevator and abruptly turned her back to the other passengers.

As the car shot upward, Jack asked with easy nonchalance, "Your floor, please?"

Again there was silence. Finally Miles said, "What's our floor?"

The key boy looked up, showing his full face for the first time—eyes set close together, a small, puffy nose, ears flat against the bald head. Franny thought it the stupidest, most brutal face she had ever set eyes on. "*Your* floor is eight, Mr. Miller," he said, barely opening his swollen lips when he spoke.

After a moment Jack repeated, "Your floor, please?"

The woman now turned her face toward the elevator boy so that Franny saw her profile. Her face was plain—neither homely nor otherwise, really—and seemed devoid of expression. Only the fact that she had turned her face toward him showed that she knew the boy expected an answer from her. It occurred to Franny that in her agitation this poor creature had forgotten what floor she was going to. At last, and as if with great effort, she did speak. "Seven for me," she said.

With a long, bony forefinger Jack stabbed the seventh-floor button. The elevator stopped almost at once, and the door slid open. The woman stepped out into the hallway, where there was a broad mirror facing her between two metal cigarette urns. Instead of turning to left or right she stopped here just outside the elevator, and for one instant her pale eyes met Franny's in the glass. Then the door closed quietly between them.

Franny had not been aware of a bouncing sensation when the elevator stopped at that floor. But when it stopped at the floor above, the sensation so upset her equilibrium that she felt positively faint. Her two feet in their fur-trimmed galoshes seemed chilled to numbness. She felt that if she tried to take one step down the hallway in the direction of the bridal chamber her knees might buckle underneath her. She wondered how she would ever manage it.

To Miles Miller, his bride had seemed not herself at all, from the time they met in the shadows of the locker room at the country club until at last they were alone in the hotel room.

But her confusion and nervousness were very understandable, he reasoned, in view of the upsetting change in their plans. And once they were alone in the room, she was indeed very much herself again. She was once again the vivacious, unaffected, ingenuous little being he had decided to marry after talking to her for five minutes during an intermission at a big début party last year. From the beginning, Miles had felt that he appreciated her special brand of innocence and even artlessness as no one else ever before had. One thing he had determined when he left college and entered upon his career in business was that he would not be the sort—the type —to marry the boss's daughter and further his career that way. He detested that type. He extended this pledge to himself even to include the daughters of prominent and influential men who might indirectly help him in his career. He extended it even to cover all the débutantes he had ever met or would ever meet. He had had no definite ideas about where he *would* find his wife, except one idea that was so childish he laughed at it himself: He had thought of meeting a perfectly unspoiled girl while vacationing in an unspoiled countryside—perhaps in the highland South, perhaps even somewhere in Europe. He had thought particularly of Switzerland. But when thinking more realistically Miles told himself simply that he would not marry for the sake of his business or social advancement. His marriage and his family life must be something altogether apart from his career.

And then, in his twenty-sixth year, he had met Franny Crowell and had had a wonderful insight. Franny was, in a most important sense, as beautifully innocent and provincial as any little mountain girl might have been. She delighted in her surroundings, accepted her relation to them without question, and would be content to remain where she was and as she was for the rest of her life. She had been practically nowhere away from home. For two years she went to boarding school in Virginia but hated dormitory life and thought it silly of girls to go East to college when they could be so much more comfortable staying at home. She had herself attended the local city university for two years and had relished meeting different kinds of people from her own home town. True, she had spent most of her summers at a resort on Lake Michigan, but even there most of her companions had been the same people she went to school with at home during the winter. Miles Miller recognized in Franny Crowell the flaxen-haired mountain girl of his childish imaginings. Her outward appearance might deceive the world but never him. She arranged her golden-brown hair always in the very latest, most sophisticated fashions. Last summer she had even let the beauty parlor put a blond streak in her hair. She plucked her eye brows, even pencilled them. The shade of her lipstick paled or darkened according to whatever was newest. But Miles perceived that all of this was as innocent and natural in his Franny as plaiting flaxen pigtails might have been.

Miles and Franny had agreed in advance that they should each have only one glass of champagne at the club on their wedding night. But among the bags that they had had brought into the hotel was Miles' genuine Gucci liquor case—a present from the men at his office. Packed with ice in the plastic compartment of the elaborate leather case were two bottles of champagne of a somewhat earlier and better year than that offered the guests by the bride's father. And into Franny's makeup bag she had managed to fit two of their very own champagne glasses. Together they had thought of everything.

In their hotel room, they spent the first half hour making toasts. They drank to Betty Manville's début ball, where they had met, drank to their first date, to their first kiss, to the night he first proposed, to the night she accepted, to the night of the announcement party. Each toast had to be followed by a kiss. Each kiss inspired and motivated another reminiscence. Finally they turned to toasting people whom they associated with events of their courtship. Since Franny was a talented and tireless mimic, Miles encouraged her to "do" each of these people. She "did" Betty Manville's mother, her own father, and then one of her bridesmaids, who had once upon a time imagined *she* was going to have Miles Miller for herself. This last was the funniest of all to Miles. He was seated on the side of the bed, leaning on one elbow, and when he had witnessed Franny's version of that poor, misguided girl he set his champagne glass on the floor and fell back on the bed in a spasm of laughter. He threshed about, still laughing aloud, and all the while wiping tears from his eyes and begging Franny to stop.

When Franny promised to stop, Miles got control of himself and sat up in the center of the bed. Wiping his eyes with his handkerchief, he looked up again and found Franny sitting on the side of the bed with her thumb pressed against her nose so hard that her little nose was flattened on her face. Her eyes were squinted up and her mouth, which was normally small and tight, was stretched and spread into a wide ribbon across her face. "You know who this is?" she asked, barely moving her lips.

"I'm glad to say I don't," Miles said, as if offended by her ugliness.

"Oh, you do," Franny insisted.

"I don't, and it's not very attractive."

"Of course it's not attractive," said Franny, keeping the thumb pressed against her nose. "It's that bald-headed bellboy, the one with the key."

"What's wrong with him?" Miles said, swinging his feet around to the other side of the bed and thus momentarily turning his back to Franny.

"You don't have to turn your back," Franny said. "See, it's still only me."

Miles looked around and smiled apologetically. Franny's face was her own again, and she was looking down at her hands very seriously. "Weren't all three of those bellboys grotesque?" she said.

"I don't think so," Miles said. "They're perfectly normal-looking human beings. I see them every day."

"Normal-looking!" Franny exclaimed, lifting her eyes to his. "How can you say so? The bald-headed one was really monstrous. And the one with the mop of hair had a really mad look in his eyes. And that pale Negro boy with the kinky red hair! How blind you are to people, Miles. You don't really *see* them."

"Maybe not," said Miles, meaning to dismiss the subject, since Franny seemed so emotional about it. Turning now, he let himself fall across the bed toward her, and again he took one of her hands between the two of his. But before he could speak the endearment he intended, something else occurred to him that he felt must be said first. It was in defense of his vision, or—he couldn't define it—in defense of something even more specially his own that had been disparaged. "Anyway," he said, "you must admit that not one of those bellhops was half as weird-looking as that painted-up creature you had your hug fest with when we were leaving the club. After the elevator ride, I don't have to tell you what *she* looked like." Though they had been in the room for more than half an hour, this was the first reference either of them had made to the woman in the elevator.

Franny withdrew her hand and stood up.

Miles said, "We're not going to quarrel about something so silly on our wedding night, are we?"

Franny was silent for a moment. Her eyes moved about the room as if taking it in for the first time. Then she bent over and kissed Miles on the top of his head. "We aren't *ever* going to quarrel again, are we, Miles?"

"Never," he said. He reached out a hand, but she pulled away. "Come back," he said in a whisper.

"Not until I've slipped into something more—more right." She smiled vaguely.

Miles lay with his head propped on one hand and watched her go to her little overnight bag and take out the folds of lace and peach silk that were her negligee and gown. Suddenly he leaped from the bed with outstretched arms. But the bride dashed through the open doorway to the bathroom and closed the door.

Miles had long since changed into his blue silk pajamas with the white monogram on the pocket when he saw the first turning and twisting of the doorknob. When Franny failed to appear at once—that is, when the knob ceased its twisting and the bathroom door didn't open—his vexation showed itself momentarily in one little horizontal crease in his smooth forehead. But the moment was so brief that even his eyes didn't reflect it, and soon a sly little smile came to his lips. . . . He would give her a signal that all was ready and waiting, and at the same time give her motivation and courage. Stepping over to the dresser he uncorked the second bottle of champagne. He managed it very expertly, taking satisfaction in his expertness. The pop was loud enough for Franny to hear and comprehend, yet there was not one bubble of wasteful overflow. The tiny golden bubbles came just to the mouth of the champagne bottle and no further. Miles had not even taken the precaution of having the two glasses handy. He was expert and he was confident of his expertness.

He watched the first bubbles appear and then shot a glance across the room at the doorknob. It was turning again. He stepped over to where the two glasses were, on the bedside table, filled them, and then returned the bottle to its ice. Still no Franny. But the doorknob was now turning back and forth rather rapidly. Miles watched it as if hypnotized. Finally he uttered a tentative "Franny?" There was no response except in the acceleration of the knob's turning. "Franny?" he repeated, striding toward the door. "What's the matter?" Still no answer. The turning was frenzied now. "Franny, do you hear me? What are you doing?"

"Of course I hear you!" Franny exclaimed through the door. "I'm trying to get out of here, you fool!"

Miles seized the knob and gave it a forceful twist.

"That's not going to help," said Franny, resentful of the overpowering yank to the knob she had been holding on to.

"The thing must be locked," Miles said, astonished. "Why did you lock it?"

Franny was silent. Then she said, "*I* didn't lock it."

"Well, *I* didn't." Miles laughed. "Anyway, try unlocking it."

"Do you think I haven't already?"

"What kind of lock is it? Is there a key?"

"No. It's one of those damned little eggs you turn."

"But why on earth would you have locked it?"

"If I did it, Miles, I did it without thinking."

Miles was now trying to see the bolt through the crack of the door. "But why would you?" he said absently.

"Why would I what?"

"Lock it without thinking."

"All decent people lock bathroom doors," she said with conviction.

"We didn't at our house," Miles said. He could definitely see the bolt through the crack. "My father used to throw away the key to the bathroom door as soon as we moved into a place."

"Don't start on your father *now*, Miles."

"My father was all right."

"Who said he wasn't? *Do* something, Miles, for God's sake."

"There's nothing to do but call the desk ·and have them take down the door."

Franny, who had for a moment been leaning against the rim of the washbowl, now straightened and grasped the doorknob again. "Miles, you *wouldn't!*"

"Don't go to pieces, Franny."

"You'd let them send up those three stooges—"

Miles burst into laughter.

"How coarse you are, Miles," Franny said, her voice deepening.

"Oh, honey, there's a regular maintenance crew, and—"

"Maybe so," she broke in, her voice climbing the scale till it was much higher than Miles had ever heard it before. "But don't you know, Miles, that Bill Carlisle would certainly know about it? Oh, God, everybody in this town would know about it before tomorrow morning!"

"In God's name, Franny, what do you propose I do?"

"What kind of man are you, Miles? Take the door down yourself. You've been living in this hotel so long you depend on them for everything. You seem to think the world's just one big hotel and that you call in the maintenance crew for any and every thing."

"O.K., Franny, I'll try," Miles said amiably. "But have you ever tried taking down a locked door?"

"Why did you have to bring me to this dump?" Franny wailed.

"And why did you have to lock the door?" he countered.

Now they were both silent as Miles went to the closet door where his Valpak hung, and dug out a small gold pocketknife. His first effort to remove the pin in the upper door hinge was fruitless. The pin wouldn't budge. Neither would the pin in the lower hinge. He decided he needed a hammer to drive the knife blade upward against the heads of the pins, and he was just turning to go and fetch his shoe for that purpose when Franny spoke again.

"Miles," she began, speaking very slowly and in a tone so grave that it stopped him, "do you remember that night at Cousin Jane Thompson's party?"

He listened, waiting for her to continue. Then he realized she expected some response from him. "Yes, Franny," he said.

"That night at Cousin Jane's," she now went on in the

same sepulchral tone, "when you said Sue Maynard's date was drunk and that she asked you to take her home." Sue Maynard was the bridesmaid who had thought *she* would have Miles for herself. Miles had been a stag at the party that night.

"Yes, I remember."

"You were lying."

"In a way, Franny—"

"In the worst way," she said flatly. "You thought I would think it was just Sue's lie and that you didn't know better, or that you knew better but were too honorable to give her away."

"Maybe."

"That's how you *thought* I would think. But I knew even that night, Miles Miller, that you engineered it all. Her date was Puss Knowlton, and you had no trouble giving *him* the shove. And don't you think I know it's more than just necking that Sue Maynard goes in for? . . . And, Miles, the night last summer, *after* we were engaged, when you couldn't come for dinner at our house with Daddy's Aunt Caroline because of the report you had to write up—you didn't have any report to write up, Miles. You went someplace out on the South Side with a little creature named Becky Louise Johnson."

By the time Franny had finished, Miles had silently crossed the room to the bedside table and downed one of the two waiting glassfuls of champagne. He had listened intently to what she said, and the more he heard the more intent he had become on getting that damned door down. In his liquor case he found a bottle opener that he decided would work better than his knife. He returned to the door with his shoe and the bottle opener, and in no time he had the top pin out of its hinge.

"Miles—" Franny began again, still in the same tone.

"Shut up, Franny!" Miles said, and at once began hammering at the lower pin. It offered a little more resistance than the other, but was soon dislodged. The door was still firmly in place, however. Twice Miles jabbed the bottle opener into the crack on the hinge side, as though he might prize the door open. Then he laughed aloud at himself.

Franny heard him laugh, of course. "Is it funny? Is it really funny to you, Miles?" she said.

"Try giving it a push from in there, on the hinge side of the door," said Miles. Franny pushed. The door creaked, but that was all.

"Miles," Franny began once again, in a whisper now, and he could tell that she was leaning against the door and speaking into the crack. "I've thought of something else I've never confronted you with."

Miles felt the blood rush to his face. Suddenly he banged on the door with his fist. "Will you shut up, you little bitch! You know, I'm not above socking you in earnest if ever I get you out of there!"

"You would sock me just one time, Miles Miller."

"It would be the second time. Don't you forget that," he said.

They were really at it now, for he was reminding her of an occasion two days after their announcement party when he had found her kissing a college kid whose name he did not even know. He had struck her with his open hand on the back of her neck—not while she was kissing the kid but afterward, as he pushed her along the terrace there at the Polo Club. He had had too much to drink that night, and that was what saved them. Franny could claim that he had deserted her in favor of the bar. She also claimed that she had not really been kissing the boy and added that, anyway, he was an old, old, old friend and therefore meant nothing to her. They hardly spoke to each other during the week following, though of course they continued going about together. And until now they had neither of them ever referred to the incident, as if by mutual agreement.

"You're no gentleman, Miles," Franny pronounced, carefully keeping away from the door now. "As Daddy said of you to start with, you have all the outward signs of a gentleman but that's no evidence you're one inside."

"I've already settled your father's hash, Franny."

"You mean he's settled yours."

It was an unfortunate word—"settled." And both of them were aware of it immediately. It quieted both of them for some time. It referred to another incident that was assumed to be closed. Franny's father had apparently suspected Miles of being a fortune hunter, and before the engagement was announced he had asked Miles frankly what kind of "settlement" he expected. Miles had stormed out of the house, and was reconciled with Mr. Crowell only after having it hammered home to him by Franny that what her father had done was merely the conventional, old-fashioned thing for a man in Mr. Crowell's position to do. Miles had finally accepted Franny's explanation, but only a few weeks ago he had had another stormy session over a similar matter. This time it was with both the bride's parents. At that very late date he had learned about certain letters of inquiry that had been sent out concerning his "background." The letters had been written to various family friends and relatives of the Crowells who had lived for many years in Santa Barbara and Laguna Beach. When Miles learned of these letters through a remark of Franny's, it was many months after the letters had been written and replied to. The revelation sent Miles into a rage. He was in such a state that Franny feared he might do real violence to her father, or even to her mother, who had actually written the letters.

She had let the cat out of the bag inadvertently. She and he were just going out to a movie one night. Franny had come down to the living room already wearing her coat and even with her gloves on, but Miles had wanted to linger and talk awhile. Before she came down, he had wandered about the room studying some family photographs taken thirty years before. These "portraits," in their upright frames on the mantelshelf and on the various tables, had reminded him of pictures in his own family's living room when he was growing up. He commenced talking to Franny about how his mother always placed the same pictures on the same tables and bureaus no matter where they were living, and then he went on to speak, as he had on several previous occasions, of how restless his father had been after he left the service. (Miles' father had been a West Point graduate and had remained in the Army until he had his first heart attack, just a few months before Pearl Harbor.) And now, as Miles had already done several times before, he began listing for Franny the towns they had lived in during and after the war. Franny, who was impatient to get on to the movie, didn't listen very carefully. When Miles hesitated, trying to think of which town it was he had omitted from his list, Franny absent-mindedly supplied "Palo Alto." But it was not Palo Alto he was trying to think of it; it was San Jose.

"Palo Alto?" said Miles. "How did you know we ever lived in Palo Alto?"

"You've told me all this before," she answered.

But he had not told her about the spring in Palo Alto! It was then that his parents had quarreled so endlessly, though he—and probably they—had never known just why. At any rate, he was always careful to leave Palo Alto out of his catalogue of towns. And he was not content now until he had wrung a confession of the whole business of the letters of inquiry out of Franny. Once she had confessed, he insisted upon taking the matter up with her parents that very night; he insisted upon *seeing* the letters. For a time, Mrs. Crowell maintained that she had already thrown away the letters. But at last she broke down. She went upstairs and returned with the packet of letters, all of which Miles read, sitting there in the family circle. He had known there couldn't be anything really bad in them, because just as there was nothing very good that could be said of his parents, there was nothing very bad, either. The worst the letters said of them was that they were "rootless people and apparently of restricted means." Miles found he could not even resent one lady's description of his mother as a "harmless little woman—pleasant enough —with a vague Southern background." The letters repeated each other with phrases like "thoroughly nice" and "well bred" and "well behaved." The sole reference to Palo Alto was "I think they lived at Palo Alto for a time. John's sister Laura met them there. She thought Major Miller very handsome. He had a small black mustache, if I recall."

The memory of all this and of the "settlement" episode occupied Miles' mind as he crossed the hotel room and picked up the glass of champagne that he had poured for Franny. The champagne had gone flat already, but he relished its flatness. He sipped it slowly, as if tasting in each sip a different unpleasant incident or aspect of their courtship and engagement—tasting all they had not tasted and toasted with the first bottle. Suddenly he put down the glass, leaving still a sip or two in the bottle, and stepped quickly over to the bathroom door. "Franny," he said, "it has just occurred to me! It wasn't your father's idea to talk about a settlement with me. You put him up to it! It was you who thought I might be after your family's money! If it had been your father's idea, he wouldn't have been so meek and mild when I called his hand. And, by God, you put your mother up to writing those letters, or she never would have given in and shown them to me."

He waited for Franny's denial, but none came. "And, Franny," he went on after a moment, "there's one more thing I know that you didn't know I knew. Your father went down to my office and asked about the likelihood of my staying on here or being transferred."

"I knew he did that, Miles."

"Darn right you knew it. You put him up to that, too. You didn't even want to take a chance on my moving you away from here." But before he had finished his last sentence, Miles heard the water running full force into the bathtub. "Franny, I'm not finished!" he shouted. "What are you doing?"

"If you don't get this door down within ten minutes"—she was speaking through the crack again—"and get it down without having Bill Carlisle up here to witness it, I'm going to drown myself in the damned bathtub."

As a matter of fact, she had begun running the water to drown out Miles' accusations, but as she spoke she became convinced that suicide really had been her original intention.

"Yes," Miles boomed, "you drown yourself in the bathtub and I'll jump out our eighth-floor window! Romeo and Juliet, that's us!"

Franny shut off the water. She opened her mouth to reply, but no words came. She burst into tears. And the poor little bride could not herself have said whether her tears were brought on by the heavy irony and sarcasm of her groom or by the thought of her dear Miles and her dear self lying dead in their caskets with their love yet unfulfilled.

Almost at once Miles began pleading with her not to cry. But it seemed that his every word brought increased volume to the wailing beyond the bathroom door. It was as if she had decided she could more effectively drown out the sound of his voice with tears than with the rush of bath water. But actually it wasn't the sound of her bridegroom's voice alone that she wished not to hear. There was the sound of another voice —other voices. She had first become aware of the other voices during one of hers and Miles' silences. Which silence she couldn't have said, because for some time afterward she tried to believe that she had only imagined hearing the other voices, or at least imagined that they sounded as near to her as they did. Finally, though, the persistence of the voices drew her attention to the fact of the other door. The other door, she finally acknowledged, must certainly lead into an adjoining room. And the voices—a man's and a woman's—came to her from that room. And now the ever-increasing volume of her own wailing was meant to conceal from herself that the woman's voice was addressing her directly through that door.

"Honey, I think we can help you." The offer was unmistakable.

"No, you can't, no, you can't!" Franny wailed.

"The gentleman in here thinks he is pretty good with locks."

"No, no, please don't come in here," Franny begged, too frightened, too perplexed for more tears now.

"Franny, what's going on?" Miles seemed on the verge of tears himself. "Darling, I'll get a doctor, you'll be all right!"

"Miles, there's another door."

"Yes?"

"And there's someone over there. Oh, Miles, make them go away."

"Keep your head, Franny. What do they want?"

"It's a woman. She says there's a man in there who can get me out of here."

"You do want to get out, don't you, Franny?" It was as though he were speaking to someone on a window ledge.

"Not that way, I don't," said Franny. Now she was whispering through the door crack. "Miles, their voices sound familiar!"

"Now, Franny, cut it out!" scolded Miles, and Franny understood his full meaning. For a moment she listened to the other voices. From the start the man's voice had been no more than a low mumbling. He didn't want his voice recognized! The woman spoke more distinctly. Franny could hear them now discussing the problem. Presently the man said something and laughed. And the woman said, "Hush, the kid will hear you." Somehow this gave Franny courage. She stepped over to the other door and said bravely, *"Will* you help me?"

Hearing her, Miles gave a sigh of relief. Then he said, "Ask them to let me come around into their room—and help."

"Will you let my—my husband come around into your room?"

She heard them deliberating. The man was opposed. Finally, the woman said, "No. He can come and meet you outside our hall door if we get this one open."

She repeated this to Miles.

"Tell them O.K.," he commanded.

"O.K.," said Franny softly.

Now the man and woman were at the door. The man was still mumbling. "Is there a latch on your side?" the woman asked.

"Yes," said Franny. "A little sort of knob."

"Tell her to turn it," the man muttered.

"Turn it," said the woman.

Franny turned it. It moved easily. "I have," she said. She watched the big doorknob revolving, but the door didn't open. There was more discussion on the other side of the door.

"It's locked with a key," said the woman to Franny. "But that's how he's going to make hisself useful." Franny's deliverer was hard at work. She couldn't tell whether it was a skeleton key or some makeshift instrument he was, using. Presently, she heard the click of the lock and heard the man say, "That's got it."

"Miles!" Franny called out. But Miles didn't answer. He was already waiting at their neighbors' hall door. There was the sound of footsteps hurriedly retreating, and then the door opened. The room itself was in darkness, but in the light from the bathroom Franny could see the man's figure outlined on the bed. The sheet was pulled up over his face. Franny looked at the woman. She was fully dressed, though barefoot, and she stood smiling at the ridiculous sight in the bed and probably at the memory of the male figure's racing across the room and jumping into the bed and pulling the sheet over its head.

"You're an angel," Franny said, without having known she was going to say it.

The woman acknowledged the compliment only by allowing the smile to fade from her lips. "He'll get up from there and try to open the other door for you in a minute," she said.

Franny gave her a grateful smile, and then she turned and walked with perfect poise toward the hall door. Her peach negligee was floor-length and its little train of lace swept gracefully along the dark carpet. When her hand was on the doorknob, she turned and said simply, "Good night." She might have been at home, turning to say a casual good night to her mother.

In the hallway, Miles had waited, fully expecting to have to carry his bride back to their room in his arms. When she appeared he was stunned by her radiance and self-possession. He had never seen her so beautiful. And Franny was equally stunned by Miles' manly beauty as he stood before her in his blue silk pajamas. For a moment they stood there beaming at one another. Finally Miles slipped his arm gently about his bride's waist and hurried her off to their room.

They found their bathroom door standing half open, and the door beyond it tightly closed. The two heavy pins still lay on the floor, but Miles quickly slipped them into the hinges. The door was now in perfect working order. Miles stood a moment gazing into the bright bathroom where Franny's clothes were heaped in one corner like a child's. "Well," he said at last, "that fellow worked fast."

"Miles," said Franny, also looking into the bathroom but with her eyes focussed on the door opposite, "did you see who it was?"

"What do you mean?"

"The woman over there—she was the woman on the elevator."

"Franny, Franny! . . . She got off at the seventh floor! How could you forget?"

"And the man—" Franny began.

"Franny, Franny, Franny," Miles interrupted, already having left her side to fetch the champagne glasses and refill them. "The man in that room is one of the conventioners from out of town. You never heard his voice or saw him before in your life."

She had been going to say that the man in the bed was Bill Carlisle. But she saw it was useless. And she knew she would never say it now. Miles came toward her slowly with the two glasses filled to the brim. They sipped their champagne, looking at one another over the glasses. In their hearts both of them were glad they had said all the things that they said through the door. As they gazed deep into each other's eyes, they believed that they had got all of that off their chests once and for all. There was nothing in the world to come between them now. They believed, really and truly, that neither of them would ever deceive or mistrust the other again. Silently they were toasting their own bliss and happiness, confident that it would never again be shadowed by the irrelevances of the different circumstances of their upbringings or by the possibly impure and selfish motives that had helped to bring them together.

An Overwhelming Question

"I don't understand you, Rudy. We've known each other all our lives, and if we can't—"

"We have not known each other all our lives, Isabel," he said flatly.

They were a comical pair at such moments. Her speech would suddenly become littered with diphthongs and elisions. His became hard and flat. A foreigner listening in at these moments might have supposed them to have grown up in two different regions of the country. But as a matter of fact, she had merely assumed the more specially feminine and he the more specially masculine form of genteel, city speech as it is spoken in the great heartland. And it signified no more than that they had reached an impasse in some kind of argument. Of far greater significance was their reference to how long they had, or had not, known each other. . . . Sometimes it was she who said they *had* known each other all their young lives, and sometimes it was he. Neither of them ever meant to say it, but in the heat of argument the untruth would sometimes slip out. Not very often, but sometimes. Otherwise,

it was acknowledged between them that they had met only
a few months before they got engaged. That was what was
real and true. Other Isabels and other Rudys whom they had
known at fourteen, at sixteen, at eighteen (and even earlier
than fourteen) had no connection with the grown-up and ma-
tured Isabel Havens and Rudy Banks.

Last winter, the grown-up Isabel and Rudy had fallen ro-
mantically and passionately in love at a Hunt and Polo Club
dance. They said yes to each other a few nights later and very
shortly now they were going to be married—in three days'
time, to be exact. Their bond was in their present and in their
future. Any memories they had in common—old awarenesses
and unawarenesses of each other, growing up as they had in
the same town—were more like memories that each might
have shared with some other boy or girl, or, still more likely,
with a succession of others. Looking back from twenty and a
little beyond, all that part of life seemed utter nonsense and
not to be thought of as in any way real.

"I just don't understand your attitude," Isabel said, trying
to begin the present argument all over again. But again words
failed her. For a full minute they stood there not saying anything. Rudy pretended to go on looking at the pieces of Danish glassware that had come in recently. (Isabel's mother liked
grouping the presents in kinds, and as their treasure had ac-
cumulated during the past eight weeks, Mrs. Havens had
managed to make this room look more and more like a well-
ordered coupon store—one for royalty, or even celestial beings.) "Lately," Isabel finally managed to continue, "lately,
Rudy, you have treated me like a leper. A mixture of a leper
and a lunatic. Or a pet that might bite you if you didn't watch
out. I am just fed up with it."

Gently he took her hand, and she at once lifted his hand
to her lips and kissed it fervently. "Right now," she said,
"even your hand is as cold as ice."

"It's cold in *here*," Rudy Banks said, shivering.

She dropped his hand, and moved over to the wall and turned up the thermostat. The room was in the basement of the house and had its own gas-fired space heater. It had been the laundry once, but a dozen years back Mr. Havens had converted it into a rumpus room for Isabel and her play-mates. More recently, Mr. and Mrs. Havens themselves had used it for a card-room on hot summer nights. And now all the furniture except the ping-pong table had been stored away and replaced by saw-horses with planks laid across them. The improvised tables and the ping-pong table and the built-in shelves held most of the wedding treasure.

From the thermostat, Isabel looked back over her shoulder at Rudy. He was fingering the Danish glass again, but his eyes were trained on her. When the gas jet in the heater flickered on, she saw him smile and shake his head. She said: "You'll be surprised how fast it will warm up."

"You *are* a wastrel," he said. "We'll be back upstairs before the blower comes on." He knew all about such heaters.

"I don't think we will." She turned to the door that led to the basement corridor, and closed it.

"Isabel," he said, "honest to God!"

"I'm serious this time, Rudy," she said.

"You aren't serious. You may think you are, but you aren't." He tossed his head back and laughed, as though that would show her she wasn't serious. "Look where we are," he said. "Just consider what the possibilities are. It gives me goose bumps to think about it. All this glass! And the cement floors!" The room was lit by a single bright globe in the center of the low ceiling. The crystal, the china, the silverware winked at them from every surface and from the open shelves. From the far end of the room, two brand-new television sets gawked. And in a nearer corner crouched an outdoor cooker, brandishing its copper and stainless-steel accoutrements.

"If I'm not serious now," Isabel said, "you'll never see me serious."

"Don't talk boloney," he said.

"It's not just talk."

"Boloney," he said, still smiling. He was not going to be drawn into more talk. If he had managed this long, he could somehow make it the rest of the way. She was really incredible, but he was confident that in another moment or so he could make her see what a ridiculous place and time she had chosen for *this* onslaught.

She moved toward him along the aisle between the tables. "Now see here, Rudy. We've been engaged for three months. We've—"

He raised three fingers and shook them at her. "And we'll be married in just three days from now," he said.

She drew nearer. He retreated around the corner of the heavily laden ping-pong table. She laughed, but he didn't feel any safety in it for him. She wasn't conceding anything. She was merely humoring him in his playfulness. He went round to the other side of the table. As he turned the corner there, his jacket brushed against a sherbet glass which fell against one of its companions and gave off an elegant tinkle.

"You'll break something," she said sharply. "You know what a clumsy ox you are." It was a sudden change in tactics on her part, but he recognized it. She was really very clever. She would make him angry, and then there would have to be a reconciliation. Then anything could happen, anywhere.

He leaned across the glassware between them and gave her a glittering smile. "You know how much I love you," he said. "Why are you so silly and persistent? You know I am not going to let you have your way."

But she had lowered her eyes to the table. She didn't seem to hear him, though of course she did hear him. She was thinking that probably she *wouldn't* have her way. She could feel the blood rising in her cheeks. And she was blaming herself for not realizing weeks earlier that he was consciously opposing her. What a dupe she had been! How she had let the time go by! Oh, the evenings they had idled away! The opportunities they had passed up! The kisses she had wasted. . . .

The space heater's fan came on—the blower. He heard its soft whirr and then almost instantly he felt the new warmth on his ankles. It seemed to him that probably she *would* have her way. For there she stood, opposite him, a picture of maidenly surrender—surrender to his refusal, which made her doubly irresistible—her eyes cast down so modestly, all her features in a gentle repose he had never imagined they had resort to, and her face and neck and even her bare shoulders pink with blushes. The warmth about his ankles rose to his knees. Or was he only imagining it? No, it kept on rising. He thought of what it must be like to drown—half with horror, half with pleasure he thought of it. And now he imagined that the whirr of the heater's motor was coming directly from Isabel herself. He knew she was going to look up at him in another moment, and he supposed there might be tears. Then he *would* drown. If she wept—he had never seen her weep, not this Isabel—then it *would* be settled.

Afterwards, he realized that she must have heard the foot-steps before he did, and that that, somehow or other, was why she never looked up. It was the first of the arrivals among the dinner guests, and they were on the basement stairs. Isabel's mother would be sending them down; every-body who came to the house had to see the presents. Rudy sprinted on tiptoe down the aisle between the tables, threw open the door to the corridor, pushed down the thermostat, sprinted back along the other aisle to Isabel. Taking her in his arms, he kissed her passionately. He observed, with relief, that there were no tears on her cheeks. . . . That's how they were when they were discovered by the utterly delighted first arrivals.

It was a fine party that night. After dinner they all went

dancing. Rudy and Isabel were rather quiet throughout the evening. They held hands a lot, and kissed frequently. But they were noticeably abstemious. Some of the young men in the party had a great deal too much to drink, and one of the girls did. She was Isabel's cousin who had come from out of town for the wedding and was staying at the Havens' house. When they returned home at half-past-two, Isabel was forced to take charge of her cousin and see her up to bed. Rudy and Isabel said only a quick good-night at the doorstep.

He telephoned at eleven the next morning—from his office. Isabel was not at home. Her cousin was still asleep, but Isabel had risen an hour earlier and had gone out by herself for a drive in her car. Rudy talked to the maid first, but Isabel's mother got on the upstairs extension and dismissed the maid. Mrs. Havens said she felt she must take this opportunity to tell Rudy that she detected a "mounting nervousness" in Isabel, and she hoped he understood it was only to be expected in a bride as "the great day" approached. He did, he did— he assured her—he did indeed. And *she* wasn't worried, was she, by Isabel's going out for a drive? He hoped not. He didn't think she ought to be. . . . Heavens, no, she wasn't. But with so much going on she was merely afraid she mightn't find another chance to speak to him privately, etcetera.

A few minutes later, Rudy stood watching them bring his car down on the elevator in the parking garage. He drove eastward a few blocks and then turned south. He had no particular destination in mind—no particular purpose. But the car seemed to know what it was doing. Was he in flight or in pursuit? he wondered. Or by keeping in motion was he trying to stand still? After last night, she might be capable of coming to his office—just barely. On the other hand, if he were in pursuit the town had grown too large during the past five years for him to think of looking for her. And it was not as though they had a trysting-place. That wasn't in Isabel's line; Isabel was a born homebody! Suddenly he began to laugh rather hysterically at his own unexpected *bon mot*— a homebody, and he only managed to check himself when he saw two men in another car eyeing him curiously.

Half an hour later, he came on her car—her long yellow convertible—parked on the edge of the golf course and near the seventh green, in Riverside Park. . . . God, he breathed. What was she thinking? Those moonlight picnics! . . . "Get your big toe out of the egg sandwiches." . . . Snipe-hunting and all that. . . . Jesus, sweet sixteen! . . . Did she—could she —think those times in Riverside Park meant anything to him or to the other boys who went along? Had the other girls thought so too—that those playful, necking-party picnics were *something?* It seemed an eternity since he had ever thought about that summer, the summer when he had come home from college and decided to try dating some of the younger girls. Had she actually been among them? Yes, he could see her sitting very near the edge of the bluff above the river and holding on to a beer bottle and trying to yodel. And possibly he was the only one near enough to her to observe that the bottle, which she finally hurled down towards the river, was still almost full of beer.

He parked his car alongside hers and got out. There seemed to be no one playing the course. He set off in the direction of the seventh green, walking south and parallel with the bluff. The only sign of life was a man riding a big power mower several hundred yards ahead. The grass he walked through had already been cut, and blackbirds and pigeons mingled indiscriminately in the area. Each time he approached them, the blackbirds rose up and moved further off. The pigeons waited till he was in their midst. His only feeling was one of boredom. Such stupid, ugly birds they were. What had they to do with him? What had re-visiting Riverside Park to do with him and Isabel? . . . He went on, despite himself, knowing she would not be glad to see him. . . . Though it was May, the sky was like pale wood ashes, with only a white disk of a sun showing through the overcast. Along the crest of the bluff, a growth of young scrub oak and sweet gum saplings hid all view of the great muddy river that was below. As he walked, he kept watching for the opening—the break in the growth. He knew it must still be there, and at last he saw it. He stepped through, and out on to the little point of eroded, red-clay earth.

She was sitting very near the edge with her plaid coat spread out beneath her, and she had on tan Bermuda shorts and a white cardigan. She looked up at him, not so much in surprise as in disappointment. Moreover, her glance accused him. Now it was he, wasn't it, who—by finding her here—said they had known each other all their lives. But no, his raised eyebrows replied, it was she who said so by being found here. He sat beside her on the plaid coat. Two hundred feet below them, down the clay bluff, the ugly, red-brown river labored energetically and senselessly. It spread before them, half a mile wide. The flat landscape to the west of it was still victim to the last of the spring floods. There were islands over there with shapes like continents, familiar looking but unnameable continents. It was a scene they both felt they had always known and never known.

They were a solemn pair, sitting there; they had met this morning in a region where they were dead to each other, where they must not and could not be otherwise. . . . One summer he had thrown pebbles at her window! No, it was a lie! But he had.

"Are you up there?"

"I'm up here."

"Coming down?"

"Have to get dressed."

"I'll be on the steps."

She was thirteen, and it was almost midnight. But he was

only a neighborhood boy, and their families were such
friends it didn't matter. And he was so much *older* than she
was. Why, she was a child. It was like having a little sister or
even a little brother to talk to. He did not like her or dislike
her. She was merely an excuse to keep from going on home.
When he came pebble-throwing at her window he had always
been somewhere else before. Probably he had spent the evening talking with boys his own age and older about whether
or not one ought to go East to college, about when and
whether-or-not the next war would come, about careers that
would take them to Africa and South America—conversations
that ended with somebody's saying: "I'll do anything so long
as it takes me away from this hell-hole." And then on the way
home, he stopped to throw pebbles at the little Havens girl's
window. She and he would sit on her porch steps and chatter
for half an hour or so. With her head of tight, black curls, and
with her lean, freckled face, and with no figure at all yet, she
looked as much like a boy as a girl. It amused him to talk to
her. It touched him, somehow. To think that two years ago
he had been that young! Poor child, she had not begun to
live. But he! Africa . . . war . . . college . . . I'll do anything
so long as it takes me away from this hell-hole!

What he did not know was that at thirteen she was already
a Roman Catholic nun. She was sent by her family to the
Methodist Sunday School every Sunday morning, but that did
not alter the larger fact. And at fifteen, the summer of the
necking-party picnics, she was soon to be the successor to
Maria Tallchief. It was one of those secrets that had to be
kept from those about you. *They* said it sounded so childish
in a girl who was already having dates. She had at least to try
to seem like the other girls. She even made fun of her dancing
lessons. But she knew her worth, and she pitied people like
Rudy Banks. Such boys were attractive to her, naturally. She
even envied them. They asked so little of life and were able
to live for the present moment only. (She knew about the

really wild girls that boys like Rudy went out with some-times.) But how would life be bearable without some high purpose like her own? . . . That was at fifteen. At seventeen, her purpose was more practical, she thought, and again more selfless. Her destiny, she knew now, was to become a social worker. Her heart went out to unwed mothers and prosti-tutes. She read serious articles in magazines. Boys like Rudy Banks were amusing still, but she knew it was a type which the society of the future must eliminate. Such men brought about the downfall of the very girls she was going to devote her life to helping. After an evening of dancing in the arms of some Rudy Banks or other, after sometimes allowing her-self to be kissed by an especially ardent admirer, she felt she could hardly wait to be released from these demands which her life made upon her. It all seemed very degrading and to no purpose.

What she did not know, of course, was that when she was seventeen and Rudy was nineteen he was making a fateful decision: Should he become a nuclear physicist or a professor of political science. . . . That year passed, and by the time he was in law school, two years later, Isabel was engrossed in her serious Junior League work. That year they were thrown together on several occasions and talked openly, not specif-ically to each other but in groups which included the other, about their absorbing interests—law and charity work. They typed each other. He heard that she was still a puritan. She knew about his affairs. But it was to be still another year before they really met. By then they were properly prepared for the meeting. Rudy Banks had finished school, and Isabel Havens had finished her Junior League apprenticeship. The time was at hand, the time for each of them to meet the right someone, to fall desperately in love, to get married. They were a sleeping beauty and a sleeping prince waking, conven-iently, at the same time and in the same place. It would have seemed a profanation of the miracle to say that in their long sleep they had dreamed anything sweeter or nobler than the love which they were created for and which was going to light them through the rest of their waking life. Whoever said so was a liar.

During the half-hour that they sat together looking at the wide river and its false islands, they spoke little. There were no kisses, and he didn't even take her hand till they rose to leave. The things that they did say were only simple things that touched on the dreariness of the scene. It seemed wrong, they said, that a brown river could not be thought as beautiful as a blue river. But the simple truth was, it couldn't. They wondered how it might be to have grown up beside a blue river with water so clear that you could see right down into its depths, a clear river in a well-defined channel cut between white limestone bluffs and with possibly a little green island in the center, very real, and possibly, even, on that island the ruins of a small castle for the eye to focus on.

That night's party was out at the Hunt and Polo Club. The hostess was Rudy's Aunt Polly—his somewhat youthful, not unworldly Aunt Polly Norris. The guests were a mixed lot. There were Isabel's attendants, of course, including her cousin from out of town, who bored everybody with her remorse and her total abstinence tonight. But the party was made up mostly from a rather frolicsome, riggish set that Rudy felt particularly at home in and from a somewhat less youthful but even more frolicsome set that his aunt belonged to. Isabel's parents, as well as Rudy's own, decided, wisely, to spend the evening at home. They said there had been so much festivity already, and there was so much to be done tomorrow and the day after, etcetera, etcetera.

It was a fine party, like all the others. There was dancing on the glassed-in terrace after dinner, which was served at ten—after drinks, which were served at seven-thirty. The little combo that Aunt Polly had hired finished playing at two a.m., as agreed upon, and departed. Before three, most of the young men, mindful of office desks that awaited them just six hours hence, dragged their young ladies away from the scene. And by that hour most husbands and wives from Aunt Polly's set had taken their leave—together or separately. Aunt Polly herself had already slipped away.

Isabel and Rudy wandered into the little corner of the lounge that the combo had occupied. It was just beside the door to the terrace, and it was banked with giant potted plants. They sat down together on the piano bench. They were holding hands, and without looking at Rudy, Isabel lifted his hand to her lips and kissed it—kissed the back of the hand, then the fingers.

"Hey now!" he said.

"Yes, hey now," she said, smiling to herself, still not looking at him.

"This morning in the park—" he began.

"In what park?" She went on, smiling. "Have you been meeting people in the park?"

"Oh," he said. "No, not I. Have you?"

"I slept all morning," she said.

"I was at the office."

"Well, then."

"Let's walk some," he said.

"Yes, let us do so." He realized that she was faking tipsiness, and an inspiration came to him.

The bar was at the other end of the big lounge. They set off in that general direction. They moved through a cigarette smog, in near darkness. Off at the drear edges of the room a few sad, last table lamps were still lit. In the mammoth fieldstone fireplace, some last embers sputtered and sent up a feeble show of sparks. But in the central gloom, Rudy and Isabel had to pick their way among tables and chairs without always knowing whether the chairs, or even the tables, were occupied by one or more persons. As they drew near the bar, they passed one final little company sitting upright around a table. Someone in the group said: "Look at 'em. They're walking on air."

Someone else said: "They think they're in love."

"What do you mean *think?*" said the first voice.

"I mean *think.*"

"What are the odds?" said a new voice. "Has he or hasn't he?"

"It's always even money."

"Not in this case. For if he hasn't, she's the only woman under forty at this party he hasn't."

"Are you speaking from experience?"

"I'm not under forty."

"Well, she's pure as the snow."

"It's always even money."

Hand in hand, they had moved on to the bar. They smiled at each other. He even bent forward and kissed her on the lips. Then, almost under his breath, he said to the barkeep, "Two whiskeys and water—heavy."

The table behind them was silent. Presently the barkeep set two bronze-colored drinks on the counter. A long, low, breathless whistle came from the table. Not-in-this-case said: "Look, he's going to slug her. That's the most loathsome sight I've ever seen."

And walking-on-air said: "With the wedding only the day after tomorrow—*really* only tomorrow now!"

Isabel looked at the drink before her on the counter, and then looked at Rudy. He gave her his glittering smile. How artless he was. Oh, how she loved him for his artlessness. She knew all about him. She loved his thinking he could use the same smile and the same drink for all his purposes. She knew who it was that had slugged her cousin from out of town last night. She knew how he and her cousin had spent that twenty minutes when he escorted her to make the long-distance telephone call to her own fiancé back home. She believed still that all that was all right for him. She believed still that she had made a mistake in her self-denial; her heart, or her mind, was still set upon remedying her mistake, upon breaking the solemn resolution which some other Isabel, in one of her other lives, had made for her. That was still her fierce, firm purpose, her overwhelming necessity even. And now something strengthened her resolve. As Rudy's smile faded, she saw a look in his eyes that was unbearable to her. . . . She *would not* serve his purpose. She would not allow him to keep the resolution made by another Rudy Banks. She would not, on their wedding night, be there merely as his idealized something or other.

She took his arm, without ever touching the glass set before her—and without his having touched his, and led him away into the gloom.

"Did you see her face?" said a voice at the table.

"Beautiful!" said another.

"Oh, God, now I've seen life's other face," said a man's voice. It would have been difficult to distinguish which among the other husky voices were male and which female. "I've seen it," the man's voice said. And then, after a moment, the same voice was giving utterance to a chain of muffled, broken sobs.

"Get hold of yourself, Doug," said a voice that was distinctly a woman's. "You're not that far out."

Two chairs scraped on the stone floor, and the barkeep was relieved of his neglected drinks.

Isabel steered Rudy in the direction of the nearest door to the glassed-in terrace. When finally they stood in the doorway, Rudy drew back. There was more light on the terrace than in the lounge, but it had been deserted by the guests. He pulled her away from the doorway, and they walked in the light along the edge of the lounge till they reached another door leading to the terrace. Isabel stepped out onto the ter-

race alone. Rudy leaned against the door-jamb and watched
her wandering about out there. She had never seemed more
maidenly, never more womanly, never more desirable, never
more precisely the very girl as she must be. He did not know
why it mattered so much to him, but at any rate he knew
that it did. He no longer regarded himself as a serious person,
he had long since come to think of himself as a kind of clown
and to think of his life's most serious activities as clownish
acrobatics which he was peculiarly well qualified to perform;
but there remained this one last absurd point of semi-serious-
ness. For it, he was willing to risk Isabel's most indignant and
righteous rage. He was, in fact, determined to risk it now,
in the light of her will to use him in the way she so clearly
intended, her will to have her cake and eat it too, her willing-
ness to make him the battleground of her conflicting purposes.

On the terrace, Isabel peered out through the glass walls
and then gazed upward through the glass overhead. "It has
cleared," she said breathlessly. "Stars are out."

Rudy burst into laughter.

Isabel seized the latch on one of the panels in the glass wall
and threw open a door to the outside. She gave one little
shriek of laughter. It seemed half in response to Rudy's laughter and half in response to her first breath of the night air—
half anguish, half delight. Without looking back at Rudy, she
ran out-of-doors.

"You can't go out there," he shouted after her, quickly
crossing the terrace to the open door. "It's all a mess!"

The mess outside was a very real one. The Hunt and Polo
had moved its location during the previous fall—very late in
the previous fall. And there had followed such a severe winter
and such a wet spring that almost no work had been done on
the grounds. Members and their guests still came and went,
between the asphalt parking area and the front entrance to
the clubhouse, over a series of rough planks laid across the
mud.

From the doorway to the glassed-in terrace there were not even any planks. When Rudy reached that doorway he saw Isabel bounding off through the mire with her white evening dress pulled up about her knees. He gave one regretful glance at his patent leather slippers and then set out after her. With his first steps he felt the mud oozing over the sides of his slippers, and it passed through ·his mind that he, Rudy Banks, might end his days a wife-beater! He might not even wait till she *was* his wife! Why hadn't he thought of that solution before? A beating just might do the trick.

He gained on her rapidly, much more rapidly than he had expected or intended. She was heading toward the woods that began a hundred feet or so distant from the clubhouse. As she approached the woods she was obviously slowing her pace. Suddenly Rudy stopped in his deep tracks. For the first time, she looked back at him. And she, too, stopped. But presently, still holding up her skirt, she began to trot along the edge of the woods where the ground was not so soft. Rudy remained where he was, lifting first one foot and then the other to shake off the mud, the way a small dog will do. When Isabel had travelled about thirty feet she turned in toward the clubhouse again. She was circling back! Before Rudy knew it, she had outflanked him and cut him off from any easy retreat to the terrace doorway.

He glanced to the right and then to the left. Isabel was moving toward him now. In an open space, several hundred feet to his left, was an assemblage of dark objects that he recognized—clumps and stacks and bunches of left-over building materials as well as certain other bulky objects. His choice was between this junk-yard and the woods, and instinct told him that he must at all costs avoid the woods. He bolted for the junk-yard.

The Hunt and Polo's new site was ten miles further from town than its old location, and in conjunction with the move (a very profitable move, the old site's having been sold at a fine figure for use as a new suburban development)—in conjunction with the move the members made one extremely sage decision: they entirely eliminated the role of horses, hounds, and polo ponies from the club's program of activities, and so were relieved from making any provision for barns, paddocks, kennels, or polo field on the new site. This was a very realistic step and would save them many thousands of dollars in years to come. And to placate a few stodgy members who disapproved, it was resolved that a good many accessories and appurtenances from the old installation should be brought along to decorate the new site and thus preserve some of the old atmosphere. If spring would only come, these ornaments would be duly set up in places appointed for them by the landscape architect. But, meanwhile, they rested with the remnants of lumber and cement blocks in the Club's private junk-yard. And it was in their precincts, on this starry April night, that Rudy Banks took final refuge from Isabel Havens.

Once he had entered that area, Isabel had difficulty catching sight of him again. The lumber piles and the stacks of cement blocks were like so many small buildings with dark little alleys of mud between. And much of what was brought from the old club consisted literally of quaint outbuildings and dependencies—a dovecote, a saddle and harness shack, a two-room playhouse for young children, as well as stacks of dog-houses, barrels, feed-troughs and drinking-troughs, even heaps of gates and rails from the old fences—and nearly all of these heaps and stacks covered over with sheets of canvas. Along the muddy passages between, Isabel pursued him doggedly. Or suddenly she did an about-face, sure she would run squarely into him around the corner she had just turned. But he was never there. Soon she ceased to imagine even that she had caught glimpses of him. She could hear the smacking and sucking of his quick footwork in the mud, and now and again she would hear him laughing to himself. She heard him mutter, "God, what's this?" Half a minute later, she heard him

say something like that again. And each time, she would presently come on the thing she supposed he had seen or perhaps
even stumbled over—first an iron hitching post, next an old
mounting block. The noises he made sounded always just
around the corner ahead or behind, or just over the nearest
bulk of canvas. She never once called out to him, or she did
not *think* she did. And she would never know how long she
went on stalking him after it was no use. She never lost her
confidence that she would find him at last.

He was never certain how close behind him she might be.
He could not hear a sound she made, but he knew always that
she was back there or maybe just ahead around the next corner. At last, he knew his only safety would be in hiding from
her somewhere. He had led her through the whole complex
of junk and rubbish, and now was back at the largest pile of
lumber. He began to climb. Beyond the lumber he could see
the gable of the children's playhouse. The climbing was very
easy. He went up and up, ever so silently. Then at the very
top, his right foot caught between two planks. Pulling the foot
free, he twisted his ankle painfully. He bent over to massage
the ankle, hopping unsteadily on the other foot. He lost his
balance, and, in an effort to regain it, whirled about, and fell
backward. As he fell, the back of his neck came down heavily
against the pointed gable-end of the playhouse.

The poor fellow died instantly. His body folded up as
though he were a life-sized Raggedy Andy, his two feet flying
upward to either side of his head. He slipped, bottom first,
down into the narrow crevice between the lumber and the
playhouse. It would be many hours before they found him
there, and meanwhile the stars shone on his uncovered head
and on the muddy soles of his dress slippers. He was wedged
in between the rough edges of the unfinished lumber and
the smooth clapboard of the playhouse. His neck was broken,
the life gone out of his body, but he was safe from Isabel at
last, poor fellow.

At The Drugstore

Matt Donelson was back home on a visit. He rose early, before any of the others were awake, and set out on foot for the drugstore, where he was going to buy a bottle of shaving lotion. He had left a pretty wife sleeping in the family guest room, two little sons snoozing away in the next room down the hall—both the wife and the sons being exhausted from the long train ride of the day before—and a mother and a father snatching early morning, old-folksy naps in their adjoining rooms at the head of the stairs. At this early hour the house seemed more like its old self than it usually did on his visits home. Though he knew it was a house that would be politely referred to nowadays as "an older house," for a moment it seemed to him again "the new house" that the family had moved into when he was aged six. His room had been the one his father now occupied. He was the baby of the family; his mother had wanted him nearby. His two big brothers had shared the room where his own two boys were sleeping this morning. And his sister, for whose coming-out year the house had been bought, had claimed the guest room for hers during the brief two years she remained at home. She and the brothers had long since, of course, had houses and families of their own. When Matt came back to see his parents he seldom caught more than a glimpse of any of them, and to their children he was a stranger.

Downstairs, just before he left the house, Matt had a brief exchange with the colored cook who was a recent comer and whose name he did not even know.

"I suppose it feels good to you to be back home," she had said.

"There's nothing like it," Matt had replied. "Absolutely nothing."

On his way to the drugstore Matt realized that this was an expedition he had not given any real forethought to. For several days before he left New York he had been intending to buy the bottle of shaving lotion, but he had kept forgetting it or putting it off—refusing somehow to let his mind focus on it. And he had risen this morning and left the house—hatless and on foot—without really thinking of *what* drugstore he was going to. It was with a certain wonderment even that he found himself hiking along a familiar thoroughfare in this sprawling inland city where he had grown up. It was a street that led through what he as a boy had thought of as a newish part of town but a part which he knew must now of course be regarded as "an older section." Once, along the way, he stumbled over an uneven piece of pavement which the roots of one of the maple trees had dislodged. Next he found himself looking up at the trees, trying to determine whether or not they had grown much since the days when he first remembered them. It seemed to him that they had not. The trees had not leafed out yet this year and even the patterns of the smallest branches against the dull March sky seemed tiresomely familiar. Somehow he felt both bored and disquieted by his observations. And when finally he stood opposite the drugstore and realized that this was his destination, the very sight of the commonplace store front was dismaying to him. How had he got here? It all seemed unreal. It was as though he had climbed out of his warm bed, without thought or care for his wife, his sons, or his aged parents, and walked off down here in his sleep—to a drugstore that he had not thought of in a dozen years.

But it was no dream, no, that is, unless all visits back home be dreams of a kind. He was wide awake, no doubt about that. He was fully and quite properly dressed, except that he wore no hat—he never wore a hat when he was back home—and he was bent on a very specific and practical piece of business. . . . But what was the business? Ah, of course, the shaving lotion! He pushed open the heavy glass door and entered the drugstore rather breezily, just as though it were any other drugstore in the world. Fluorescent lights, giving everything an indigo tint, gleamed overhead and behind the counters and even inside some of the glass cases, as they would have done in any other modernized, up-to-date drugstore. But it was still so early in the day that there wasn't another customer in the place. In the artificial light and in the silence, there was the timeless quality of a bank vault. Or, more precisely, the atmosphere was that of a small, out-of-the-way museum where the curator doesn't really expect or welcome visitors.

To call attention to his presence Matt began dragging his leather heels on the tile floor. But at once he checked himself. The black and white tile under foot had suddenly caught his eye! How well he remembered the maddening pattern of it! And he was struck by the thought that this tile was the only feature of the once-familiar drugstore that remained unchanged. Even more striking to him, however, was the coincidence that last night in the railroad station he had had very nearly the same experience. The old Union Depot had, sometime very recently, undergone complete alteration, and when Matt had walked into the lobby just after midnight, he had believed for one moment that he was in the wrong city. During that terrible moment he had looked over the heads of the two sleepy boys at his wife and had given such a hollow laugh that Janie took a quick step toward him, saying, "What is it, dear? What is it, Matt?" Then the expanse of two-toned beige tiling, on which he had long ago played hopscotch, had seemed to come right up at him, and he felt such relief that he had sighed audibly.

Now in the drugstore, with his eyes fixed on the hypnotic black and white diamonds and octagons, he gave another such sigh. He felt relieved all over again not to have gotten Janie and the boys off the train in a strange city in the middle of the night. It really was not something he could possibly have done, of course, but that didn't diminish the relief he felt— last night or this morning. And while he continued to wait in the front part of the drugstore for someone to take notice of him, his mind dwelt further on his confusion last night. . . . "What is it?" Janie had asked still again, placing a gloved hand on his sleeve. He had tried to turn his sigh into a yawn, but that had not deceived Janie for one second.

"It's nothing," he had said, watching now for the porter to bring in their luggage. "I was only thinking how I used to play a kind of hopscotch on this floor whenever we came here to meet people."

Janie had looked at him with narrowed eyes, not at all convinced; on their visits home—especially just before they arrived—she always developed her own peculiarly mistaken ideas about what thoughts he was having. "Surely," she said now, "surely you can't have expected anyone to meet us at this hour, Matt. Especially after you insisted so that they not." . . . He wasn't even annoyed by her misreading of his thoughts. In fact, he had had to smile. And he even seized the hand that was resting on his sleeve and whispered, "My little worry-wart!" It was so *like* the notions she always took about his homecomings. She was ever fearful that on these occasions there would be some misunderstanding or quarrel between him and his father, or between him and one of his brothers, or even his gray-haired brother-in-law. Moreover, he knew that in her heart she was firmly convinced that there was some old quarrel between him and his family that had sent him to live away from home in the first place—some quarrel that he would not tell her about. In the early years of their marriage she had not let it bother her very much. But ever since the first baby came she had devoted considerable time to "winning him back to his family." She never put it into so many words—they were *his* words—but he knew what her thoughts were. (She had taken to writing regularly to his mother and even began remembering his father's birthdays.) It had originally seemed to him a good joke on her that she thought there were hidden wounds to be healed, but the joke had gone too far and she had at last become too serious about the matter for him to do more than smile and call her a worry-wart. Yet it really was laughable, almost incredible, to think how little she understood him with respect to his relations with his family—His was simply not a quarreling kind of family! They didn't have the passionate natures for it!—and particularly with respect to how he was affected by the prospect of a short visit with just his two parents.

His confusion last night, however, had been a rather extraordinary thing. And he had to acknowledge that it was due partly to the fact that none of the family was there to meet him. Always in the past at least one of them had been here. They thought it silly of him to insist upon coming home on the train instead of flying (They didn't understand what he meant by the transition's being too abrupt. And the difference in the fares was *so* trivial), but still one of them had always trekked down to the dingy old railroad station to welcome him—him and his family. Usually it was his father or one of his two brothers who came, because they considered it strictly a man's job to meet a train that arrived so late at night. They usually seemed amused to find themselves in the Depot again. They hadn't been there since the last time Matt came home! (Who else rode the trains nowadays but Matt?) And Matt was merely amused at their amusement. Why should he take offense at their condescension when he would only be home for a few days? . . . With whoever came to meet the train—father or brother—Matt and Janie and the boys would walk the length of the great Depot lobby, between the rows of straight-back benches on one of which a pathetic family would be huddled together and on another a disreputable looking old bum would be stretched out, asleep with his head on his bundle and with his hat over his eyes. And when the party came directly under the vast dome that rose above the lobby, Matt's father or brother would tell the boys to look up and see the bats whoozing around up there or see the absurd pigeon that had got himself trapped in the dome and was flapping about from one side to the other.

It had been a very different scene last night, however. The dimly lit lobby of old had been transformed. A false ceiling had been installed no more than ten or twelve feet above the floor. And a new, circular wall, with display windows for advertisers and with bright posters declaring how many people still rode the trains, altered the very shape of the room, hiding the rough stone columns around which children had used to play hide and seek. As for the wooden benches, they were replaced by plastic, bucket-bottomed chairs on which huddling together would have been difficult and stretching out alone quite impossible. And the lighting, though indirect, was brilliant; there were no dark corners anywhere.

In view of these changes Matt felt his moment of consternation and confusion upon entering the lobby a very natural response. He did not have to lay it, even in part, to his weariness from the long train ride. Yet when the porter had finally appeared with their luggage and he and his little family had passed out of the lobby and into the large vestibule at the main entrance of the Depot, something even more absurd, if no more confusing, happened. In a huge wall mirror which had always occupied its place there in the vestibule, Matt saw his own reflection; he mistook that reflection for some other male member of his own family. "Oh," he said under his breath. But his "oh" was not so soft that Janie didn't hear it. She perceived at once the mistake he had made. This time he might almost have shown annoyance with her. Her smile said, "You see, you *were* expecting to be met," but the smile was also full of love and was so overly sympathetic—be it sympathy ever so uncalled-for—that he could only gently push her and the boys through the doorway and follow them silently to the waiting taxi.

In the drugstore none of the clerks had come to work yet. Only the druggist himself was there, and as soon as he appeared, Matt apprised him of the business he had come on. "What kind will it be—what brand?" the old fellow asked. Matt gaped across the counter. He couldn't believe his eyes at first. It was the same old Mr. Conway who had been the druggist there twenty-odd years before. It was the same old Mr. Conway, and yet of course he didn't recognize Matt.

"I don't know, sir," Matt said respectfully. "Any kind."

The old druggist looked up suspiciously and with obvious irritation. "*Any* kind?"

Matt began to smile, but then he realized his mistake. One large vein stood out on the druggist's forehead precisely as it had used to do whenever he was vexed. . . . (Incredible, incredible that he should remember Mr. Conway's vein!) . . . The broad, flat nose twitched like a rabbit's. . . (To think that he should remember. How annoying it was.) . . . One more thing. The small, close-set eyes seemed to draw closer together as the druggist bent across the counter peering up at him. Then the total personality of the man came back to him,

and somehow it was all too much to be borne at this hour of
the morning. He shifted his gaze away from Mr. Conway.
But in the mirror behind Mr. Conway he saw another familiar face (oh, *too familiar*) and was struck by the guilty
expression in the round eyes that ogled back at him there.

"*Any* kind?" Mr. Conway was saying again. For a moment
the voice seemed to be coming from away at the back of the
store. But that was absurd. Mr. Conway was right here before
him. There was something back there, however, tugging at
Matt's attention.

"Yes, *any* kind," he repeated. They were like two birds or
two insects answering each other. Finally Matt broke the
rhythm of it. In the most impersonal, hard, out-of-town voice
he could muster, he said, "Any kind, my friend. And I'm
afraid I'm in a hell of a hurry."

He even managed to sound a little breathless. Unfortunately, though, it wasn't a very manly breathlessness. It was
a boy's breathlessness. It was as if this very morning he had
run all the way from home with his school books under one
arm and his yellow slicker under the other and was now
afraid that the streetcar—the good old Country Day Special
—would pass before he could get waited on. How terrible it
had been being a boy, and the world so full of Mr. Conways.

Mr. Conway turned away toward the shelves on the wall
behind him, to the left of the mirror and toward the rear of
the drugstore. (Still, still there was something back there
trying to claim Matt's attention. But he couldn't, or wouldn't,
look.) He tried to watch Mr. Conway as he examined the
various bottles. He was of course searching out the most
expensive brand. The old guy's rudeness was insufferable
and at the same time fascinating. As soon as his back was
turned, Matt felt himself seriously tempted to snatch up some
article off the counter and slip it into the pocket of his topcoat. As a boy he had never for a moment been tempted to
do such a thing, though he had seen other boys do it. They

had taken the most trivial and useless articles—ladies' lip-sticks, manicure scissors, get-well cards, though they would not have stooped to stealing candy or chewing gum. Not Country Day boys! But something distracted Matt from his temptation, and distracted him also from watching Mr. Con-way's evil, grasping fingers. (The fingers moved with awful deliberation and seemed bent on strangling every bottle they picked up.) What distracted Matt, of course, was that same familiar face in the mirror, his view of it now unobstructed by the figure of his malefactor.

Yet somehow or other it wasn't the same face in the mirror this time. The eyes weren't the guilty eyes of a school boy. The face wasn't really familiar at all—not *here*. The person in the mirror now eyed him curiously, even incredulously, and momentarily he resented the intrusion of this third, un-familiar person on the scene, a person who, so to speak, ought still to have been asleep beside his wife back there in the family's guest room. But he accepted the intrusion philo-sophically. In effect said to himself, "Look, look, look! Have your fill and let me get back to my important business with Mr. Conway." But the face had a will of its own. It had an impersonal, hard, out-of-town look, like the faces one gets used to seeing everywhere except in the mirror. It was one thing consciously to put those qualities into your voice; it seemed quite another to find them translated and expressed in your face without your even knowing about it.

But the impression lasted only for a moment. The eyes in the mirror grew warm and sympathetic. They were the same fine old eyes. It was the same fine nose too, just the littlest bit beefier than the boy's nose had been. The blond hair was as thick as ever through the temples. (If it lay flatter on top, you could not say for certain that it was really thinning even up there.) And the ruddy complexion was the same as of old, or was except for the "slight purplish cast" that his mother was always imagining when he came home, and had got his wife to imagining, and now had him half believing in.

By the time Mr. Conway had set the bottle on the counter before him, Matt Donelson had recovered himself—had been recovered, that is, by the grown-up self. The thought of his mother and wife had reminded him of the real circumstances of this day in his life. At seven forty-five a.m. on a Saturday morning he was in the drugstore where he used to hang out as a boy. It was the man to whom the strange cook had spoken so politely and respectfully that looked at Mr. Conway now —the mature Matt Donelson, aged thirty-five, a man with a family of his own but still a faithful and attentive son, a man whose career was such a going thing that he could easily spare an occasional four or five days for visits back home.

Poor old Mr. Conway. His hand trembled as he set the bottle down. Matt seemed to feel something inside himself tremble. Pitiable little old fellow, he thought. What kind of a career had he had? Probably the most that could be said for him was that he had held his own and kept up with the times. Instead of the white linen jacket that had once upon a time made him look like a butler, he now wore a sleazy, wash-and-wear tunic (with short sleeves and a tight collar) that suggested he was an elderly surgeon fresh from the operating room. Besides the addition of fluorescent lights, his drugstore had been refurbished throughout. The soda fountain was no more, and of course the tables and the booths were gone. There was now a large toy department, a hardware counter, shelves containing men's socks and jockey shorts, a serve-yourself freezer with half-gallon packages of ice cream, cartons of milk, even loaves of bread. Instead of the old lending library, innumerable paper-backs were offered for sale on two revolving stands. Mr. Conway—bless him, dear old fellow —had always had an eye for what brought in the money. No doubt he had a goodly sum stashed away. No doubt he was highly respected by the other storekeepers along this street. Within his lights, he was probably a considerable success. Perhaps his kind was, as everybody always said, the backbone of the community, even the backbone of the country. Matt was on the verge of making himself known to the old man and of reminding him of the days when Country Day boys waited for the streetcar in his store. He was on the verge; then he pulled back.

What was it now? Out of the corner of his eye he had caught a glimpse of the giant mortar and pestle that squatted on a shelf above the entrance to the pharmacist's prescription room. It had squatted up there in the old days; it seemed to be the only piece of the old décor that had been allowed to remain. The bowl was about the size and shape of a large wastebasket, and the boys, who had somehow always hated the sight of it, used to toss candy-bar wrappers and other trash up into it. . . . Was that what had made him pull back? Was it only this that had been calling for his attention back there all along? Or was it the electric light burning with such fierce brightness in the prescription room beyond the door· way? (How keenly he had felt the fascination of that intense light when he was fourteen.) But presently he answered his own question very positively. It could not be any of that. Surely not. No, it was the bottle of shaving lotion itself that had made him recoil and refuse to introduce himself to Mr. Conway. For, almost without realizing it, he had observed that Mr. Conway had actually set before him—albeit with trembling hand—the most expensive brand that such a drug-store as this would be likely to stock. Matt recognized the label, and despite the bottle's being tightly sealed and neatly cartoned he imagined he could detect the elegant scent.

"Didn't you have something cheaper?" he said.

Mr. Conway grinned, showing—yes—the same old dentures, row upon regular row. And when he spoke there was the familiar clamp and clatter. "I thought you didn't mind what brand," he said. His hand rested solidly on the carton now.

Without seeing himself in the mirror, Matt knew his face was coloring. His lips parted to speak, but at that instant he heard the sound of footsteps in the front part of the store. Someone else had come in.

"You want something cheaper, then," Mr. Conway said, in a loud voice.

"This will do," said Matt.

He quickly drew out a bill and handed it to the druggist. Just as quickly the old man drew change from the cash register and counted it into Matt's open palm. Before Matt's fingers had closed on the change, he glanced over his shoulder to see who it was that had come in. From the first sound of the footsteps he had felt an unnatural curiosity to know who this other person was. He had imagined that it might be someone he knew. But his shock upon glancing back now was greater than any he had received from the face in the mirror.

A rosy cheeked young man had come up directly behind him—a man ten years or so younger than himself. And the face of this young man, who was at the moment removing from his head a checked cap which matched the checked raglan coat he wore, was indisputably the face of old Mr. Conway as it had been forty years ago—long before even Matt had ever set eyes on him. A black fright seized Matt Donelson. Either this *was* a dream from which he could not wake himself or he was in worse trouble than any of those friends of his and Janie's back in New York—the ones they laughed at so for feeding the revenues of the analysts.

He looked back at Mr. Conway to make out if he saw the apparition too. But Mr. Conway's eyes were on the big clock above the entrance to the store. Matt looked up at the clock; and now he had to concede that there was, after all, another fixture that had been here in the old days. But *had* the clock been there when he came in five minutes ago? Perhaps before his eyes this modern drugstore was going to turn back into the place it had once been. Worst of all, the clock hands said that it was ten minutes to eight!—the time when the Country Day Special was scheduled to pass this corner. *Would* have been the time, that is, on a week day. *Had* been the time, that is, in the era of streetcars. Nowadays, he reminded himself, the boys rode to school on buses. . . . He put his two hands to his head and massaged it gently. He felt a swimming sensation.

"It's ten minutes to eight," Mr. Conway said flatly. Matt sensed at once that the old man wasn't addressing him. He felt better, and removed his hands from his head.

From behind him came the equally flat response: "I know."

And now Matt had no choice but to turn around and determine finally whether or not the young man were real. When he confronted him it was really as if he himself were the ghost, because the young man with the rosy cheeks and the shock of dark brown hair did not seem to see *him*. The young fellow was real enough all right but he seemed lost in a dream of his own.

Despite his being the youthful image of old Mr. Conway, with the same squashed nose and small, close-set eyes, he was a pleasant looking young man. And judging from the dreamy expression on his face, from his snappy clothes, and from the easy way he was now slipping out of his coat, he was a person fairly pleased with the world and not totally displeased with himself. Matt was a trifle offended by the way he seemed to be blind to *his* presence, regarding him as a mere customer and therefore not worthy of his direct gaze. (A family trait, no doubt, since this was certainly Mr. Conway's own flesh and blood.) But still, even before he heard him speak again, Matt was more attracted to the young man than put off by him.

Matt had already turned away and was moving toward the front of the store when he heard the young Conway addressing the old man: "We've morning sickness at our house again this morning." The voice was very masculine, very gentle, expressing keen pleasure in the tidings he brought. "It's a pretty sure thing now," he said.

Matt could not resist taking another glance over his shoulder. He saw that old Mr. Conway was already off to his prescription room, padding down the aisle behind the counter. He responded to his son's good news without bothering even to look at him. But he was clacking away as he went along, his plate making more noise than his footsteps, and speaking so loud that Matt heard him quite distinctly: "Well, that doesn't alter its being ten to eight when you turned up. And there have already been four prescriptions called in which I haven't got started on good."

The old Scrooge, the old bastard! ... Tyrannizing over this easy-going young fellow! ... Making no concession even at such an important moment! ... Matt felt it behooved him almost to go back and shake the young man's hand. But he didn't, of course. He had almost reached the front door now. He halted by the long magazine rack just to the left of the door. (Yes, there had always been such a rack there. Yet the rack was something else he hadn't noticed at first.) From the rear of the store he could hear the young Conway whistling. He let his eye rove over the display of magazines. Somehow he could not bring himself to leave. He tried to identify the jazzy tune young Conway was whistling, but it was something too recent for him. He continued to study the magazines. There was the same old selection. Only *Collier's* was missing. He remembered how the Country Day boys had been forbidden to touch a magazine they were not going to buy.

Presently the whistling was interrupted by the old druggist's voice.

"Is the music necessary?"

The reply was cheerful enough: "Not if you say so."

There was a moment's silence. Then, lowering his voice so slightly that it was only the more insulting to Matt, Mr.

Conway asked, "Is that the same customer up there, still hanging around?"

"Yep. The same."

"Better keep an eye on him. He let on to be in 'one hell of a hurry' when he came in."

"All right," said the young man, and Matt thought he heard an indulgent snicker. Boldly Matt turned around and looked the length of the store at the two men. The older man stepped back into the prescription room. Matt could not be certain but he believed the younger man, who was now in shirtsleeves, winked at him.

He turned back toward the magazines and gazed unseeing through the broad window above the rack. He was reflecting on the young man's undisturbed good spirits, on his indulgence toward his crotchety father. Mr. Conway was lucky indeed to have a son with such an understanding and forgiving nature. And suddenly it was as though the young Conway had communicated to Matt an understanding of the old man's ill humor and impatience this morning: It was due to Matt's interruption while he was trying to get those prescriptions filled. Matt could not restrain a malicious little smile. It was *so* like old times. They had always delighted in interrupting Mr. Conway when he was at work back there in the prescription room. Poor guy seemed to have had a lifetime of having his most important work interfered with. Whenever there was a piece of rough-house up in the front part of the drugstore and Mr. Conway had to be called from his "laboratory" to deal with it, the boys became almost hysterical in their glee. They were apt to be good as gold if he stood idly here by the front window with his hands behind his back. But somehow they could not bear his being at work in the prescription room crushing a mysterious powder with his pestle or turning up the blue flame of his Bunsen burner under a vial. It was wonderful the things they used to do in order to distract the druggist.

At the soda fountain, in those days, there was a youngish black-haired woman who was believed by some of the boys to be Mr. Conway's wife. Sometimes four or five of the boys would line up on the stools at the soda fountain and place orders for cokes. Then when the glasses were set before them they would pretend to have no money. At first the dark-haired woman would merely threaten to call "Dr. Conway." The boys, winking at each other, begged her not to, and even pretended to try to borrow the money from some of the other boys who were looking on. Finally the woman would throw back her head and call out at the top of her voice: "Oh, Dr. Conway! Dr. Conway!"

But the boys continued to search their pockets until the very moment the druggist appeared. (Apparently he worked with his plates out, because he always came through the door of the prescription room with his hand to his mouth as though he were just shoving them in.) Only at that moment did each of the boys make the miraculous discovery that he had the needed money after all. With one accord they all bent forward and plunked their money down on the marble counter. And when they had done this they would be overcome by such a fit of giggling that they couldn't drink their cokes. Sometimes they would have to go off to school without tasting the drinks they had ordered and paid for.

At another counter in the drugstore, where cigarettes and toilet articles and candy-bars were sold in those days, there was usually a somewhat older woman, a woman who was generally believed to be Mr. Conway's mother. Sometimes Mr. Conway himself presided at that counter; that was when the boys actually swiped the useless articles they found on display. But when his "mother" was in charge they always made a point of fumbling. . . . As a matter of fact, there was a school of thought which maintained that this older woman was the druggist's wife and the younger woman was his daughter. Since in the boys' eyes Mr. Conway was of an indeterminate age, all of them conceded that the truth might lie either way; and the women themselves would not tolerate questions about their identity. It remained always a mystery. . . . At any rate, in an emergency, "mother" Conway would place her two hands on the glass case before her, fix the suspect with her feline eyes, and call out in a coarse, plangent voice: "Do—oc—to-or!"

And the thief stood looking at her blankly until at last the druggist came in sight. The trick at this point, for the boy, was to stoop down and pretend to find the missing article on the floor where he had unknowingly knocked it. Then, handing it to the druggist himself, his next move was to begin making profuse apologies which could not be heard above the gleeful convulsions of the other boys and which continued until some boy at the front door shouted, "Special! Special!" After that, came the chaos of a general exodus. Amid the grabbing up of books and football gear and sheepskin coats, and against the clamor that accompanied the rush for the door, Mr. Conway was helpless. He stood watching them go, his nose twitching, the vein standing out on his forehead, his false teeth no doubt clacking, and holding in his hand a dented lipstick case or a pocket comb with possibly half its fine teeth broken.

Matt felt that he had seen each of these pranks played at least a dozen times. But Mr. Conway seldom took any action against the pranksters; these Country Day boys were the children of his best customers; their parents had the biggest charge accounts on his books; and Mr. Conway had always had a good head for business. Matt had seen even worse tricks than these played on the old man, though he himself had always been a little too timid, a little too well brought up, to have any part in them. He had generally looked on with amusement, but also with a certain disapproval. He had never so much as snatched up a magazine and stuck it under his jacket, or even broken the rule against glancing through a magazine one was not intending to buy. Suddenly now he realized he was at this very moment holding a copy of a news magazine in his hand. He pushed it back into the rack. Then he eased it out again. He held it in his two hands a moment, gazing blankly at the newsworthy face on the front cover. And before he could stop himself he stole a glance over his shoulder. . . . From beside the cash register the young Conway was watching him. . . . Slowly Matt turned around and, with the magazine he didn't want in one hand and with his other hand delving into his pocket for change, he walked back toward the young man. He had got sufficiently ahold of himself to make it a thoroughly casual performance.

The young Conway accepted the payment for the magazine with a positively friendly kind of smile. In fact, when Matt turned away he was again not sure that the young man had not winked at him. Despite his unfortunate resemblance to his father, the young man was obviously a sensitive, reasonable, affable sort. Matt felt drawn to him, wished they could have some conversation, longed to congratulate him on his wife's morning sickness. Matt felt also that there was some other purchase he had been intending to make which had escaped his mind this morning; surely there was *some* reason why he should not leave the drugstore yet.

This time he stopped before one of the revolving stands that held the paper-back books. He began turning the thing slowly. What else was it he had recently been intending to buy in a drugstore? He imagined that it had almost come to him the first moment he had looked back and seen the young Conway removing his checked cap from his head. Perhaps if he went back and made conversation with him now, the thing would come to the surface of his mind. Maybe the young Conway would enjoy hearing about the pranks that the school boys used to play on his father. No, that would not do. Especially not if one of those women who used to clerk in the store had been his mother; because, somehow, the worse the prank had been, the more it had always involved one or both of those women. It did seem to Matt in retrospect, however, that probably neither of the women was the real Mrs. Conway. Very likely they were both merely hired clerks, and the real Mrs. Conway—and her mother-in-law too, and the daughter if there were one—kept at home and looked after the young Conway, who would have been a mere infant at that time. Yes, there was a gentleness about the rosy cheeked young Conway, as seen today, that suggested a careful upbringing by women who didn't go out to work. . . . Yet one could not be sure, because those two women clerks, even if they were not in the mother-wife-daughter category, could not possibly have been more respectful of Mr. Conway than they were, or seemed more dependent upon him for protection. They believed absolutely in the old man's authority, and their confidence in him was resented by the boys. What strange power had he over those two women? This question, in the boys' minds, was lumped in with all the other questions they had about Mr. Conway. And all their pranks, if not intended to satisfy their curiosity, were at least intended to show that they knew there was something to be curious about. . . . There was the time, for instance, when Ted Harrison threw the stink bomb. The stench of the sulfur made Matt shake his head even now. The memory of it was that vivid. The two women didn't understand what had happened. The odor hadn't yet reached their nostrils when some of the boys began exclaiming in girlish voices: "O, that *awful* Mr. Conway! That *dreadful* Mr. Conway!" The two women stared at each other across the store for a time, then each of them began to spread her nostrils and sniff the malodorous air. The boys all set their faces toward the back of the store, focussing their eyes on the lighted doorway beneath the huge mortar and pestle. Presently, in a dramatic stage whisper, Ted Harrison asked: *"What* can Mr. Conway have *done?"*

Matt himself, standing near the soda fountain that day, had

fixed his attention on the face of the younger woman. He was watching her when she inhaled the first whiff of the stink bomb. Suddenly her nostrils quivered, her swarthy skin took on a curious glow, her dark eyebrows contracted. He could tell that her eyes had met those of the older woman, who was behind him at the other counter. Then simultaneously the two women fled their posts, running behind the counters toward the rear of the store. What indeed *had* their Dr. Conway done? They met at the entrance to the prescription room and disappeared through the doorway. There came the sounds of the three excited voices back there, and then presently Mr. Conway emerged, pushing in his dentures. The two women followed close behind him, but he soon sent them scurrying back to their places.

As Mr. Conway approached from the rear, the boys drew away from him toward the front of the store. They really were afraid of him. With downcast eyes they pretended to be looking and smelling all about to find where the stench came from. But suddenly Ted Harrison made a dash for it; he rushed right past Mr. Conway. "It's somewhere back here, I think," he shouted. He rounded the big glass case where hot water bottles and syringes and enema bags were displayed. And then, to the consternation of all, Ted Harrison passed beneath the mortar and pestle and through the bright doorway. He was out of sight for only one second, certainly not long enough to have done any damage or to have had more than a glimpse of the sacrosanct prescription room, but when he reappeared a cheer went up from the other boys. In fact, Ted was already outside again by the time Mr. Conway roared back at him to "get the hell out of there." And when the old druggist slipped in between the counters to try to head him off, Ted was already among his companions again in the front part of the store. Somebody shouted, "Special!" The front door was flung open. The crowd surged out onto the sidewalk, and without slowing their pace moved on into the street, and then, heedless of angry horns and shrieking tires, clambered aboard the waiting streetcar, some of them still chanting, "Special, Special!" until the streetcar doors were safely closed behind them.

There was probably never a worse incident than that one —except one, except one. There was that morning when some boy wrote with soap on the mirror behind the soda fountain. Another boy, probably an accomplice, had fallen or been pushed out of his chair at the little round table where he had gone to drink his morning coke. As he fell, his knee struck the tile floor—or so he pretended—and presently he lay on the floor moaning and groaning, and writhing in his pain. Of course the two clerks, those same two helpless, artless females, came hurrying to his succor. But he would not let them come near enough to examine the injured knee. "It's killing me!" he wailed, and he began thrashing about as though he were going into a fit. What else were the two honest women to do but cry out for their lord and master? And what else could Mr. Conway do but come forward?

He came warily, though, this time, shoving at his dentures and keeping an eye out for anyone who might make a rush for the prescription room. But his wariness and his precaution were needless and to no point on this occasion. Even before he appeared, a hush had come over the dozen or so boys who were present. Further, silently they had begun to gather up their possessions and to creep toward the front entrance. There was no cry of "Special" this time, and nothing false or pretended about the urgency they felt to be out of the place. Literally they had seen the handwriting on the wall. Clearly the consensus was that this time someone had gone too far. Matt, like a good number of the others, probably had not really seen which of them had done the writing. His whole attention had been directed toward the boy who squirmed on the black and white tile in the center of the store, and as Matt moved with the group toward the entrance, his eyes avoided another contact with the soapy writing on the mirror. But he had no need to see it again. It was written before his mind's eye forever. Twenty years later he could still see it just as distinctly as he could smell the sulfur of the stink bomb: the crude, hurriedly written letters spelling out the simple sentence, "Mr. Conway sleeps with his mother."

And at the door, as he passed out with the others, Matt had looked back to see that the boy on the floor had got to his feet and, with only the slightest pretense at a limp, was running on tiptoes to join his schoolmates.

Nobody waited to see how the writing on the mirror would affect Mr. Conway or the two women. But during the following two weeks Mr. Conway stationed himself at the entrance each morning and would not let the Country Day boys come inside the drugstore. It was in the dead of winter, and the boys had to wait outside in the cold, stamping their feet and beating ther hands together until the Special arrived. When at last Mr. Conway did relent, there was a period of a month or more when the boys came into the drugstore every morning and behaved like the real little-gentlemen that Country Day boys were sempiternally and without exception supposed to be. And during that period it was only with the greatest difficulty that Matt had been able to look directly into the eyes of either of the two women clerks. Whenever he wished to make a purchase he couldn't find his voice. If he did finally find his voice it would be either too soft or too loud. Or in the midst of whatever he tried to say his voice would break and change its pitch from high to low, or the other way round. The most painful part, though, was that before he could speak he would stand before the one or the other of the two women for several seconds, scratching his head and looking down at his feet.

That memory of the head-scratching! It was to mean Matt's release and salvation after standing there so long hypnotized by the revolving book stand. He came out of his trance, and he realized that he was actually at this moment scratching his head. And that was it. It was something to soothe his troublesome scalp that he had been meaning to buy in a drugstore. With great self-assurance he strode back to the counter where the young Conway was still on watch.

But when he stood face to face with the amiable sentinel there—so smiling, so fresh complexioned, so luxuriantly thatched (and with the luxuriant thatch so lovingly groomed) —he understood that it was not really he that he wanted to see again. It was the older man. And once again, some twenty feet from where he now stood, it was the giant mortar and pestle with the bright doorway underneath that caught his eye. It was a red flag waved before him—maddening. Ted Harrison had actually got inside the prescription room. But Matt Donelson had never even taken part in any of the pranks. He heard himself saying to the young Conway, "There's a matter I'd like to speak with the pharmacist about. I'd like to get some advice. I'd like him to recommend something."

The young man stopped smiling, and tried to look very serious and professional. "Maybe I can help you," he said. "As a matter of fact, I am a pharmacist myself. And my father is tied up with some prescriptions just now."

Matt continued to look at him for a moment or so without saying more.

The gentleness and sensitivity that showed perpetually in the young man's eyes was momentarily translated into a look of professional consideration for the feelings of a customer. But Matt would have none of that. The young Conway was obviously a mere slave—no man at all really. Else how could he consent to live under the domination of that brute of an old man? Moreover, Matt could tell that the young man thought he had guessed the nature of his ailment. He thought it was hemorrhoids that Matt was so hesitant to mention. "It's my scalp," Matt said abruptly. "I have a more or less chronic scalp complaint. No dandruff, but itching and an occasional breaking out."

"Ah, yes, I see," the young pharmacist began. And lifting his eyebrows he actually looked directly at Matt's head.

Matt looked back at *his* head. "If you don't mind," he said, "I'd like to speak with the senior pharmacist." He relished that last phrase, and he was pleased to observe that finally he had managed to offend the junior pharmacist.

Now the young Conway looked at Matt for a moment without speaking. Presently the inane smile returned to his lips. "Just one moment, please," he said to Matt. He turned and walked away, back to the prescription room. Matt could barely restrain himself from following. The young man stood in the doorway, leaning one shoulder against the jamb while he spoke with his father. Then he came back with a message.

"My father," he said quietly, "suggests that you probably ought to see a doctor."

Matt understood at once that there was more than one interpretation that could be made of that message. "I believe I'd like to speak to the pharmacist myself," he said, and was already striding alongside the counter and toward the doorway to the prescription room. But the young Conway was moving at the same speed behind the counter. They converged at the entrance to Mr. Conway's prescription room. And simultaneously the figure of the old druggist was framed in the doorway. Matt went up on his toes and peered over Mr. Conway's shoulder! He saw it all, the white cabinets and the bottles and the long work shelf, all so like a hundred other pharmacists' shops he had had passing glimpses of. Everything about it looked so innocent and familiar and really quite meaningless. There was no satisfaction in it for him at all— not even in the glass of water which he identified as the receptacle for Mr. Conway's teeth. But what kind of satisfaction should he have got? he asked himself. What had he expected? Something inside him which a moment before had seemed to be swelling to the bursting point suddenly collapsed.

"You told my father you were in a hurry," he heard the young pharmacist say. "I think you'd better get going now."

Looking at the young man, Matt observed that he definitely had a nervous tic in one eye. And all the blood had gone out of his cheeks now. He was in a white rage. Why, he even had his right fist tightened and was ready to fight Matt if necessary to protect the old druggist. The incredible thing was that only a moment before, Matt himself would have been willing to fight. Why? What had possessed him? Already the whole incident seemed unreal. Surely he had been momentarily insane; there was no other way to explain it. He backed away from the two men, turned his back to them, and quickly left the drugstore.

On his way back to his parents' house he kept shaking his head as if to rid himself of all thought of his absurd behavior in the drugstore. But at the same time he kept reminding himself of how near he had come to getting into a scrap with the young druggist, and perhaps the old druggist too. How unlike him it would have been, what an anomaly, how incongruous with everything else in a life that was going so well. He would never have been able to explain it to anyone. But even without the incident's ending in a real brawl, his behavior was nonetheless appalling. The only difference was that nobody ever need know about it. Finally he would be able to put it out of his own mind.

Back at the house, he found everyone up and stirring. The odors of the coffee and bacon greeted him in the front hall. From the living room he heard the voices of his two little boys commingled with those of his parents. "There he is now," he heard his mother say. He stepped to the cloak closet and hung up his topcoat, and while still at the closet he slipped the bottle of shaving lotion into the pocket of his jacket. He hesitated a moment, undecided about what to do with the magazine he had bought. It was a magazine he never read himself and one his father "thoroughly detested." Suddenly he stuffed it into the pocket of his father's heaviest winter coat. He knew it wouldn't be discovered there until his mother packed away the winter clothes the first week in May, and it pleased him to think of the mystery it would make and how they would talk about it for days. . . . As he left the closet, his father hailed him from the living room doorway with: "Where have you been?"

"Just out," Matt said, and then out of long practice was able to soften such smart-aleckness toward his father with: "Just out for a walk."

"I might have gone with you if you had given me a knock," said his father. The two boys appeared now on either side of their grandfather.

"So would I," said the older boy. He was ten and was beginning to want to dress like a man. He had put on a tie this morning and kept running a finger around the inside of his collar.

"Me too," said the little brother, who was eight and affected nothing.

Matt eyed the three of them. He observed that the old man was wearing the silk smoking jacket he and Janie had sent him at Christmas. "You were both slugabeds," he said to the boys. He went past them and into the living room to kiss his mother on the forehead. "That's a good-looking smoking jacket *he's* wearing," he said to her. His father shrugged, feigning indifference.

"He saves it for special occasions," his mother said. "It's very becoming to him."

"I'm going to run up and shave," Matt said.

On the stairs he met Janie. She had done her long, dull-gold hair in the way his mother liked it, *not* with the dramatic part in the center the way she and he liked it best but parted on the side and brushed softly across her brow and low over her ears to an upswept ratted effect on the back of her head. She looked old-fashioned, like some girl in a 1917 poster.

"Early bird," she said, as he came up toward her.

As they passed, he gave her hand a quick squeeze. "I must

shave," he said, rubbing a hand upward over his cheek. "They wouldn't like it this way."

"Oh, must you?"

"I don't look civilized," he said. "I'll hurry."

"No, don't hurry. You're sure to cut yourself if you hurry."

"Worry-wart, I never cut myself," he said.

From the top of the stairs he heard her addressing his parents a good morning. . . . It was wonderful being home. It was wonderful having his wife be so attentive to his parents, and his parents so admiring of Janie. It was fine having his parents enjoy the boys, and the boys and Janie enjoy his parents, and fine enjoying them himself the way a grown man ought to do.

He felt that everything was under control and that it was going to be a good visit. Once while he was shaving, in the bathroom, he saw his hand tremble slightly just before he was going to bring the razor up to his bristly throat. But he steadied the hand, and a little smile came upon his lips as he did so. He had already shaved around his mouth, and in the mirror above the lavatory be observed there was a certain cynicism in the smile. It was strange.

When he came down to breakfast, the others had already taken their places around the big dining table. They were all sipping at some kind of juice, but at his plate there was an orange and a fruit knife—as of old. His mother was watching his face, and he smiled at her appreciatively. There was also a box of cigars at his place. He picked up the box, examining it and reading the brand name, holding it gingerly in one hand as though trying to guess its weight. "I haven't had any of these in a long time," he said to his father, who pretended not to be listening. "I can't afford them." He took the box over to the sideboard, aware that his father was watching him, and put it down there. "You'll have to join me in one after breakfast," he said to his father.

"Not for me," the old man said. "Not any more."

Matt stood with his back to the room, looking down at the

cigar box on the dark sideboard. Somehow his father's words
held him there; he could not turn away. And suddenly a great
wave of despair swept over him. It caught him completely
off guard. He felt his heartbeat quicken beneath his shirt, and
he realized that his shirt was soaked with what must be his
own sweat. He placed his two hands on the sideboard as if
bracing himself against another wave, which came on now
with more fury than the first and which was not of despair but
of some other emotion less easily or less willingly identified.
It was like regret for lost opportunities, or nearly like that—
but already it had passed and already still another wave was
imminent. And then it came, the inevitable feeling that Janie
had been right last night, and always, about what was happening inside him at these homecomings. His first impulse
was to hurl the whole weight of his great good sense and
reason against the flood of feeling, but the deeper wisdom
of a long-time swimmer in these waters prevailed. He yielded
a little to the feeling and let himself be carried out a certain
distance, striving only to keep his head clear; and meanwhile
he kept telling himself, warning himself, in big, easy
strokes. . . .

"What are you doing over there?" his father was saying
now. Matt rummaged in his pocket for the small silver knife
he always carried (mainly for the purpose of paring his nails).
He opened the knife and began slitting the paper that sealed
the cigar box. He did a very precise job of it, careful not to
dig into the surface of the soft wood because he knew one
of the boys would want the box. Presently he turned to the
table with the lid of the box open and exhibited its fragrant,
orderly contents. Everyone strained to see. The smaller boy
stood up beside his chair and peered across the table. Apparently everyone took satisfaction from the symmetry of the
cigars and the orderly way they were lined up inside the box.

Matt stepped toward his father and said, "Take one for
after breakfast."

"I told you I've given up all that," his father said calmly, looking Matt in the eye. His father always sat very erect in his chair, especially at breakfast. And at that hour the old man's bald pate had a smoother, rosier look than it would have later in the day. His face stayed always the same, but by noon the top of his head would have a tired look.

"We'll see," Matt said, winking at his mother, and flipping the box lid closed. He had never felt more self-possessed.

But when he turned again and replaced the cigar box on the sideboard, he again found that something barred his rejoining the family group. This time there was no nonsense about waves sweeping over him or about keeping his eye on the shore. There was a different kind of nonsense: It seemed to him now that he had gone to that drugstore on purpose this morning, that he had planned the whole adventure before he ever left New York. It had been intended to satisfy some passing and unnamed need of his, but the adventure had cut too deep into his memory and into what was far more than mere memory. Inadvertently he had penetrated beyond all the good sense and reasonableness that made life seem worthwhile—or even tolerable. And through the breach, beyond, behind or beneath all this, he was now confronted by a thing that had a face and a will of its own. It was there threatening not only him and his father but the others too. Its threat was always present really, in him and in every man. It was in women too, no doubt, but they were so constituted that they never lost sight of it, were always on their guard, were dealing with it every moment of their lives.

Above the sideboard hung a dark still-life done in oils. It was protected, in the fashion of an earlier day, by a rather thick pane of glass. Behind this glass a dead fish lay upon a maroon platter, and beside the platter were stretched two dead pheasants in full plumage, their necks drooping over the edge of what seemed to be the same sideboard that the picture hung above. They were not very colorful pheasants, all dull browns and reds; and the leaden-eyed fish, with its lusterless scales and its long, tapering tail, bore more resemblance to a dead rodent than to any game fish. He had been at once fascinated and repelled by the picture as a child, then when he was older he had come to despise its triteness, and later he had learned to find it amusing. It had been painted by one of his great-grandmothers, and like the mahogany sideboard was counted among the family treasures. Suddenly now the limp tail of the dead fish stiffened and moved! Or perhaps it was the neck of one of the lifeless pheasants! . . . It was neither of course. The movement had been the reflection of his own face as he lifted it. He was not amused by the illusion. Momentarily the dim reflection of his face in the glass, superimposed upon the dark, unreal fish and pheasants, appeared to him as the very face of that Thing he had uncovered. The dark face loomed large in the glass and it was a monstrous obtrusion on the relatively bright scene that was reflected all around it—the innocent scene at the breakfast table behind Matt. In the glass he could see his mother nodding her head as she spoke. She was saying that one of his brothers was going to stop by the house to see them on his way to work this morning. And he heard Janie asking whether that brother's oldest child was going to graduate from high school this year. . . . How dearly he loved them all! And how bitterly the Thing showing its face in the glass hated them!

"Only out for a walk, eh?" his father was saying, just as though Matt's back were not turned to the room. The tone was playfully sententious. It was their old accustomed tone with each other. Matt massaged his face, as if to transform his features before presenting his face to the family. He reached into the cigar box and took out one cigar for himself, then headed toward the empty chair beside his mother.

"Yes, only out for a walk," he replied cheerfully. "And why not?"

"I don't know. You had a guilty look when you came in."

Matt was standing behind his chair at the table. Already he was able to laugh inwardly about the business of the boogy man in the glass. What nonsense! Perhaps it was a sign of age, letting a visit home upset him so. The truth was, it wasn't just waking up in his father's house and the visit to that drugstore. He had come to the age where waking up anywhere but in his own apartment or in any city but New York could throw him out of kilter. And he reflected that ever since he could remember, his father had disliked sleeping anywhere but in his own bed. It was very wise of the old man, very wise.

As he was getting into his chair he heard the older boy say to his grandfather, "Yes, he looked guilty all right. I noticed it."

"Yes, he sure did," added the younger boy.

"You two little parrots," Matt said fondly. And to his father he said, *"They're* just *like* you."

Janie burst out laughing. He could feel her relief. And his mother said, "You men."

Matt smiled at his father, waiting a moment before taking up his napkin from the table. He was aware that his smile was the same smile he had given his trembling hand upstairs.

"Just out for a walk, eh?" his father said again, childlike in the pleasure he took from the attention his remark had drawn the first time, and even more childlike in his effort to repeat or extend the pleasure. But Matt knew he wouldn't pursue the subject further. He felt that in a sense his father understood him better even than Janie did. And the old man had his own way of communicating it. Yes, it seemed to Matt that he and the man sitting at the head of the table had long, long since reached an understanding and come to terms with one another. Surely no one could say that either he or his father had not made those adjustments and concessions that a happy and successful life requires. They played at being father and son still, played at quarrelling still, but they had long ago absolved each other of any guilt. They were free of all that. As two men, they respected each other and enjoyed each other's company. All the rest was nonsense!

Presently the conversation around the table became general. Everyone chattered while they waited for the cook to come and remove the fruit juice glasses. The two boys were behaving extremely well with their grandparents, and Janie had never seemed easier or more at home in the house of her in-laws. Everything was going splendidly. Matt unfolded his napkin and stretched it across his lap. He experienced an exhilarating sense of well-being. He took up his fruit knife and began to peel his orange. He worked with a steady hand, displaying consummate skill, and was conscious that everyone else was looking on admiringly while he performed the rite. As he peeled away at the orange, making the coarse rind come out in long curls like apple peels, it was as though he could already taste the fruit in his mouth. Yet when finally he had put down his knife he observed with satisfaction that there was nowhere a break on the thin, inner pellicle of the orange. His satisfaction was so complete, in fact, that he could not resist lifting up the piece of fruit—unscathed and whole— between the fingertips of his own hands for a general inspection. Then for a moment he sat looking over the orange and into the faces of his loved ones, and he did not wonder at their grateful smiles.

Sky Line

"Is it God knocking?"

"No, no. That isn't God. That isn't God."

"Then it's the hanging baskets. The wind is blowing the vine-baskets against the house."

"After the wind has died, you may go out on the porch and look at the wall of the house, at the places where the wire baskets have chipped more paint off the boarding."

"They are Grandmother's baskets."

Then his little humpbacked grandmother is found dead in her bed one morning, and he must play in his room upstairs for two days. Out his window he watches automobiles coming from far off. They turn on streets which wind for no reason through a field, wide streets with sidewalks but with few houses and no trees along their borders. Down his street there is only the house on the corner and the speckled stucco next door where the little girl comes and leans against one of the porch pillars.

Everywhere in the fields are white signs with blue and red lettering that hurts the eye.

During the second day the Negro cook Cleo comes up and plays parcheesi with him while downstairs the music and the preaching go on. From his window he watches the hearse drive away with the long line of cars following it. On the winding street through the fields the long line moves like a black snake. Cleo says, "She wuz lyin' 'ere in bed when we find 'er—just like she be asleep."

Cleo leads him down the stairs by his hand, and they watch the Negro men loading stacks of folding chairs on a truck.

After the funeral some big wicker baskets are left sitting about in the front hall and on the porch. Just at twilight one day everything outside the living room window looks yellowish. Then the rain comes like a burst of tears; and the wind blows the wicker baskets over, and the tin cans from inside them roll about the porch floor. The tin cans and the wicker stands and the swinging baskets make a clatter like a jazz band. Even his mother goes to the window and looks out. And he says to her, "The wood will look pinkish in the spots where the paint is gone."

All the wicker baskets are at last stacked behind the garage and burned like old boxes. The tin cans serve in turn, as one after another rusts, for watering troughs to the white pointer which runs on a wire in the back yard. And the swinging baskets ("your poor grandmother's last efforts at gardening") are missing from the porch. After dinner on Sunday Cleo wraps them in newspaper and goes off toward the trolley with one under each arm.

The painters arrive that spring with ladders and spotted canvas, and paint his house a fresh white. Ever after he can see only sunken places on the white clapboard where the baskets knocked for years.

His father and the father of the little girl next door like to play "catch." They play on Sunday afternoons through every spring. Then his father wears a black sweater with yellow stripes that go around him like tiger stripes; and her father, whose hair is gray, wears a sweater that buttons down the front. Each of the men has a big five-fingered glove, and they sit on the porch the first spring-like Sunday and oil their gloves. Sometimes Joseph, the Negro who works next door, plays with them, and then the three men will yell such things as, "Out on first!"

Once the little girl's mother calls Joseph into the house, and Joseph throws his glove to the boy as he runs toward the kitchen. His father whistles through his fingers and shouts, "Replacement on third!" Joseph's glove smells sweatier than his father's. It has more stuffing and no fingers outside; and it's wet inside. But the boy soon forgets, for he has caught the first baseball ever thrown to him.

In a few weeks he is thinking, "I can catch about as well as either of them." And after his own yellow mitt comes and a ball and a bat with black taping, he plays catch with other boys during school recess. There he sometimes recalls Joseph and his smelly mitt and wonders what ever has become of the two, for the little girl's mother now has a Negro who doesn't like to play catch.

After two years of baseball he is certain that he can catch as well as the men, though he can't throw as hard as they might. He plays with them often.

A ball comes so straight and hard from the little girl's father that the boy throws off his glove and rubs his palm on his pants leg.

His father, without a word, speeds toward him and picks up the ball.

The boy did not have to take off his glove. He just feels disgraced because he cannot throw one back as hard.

His father hurls the ball at the neighbor, who sees it barely in time to shield his glasses with his forearm. But the ball strikes the man's elbow and falls to the ground. As he straightens his arm, he winces. But he makes a sudden lurch and sweeps the ball from the ground with his right hand. His upper lip shortens under his nose, showing his purplish gums. He squints and sends the ball back to the younger man.

The boy watches the ball as it flies. With a quick wave of his hand his father motions him to go. He feels his way backward toward his house, his eyes on the two men who have never before thrown much harder than he.

The ball bounces from his father's glove, but he catches it in the air and shoots it back.

The older man is smiling. His face is red and moist.

The ball goes straight back and forth.

They stand about sixty feet apart with the big round bed of zinnias and petunias between them.

Again the ball bounces from the younger man's glove. It falls on the grass. He stoops slowly to pick it up, his gaze on his neighbor. The sod is a fresh green and his body makes no shadow on it, for dark clouds have been gathering in the sky of the March afternoon. The father takes a slow, deliberate wind-up which seems so professional to the boy that his mouth falls open.

But the neighbor laughs aloud and sends a ball back that jolts the boy's father. The boy blushes.

The speed of the ball is slow for a few throws, then gathers speed, then slows, and suddenly speeds again.

The boy's back is to the white clapboard of his house. He is breathing heavily, his little chest rising and falling. Across the lawns he sees the little girl leaning against a pillar on her own porch. She is bouncing a red rubber ball, and he thinks, "Why, the dumb thing doesn't see it at all." He is sweating as hard as the men when the rain begins to fall; but he feels only an occasional drop, for he is under the eaves of the house. As the rain comes harder and the two men pay no heed, he sees the little girl give closer attention to the game of catch. He smiles in his scorn for her as she steps to the edge of the porch and stands in the afternoon light which is yellow now.

The rain streams now like a waterfall.

It pours off the eaves of the house as from a pitcher and runs about his feet.

Either man can hardly hold the ball. It will slip from his fingers, and he will pick it up and hurl it toward the other. The striped sweater and the buttoned sweater both are heavy and are dripping water.

The older man takes off his fogged glasses and puts them in the pocket of his sweater, and then he throws the ball straight again.

The boy's father shoots it back quickly, with an oath.

His neighbor stops the ball high above his head and laughs. He dries the ball on the underside of his sweater before he throws it this time.

Now the little girl has begun to cry. She lets her red rubber ball go, and it rolls off the porch and into the rain.

The boy's father slips and falls on the grass when he stops the baseball in his wet glove, but he jumps up, dries his hand and the ball, and throws the ball again. It smacks the wet leather of the older man's glove, and he stands shaking a stinging hand, and he has begun to cough now. As he draws back his arm to throw, the little girl begins bouncing herself up and down on the porch and calling to him. And the baseball crashes through his neighbor's garage window.

The two men stand in the rain, each with his gaze fixed on the blurred figure of the other. Then the boy's father turns his back and starts slowly through the rain toward his own house. The little girl runs to meet her father, but he pushes her and looks back once more toward the little boy and his father.

The boy and the little girl walk on opposite sides of the street from that time, but, anyway, he is now too old for girls. There are little boys who live in new houses which are now scattered along the winding streets and along his own block, and he is learning to fight with his fists. One day he tears the scab off a sore on his deskmate's wrist. After school they fight behind a white and red and blue For Sale sign in the lot where the Catholic church is going to be built. During his bath after the fight he finds that the deskmate has given him a bruise on his thigh, and the bruise is still there the next Friday when the deskmate's sore has gotten a new scab; so he, all of a sudden, tears off the second scab with his fingernail. This time the deskmate goes to the teacher and shows her his sore. The teacher changes their seats. And the last he remembers of the matter is his former deskmate's writing on the blackboard with a white bandage on his wrist.

The new Catholic church is hardly finished in August when the new school building is started in the next block. The church is of yellow brick with a great round window above the main doorway. And for the new school the workmen are digging in the ground all through August. The lot they work in has always been covered with waist-high yellow grass, and every day the boy looks at the grass which the workmen have trampled down until it lies flat like the hair on a boy's head. He has never played in that lot with its high grass as he once used to do in the church lot, and has felt that it looked like "the central plains of Africa." But the workmen dig deep, and now the heaps of red dirt look like the "forbidding Caucasian mountains."

By Christmas the workmen have only laid the concrete in the long, narrow basement and put up a few concrete shafts, and the thing stands like that until spring. Finally he gets used to the lot looking that way.

Some of the children, especially the new children, like to climb down into the long basement, and they build a snow man there during the last snow in March. But a feeling that the lot isn't completely changed and yet isn't as it has been keeps the boy away. Things have changed in the suburb; repeatedly he has told the new children how things once were, he is that conscious of it; but something forever keeps him from trying to observe too closely just how the new buildings go up.

One day the little girl's father is dead. The boy's own mother and father talk for a long while in their bedroom with the door closed. Afterward his father goes next door, and still later the Negro man comes and asks his mother to come. The boy sits at the window of his little room upstairs all afternoon and watches the other neighbors come and go across the lawns.

Two young neighbor women stand on a lawn across the street and talk, gesticulating; and one keeps shrugging her shoulders. The little girl appears outside the back door of her house with a pair of scissors which glisten in the sunlight. Her dress is white and it's so plain and long that her legs look short and her body very long. She goes to the round zinnia bed and looks ponderously at the flowers.

The window is up, and the boy sits on the sill, his head leaning against the screen. The girl bobs up and down among dull-colored flowers, very soon holding an armful of zinnias.

The boy begins to whistle a doleful cowboy tune.

She looks up from the center of the zinnia bed. He stops short. She scans the windows of the house, but she cannot make out his figure through the black wire screen. She stoops again, and he whistles one high note. She peers suddenly up at his window, opens her mouth and, sobbing, scampers on her short legs into her house.

And he stays at the window, looking out over the tile and shingled rooftops of the new houses and at the yellow tower of the new Catholic church.

Soon after school starts that fall the house next door is sold, and the little girl and her mother are moved into his own mother's guest room, the room which was once his grand-mother's.

"I'll miss having a guest room," his mother says, "but it's not permanent."

One afternoon people come in automobiles and on foot from the neighborhood, and the furniture is moved out of the stucco house into the yard and sold. The boy sits on the edge of the porch and thinks, This is a sight I won't forget —beds and tables and easy chairs on the lawn, especially with men and women dropping down into the chairs and then getting up and looking at them with their heads cocked to one side.

What didn't sell is brought into his house, and the sitting room seems a different place with the new green chair and footstool which doesn't match the set.

The little girl is a grade ahead of him and so goes to the new school which is called "Junior High." She has to go to school earlier than he, and he is grateful for this. For she is now an inch taller than himself, and it makes him uncomfortable to walk with her.

One Saturday at noon, as he comes in from baseball, she meets him at the front door.

"Something's happened," she says.

He is putting his mitt and ball into the closet under the stairs. He looks at her and feels that she is somehow too tall to be wearing the plaid knee socks.

"Your daddy's lost his job," she says.

The boy answers resentfully that his father will get another as quickly as he has lost this one, and he goes upstairs. But as he passes his father's room he sees him stretched across the bed and sees the two women seated in rocking chairs, looking at one another. He tiptoes back downstairs and goes into the sitting room where the little girl is reading a magazine. He sits down and looks at her—lounging in the green chair with her round, bare knees over the green stool. She puts the magazine aside.

"Mama's going to work," she says. "And I guess I will, some way."

The changes that will come flood his imagination. The past

seems absolutely static in the light of what he feels is to come.

"So will I," he says.

Soon he is able to get a paper route, and now his mother rouses him at three every morning and gives him coffee before he goes out. Through the winter he wears a pair of his father's hunting boots with several pairs of socks to make them fit. One morning his mother runs barefooted through the snow on the lawn, shining the flashlight that he has forgotten. She calls to him:

"Your light! Your light! You forgot your light!"

The sight of her there in the dark and cold, barefooted and in her kimono, is so literally dreadful to him that he turns and runs from the sight. And he can hear her calling, "Your light! Your light! Your light!" until he is almost to the trolley line where he picks up his papers.

The boy's imagination is soon conjuring pictures of the two families on the fourth floor of a downtown tenement house. Several families on his block have had to move from their houses during this fall, and other houses on his route have been found empty on collection day. But his mother will say to him over his cup of coffee, "The house is mine. I'll work my fingers to the bone to keep it." She finally has to give up Cleo, the cook; and they only feed the Negro man who has worked for the little girl's mother, until he can pick up another job.

The little girl's mother has started to business school. She and his father leave in the automobile each morning. He can see them pass from the schoolhouse window and realizes that the automobile is getting to be an old number. When he comes home in the afternoons, his mother will sometimes be washing or ironing the clothes in the kitchen. It's when he comes in one day and sees her on her knees waxing the dining room floor that he first observes how narrow her hips have got; and he turns from her and goes up the stair, two steps at a time, to his room. He looks at the school pennants about the walls, and his tears blur the scene. He looks out his window over the rooftops of the suburb and hears the boys yelling down behind the new school. And he takes off his leather jacket and slips his black football jersey on over his head.

But it seems that even his father's loss of his job hasn't been as simple and as quick as he had supposed. His father's whole company is going out of business, and there are articles about it in the newspaper every few days, his father's testimony in the courtroom being quoted once. During the weeks that his father is at home, before he has found the new job "on commission," he will sometimes walk up and down the front porch with his hat and coat on; and the boy's mother will look out the window at him and say to her son or to the little girl, "Through the whole litigation his innocence, honesty, and integrity were not once questioned."

By spring the little girl's mother has an office job at the same place his father sells from. They have not renewed the automobile license this year, and every morning the two breadwinners walk three blocks, by the little hedges and young Lombardy poplars, to the trolley.

One Saturday morning the boy comes back from his paper route late and passes the pair on the sidewalk. The little girl's mother says something to his father, who calls out to him, "Hold yourself up straight!" and calls him, "Longlegs." So he throws his shoulders back and begins to run. He hears them laughing until he turns the corner, and then he feels shaken up inside and hot about the forehead.

His mother is at her sewing machine by her bedroom window. He comes and stands beside her and with a half smile on his face says, "I'm catching lockjaw, I guess. I feel stiff in my jaw, under here, and everybody says that's the first symptom." His mother slips two fingers down his shirt collar, feeling the nape of his neck.

"Why, you're cooked with fever," she says. And she hasn't got him into bed in his little room before he begins to cough from his chest. It had poured rain through the first half of his route that morning; and she had tried to persuade him to wear his "rain things." "You've caught your death of cold in that rain," she says.

By the next afternoon he is considered "a very sick boy." His temperature is 103½. The doctor comes and says that it may turn into pneumonia.

"Now, if this does take a turn for the worst, it will be best to have him in a hospital."

"No, I want him at home."

"*They* can take better care of him."

"I think not, Doctor."

"You'll need a nurse."

"I must take care of him, Doctor."

The voices sound like echoes, and the human figures seem far away. Later he can hear the murmur of voices in his mother's room. His father and the little girl's mother are arguing with her, and they sound as though they may be away in some valley.

The next day, Monday, his mother tiptoes about his room, and the doctor comes twice. He can hear the doctor's voice more distinctly in the front hall downstairs than when he is by his bed talking to him.

Sometimes the little girl will sit in the room with him and read her magazine. He lies there during the afternoon with flannel and plasters about him, content to look at the walls and think of the other wallpapers that he remembers there. One can hardly see the wallpaper, for it is decorated with pennants and calendars.

In the middle of the night he wakes and sees that the light is wrapped in a piece of blue tissue paper. His mother says, "You've been out of your head for five hours."

"How sick am I, Mother?"

"You haven't pneumonia."

The doctor comes in a while and tells him he'll begin to get better now.

His father comes too and pats him on the back of his warm, limp hand, but says nothing. And when he leaves the room, the boy remembers the dreams of his delirium: His father and the mother of the little girl lay dead on the streetcar tracks. Cleo, the cook, was back in the kitchen, and his mother was telling her, "You can't really call the accident a tragedy." And he and his mother broke into gales of laughter.

The next fall the boy himself goes to Junior High. But the little girl dresses and acts so much older than he does now that he doesn't mind walking with her. She has gotten very fat, and he teases her about that and about the boys that talk to her at recess. Occasionally she will lend him money, but it is only to keep him from teasing her about the boys during dinner at night. She is so fat and so polite in public now that she seems a different person from "the little girl," as different as his mother is from her former self, as different as the corner on the trolley line is with the new drug store on it.

He works in the drugstore after school. He serves sodas to the high-schoolers in automobiles and wears a white apron and a white fatigue cap on the side of his head. One afternoon he sees, through the drugstore window, a tall, thin woman approaching the store. It is a familiar figure, yet he can't identify it as his mother for several seconds. She rarely leaves their street now that the automobile is shut up in the garage without any license, and she has lost even more weight in the past months. He thinks, I have a right to resent her coming to the store if it is not on business. He steps away from the window and waits.

When she doesn't come through the door, he looks out again; and it is just in time to see her step up into the trolley car that rumbles off toward town.

And yet it is not many days after this that he hears her tell his father over the telephone that she won't meet him in town for dinner because she dislikes to ride the trolley.

The little girl's mother and his father stay in town to work two, sometimes three, nights a week, and they never come out on Saturday afternoons now. They usually call and try to get his mother to meet them somewhere. When they come to dinner on Saturday nights his father invariably smells of whisky, and the boy sometimes feels certain that a part of the odor comes from the little girl's mother. His father will say at the dinner table, "I'll tell you this selling game is different. Sociability counts for everything."

Again and again he sees his mother take the trolley for town in the afternoons. He suspects her of going in the mornings some days, for twice he has found her making the beds when he comes by home to leave his books after school. He wonders, sitting in the glare of the many-windowed schoolroom, if his mother is this very minute on one of her mysterious missions and if his father and the little girl's mother are drinking with someone over a sale downtown. If so, his house, a few blocks away, is empty. Not even the white pointer runs in the yard, for his father never hunts any more and has said that he's not mean enough to keep a dog and not hunt him. It pleases the boy to think of the house totally empty and to reflect that under the paint the marks that the vine-baskets made are actually still there.

At home he listens. He pretends to sleep on the couch after dinner at night. Spring comes, and he sits on the porch— under the window. He never closes the door to his room. He listens, and at last he hears.

He stands in the upstairs hall one night, poised, ready to move to the bathroom if the parents' door opens. His mother has made some sort of confession, and his father is saying, "Why didn't you tell me?" Those are the only audible words. But in a few days his father tells him that his mother is going to the hospital. She is going to have a mighty serious operation.

And she packs a little Gladstone bag at bedtime one night. He watches her from the hall, putting in the pink silk night-gowns, the quilted bathrobe, and her hair brush. In the morning his father and the little girl's mother and his mother go into town on the trolley together.

He is called to the principal's office from his geometry class. The principal, Miss Cartright, is an unpredictable, white-haired woman behind a pair of horn-rimmed glasses. The expression on her face is an absolutely new one this time.

"My child . . ."

"Yes, ma'am, Miss Cartright."

"You are a young man now. Do you understand?"

"Yes'm."

"I feel that you are unprepared for what I have to tell you, but you must accept it bravely."

"Yes'm."

"You are aware that your mother has not been well?"

"She's in the hospital. She's not dead, is she?"

"She died this morning . . . under the knife."

"May I get my books?"

"Yes, but wait a moment, child."

"Hadn't I better hurry home?"

"Wait, child. We must be sure that you know what this means."

"I know."

"You'll not see your mother alive again. You'll not have her careful, guiding hand to help you."

"Yes'm, I know, Miss Cartright."

"There will be hours of loneliness. And your father's not your mother. He can't take her place, however hard he try. . . . There, there. None of this in a big boy like you. Come to me. I want to be some comfort to you, not just a teacher."

The funeral is held in the undertaker's parlor, and the boy looks in the coffin at his mother's powdered face. At the ceme-

tery, when they are arranging the flowers over the grave, he
recalls how the wicker baskets blew about the porch after his
grandmother's funeral and how his mother went to the window and looked out.

For several weeks he waits to hear of his father's plans to
sell the house. The other two argued with his mother over
that the night before she went to the hospital, and he heard
his father say after the funeral that it would have added ten
years to her life if she had sold the house. "This house," he
said, "was the biggest tumor she had." But nothing was said
of a sale after that.

All that summer the boy keeps the yard as though his
mother were alive and nagging him about it. The girl does
the housekeeping with the help of a Negro woman named
Jessie. Their parents take them to a downtown picture show
at least one night a week now. Coming back one night on the
trolley he says to the little girl's mother, "Why doesn't Daddy
sell the place and move to town?" But she changes to another
topic for conversation as though she had not heard him.

When he and the girl are at the top of the stairs that night,
she whispers, "Don't you know, Foolish, that you own the
house and can't sell it till you're twenty-one?"

This year the girl has begun at the high school; so she has
to take the trolley into town with her mother and his father.
She wears silk stockings all of the time and she fixes her black
hair in a knot on the back of her fat, white neck. She has a
friend named Susie who uses quantities of lipstick and cheek
rouge and who comes home with her many afternoons. The
boy pays little attention to them until one night Susie stays
for dinner, a night when the grown people don't come home.
During dinner the girls tell long stories with elements in
them which he thinks are very funny but which he thinks they
don't understand, being girls. After this he likes to talk with
them and to try to find out how much they do understand.
He will sit sometimes and just watch them file their finger-

nails. But when Susie offers him her picture once, he says he doesn't want it.

Then his father calls him into the living room one Sunday and tells him that the girl is a young lady now; and tells him that he must let her have his room and that he must move his belongings into his father's room. The boy hangs his head in protest. Finally he looks up and says, "I don't want to, Daddy."

The girl's mother is sitting across the room, and she looks at him soberly and says nothing. He sees, as if for the first time, that she wears as much lipstick and cheek rouge as Susie, and that her hair, gray on top, is bobbed and combed close to her head like a man's. His father stands up; he goes and sits on the arm of her chair. "You'll move your things after dinner tonight," he says. As the boy leaves the room, the father calls, "I'll help you, old man." And the girl's mother says something in too hushed a tone for him to hear her words.

But he likes rooming with his father. He is allowed to put his pennants on the walls of the big room and is told that he can arrange the furniture any way he likes. Often the two will go to bed at the same time and will lie in the dark talking of baseball. He sees the whole household with a different perspective. And now it is his father who is a different person.

There are times when he hears his father come into the room long after he has been in bed. And when the heavy body slips under the cover beside him, he can smell the alcohol and feel and hear the heavy breathing. Then he dreams of a day, certainly not more than a year or two hence, when he will be able to ask his father for a cigarette.

One night the boy and his father are in bed in their dark room when the clock thumps past ten.

"Are you awake still, son?"

"Wide awake."

"Tell me how much you are saving of what you earn."

"All right, s'r. Half of it."

"You must learn just how much it means to save money. If you don't save, then you will have to work when you are tired."

"When I'm old?"

"You may get tired before you get old. And if you're tired and know you'll never be able to rest, you'll get desperate."

"Oh, I suppose that *would* make you turn crooked."

"It might, if you could let yourself. If you can't let yourself turn crooked, despair will make things bad in a hundred other ways, anyhow."

"How much money do you make, Daddy?"

"In a good month?"

"Yes, that'll do."

"Enough to pay back what I borrow in a bad month."

"You aren't mentioning figures, I guess?"

"I didn't press *you*, did I?—for how much you save."

"I'll tell you."

"No. No, don't."

"It's a good deal."

"Yes. I'm afraid of how much it might sound like to me."

One night the boy is awakened by the sound of heavy rain. "I must put down the window," he thinks. But presently someone, barefooted, tiptoes through the bedroom door, across the room, toward the window. It is his father; and he removes the prop and lowers the window noiselessly but for the squeak of the sash, and he leaves the room again. Then quite distinctly his voice comes from the hallway: "Both of them." And presently the door to Grandmother's former bedroom scrapes the floor as it closes, and the boy tries to visualize the dark scene on his mother's guest room bed.

It is a day when the wind rustles the treetops, even the tops of slender poplars; and yet the wind is so soft, nearer to the earth, that it barely stirs the flaps of the boy's shirt collar. The sky is turquoise, and the hurried clouds look pink in their centers. The boy stands in the middle of the circular flower bed, surveying his work. His shirt is khaki and his trousers are faded blue jeans. His height measures somewhat over five feet, and atop his head his straight, brown hair stirs gently with the flaps of his shirt collar. His shirt sleeves are rolled above the elbows of his long, thin, white arms. In his right hand he holds a rusty trowel.

One third done, he says. From his feet, in the center of the flower bed, a section of broken earth, cleared of all the green spring shoots but the little zinnia and petunia plants, stretches out to the rock border. One hundred and twenty degrees, he says; and he turns to the other two thirds of the bed, which are green with clover and grass and dandelion. His long shadow falls across those two thirds to the border and divides them evenly. He points with the trowel to the section on his left and pronounces: "Four-thirty." Then he points to that at his right hand and says: "Five o'clock." He stoops, drives the trowel around the roots of a dandelion plant, and shaking the dirt from the root throws the weed beyond the stone border of the bed.

Inside the house the telephone is ringing. It rings for so long a time that he stands up and looks over his shoulder toward the house. The ringing ceases, and he stoops again and digs. It is not long before the girl is walking along the wall of the white clapboard house. The boy is on his knees working carefully between two tiny zinnia shoots. He watches her approach from the corner of his eye. She wears high-heeled brown and white shoes and no stockings on her legs, which are fat and at the same time muscular. Her skirt, a plaid material with a predominance of green and orange, is stretched around her big hips. And her tan sweater fits too closely under the arms and is drawn across her matronly breasts too tight to be less than obscene.

She stands close to him with her shaven legs far apart. He

looks up at her; she is standing with her hands on her hips, and he thinks that her clothes fit her as the shrunken summer covers do the big living room chairs. Her brown, bobbed hair blows in the wind, and one strand plays over her unpowdered face.

"Jim, darling," she says, "they're married."

"Who's married?" he says as though to deny the possibility.

"Mother and . . . Mommy and your father."

"And you're glad?" he asks.

She weighs the question for a moment. "I don't think I care a snap, Jim."

He looks at his trowel and then inquires with indifference in his voice: "Did you know they would?"

"Only by conjecture. But Mommy just called on the phone, and I talked to both of them."

With some deliberation he digs his trowel into the ground and pulls up a clod of dirt with grass on it; but she remains before him. Then he asks, "Will they be out to dinner to-night?"

"No," she says, brushing the strand of hair from her face with her pink hand, "they've gone to Chicago for the week end. I think they'll stay even longer. It's a long way up to Chicago."

The girl has turned and is walking toward the house. She walks over the grass on the balls of her feet. And he gazes after her heavy figure.

He is digging in the last green third. Of a sudden his breath seems to catch in his chest and his temples grow hot. He is squatted, resting his haunches on his heels. He raises his head in surprise at his own sensation, and he speaks out loud to himself: "I'm not sorry about *them*." But he cannot say what it is.

The light of the afternoon has a yellow tint in it. He looks at the sky. The whole western sky is a black mass, one that is advancing rapidly to meet the puffy gray clouds which clutter

the eastern horizon and the sky overhead. He digs his trowel
into the earth, uproots, tears, and digs again.

The shrill whistles in the distance have blown for five
o'clock, and he is working assiduously at the blades of grass
that grow from between the rocks of the border. He has finished the last third of the bed, but he works on. He does not
raise his head; his eyes follow his fingers plucking grass from
between the rocks. Something has filled him with a dread of
quitting. It isn't, he tells himself, the thought that he must
realize the marriage of his father to the mother of the girl,
that he must go into the house with only that to occupy his
mind. And yet he can't assure himself that it is only a dread
of the memories that the yellow light will bring when he looks
up into it. He feels the first drop of water on the back of his
neck at exactly the moment that he hears the voice of the girl:

"Jim, darling, do come in out of the rain."

He stares up at the white clapboard house through the
bilious light and discerns the figure of the girl at the window
of her bedroom, the room which once was his own.

He drops his trowel on the grass and walks, with his heart
beating under his tongue. The electric light burns in the
girl's room, and he can see her in the window through the
black screen. He walks with his arms hanging straight at his
sides as though he carries two heavy pails of water in his
hands. In that strange light his eyes meet the girl's eyes
through the fine mesh of the screen. Her eyes are darker than
her hair.

A clap of thunder jerks the eyes of both toward the sky,
and the rain bursts upon him. He runs three steps and leaps
over the shrubbery onto the end of the porch. There he turns
his face toward the yard and stands rigid, and his pulse throbs
in his wrists. He senses that the girl is still at the window.

His hand turns the cold brass knob of the front door, and
he flings open the door. The furniture of the hall is a group
of strange objects to him. How weird are the roosters in the

design of the floor rug, the crack on the table top mended
with yellow plastic wood, and the crazy angle of the mirror.
He is unbuttoning his wet shirt as he runs up the stair and
he tears it off as he shoves open the door to the room in which
he once used to sleep.

The bed is between him and the girl, who is wearing a
crepe de Chine negligee. She sits down on the other side of
the bed, puts one hand softly on the pillow, and says, "What
do you want, Jimmy?" He crosses the room. She twists her
body and throws herself face downward on the bed. The boy
stands over her, his wet shirt in his hand, looking at the back
of her head. The girl rolls over on her back and smiles up
at him.

He looks into her brown eyes under her heavy low brow
and sees, he feels, the innocence of someone years younger
than himself, the innocence of a very little girl. Her head is
sunk in the fat, white pillow. She crooks her elbow behind
her head and smiles up at him. She shifts the position of her
body and rubs her bare feet together. Her eyes, he thinks,
are like the brown eyes of a young dog. His temples are ablaze
and presently he knows that his whole face and perhaps his
whole bare chest is the color of the girl's rouged cheeks. He
quickly turns his back to her and finds himself looking out
the window through falling rain at the rooftops of the suburb.
While his eyes are fixed on the yellow tower of the Catholic
church and he stands braced by his hands on the window sill,
the sudden loud laughter of the girl on the bed slaps his ears.

He doesn't know how long the laughter lasts. The rain falls
outside the open window, and now and again a raindrop
splashes through the screen onto his face. At last it is almost
night when the rain stops, and if there is any unnatural hue
in the light, it is green. His heart has stopped pounding now,
and all the heat has gone from his face. He has heard the
hanging baskets beat against the house and felt the silence
after their removal. He has heard the baseball smacking in

the wet gloves of the men and seen the furniture auctioned on the lawn. The end of his grandmother, the defeat of his mother, the despair of his father, and the resignation of his new stepmother are all in his mind. The remarkable thing in the changed view from the window which had once been his lies in the tall apartment houses which punctuate the horizon and in the boxlike, flat-roofed ones in his own neighborhood. Through this window the girl too, he knows, must have beheld changes. He takes his hand from the sill and massages his taut face on which the raindrops have dried.

When he faces her again, he says that they must prepare some sort of welcome, that they must get busy.

A Strange Story

How are they to be explained, the voices one heard as a child?
I was seven. My father had left me waiting in the car for more
than an hour while he walked over a tract of densely wooded
bottom land he owned. I was not alone in the car. My older
brother was there with me, but he soon fell asleep. I wasn't
frightened; I was merely hot and bored. Since my brother
had fallen asleep with his head against my shoulder, I dared
not move a muscle. As a kind of consolation, I suppose, my
father had left his pocket watch with me. It was a big, gold
watch, thick as a biscuit, and it had once belonged to my
grandfather. On the gold lid that snapped over the face were
engraved the letters LP, which were my grandfather's initials,
as they were also my father's and my own. On the face of the
watch the hours were marked in black Roman numerals that
I could not yet read with any certainty. I sat watching the
second hand go round . . . The minutes passed very slowly.
I heard the dry sounds of the insects in the tall grass nearby
and listened to the thirsty cries of the birds flying over the

low-lying woods towards the bayou. When my father finally returned, I told him about a voice that had spoken to me during his absence. At first the voice had repeated my name very softly several times, "Louis Price . . . Louis Price . . . Louis Price." Then later in an even softer tone it had said to me, "You are not Louis Price. You are the Lost Dauphin." My father laughed merrily when I told him, and afterward it became a family joke. One of my uncles said I was already manifesting a strong family trait—delusions of grandeur. The only thing about the incident that irritated my father was that I should maintain I did not know who the "Lost Dauphin" was and that I had never heard of him before. But I maintain to this day that I did not and had not.

Now and then, I find myself in conversation with someone who insists that he never heard voices as a child—voices he could not explain. But I believe him no more than I believed the man I knew in the army who said he never dreamed at night and was not able to imagine what a dream was like. Obviously, that man in the army was lying, and only for the sake of making himself interesting. But that's not the psychology of those who say they never heard voices when they were children. You will notice one thing about such people; it is not only the voices they don't remember. They remember almost nothing about their childhood. Whatever they do remember will be related, more often than not, to some experience connected with growing up, with putting childhood behind them, with mere recognition of the adult point of view. My brother, for instance, takes no stock nowadays in my talk about voices. He says I never heard anything he didn't hear, by which he means to say I heard nothing. But, mark you, though my brother is two years older than I, he has only the vaguest recollection of anything about that day our father took us with him to the low ground near the Forked Deer River, whereas I can recall almost every detail of the expedition—the deep-rutted, red clay road we travelled from town, the elderberry bushes that scratched the sides of the car, a dead sycamore tree that stood alone on a little knoll ten yards from where we were left waiting, the sounds of the insects, the cries of the birds. But, on the other hand, why my brother and I happened to be taken along that day I have no idea. And when and why my father had acquired that tract of land, and when and how he disposed of it are matters I know nothing about. These are questions that my brother might be able to answer.

When I was even younger—I will not say how much younger, for fear of not being believed—a voice once interrupted my play to speak prophetic words to me. On our front lawn, there in the little town in West Tennessee where I spent the first eight years of my life, were two giant chestnut trees. Since this was in the days before the blight, they were real chestnuts, not horse chestnuts. In September, the burs fell from the branches and covered the ground underneath. I learned early in life to open the burs with a minimum of finger pricking. And I devoured the meat of the nuts with such relish that the sound of my "m'mmms" sometimes reached my mother's ears through the open window of her sitting room. She declared that the first time she heard me out there she mistook the noises I made for the humming of bees under the apricot trees that grew nearer the house.

I not only ate the chestnuts; I used to play for hours with the burs, stacking them into neat pyramids or fashioning mountainous landscapes like none I'd ever seen, like none that ever existed except perhaps on some other planet. It was while I squatted there at my play one afternoon that I heard the slow clop-clop of a horse's hoofs on the macadam street that went past our house. I may have experienced some premonition of who the rider would be before I looked around, I cannot be sure about that. I am sure only that before I looked I heard a voice that seemed to come right out of the tree trunk saying, "Ruin. Ruin." When I glanced over my shoulder I saw that the horseman was our Cousin Talbot Williamson. He was a big, barrel-chested man and he sat very straight in the saddle. I got up off the ground and walked down to the iron fence that enclosed our lot and I stood there watching the erect figure on the horse until horse and rider had passed all the way up the street and over the rise beyond which I knew the town street turned into a country road. The sight of the straight figure sitting astride the horse stirred in me strange feelings of envy and admiration—and of dread. And when the figure had passed out of sight, the memory of it seemed no less mysterious to me than the voice I had heard coming out of the tree trunk.

Cousin Talbot Williamson was a man of about my father's age and he lived five miles from town in an old hip-roofed, clapboard house that my great-grandfather had built in ante-bellum days. He farmed the old home-place, and he and his wife lived out there without an automobile, without servants, even without electricity or plumbing in the house. All the relatives thought it their privilege and perhaps their duty to pay calls on Cousin Talbot and Cousin Carrie from time to time. A visit usually included a tour of the house lot, a look through the house, and then a half hour of talk about "old times." The women in the family disliked Cousin Talbot. They said he was a "vain egotist" and that he imagined himself a lady-killer. But they felt sorry for Cousin Carrie, who at thirty already seemed an old woman, and they thought her entitled to a little female company now and then.

I believe it was on a Thursday or a Friday afternoon that I watched Cousin Talbot ride past our house. At any rate, on the following Sunday, my father decided it was time for us to pay a visit to the home-place. I believe there was nothing unusual about our visit that Sunday. Actually, it is the only such visit I can remember making, but in later years my mother assured me that we had spent many a Sunday after-noon out there. She said my father always imagined that we were more welcome at Cousin Talbot's than we actually were. And I am absolutely certain that I had been there before, because in my memory of that day nothing seems unfamiliar. After the preliminary walk about the place, the adults retired to the kitchen for their talk. My impression is that Cousin Talbot and Cousin Carrie occupied only two or three rooms toward the rear of the ground floor. The rest of the house was like a barn, and we children were turned loose to amuse ourselves wandering through the empty hallways and rooms.

We found little to interest us and we didn't have a very lively time. In what had been the front parlor, my two sisters, both older than I, (Q.A.) discovered a ragged and faded old corset and they quarreled over who had seen it first. But when the younger girl, who was my brother's twin, began to cry, my brother took her part, and the older girl had to give in. She had a moral victory, however, because as soon as she had relinquished the corset she pointed out that the stays had already been removed. There was nothing useful to be salvaged from it. Everywhere else, we found only stacks of old newspapers and empty cardboard boxes. In one of the upstairs rooms, Cousin Talbot kept rabbits, but since we had been warned not to go in there we had only glimpses of the rabbits through the keyhole. None of us held back when Mother called from the foot of the staircase to say it was time to go home and fix Sunday night supper.

We must have left for home no later than four-thirty or five. Six hours later, the old house my great-grandfather had built had burned to the ground. Talbot Williamson was not there when the fire broke out, and when the nearest neighbors arrived, Cousin Carrie was hysterical and could not make it clear whether or not she knew where her husband was. I suppose she might probably have been able to guess, but even afterward she never made it clear what or how much she knew. By the time Talbot arrived on the scene, his wife had been taken away by some of her own kinspeople. The two of them never saw each other again.

Those who were present at the fire reported that it was not long before midnight when Talbot Williamson came galloping up. His horse was in a terrible lather. Someone rushed up to assure him that his wife was safe, but the information seemed to make no impression on him. Without dismounting, he looked about him at the assemblage of neighbors and for several minutes gazed into the flames that were by then consuming the last of the oak timbers. Finally he turned his horse away and rode off at a walk toward the watering trough and the barn. Everyone waited expectantly for him to reappear on foot. Instead, after ten minutes or so, he came galloping up from the barn on his horse, and without looking to left or right and yet choosing a course between the onlooking neighbors and the fire he galloped through the house lot, out the gateway in the picket fence, and down the lane to the main road. It was the last his neighbors would ever see of him; his relatives had already seen their last. Next morning, the body of his dead horse was found at the roadside ten miles away. Two days later, news came that a married woman in a neighboring town, whose name had long been connected with Talbot's, had vanished that same night.

I heard these details and others reported to my parents by eyewitnesses of the scene. I knew, without their saying, how erect he must have held himself as he rode back past the burning timbers of the house. And the image aroused in me the same feelings of envy, admiration and dread that I had known standing by the iron fence a few days before.

Please do not attempt to find any consistency or try to uncover any *buried* significance in the kind of utterances I heard. Sometimes they were prophetic, at other times either genuinely profound or crudely sententious. Sometimes they were amusing, even joshing. They were exactly like the voices you remember hearing, unless, or course, you happen to be one of the number who have forgotten childhood and who think that a child is merely an immature man or woman. If that is the case, you will already have decided that I was an abnormal child and that I have never quite got over it. I can assure you that I have completely got over it—if abnormal I was! I move about the world like anyone else and enjoy a reasonable success in my chosen profession. And I abhor mystics! I shall not be making references to myself as an adult after this, but it may interest you to learn that I now have two adolescent children who already know next to nothing about what it was like to be a child. Further, like yourself, perhaps, I have been married, not once but several times, and in each instance—But, no, I have already said enough to convince you that my adult life has not been so very different from yours, or at any rate not so different from that of a certain number of your friends. No more about any of that.

Even when you are a child, it is difficult to get other children to admit to the voices they hear. And the mistake I made from a very early timé was in speaking so frankly on the subject. I don't specifically remember telling anyone about the voice that came from the trunk of the chestnut tree. Possibly at that age my voices seemed such an ordinary part of experience that I didn't always bother to mention them. But a few years later I was forever making that mistake. I can still see the queer look—it was always the same—on the faces of children I made listen to me. It was not an expression of disbelief but one of disgust. They seemed to say, "Don't you know it is in bad taste to speak of such things?" A few years later, after I had given up hearing any voices but those of the people around me, I once saw precisely that same expression come over the face of an older boy in whom I had confided that when I got out of school I wished to become either an actor or an artist. I knew before I said it that the boy had similar ambitions. But after that day he ignored my existence and never gave me a chance to speak to him again.

You can see that, though I always did well enough in school, I was never quick to learn what people expected of me otherwise. I was born without the instinct to defend myself in a fight, or even the instinct to pursue an ordinarily polite conversation with people I wished to make friends of. And yet these deficiencies of mine did not seem to matter so much in those days before I consciously began listening to the voices of other people and formally foreswore hearing voices that came out of the air, from the trunks of trees, and even sometimes out of the mouths of small animals.

I was standing on the school steps one afternoon, waiting for my brother's class to be let out. Again, I was feeling rather bored with life. We were no longer living in the old town in West Tennessee. My brother and I were in a city school, and my brother's class was kept an hour later than mine. Every day, I waited there on the steps until the hour when he was let out and our colored chauffeur came to pick us up. Sometimes there were other small children waiting, but on this particular day I was alone. All at once, I saw a big dun-colored rabbit hopping across the green lawn. I hadn't then lived in a city long enough to know how thickly populated by rabbits and squirrels such "residential" neighborhoods often are. When presently the rabbit stopped and spoke to me, I was hardly more amazed than I had been by his very appearance there. He stopped in the center of the school lawn, lifted up one front foot rather daintily, and said to me, "Good morning to you, Bonaparte." That he should call me "Bonaparte" and that he should say "good morning" when it was really afternoon seemed hilariously funny to me and sent me into gales of laughter. At the sound of my loud laughter, of course, the rabbit hopped briskly away into the hedge.

I was still laughing when my brother and his classmates burst through the doorway behind me. They wanted to know at once what it was I was laughing about, but as I began telling them I saw the angry patches of red coming into my brother's face. Before I could dodge the blow he had struck me on the temple with the heel of his hand. I did not fight back and I did not cry. I simply sat down on the steps and remained there until all the others except my brother had gone. He leaned against the rail on the far side of the steps, looking at me with hatred. Finally I got up, and we walked together in silence to the car, where the chauffeur was waiting, as always, slouched behind the afternoon paper.

There is one incident from the earlier time—before we had moved, that is—which I very naturally find embarrassing but which must be recounted because it is such a happy memory. I was seated on the toilet in the downstairs bathroom that opened off the back porch. It was summertime, and the door stood open. I had watched the cook pass along the porch several times, performing little last-minute tasks. In those days, small-town cooks went home after midday dinner and returned at sundown to fix supper. Presently, I saw Alice start across the porch to the back steps, wearing her hat. She hesitated a moment and looked in through the bathroom doorway at me. She had been my nurse until a year or so before, when the old cook quit. I was fond of her, and I knew that she was fond of me. She looked in at me with her lips pressed tightly together, but I heard a voice like hers asking, "Are you going to sit on that Christmas-tree all day?" My voices rarely had such a definite character as that one had, and somehow that accounts for part of the pleasure I derived from the incident.

Alice disappeared for a moment but soon came into my line of vision again as she walked down the path through my father's big vegetable garden. She carried a paper sack under one arm and at the foot of the garden she slowed her pace and began rather boldly filling her sack with a half-dozen or so of his ripe tomatoes and two or three cucumbers. When she had filled it she lifted her free hand and waved to me. And when I waved back, it gave me a feeling of immense satisfaction.

As soon as she had passed on into the alley beyond and out
of my sight, I heard another voice—one of my usual voices,
without any special quality or character—say, "Now what
have you done?" The tone was both accusing and exultant. I
thought about what had been said by both voices for a moment and then I burst into laughter. I found the whole incident highly amusing.

It is a much later time. It is a Saturday morning. I have
somehow been roped into a game of baseball. Since I have no
instinct for throwing or catching a ball—and as yet no learned
ability—I am sent to the outfield, where I won't matter so
much. The team at bat has one out and two men on base.
Their best hitter steps up to the plate and hits a high, easy
ball that begins an arc that I know is going to end right in
my glove. I am hypnotized by the little planet moving so
inevitably toward me and I could not run away from it if
I tried. And then there is the "plop" in my glove and I am
holding onto the ball desperately. As if from far, far away
I hear the cheers of my team mates; immediately and from
the same far distance, they are calling out for me to throw
the ball. Almost any throw will mean a double play and the
retirement of the other team. I lift the ball in my right hand,
draw back my arm. And over that shoulder comes the quiet
voice: "Time passes. You haven't got forever." I freeze.
I remain frozen there, holding the ball high above my head.
I know that I am not going to throw it. I understand that
the words do not refer to my throwing the ball. Voices never
instruct about practical things of the moment. It is only cruel
irony when they seem to. Better for me to avoid even the appearance of not understanding them when I do. I could, in
my clumsy fashion, get the ball at least as far as second base.
It would be to my inestimable benefit and gain. But I continue to stand there holding onto the ball. I do not listen to
the shouts of the other boys. I am tempted to listen, but the

incentive is not great enough—is not clear enough yet. I must go on listening to the other voices for a few more years yet. I see my brother advancing toward me across the field, accompanied by a boy who is even younger than I am and who will be my replacement. My brother comes toward me with a look that warns I had just better not dare try one of my explanations on him. He is on to me now—for life.

I hand him the ball and give up my glove to the other boy. As I amble off in the direction of the new, big house our family has recently moved into I feel no humiliation or regret at having been put out of the game. I only feel depressed by what the voice said. It makes no sense whatever to me; I understand it perfectly. I am filled with a deep, unhappy satisfaction. That's how it was.

I was eight and a half when we moved away from the country town. After the move, my mother and father were never happy together again. But they were not finally divorced until I was in high school, and their discontent with each other as man and woman did not seem to affect very much the happiness of our family life during those years. They never quarrelled violently, or not in the presence of us children. Usually, I was no more disturbed by the quarrels that I did hear between them than by the bickering that increased among us children as we grew older. It seemed natural and inevitable. And when the divorce came at last, that seemed merely the same kind of event as the graduation of my oldest sister from college or the twins' graduation from high school. Perhaps it was because I didn't really listen to their quarrels that I was not usually disturbed. Sometimes, though, without even listening to what they were actually saying, I *would* experience a vague disquietude—really more of a dissatisfaction with my own state than with theirs. I sensed that whereas our bickering always seemed pointless, their quarrelling had a mysterious point to it that made it worthwhile.

After they had got their divorce, I was to hear each of my parents explain in almost identical terms what had happened to their marriage. They said that, following the move, the changed circumstances in their lives had let them see how really unsuited to each other they had always been. This was the easiest thing for them to say and to try to believe, so long afterward. But I don't suppose they truly believed it. They were no more ill-matched than most couples are, and I doubt that their first misconceptions about each other had been very extraordinary ones. I suspect the fact is that they had once been very much in love and that the babies born of that love gave them great satisfaction. Perhaps the satisfaction was so nearly complete that by the time their babies were no longer babies but little people racing in and out of the house, they knew the need, once again, to feel and make felt their own separate individualities. It is not too shameful a possibility to consider, I think—not when you reflect that that is all that seems real to most of us beyond a certain point, and that beyond that point we are committed to nothing but pursuing that reality. I remember all too clearly the elation both of them had expressed at the prospect of leaving the town where their children had been born and had grown out of babyhood. I believe their elation was a joyful anticipation of something more than just my father's rise in the world. What I am most certain of is that the changes in their life— the move and their altered relationship—only just happened to coincide and that it was for us children the happiest of coincidences. It was like meter and rhyme. The one thing made the other seem natural and inevitable. And if it had not happened so, we children might not have got the right impression about the naturalness and inevitability of either thing.

There is not much more I have to say about either of my parents. In his new life, my father took up tennis and handball. I never saw him play handball, but I know that he never got to be any real good at playing tennis singles and that he disliked doubles. My mother teased him about persevering so in something that he could not excel in and said she believed he fancied himself in his white tennis shorts and sport shirt. He was no more than forty at the time, and it was true that he did look rather like a college boy whenever he set out for the University Club in his tennis garb.

I remember his coming home late for dinner one night and explaining to us that he had been playing handball. My mother laughed skeptically and said, "Handball, indeed!" Father blushed and then he looked at her for some time without speaking. There was no quarrel, but on another occasion I remember his making a comparable remark to her. She was an excellent horsewoman. In the country town, and while her children were small, she had not ridden much. But in her new surroundings that was all changed. There was the fall horse show and the spring horse show, and it seems to me that she was always preparing for the one or the other. We usually went to see her ride and sat in a box applauding her every time she went by. Sometimes she rode her own horse, but more often it was the horse of one of her friends. Father had bought a small suburban estate, and some of our neighbors kept fine stables. Mother often rode before breakfast. Once she returned just as Father was leaving for his office. "We missed you at breakfast!" he called to her from his car.

"Sorry I didn't make it," she replied, peering down into the car from her horse.

"Out riding with the young squires again, eh?" he said. Then he drove off, without any further exchange between them. I am not really sure whether he said "squires" or "squire," but I don't think it makes much difference which it was.

I became fast friends with both my parents after I was grown, and I make it a rule never to inquire into those parts of my friends' lives, past or present, that don't concern me.

In the case of my parents as friends, I have possibly been spared gossip that mutual friends would ordinarily have supplied. And possibly, because they *were* my parents, my memory has spared me a good deal, too. But my memory has not spared me with regard to a dream I once had. It was a year or so after I had given up hearing my voices. In the dream I saw my mother and father seated side by side in a rope swing. They were terribly crowded, of course, and couldn't make themselves comfortable. Everytime the swing went up in the air, one of them would almost fall out. And then I dreamed I heard one of my old voices saying, "Oh, ouch, oh, ouch, ouch, ouch!" I woke up laughing, and what seemed so funny to me was that that was not the kind of thing my real voices would ever have said.

Before I conclude, before I tell you about how I finally hushed the voices I heard as a child, I must relate two incidents that involve my brother's twin sister. She was ten years old when we left the country town. From that time, she and our older sister were sent to a girls' day school. And from about that time, the old closeness and loyalty between her and her twin brother ceased to exist. Suddenly it was as though she were two or three years older than he, and during the rest of their lives they have remained almost totally indifferent to each other. But she began to take an interest in me. She mothered me and played babyish games with me that she would not have played with anyone her own age—games of hide-and-seek, usually, in which even I didn't take much pleasure at my age.

Since our parents did a good deal of travelling in those days —sometimes together, sometimes separately—we children were left alone in the house for relatively long periods with only the servants to look after us. (These servants, I should point out, were always imported from our country town and were almost like relatives to us. One of them was a woman of some education. She had gone up North to a Negro college and had even taught school for a while when she first came home. She used to help me with my lessons, and one night when we had put aside the books I confided in her that I wanted to be an artist when I grew up. "Do you love Nature?" she asked. I was stunned by the question and, after some deliberation, I had to admit that I did not *love* Nature. "Then you can't ever be an artist," she said. She was a superior kind of woman, but I am afraid I have never quite forgiven her for not pursuing her education further before she came to work in our kitchen. Another of these servants was a palmist, and she read in my palm that I was going to be a fine musician. "You'll probably play the fiddle, like your granddaddy," she said. But I knew even at that age that I was tone-deaf, and I was a long time in regaining my faith in palmistry.) When we children played, the whole house was our province, and no games were too rough. Things got broken now and then, but it didn't seem to matter much. My brother and one of his friends, seizing two curiously shaped sticks that I had brought home from a walk in the woods, played at jousting one night in the front drawing room. Suddenly the friend lifted his stick above his head and struck directly into the crystal chandelier. It was an enormous antique fixture that my mother had bought in New Orleans. When he heard the crash above him the boy threw down the stick and covered his face with his hands, but he didn't move from beneath the chandelier. For at least three or four minutes, he stood there with his hands over his face while the prisms dropped all about him like melting icicles. Another time, our older sister and one of her beaux, in a fit of high spirits and for no other good reason, rode their horses up on the front porch and into the front hall. The scars that the horseshoes made in the floor were too deep ever to be removed. But I don't believe there were complaints from my parents in either instance.

Whereas in the country (country town) we had been made to feel that nothing in our house was replaceable, now everything was apparently replaceable or expendable. I remember thinking that this was merely a sign of our increased prosperity, and in part it may have been that. At any rate, my sister and I seldom broke anything during our games. We played quietly, hiding from each other in such incredible places that it sometimes took three quarters of an hour for one of us to find the other. One afternoon, I had hidden in a compartment of the sideboard in the dining room. I had been there for quite some time. I was in an especially cramped position, because this was the compartment in which my mother's cut-glassware wedding presents were kept and I had managed to coil myself about cruets, pitchers, and decanters without actually touching a single piece. Before my sister finally found me, I had got in very depressed spirits and had heard a voice saying to me in the darkness, "There is no one god. And there was no beginning and there will be no end."

When my sister opened the compartment door, I told her immediately that I had heard a voice that said "There is no god." I don't know why I censored it. Possibly I knew that "There is no god" would not sound so blasphemous to her as "There is no one god."

She looked in at me curiously, observing how I was coiled about the glassware. "You had better be careful," she began, and I thought she was going to say that I was apt to break a piece of the glass getting out. "You had better be careful," she said, "or you *will* turn out to be some kind of preacher, or something, the way everybody says."

This was the first inkling I had ever had that there was something "everybody" said about me, and it gave me a shock that I don't suppose I ever entirely recovered from. For the moment, however, I stuck it off somewhere in the back of my mind. And its only immediate effect was to make me kick over one of the decanters as I was crawling out of my hiding place. The glass stopper rolled out onto the floor, and though the decanter didn't break, to my astonishment—and to my sister's—the thing turned out to be filled with a dark, sweet smelling wine. Before I could right the bottle, some of the wine had gushed out onto the carpet and left a stain there that no amount of scrubbing and cleaning, on our parts or the servants', could ever expunge.

Several days passed, or perhaps even more time, before I thought again of what the voice had said to me when I was hidden in the sideboard. Possibly this lapse of time and the revelation my sister had made to me combined to rob the message of any powerful impact. It was the only religious or irreligious—whichever—utterance I ever heard from my voices, and the impression it made was not very considerable. Any suggestion of infinity, however, could always depress me somewhat when I was a child. For instance, on the cover of my Baby Ray reader, in the first grade at school, was a picture of Baby Ray himself holding a copy of his Baby Ray reader with a picture of Baby Ray himself holding, etcetera, etcetera. A glance at that cover could put me into a morbid frame of mind for the rest of the school day. I shall never forget the joy I knew when the teacher set aside the last hour of school one afternoon to instruct us in making brown-paper jackets for our readers; I believe the quickness and thoroughness with which I dispatched the job made a lasting impression on the teacher and may account for my getting off to a very good start in school. I used to be similarly affected by the seeming infinity of reflections in barbershop mirrors, and I would sometimes embarrass my brother by sitting through a whole haircut with my eyes closed. Anyway, the recollection of what I heard in the sideboard affected me no more profoundly or lastingly than those experiences did.

Though my sister befriended and mothered me during this period, she was also my chief tormentor. She tormented me, that is, with her confidences. I don't precisely remember it, but I am sure that she must have begun pouring out her sorrows to me as soon as I had crawled out of the sideboard that day. I am sure of it, because that is the way it always was. At least half the time we spent together was given over to my listening to her accounts of injuries other people had done her and to her grievances against her fate in general. I usually listened in silence and at night I tossed in my bed, thinking of how unjustly she was used and of how unhappy she was. She said she was the most unpopular girl in her class at school. The other girls ignored her and thought her clothes were tacky. And why shouldn't they think so, she would ask rhetorically. For although we had as much money as anybody else, didn't Mother make her wear some of the dresses her own sister had worn to the same school two and three years before? And Mother and Father frequently included Sister in their social plans, but said *she* was too young. They encouraged Sister to try out for the steeplechase, but said *she* was too young. It was easy enough to see who *their* favorite was. None of her teachers valued her, either, and some of them went out of their way to find fault with her work and humiliate her before her classmates. She could not blame her own twin brother for being ashamed to walk down the street beside her. After all, she was already two inches taller than he, and there was no predicting how tall she might get to be before she was even given a chance to put on high heels . . . She had inherited all the worst physical traits from both sides of the family . . . She had never met a boy her own age who did not find her repulsive. . . .

One day, I made a drawing of her, working entirely, so I thought, from a small snapshot. I believe it was my very first attempt at human portraiture. Previously, I had spent many, many hours copying pictures of animals out of magazines and sometimes drawing our pets from life. My efforts had been very well received by all the family. My brother was especially admiring of my horses. I think it was the only accomplishment of mine he ever respected, though eventually he became disgusted with me even about that. At first, he took my horse pictures to school as gifts for his friends. Later, he began selling them to the other boys. He grew impatient, however, when I could not fill his orders fast enough. When I was unable to teach *him* to draw the horses as I did, in order to supply the demand, he was irritated beyond measure. He would not believe that I knew no principles, no guiding rules that I could pass on to him. He stormed at me, he broke his own pencil across his knee, tore up his paper. I was dismayed and gave up drawing altogether for a while.

But after dinner one night I brought out the drawing I had made of my sister. Both my parents were present and both were delighted with the drawing. They exchanged the kind of warm glances that only something one of us children said or did could call forth in those days. They could hardly believe it was my handiwork. Even my older sister and my brother were astonished by the "real likeness." But while these others admired the portrait, the subject herself remained in a far corner of the big sunroom where we had gathered. As I have already stated, I was convinced that I had worked entirely from the snapshot, but there can be no doubt that I had also worked from memory—from the image of my sister's face as it appeared during those long confidences I had listened to. Presently my mother said to my sister, "Come over here and see yourself. It's a fine likeness, and you're very beautiful." Then, laughing quietly, with her eyes, on the drawing, she added, "He makes you out rather a mournful beauty, I must admit, but—"

At that moment my sister, whose eyes had been directed toward me all along, suddenly sprang from her chair, shouting at me, "How hateful of you! How dreadful you are! How cruel!" She had not even seen the picture, and I don't think it was Mother's description that inspired the outburst. She made a dash from the room, but she chose a route close enough to where the rest of us were gathered to get a glimpse of my drawing. "Hideous!" she said as she went by.

"I thought she might like it," I said after she was gone, though I am not sure I was telling the truth.

"You had better put it away for a while," Mother said. "It is just that she is at a very self-conscious age."

Regardless of whether or not I had thought she would like my doing the picture, I was genuinely sorry that I had so wounded her and wished that I had not shown the drawing to anyone. I did not understand her self-consciousness. She was a great mystery to me. And though I wished to explain to her what it was that had moved me to draw her picture, I did not even know where to begin. I was no more able to tell her *why* I drew it than I would have been able to tell my brother *how* I did it. All was over between my sister and me from then on. Like my brother, she was now on to me—for life.

I was not yet on to myself, however. My voices continued to speak to me now and then for another three years, until I was a year older than my sister was that day. As an adult, I can see some kind of connection—I will not deny it—between that episode and what began soon afterward. But the connection is not relevant to my purpose. My purpose is to keep always in mind the value the events had to the child I still was, the child whose experience and logic I still do not contradict.

When I was about fourteen years old, I began imagining myself in love with nearly every little girl who came into my acquaintance. I say "imagining" because of course I know that I could not have been in love as often as I seemed to be. I knew this even at the time. I knew that in some instances my love was self-deceptive and in others was real. If I should take the trouble I could distinguish for you even now between the little girls I was truly in love with and those I deceived myself about. I recently came across an old school book of mine in which the names of twenty-seven girls were listed in my handwriting on the fly leaf. Glancing down the list I felt my pulse quicken as I caught sight of certain names. Others only brought a smile, or sometimes a frown when I could not quite recall a face or even recollect whether it was a girl I had known in our neighborhood or at the skating rink or at school or at dancing class. I find no difficulty in accounting for the large number. It was almost inevitable, since my attentions were invariably rejected. The little brunette or blonde or redheaded object was either frightened or sent into giggles by my sudden determination to walk beside her down the school corridor, or to skate beside her, with hands criss-crossed, around the rink.

I am sure it was my complete silence that made me seem so sinister or so outrageously funny to all those little girls. But speak to them I could not. My attentions were always solemn and wordless. At dancing class, I once wrote the same girl's name after every number on my program and then walked over to where she was standing and held up the card for her to see, exactly as though she and I were two deaf-mutes. Unfortunately, from the girl's point of view, I had got to her before any other boy had had a chance to ask her for a dance, and she responded by bursting into tears. The dancing master reprimanded me, of course, but I can still remember how beautiful she looked with her face flushed and her eyes moist with tears, and I wasn't altogether sorry for what I had done. Before the next meeting of the dancing class, I had already given my heart to someone else; because it is quite as true for a child as it is for an adult that once he has been in love, being out of love is an unbearable state and one that he will not endure a moment longer than he must.

To some people, the child they once were is like a brother or a sister who died young. My father had a brother who

lived to be only eleven; my mother had a sister who died at
eight. How tenderly each of them has always remembered
the child in the family who died—how tenderly and how
dimly! That child who died is the child they remember the
most about, and the least. What a wealth of details and anecdotes can be recalled! But what the true nature of the child's
experiences were, what life really seemed like to him, is all
beyond knowing and beyond mattering. The child is *dead.*
The only difference is that the child who went on to death,
instead of to adulthood, will have many allowances and concessions made with respect to magical experiences he was
said to have had. He wasn't like other children! He was in
such harmony with the natural world about him! Or: It was
almost as though she were never fully committed to life in
this world! Or: On his deathbed, only a few minutes before
he was taken, he rose up from his pillow and said to his
mother, "Don't you hear that lovely singing? Is it the angels,
Mother?"

My voices, whatever they were, were not the voices of
angels. They never spoke except when they had something
interesting or amusing to say to me. And I might never have
given up hearing them had they themselves not been finally
so amenable to the break and at the same time disposed to
let the decision be mine. Angels could not possibly have been
so self-effacing or so unwilling to stand in the way of all the
future happiness and unhappiness to which I was entitled.

Dancing class was held from eight until nine-thirty on Friday evenings. My brother and I were regularly delivered and
fetched home by the chauffeur. During the first half hour, the
boys and girls, in two separate rooms, were given instruction
in the dance steps of the day. At precisely eight-thirty, the
little girls were herded in through a door at one end of the
main ballroom, the boys through a door at the opposite end.
For several minutes, the girls remained huddled together
down at their end, and the boys milled about at the other—

each group trying to appear unaware of the other's presence. But at last the dancing master took his place in the center of the parquet, bowed formally to the balcony, where there would be a scattering of parents and a somewhat larger number of maids and chauffeurs, and then he raised his hand high above his head and clacked his black castanets.

For the girls this was the signal to fan out across their end of the room and take their "separate and individual" stances. It was the signal for the boys to advance on the girls. And advance we did, armed with our little purple pencils dangling on gold cords from our program cards, and each of us—consciously or unconsciously—trying to imitate the gait of a father or the strut of some older boy admired at school. As we approached the girls, a whispering went up from them like the whispering of trees, and we marched fiercely and possessively into their midst as into a lovely woods that we had been ordered to take at any cost—at any cost to ourselves, at any cost, presumably, to the lovely woods. Invariably, after such a beginning, everything about the hour of fox-trotting and two-stepping that followed seemed anticlimactic. The presence of the dancing master, his wife, their two assistants, as well as that of the observers in the balcony, insured its being a dull, tedious, uneventful time.

But it was the custom that after class small private parties should be held at the houses of the members. And the time came when my brother got up one of these parties. Since it was to be held at our house, I was told that I might—that I must, in fact—invite one of the girls to come as my "date." The girl I chose was one whose name appears on that list in the old school book I came across, and hers was one of the names that could, as recently as a few weeks ago, still cause my pulse to quicken. An unlikely kind of name it was, too, yet there it is in the old book, written down correctly, with all its many consonants accounted for and in their right order: "Yvonne Schmidt." (Alas, these few more weeks have not lessened its effect.) When I stood before her, holding on tightly to my little pencil and twirling the program card at the other end of the cord, and asked her in a whisper if she would come with me to the party at our house, I could not really hear my own voice above the chatter there in the ball-room. Afterward, I was not certain that I had spoken the words. Perhaps Yvonne read my lips, or perhaps she read the invitation in my eyes, or perhaps she had wanted so for me to ask her that she imagined that she actually heard the question. She accepted immediately.

There is no need holding back what happened at the party at our house. As soon as we had walked through the front door, Yvonne ditched me. She ditched me for the one she loved. I had not guessed it—there was no way I could have—but she was mad for my brother, and she wouldn't have scorned any means of obtaining an invitation to his party.

But from the moment she accepted until the moment when we walked together through the front door of my house was by no means a short period of time for one of my attachments to last. Even in retrospect it seems like a rather long time. Remember that I was a child still and that time passes differently in childhood. At any rate, the experience—if not quite the duration of time itself—was comparable to an unfortunate first marriage that influential parents manage, by hook or crook, to end with an annulment. Yes, like that—followed by the same feelings of frustration, emptiness, betrayal. But in one sense it was also like that second marriage about which one has so many illusions and would do almost anything to save except that one has, quite by chance, overheard those very amusing and unforgettable remarks about oneself exchanged between the wife of one's bosom and her lover. Yes, there was some of that same disenchantment with world and with self.

I rode home from dancing class with Yvonne at my side, the two of us sitting on the little jump seats in my mother's limousine. My brother and his girl were in the back seat. They kept up a steady flow of conversation. It never occurred to me to imitate their kind of drivel. Most of the way, I sat looking out the window, wishing I knew what kind of things Yvonne would most enjoy hearing me say. I decided that probably it would just come to me naturally once we were out of the car and inside the house. But I never had a chance to find out whether or not anything would have come to me.

Although dancing class was always so heavily chaperoned that we could hardly wait for the time to pass, the parents afterward were frequently without any real chaperonage at all. Apparently it was only the public appearance and the good opinion of the dancing master that mattered to the parents of our generation. Sometimes a yawning father or a preoccupied mother would pass through the rooms of the house where a party was being given, but, often as not, they did not even bother to make an appearance. On the night of the party at our house, both our parents were away. The servants were on duty to see after our needs, however, and our older sister had been deputized to be on hand with her beau. My brother's twin, who considered herself too old for the dancing class set, was also at home that night. But she could hardly be thought of as a chaperone, and when urged to come down and join the party, she declined, saying that she had letters to write.

The rugs in the front hall had already been taken up when we came in. That was where those who wished to would be encouraged to dance. Also, the piano had been rolled out from the drawing room to a place near the foot of the stairs. When we came into the vestibule, my sister was seated at the piano in the hall, and her beau was standing beside her with one hand on her shoulder. They turned around immediately, and at the sight of me holding the door open for Yvonne, my sister's lovely face was suddenly made lovelier for me by a broad smile of approval. And then as she stood up she threw me a kiss. It was an exhilarating moment. I turned to Yvonne, but she had already passed ahead of me into the hall. My brother and his girl had come inside now, too, and almost at once other guests began streaming in. My sister introduced herself to the girls and led them back to the sunroom where they would leave their wraps.

My sister's beau came up to me and asked, "What's your girl's name?"

"Her name's Yvonne."

"She's a very pretty girl," he said. "You've got taste."

And when my sister returned, I heard him say to her. "Her name's Yvonne."

I drifted into the drawing room with the other boys. When the girls joined us there, Yvonne would not even let me stand beside her. She kept slipping away from me until at last I went out into the hall, where our chauffeur, having now changed from his driver's uniform into a white housecoat and dark trousers, was seated at the piano and was beginning to sound a few chords. He often played for us children and he had welcomed the opportunity to provide the music on this occasion. I knew that though he could not read music he liked to have someone stand beside him and turn the pages of whatever sheet music happened to be on the rack. I stood there turning the pages for him almost as long as I remained at the party.

Once or twice, I saw my sister and her beau eyeing me. Obviously they suspected something had gone wrong. Finally, the terrible moment came when my brother and Yvonne had been dancing together at the rear of the hall for some fifteen or twenty minutes. During most of this time there were three or four other couples dancing, too, but the other couples were continually changing partners there on the floor or going out for refreshments and returning with different partners. More than once I saw my brother's girl come to the drawing room door, glance out at him, and then look re-

proachfully at me. But it was my sister and her beau who
finally spoke to me. They came from the dining room, where
the refreshments were set out, and as soon as they had crossed
the threshold they began dancing. The young man guided
my sister almost directly across the hall to me. When they
got very close they stopped dancing, but remained in each
other's arms while they spoke.

"Go and break on him, you little nut," my sister said.

"Yes," said her beau, "show that little Yvonne what it's
like to *really* dance."

I had no choice. I set out down the hall toward the pair.
But when I was only a few feet away from them I heard
Yvonne say very distinctly, "Why is he the way he is? What's
the matter with him?"

"Haven't you heard?" my brother said, smiling. "He hears
voices."

"Not ours, I hope," she laughed.

"No, not ours. That's the trouble. *Other* voices."

"You're kidding."

Both of them saw me coming toward them, but I suppose
they thought I really wouldn't hear *their* voices. And just
as I was about to reach out my hand and touch my brother's
shoulder, they turned and walked away in the direction of
the dining room.

I shuffled back toward the piano. My sister and her beau
were still dancing there, but they wouldn't look at me. I felt
the chauffeur's resentful gaze when I didn't stop and begin
turning the pages for him again. I put my hand on the bannister rail and started up the stairs. My other sister was seated
at the top of the flight, peering down into the hall, but when
she saw me she began writing on a pad of paper that she held
on her knee. When I came up to where she was, she said,
"Did you see Sister dancing with her eyes closed? Isn't she
disgusting?" Without answering, I went on up to my room.

I had switched on the light and was closing the door to my

room when a voice said to me, "The number of steps in the stair remains always the s—"

"Hush!" I interrupted, closing my eyes and running my hand through my hair. "Won't you hush?"

"We can never hush," said the voice.

I opened my eyes and looked about at all my dear possessions that cluttered the room. It seemed to me that the voice had come either from the sea shells on the bottom shelf of my bookcase or from the leaf fossils there beside them. I took a step in that direction. It was the first time I had ever spoken back to my voices; it was the first chance they had had to answer me.

"Hush for a year," I said suddenly, "or for five years, and then come back."

"We can never hush." This time it came from another part of the room, from the corner where my collection of knotty sticks and pieces of driftwood was kept. "But you may stop hearing us whenever you wish." I did not turn around. And after that the voice seemed to come from no particular object or direction. "You might as well stop hearing us," it said. "You have everything to gain, and nothing to lose."

"But who are you?" I said. "I don't want to hear you, but I want to know who you are. I don't want to forget you." And suddenly, when I had said that, the room was filled with such a loud laughter that I thought my eardrums might burst. I whirled about to make sure I was still alone there. I *was* alone. I clapped my hands over my ears, but the volume was not diminished. I ran to the corner, seized one of my sticks and began knocking all my pretty objects off the shelves and off the bureau top and smashing the glass that covered my moth collections. At last I raised my voice and shouted, "I will stop hearing you, you demons who persecute innocent children!" The laughter ceased abruptly, or so it seemed to me.

The silence was awful for a moment. But presently I heard my sister, who had looked at me so approvingly two hours before, speaking to me through the door. "Your guests are leaving," she said. "You'd better come down." She had opened the door now. When I turned around and faced her I could tell from her expression that she had not heard the racket I had been making. "This is not a very mature way for you to react," she said, glancing all about. "I can see you've got a lot to learn, Brother. Do you think you are so much better than everybody else that you are never going to be jilted?"

"Has the little wench gone?" I said through my teeth. And I threw aside my stick.

My sister laughed. "That's more the spirit," she said. Then she took a step backward. "You had better not come down, after all. Stay up here and pick up the pieces." At the door, just before she went out, she elaborated. "Pick up the pieces, Little Brother. Tomorrow is another day. And if it's not perfect, the next one may be." It sounded trite to me even at the time, and I am not sure she was not quoting some popular song of the day. But she was trying to speak to me, and I loved her for it, and I pitied her for having to say it that way. She was only seventeen—not yet out of high school, even. Maybe for a girl that is not so very young. But I know that when I got to be her age I was still only beginning to grow up. Though I stopped hearing the mysterious voices one hears as a child that night in my room, at seventeen I was still learning to listen to the voices of people—still discovering just how carefully, for love's sake, one must always listen. And I was thirty before I felt that love's recompense was adequate to let me say with honesty the kind of thing that my sister had said at seventeen.

But, still, how am I to explain the voices I heard as a child? Why did I hate so to give them up? And why do I insist so upon remembering them? . . . Well, I reject your explanation, whatever it is. And, after all, they are *my* voices. The truth is, I have come to like having them there at my beginning, unexplained, a mystery. I *will* not have you, or anyone, explaining them. My liking for the mystery of them has increased with every bit of other learning I have had to do. Such a mystery becomes, finally, a kind of knowledge. It instructs and informs us about the arbitrary nature of most of the things we have to learn in order to walk the world as adults. Learn those things we *must,* but we possess the knowledge in our hearts that it might have been different. Our requirement might have been to make sense out of what the voices were saying, and, in that case, those of us whose inclination was to go on listening always to our voices would be the normal ones and not the rare birds we are.

After seventeen, I became obsessed with learning from people—about people and the world. I listened to everybody. I became a wonderful listener, and still am. Everybody says so. The unfortunate thing, however, is that I have become eccentric in ways you might not expect. For instance, every time the season changes nowadays, I wonder what in the world has come over me and why I am so uncomfortable, until one day somebody happens to say in my presence, "Winter is really here now. This is the coldest day we have had," or, "Well, the hot weather is upon us, no mistaking it." After that, I change to clothing of appropriate weight, and I am all right again. One more thing, too. I *have* learned to love Nature. And the memory of my unexplained voices has been instructive there. Whenever I return to the scenes of my childhood and admire the pale beauty of the sycamore trees and the glossy leaves of the oaks—almost like magnolias, some of them—I understand how far, in my mind, I have had to withdraw from trees in order to learn to love them. I go for walks in the woods with my family sometimes, on my visits back home, and often I cannot help remarking on the absence of any chestnut trees in the woods. My family finds it very curious that I remember the chestnuts at all and tell each other it is evidence of how much I have always loved Nature. But that isn't so. It is something I have learned. It is something strange and wonderful that I have learned to do.

The Fancy Woman

He wanted no more of her drunken palaver. Well, sure enough. Sure enough. And he had sent her from the table like she were one of his half-grown brats. *He,* who couldn't have walked straight around to her place if she *hadn't* been lady enough to leave, sent *her* from the table like either of the half-grown kids he was so mortally fond of. At least she hadn't turned over three glasses of perfectly good stuff during one meal. Talk about vulgar. She fell across the counterpane and slept.

She awoke in the dark room with his big hands busying with her clothes, and she flung her arms about his neck. And she said, "You marvelous, fattish thing."

His hoarse voice was in her ear. He chuckled deep in his throat. And she whispered: "You're an old thingamajig, George."

Her eyes opened in the midday sunlight, and she felt the back of her neck soaking in her own sweat on the counterpane. She saw the unfamiliar cracks in the ceiling and said, "Whose room's this?" She looked at the walnut dresser and the wardrobe and said, "Oh, the kids' room"; and as she laughed, saliva bubbled up and fell back on her upper lip. She shoved herself up with her elbows and was sitting in the middle of the bed. Damn him! Her blue silk dress was twisted about her body; a thin army blanket covered her lower half. "He didn't put that over me, I know damn well. One of those tight-mouth niggers sneaking around!" She sprang from the bed, slipped her bare feet into her white pumps, and stepped toward the door. Oh, God! She beheld herself in the dresser mirror.

She marched to the dresser with her eyes closed and felt about for a brush. There was nothing but a tray of collar buttons there. She seized a handful of them and screamed as she threw them to bounce off the mirror, "This ain't my room!" She ran her fingers through her hair and went out into the hall and into her room next door. She rushed to her little dressing table. There was the bottle half full. She poured out a jigger and drank it. Clearing her throat as she sat down, she said, "Oh, what's the matter with me?" She combed her hair back quite carefully, then pulled the yellow strands out of the amber comb; and when she had greased and wiped her face and had rouged her lips and the upper portions of her cheeks, she smiled at herself in the mirror. She looked flirtatiously at the bottle but shook her head and stood up and looked about her. It was a long, narrow room with two windows at the end. A cubbyhole beside the kids' room! But it *was* a canopied bed with yellow ruffles that matched the ruffles on the dressing table and on the window curtains, as he had promised. She went over and turned back the covers and mussed the pillow. It might not have been the niggers! She poured another drink and went down to get some nice, hot lunch.

The breakfast room was one step lower than the rest of the house; and though it was mostly windows, the Venetian blinds were lowered all around. She sat at a big circular table. "I can't make out about this room," she said to the Negress who was refilling her coffee cup. She lit a cigarette and questioned the servant, "What's the crazy table made out of, Amelia?"

"It makes a good table, 'spite all."

"It sure enough does make a strong table, Amelia." She kicked the toe of her shoe against the brick column which supported the table top. "But what *was* it, old dearie?" She smiled invitingly at the servant and pushed her plate away and pulled her coffee in front of her. She stared at the straight scar on Amelia's wrist as Amelia reached for the plate. What big black buck had put it there? A lot these niggers had to complain of in her when every one of them was all dosed up.

Amelia said that the base of the table was the old cistern. "He brung that top out f'om Memphis when he done the po'ch up this way for breakfas' and lunch."

The woman looked about the room, thinking, "I'll get some confab out of this one yet." And she exclaimed, "Oh, and that's the old bucket to it over there, then, with the vines on it, Amelia!"

"No'm," Amelia said. Then after a few seconds she added, "They brung that out f'om Memphis and put it there like it was it."

"Yeah . . . Yeah . . . go on, Amelia. I'm odd about old-fashioned things. I've got a lot of interest in any antiques."

"That's all."

The little Negro woman started away with the coffee pot and the plate, dragging the soft soles of her carpet slippers over the brick floor. At the door she lingered, and, too cunning to leave room for a charge of impudence, she added to the hateful "That's all" a mutter, "Miss Josephine."

And when the door closed, Miss Josephine said under her

breath, "If that black bitch hadn't stuck that on, there wouldn't be another chance for her to sneak around with any army blankets."

George, mounted on a big sorrel and leading a small dapple-gray horse, rode onto the lawn outside the breakfast room. Josephine saw him through the chinks of the blinds looking up toward her bedroom window. "Not for me," she said to herself. "He'll not get *me* on one of those animals." She swallowed the last of her coffee on her feet and then turned and stomped across the bricks to the step-up into the hallway. There she heard him calling:

"Josie! Josie! Get out-a that bed!"

Josephine ran through the long hall cursing the rugs that slipped under her feet. She ran the length of the hall looking back now and again as though the voice were a beast at her heels. In the front parlor she pulled up the glass and took a book from the bookcase nearest the door. It was a red book, and she hurled herself into George's chair and opened to page sixty-five:

nity, with anxiety, and with pity. Hamilcar was rubbing himself against my legs, wild with delight.

She closed the book on her thumb and listened to George's bellowing:

"I'm coming after you!"

She could hear the sound of the hoofs as George led the horses around the side of the house. George's figure moved outside the front windows. Through the heavy lace curtains she could see him tying the horses to the branch of a tree. She heard him on the veranda and then in the hall. Damn him! God damn him, he couldn't make her ride! She opened to page sixty-five again as George passed the doorway. But he saw her, and he stopped. He stared at her for a moment, and she looked at him over the book. She rested her head on the back of the chair and put a pouty look on her face.

Her eyes were fixed on his hairy arms, on the little bulk in his rolled sleeves, then on the white shirt over his chest, on the brown jodphurs, and finally on the blackened leather of his shoes set well apart on the polished hall floor. Her eyelids were heavy, and she longed for a drink of the three-dollar whisky that was on her dressing table.

He crossed the carpet with a smile, showing, she guessed, his delight at finding her. She smiled. He snatched the book from her hands and read the title on the red cover. His head went back, and as he laughed she watched through the open collar the tendons of his throat tighten and take on a purplish hue.

At Josephine's feet was a needlepoint footstool on which was worked a rust-colored American eagle against a background of green. George tossed the red book onto the stool and pulled Josephine from her chair. He was still laughing, and she wishing for a drink.

"Come along, come along," he said. "We've only four days left, and you'll want to tell your friend-girls you learned to ride."

She jerked one hand loose from his hold and slapped his hard cheek. She screamed, "Friend-girl? You never heard me say Friend-girl. What black nigger do you think you're talking down to?" She was looking at him now through a mist of tears and presently she broke out into furious weeping. His laughter went on as he pushed her across the room and into the hall, but he was saying:

"Boochie Boochie. Wotsa matter? Now, old girl, old girl. Listen: You'll want to tell your girl-friends, your *girl-friends*, that you learned to ride." That was how George was! He would never try to persuade her. He would never pay any attention to what she said. He wouldn't argue with her. He wouldn't mince words! The few times she had seen him before this week there had been no chance to talk much. When they were driving down from Memphis, Saturday, she had gone through the story about how she was tricked by Jackie Briton and married Lon and how he had left her right away and the pathetic part about the baby she never even saw in the hospital. And at the end of it she realized that George had been smiling at her as he probably would at one of his half-grown kids. When she stopped the story quickly, he had reached over and patted her hand (but still smiling) and right away had started talking about the sickly looking tomato crops along the highway. After lunch on Saturday when she'd tried to talk to him again and he had deliberately commenced to play the victrola, she said, "Why won't you take me seriously?" But he had, of course, just laughed at her and kissed her; and they had already begun drinking then. She couldn't resist him (more than other men, he could just drive her wild), and he would hardly look at her, never had. He either laughed at her or cursed her or, of course, at night would pet her. He hadn't hit her.

He was shoving her along the hall, and she had to make herself stop crying.

"Please, George."

"Come on, now! That-a girl."

"Honest to God, George. I tell you to let up, stop it."

"Come on. *Up* the steps. *Up! Up!*"

She let herself become limp in his arms but held with one hand to the banister. Then he grabbed her. He swung her up into his arms and carried her up the stairs which curved around the back end of the hall, over the doorway to the breakfast room. Once in his arms she didn't move a muscle, for she thought, "I'm no featherweight, and we'll both go tumbling down these steps and break our skulls." At the top he fairly slammed her to her feet and, panting for breath, he said without a trace of softness:

"Now, put on those pants, Josie, and I'll wait for you in the yard." He turned to the stair, and she heard what he said to himself: "I'll sober her. I'll sober her up."

As he pushed Josephine onto the white, jumpy beast he must have caught a whiff of her breath. She knew that he must have! He was holding the reins close to the bit while she tried to arrange herself in the flat saddle. Then he grasped her ankle and asked her, "Did you take a drink upstairs?" She laughed, leaned forward in her saddle, and whispered:

"Two. Two jiggers."

She wasn't afraid of the horse now, but she was dizzy. "George, let me down," she said faintly. She felt the horse's flesh quiver under her leg and looked over her shoulder when it stomped one rear hoof.

George said, "Confound it, I'll sober you." He handed her the reins, stepped back, and slapped the horse on the flank. "Hold on!" he called, and her horse cantered across the lawn.

Josie was clutching the leather straps tightly, and her face was almost in the horse's mane. "I could kill him for this," she said, slicing out the words with a sharp breath. God damn it! The horse was galloping along a dirt road. She saw nothing but the yellow dirt. The hoofs rumbled over a three-plank wooden bridge, and she heard George's horse on the other side of her. She turned her face that way and saw George through the hair that hung over her eyes. He was smiling. "You dirty bastard," she said.

He said, "You're doin' all right. Sit up, and I'll give you some pointers." She turned her face to the other side. Now she wished to God she hadn't taken those two jiggers. George's horse quickened his speed and hers followed. George's slowed and hers did likewise. She could feel George's grin in the back of her neck. She had no control over her horse.

They were galloping in the hot sunlight, and Josie stole glances at the flat fields of strawberries. "If you weren't drunk, you'd fall off," George shouted. Now they were passing a cotton field. ("The back of my neck'll be blistered," she thought. "Where was it I picked strawberries once? At Dyersburg when I was ten, visiting some God-forsaken relations.") The horses

turned off the road into wooded bottom land. The way now
was shaded by giant trees, but here and there the sun shone
between foliage. Once after riding thirty feet in shadow,
watching dumbly the cool blue-green underbrush, Josie felt
the sun suddenly on her back. Her stomach churned, and the
eggs and coffee from breakfast burnt her throat as it all gushed
forth, splattering her pants leg and the brown saddle and the
horse's side. She looked over the horse at George.

But there was no remorse, no compassion, and no humor in
George's face. He gazed straight ahead and urged on his horse.

All at once the horses turned to the right. Josie howled. She
saw her right foot flying through the air, and after the thud of
the fall and the flashes of light and darkness she lay on her
back in the dirt and watched George as he approached on
foot, leading the two horses.

"Old girl . . ." he said.

"You get the hell away from me!"

"Are you hurt?" He kneeled beside her, so close to her that
she could smell his sweaty shirt.

Josie jumped to her feet and walked in the direction from
which they had ridden. In a moment George galloped past
her, leading the gray horse and laughing like the son-of-a-
bitch he was.

"Last night he sent me upstairs! But this is more! I'm not
gonna have it." She walked through the woods, her lips moving as she talked to herself. "He wants no more of my drunken
palaver!" Well, he was going to get no more of her drunken
anything now. She had had her fill of him and everybody else
and was going to look out for her own little sweet self from
now on.

That was her trouble, she knew. She'd never made a good
thing of people. "That's why things are like they are now,"
she said. "I've never made a good thing out of anybody." But
it was real lucky that she realized it now, just exactly when she

had, for it was certain that there had never been one whom more could be made out of than George. "God damn him," she said, thinking still of his riding by her like that. "Whatever it was I liked about him is gone now."

She gazed up into the foliage and branches of the trees, and the great size of the trees made her feel real small, and real young. If Jackie or Lon had been different she might have learned things when she was young. "But they were both of 'em easy-goin' and just slipped out on me." They *were* sweet. She'd never forget how sweet Jackie always was. "Just plain sweet." She made a quick gesture with her right hand: "If only they didn't all get such a hold on me!"

But she was through with George. This time *she* got through first. He was no different from a floorwalker. He had more sense. "He's educated, and the money he must have!" George had more sense than a floorwalker, but he didn't have any manners. He treated her just like the floorwalker at Jobe's had that last week she was there. But George was worth getting around. She would find out what it was. She wouldn't take another drink. She'd find out what was wrong inside him, for there's something wrong inside everybody, and somehow she'd get a hold on him. Little Josephine would make a place for herself at last. She just wouldn't think about him as a man.

At the edge of the wood she turned onto the road, and across the fields she could see his house. That house was just simply as old and big as they come, and wasn't a cheap house. "I wonder if he looked after getting it fixed over and remodeled." Not likely. She kept looking at the whitewashed brick and shaking her head. "No, by Jesus," she exclaimed. "*She* did it!" George's wife. All of her questions seemed to have been answered. The wife had left him for his meanness, and he was lonesome. There was, then, a place to be filled. She began to run along the road. "God, I feel like somebody might step in before I get there." She laughed, but then the heat seemed to strike her all at once. Her stomach drew in.

She vomited in the ditch, and, by God, it was as dry as corn-flakes!

She sat still in the grass under a little maple tree beside the road, resting her forehead on her drawn-up knees. All between Josie and her new life seemed to be the walk through the sun in these smelly, dirty clothes. Across the fields and in the house was a canopied bed and a glorious new life, but she daren't go into the sun. She would pass out cold. "People kick off in weather like this!"

Presently Josie heard the voices of niggers up the road. She wouldn't look up, she decided. She'd let them pass, without looking up. They drew near to her and she made out the voices of a man and a child. The man said, "Hursh!" and the voices ceased. There was only the sound of their feet padding along the dusty road.

The noise of the padding grew fainter. Josie looked up and saw that the two had cut across the fields toward George's house. Already she could hear the niggers mouthing it about the kitchen. That little yellow Henry would look at her over his shoulder as he went through the swinging door at dinner tonight. If she heard them grumbling once more, as she did Monday, calling her "she," Josie decided that she was going to come right out and ask Amelia about the scar. Right before George. But the niggers were the least of her worries now.

All afternoon she lay on the bed, waking now and then to look at the bottle of whisky on the dressing table and to wonder where George had gone. She didn't know whether it had been George or the field nigger who sent Henry after her in the truck. Once she dreamed that she saw George at the head of the stairs telling Amelia how he had sobered Miss Josephine up. When she awoke that time she said, "I ought to get up and get myself good and plastered before George comes back from wherever he is." But she slept again and dreamed this time that she was working at the hat sale at Jobe's and that she had to wait on Amelia, who picked up a white turban and asked Josie to model it for her. And the dream ended with Amelia telling Josie how pretty she was and how much she liked her.

Josie had taken another hot bath (to ward off soreness from the horseback ride) and was in the sitting room, which everybody called the back parlor, playing the electric victrola and feeling just prime when George came in. She let him go through the hall and upstairs to dress up for dinner without calling to him. She chuckled to herself and rocked to the time of the music.

George came with a mint julep in each hand. His hair was wet and slicked down over his head; the part, low on the left side, was straight and white. His cheeks were shaven and were pink with new sunburn. He said, "I had myself the time of my life this afternoon."

Josie smiled and said that she was glad he had enjoyed himself. George raised his eyebrows and cocked his head to one side. She kept on smiling at him, and made no movement toward taking the drink that he held out to her.

George set the glass on the little candle stand near her chair and switched off the victrola.

"George, I was listening. . . ."

"Ah, now," he said, "I want to tell you about the cockfight."

"Let me finish listening to that piece, George."

George dropped down into an armchair and put his feet on a stool. His pants and shirt were white, and he wore a blue polka dot tie.

"You're nice and clean," she said, as though she had forgotten the victrola.

"Immaculate!" There was a mischievous grin on his face, and he leaned over one arm of the chair and pulled the victrola plug from the floor socket. Josie reached out and took the glass from the candle stand, stirred it slightly with a shoot of mint and began to sip it. She thought, "I *have* to take it when he acts this way."

At the dinner table George said, "You're in better shape to-night. You look better. Why don't you go easy on the bottle tonight?"

She looked at him between the two candles burning in the center of the round table. "I didn't ask you for that mint julep, I don't think."

"And you ain't gettin' any more," he said, winking at her as he lifted his fork to his lips with his left hand. This, she felt, was a gesture to show his contempt for her. Perhaps he thought she didn't know the difference which, of course, was even more contemptuous.

"Nice manners," she said. He made no answer, but at least he could be sure that she had recognized the insult. She took a drink of water, her little finger extended slightly from the glass, and over the glass she said, "You didn't finish about the niggers having a fight after the chickens did."

"Oh, yes." He arranged his knife and fork neatly on his plate. "The two nigs commenced to watch each other before their chickens had done scrapping. And when the big rooster gave his last hop and keeled over, Ira Blakemoor jumped over the two birds onto Jimmy's shoulders. Jimmy just whirled round and round till he threw Ira the way the little mare did you this morning." George looked directly into Josie's eyes between the candles, defiantly unashamed to mention that event, and he smiled with defiance and yet with weariness. "Ira got up and the two walked around looking at each other like two black games before a fight." Josie kept her eyes on George while the story, she felt, went on and on and on.

That yellow nigger Henry was paused at the swinging door, looking over his shoulder toward her. She turned her head and glared at him. He was not even hiding this action from George, who was going on and on about the niggers' fighting. This Henry was the worst hypocrite of all. He who had slashed Amelia's wrist (it was surely Henry who had done it), and probably had raped his own children, the way niggers do, was denouncing her right out like this. Her heart pounded when he kept looking, and then George's story stopped.

A bright light flashed across Henry's face and about the room which was lit by only the two candles. Josie swung her head around, and through the front window she saw the lights of automobiles that were moving through the yard. She looked at George, and his face said absolutely nothing for itself. He moistened his lips with his tongue.

"Guests," he said, raising his eyebrows. And Josie felt that in that moment she had seen the strongest floorwalker weaken. George had scorned and laughed at everybody and every situation. But now he was ashamed. He was ashamed of her. On her behavior would depend his comfort. She was cold sober and would be *up* to whatever showed itself. It was her real opportunity.

From the back of the house a horn sounded, and above other voices a woman's voice rose, calling "Whoohoo!" George stood up and bowed to her beautifully, like something she had never seen, and said, "You'll excuse me?" Then he went out through the kitchen without saying "scat" about what she should do.

She drummed on the table with her fingers and listened to George's greetings to his friends. She heard him say, "Welcome, Billy, and welcome, Mrs. Billy!" They were the only names she recognized. It was likely the Billy Colton she'd met with George one night.

Then these *were* Memphis Society people. Here for the night, at least! She looked down at her yellow linen dress and straightened the lapels at the neck. She thought of the women with their lovely profiles and soft skin and natural-colored hair. What if she had waited on one of them once at Jobe's or, worse still, in the old days at Bernstein's? But they had probably never been to one of those cheap stores. What if they stayed but refused to talk to her, or even to meet her? They could be mean bitches, all of them, for all their soft hands

and shaved legs. Her hand trembled as she rang the little glass
bell for coffee.

She rang it, and no one answered. She rang it again, hard,
but now she could hear Henry coming through the breakfast
room to the hall, bumping the guests' baggage against the
doorway. Neither Amelia nor Mammy, who cooked the evening meal, would leave the kitchen during dinner, Josie knew.
"I'd honestly like to go out in the kitchen and ask 'em for a
cup of coffee and tell 'em just how scared I am." But too well
she could imagine their contemptuous, accusing gaze. "If only
I could get something on them! Even catch 'em toting food
just once! That Mammy's likely killed enough niggers in her
time to fill Jobe's basement."

Josie was even afraid to light a cigarette. She went over to
the side window and looked out into the yard; she could see
the lights from the automobile shining on the green leaves
and on the white fence around the house lot.

And she was standing thus when she heard the voices and
the footsteps in the long hall. She had only just turned around
when George stood in the wide doorway with the men and
women from Memphis. He was pronouncing her name first:
"Miss Carlson, this is Mr. Roberts, Mrs. Roberts, Mr. Jackson,
Mrs. Jackson, and Mr. and Mrs. Colton."

Josie stared at the group, not trying to catch the names. She
could think only, "They're old. The women are old and
plump. George's wife is old!" She stared at them, and when
the name Colton struck her ear, she said automatically and
without placing his face, "I know Billy."

George said in the same tone in which he had said, "You'll
excuse me?" "Josie, will you take the ladies upstairs to freshen
up while the men and I get some drinks started? We'll settle
the rooming question later." George was the great floorwalker
whose wife was old and who had now shown his pride to Josie
Carlson. He had shown his shame. Finally he had decided on a
course and was following it, but he had given 'way his sore

spots. Only God knew what he had told his friends. Josie said to herself, "It's plain he don't want 'em to know who I am."

As Josie ascended the stair, followed by those she had already privately termed the "three matrons," she watched George and the three other men go down the hall to the breakfast room. The sight of their white linen suits and brown and white shoes in the bright hall seemed to make the climb a soaring. At the top of the stairs she stopped and let the three women pass ahead of her. She eyed the costume of each as they passed. One wore a tailored seersucker dress. Another wore a navy blue linen dress with white collar and cuffs, and the third wore a striped linen skirt and silk blouse. On the wrist of this last was a bracelet from which hung a tiny silver dog, a lock, a gold heart.

Josie observed their grooming: their fingernails, their lipstick, their hair in tight curls. There was gray in the hair of one, but not one, Josie decided now, was much past forty. Their figures were neatly corseted, and Josie felt that the little saggings under their chins and under the eyes of the one in the navy blue made them more charming; were, indeed, almost a part of their smartness. She wanted to think of herself as like them. They were, she realized, at least ten years older than she, but in ten years, beginning tonight, she might become one of them.

"Just go in my room there," she said. She pointed to the open door and started down the steps, thinking that this was the beginning of the new life and thinking of the men downstairs fixing the drinks. And then she thought of the bottle of whisky on her dressing table in the room where the matrons had gone!

"Oh, hell," she cursed under her breath. She had turned to go up the two steps again when she heard the men's voices below. She heard her own name being pronounced carefully: "Josie Carlson." She went down five or six steps on tiptoe and stood still to listen to the voices that came from the breakfast room.

"You said to come any time, George, and never mentioned having this thing down here."

George laughed. "Afraid of what the girls will say when you get home? I can hear them. 'In Beatrice's own lovely house,' " he mocked.

"Well, fellow, you've a shock coming, too," one of them said. "Beatrice has sent your boys down to Memphis for a month with you. They say she has a beau."

"And in the morning," one said, "your sister Kate's sending them down here. She asked us to bring them, and then decided to keep them one night herself."

"You'd better get *her* out, George."

George laughed. Josie could hear him dropping ice into glasses.

"We'll take her back at dawn if you say."

"What would the girls say to that?" He laughed at them as he laughed at Josie.

"The girls are gonna be decent to her. They agreed in the yard."

"Female curiosity?" George said.

"Your boys'll have curiosity, too. Jock's seventeen."

Even the clank of the ice stopped. "You'll every one of you please to remember," George said slowly, "that Josie's a friend of yours and that she met the girls here by appointment."

Josie tiptoed down the stairs, descending, she felt, once more into her old world. "He'll slick me some way if he has to for his kids, I think." She turned into the dining room at the foot of the stairs. The candles were burning low, and she went and stood by the open window and listened to the counterpoint of the crickets and the frogs while Henry, who had looked over his shoulder at the car lights, rattled the silver and china and went about clearing the table.

Presently George had come and put his hand on her shoulder. When she turned around she saw him smiling and holding two drinks in his left hand. He leaned his face close to hers and said, "I'm looking for the tears."

Josie said, "There aren't any to find, fellow"; and she thought it odd, really odd, that he had expected her to cry. But he was probably poking fun at her again.

She took one of the drinks and clinked glasses with George. To herself she said, "I bet they don't act any better than I do after they've got a few under their belts." At least she showed her true colors! "I'll keep my eyes open for their true ones."

If only they'd play the victrola instead of the radio. She liked the victrola so much better. She could play "Louisville Lady" over and over. But, *no*. They all wanted to switch the radio about. To get Cincinnati and Los Angeles and Bennie this and Johnny that. If they liked a piece, why did they care who played it? For God's sake! They wouldn't dance at first, either, and when she first got George to dance with her, they sat smiling at each other, grinning. They had played cards, too, but poker didn't go so well after George slugged them all with that third round of his three-dollar-whisky drinks. Right then she had begun to watch out to see who slapped whose knee.

She asked George to dance because she so liked to dance with him, and she wasn't going to care about what the others did any more, she decided. But finally when two of them had started dancing off in the corner of the room, she looked about the sitting room for the other four and saw that Billy Colton had disappeared not with his own wife but with that guy Jackson's. And Josie threw herself down into the armchair and laughed aloud, so hard and loud that everybody begged her to tell what was funny. But she stopped suddenly and gave them as mean a look as she could manage and said, "Nothin'. Let's dance some more, George."

But George said that he must tell Henry to fix more drinks, and he went out and left her by the radio with Roberts and Mrs. Colton. She looked at Mrs. Colton and thought, "Honey, you don't seem to be grieving about Billy."

Then Roberts said to Josie, "George says you're from Vicksburg."

"I was raised there," she said, wondering why George hadn't told her whatever he'd told them.

"He says you live there now."

Mrs. Colton, who wore the navy blue and was the fattest of the three matrons, stood up and said to Roberts, "Let's dance in the hall where there are fewer rugs." And she gave a kindly smile to Josie, and Josie spit out a "Thanks." The couple skipped into the hall, laughing, and Josie sat alone by the radio wishing she could play the victrola and wishing that George would come and kiss her on the back of her neck. "And I'd slap him if he did," she said. Now and again she would cut her eye around to watch Jackson and Mrs. Roberts dancing. They were at the far end of the room and were dancing slowly. They kept rubbing against the heavy blue drapery at the window and they were talking into each other's ears.

But the next piece that came over the radio was a hot one, and Jackson led Mrs. Roberts to the center of the room and whirled her round and round, and the trinkets at her wrist tinkled like little bells. Josie lit a cigarette and watched them dance. She realized then that Jackson was showing off for her sake.

When George came with a tray of drinks he said, "Josie, move the victrola," but Josie sat still and glared at him as if to say, "What on earth are you talking about? Are you nuts?" He set the tray across her lap and turned and picked up the little victrola and set it on the floor.

"Oh, good God!" cried Josie in surprise and delight. "It's a portable."

George, taking the tray from her, said, "It's not for you to port off, old girl."

The couple in the center of the room had stopped their whirling and had followed George. "We like to dance, but there are better things," Jackson was saying.

Mrs. Roberts flopped down on the broad arm of Josie's chair and took a drink from George. Josie could only watch the trinkets on the bracelet, one of which she saw was a little gold book. George was telling Jackson about the cockfight again, and Mrs. Roberts leaned over and talked to Josie. She tried to tell her how the room seemed to be whirling around. They both giggled, and Josie thought, "Maybe we'll get to be good friends, and she'll stop pretending to be so swell." But she couldn't think of anything to say to her, partly because she just never did have anything to say to women and partly because Jackson, who was not at all a bad-looking little man, was sending glances her way.

It didn't seem like more than twenty minutes or half an hour more before George had got to that point where he ordered her around and couldn't keep on his own feet. He finally lay down on the couch in the front parlor, and as she and Mrs. Roberts went up the stairs with their arms about each other's waists, he called out something that made Mrs. Roberts giggle. But Josie knew that little Josephine was at the point where she could say nothing straight, so she didn't even ask to get the portable victrola. She just cursed under her breath.

The daylight was beginning to appear at the windows of Josie's narrow little room when waking suddenly she sat up in bed and then flopped down again and jerked the sheet about her. "That little sucker come up here," she grumbled, "and cleared out, but where was the little sucker's wife?" Who was with George, by damn, all night? After a while she said, "They're none of 'em any better than the niggers. I knew they couldn't be. Nobody is. By God, nobody's better than I am. Nobody can say anything to me." Everyone would like to live as free as she did! There was no such thing as . . . There was no such thing as what the niggers and the whites liked to pretend they were. She was going to let up, and do things in secret. Try to look like an angel. It wouldn't be as hard, since there was no such thing.

It was all like a scene from a color movie, like one of the musicals. It was the prettiest scene ever. And they were like two of those lovely wax models in the boys' department at Jobe's. Like two of those models, with the tan skin and blond hair, come to life! And to see them in their white shorts spring about the green grass under the blue, blue sky, hitting the little feather thing over the high net, made Josie go weak all over. She went down on her knees and rested her elbows on the window sill and watched them springing about before the people from Memphis; these were grouped under a tree, sitting in deck chairs and on the grass. George stood at the net like a floorwalker charmed by his wax manikins which had come to life.

It had been George's cries of "Outside, outside!" and the jeers and applause of the six spectators that awakened Josie. She ran to the window in her pajamas, and when she saw the white markings on the grass and the net that had sprung up there overnight, she thought that this might be a dream. But the voices of George and Mrs. Roberts and Phil Jackson were completely real, and the movements of the boys' bodies were too marvelous to be doubted.

She sank to her knees, conscious of the soreness which her horseback ride had left. She thought of her clumsy self in the dusty road as she gazed down at graceful boys on the lawn and said, "Why, they're actually pretty. Too pretty." She was certain of one thing: She didn't want any of their snobbishness. She wouldn't have it from his two kids.

One boy's racket missed the feather thing. George shouted, "Game!" The group under the tree applauded, and the men pushed themselves up from their seats to come out into the sunlight and pat the naked backs of the boys.

When the boys came close together, Josie saw that one was

six inches taller than the other. "Why, that one's grown!" she thought. The two of them walked toward the house, the taller one walking with the shorter's neck in the crook of his elbow. George called to them, "You boys get dressed for lunch." He ordered them about just as he did her, but they went off smiling.

Josie walked in her bare feet into the little closet-like bathroom which adjoined her room. She looked at herself in the mirror there and said, "I've never dreaded anything so much in all my life before. You can't depend on what kids'll say." But were they kids? For all their prettiness, they were too big to be called kids. And nobody's as damn smutty as a smartalecky shaver.

Josephine bathed in the little, square, maroon bathtub. There were maroon-and-white checkered tile steps built up around the tub, so that it gave the effect of being sunken. After her bath, she stood on the steps and powdered her whole soft body. Every garment which she put on was absolutely fresh. She went to her closet and took out her new white silk dress and slipped it over her head. She put on white shoes first, but, deciding she looked too much like a trained nurse, she changed to her tan pumps. Josie knew what young shavers thought about nurses.

She combed her yellow hair till it lay close to her head, and put on rouge and lipstick. Someone knocked at the bedroom door. "Yeah," she called. No answer came, so she went to the door and opened it. In the hall stood one of the boys. It was the little one.

He didn't look at her; he looked past her. And his eyes *were* as shiny and cold as those on a wax dummy!

"Miss Carlson, my dad says to tell you that lunch is ready. And I'm Buddy."

"Thanks." She didn't know what the hell else she should say. "Tell him, all right," she said. She stepped back into her room and shut the door.

Josie paced the room for several minutes. "He didn't so much as look at me." She was getting hot, and she went and put her face to the window. The people from Memphis had come indoors, and the sun shone on the brownish green grass and on the still trees. "It's a scorcher," she said. She walked the length of the room again and opened the door. Buddy was still there. Standing there in white, his shirt open at the collar, and his white pants, long pants. He was leaning against the banister.

"Ready?" he said, smiling.

As they went down the steps together, he said, "It's nice that you're here. We didn't know it till just a few minutes ago." He was a Yankee kid, lived with his mother somewhere, and rolled his *r*'s, and spoke as though there was a lot of meaning behind what he said. She gave him a quick glance to see what he meant by that last remark. He smiled, and this time looked right into her eyes.

After lunch, which Josie felt had been awful embarrassing, they traipsed into the back parlor, and George showed off the kids again. She had had a good look at the older one during lunch and could tell by the way the corners of his mouth drooped down that he was a surly one, unless maybe he was only trying to keep from looking so pretty. And all he said to the questions which George asked him about girls and his high school was "Yeah" or "Aw, naw." When Henry brought in the first round of drinks, and he took one, his daddy looked at him hard and said, "Jock?" And the boy looked his daddy square in the eye.

Buddy only shook his head and smiled when Henry offered him a drink, but he was the one that had started all the embarrassment for her at lunch. When they came into the dining room he pulled her chair out, and she looked back at him— knowing how kids like to jerk chairs. Everybody laughed, but she kept on looking at him. And then she knew that she blushed, for she thought how big her behind must look to him with her bent over like she was.

The other thing that was awful was the question that Mrs. Jackson, the smallest matron and the one with the gray streak in her hair, asked her, "And how do *you* feel this morning, Miss Carlson?" It was the fact that it was Jackson's wife which got her most. But then the fool woman said, "Like the rest of us?" And Josie supposed that she meant no meanness by her remark, but she had already blushed; and Jackson, across the table, looked into his plate. Had this old woman and George been messing around? She wondered. Probably Mrs. Jackson hadn't meant anything.

As they all lounged about the sitting room after lunch, she even felt that she was beginning to catch on to these people and that she was going to start a little pretense of her own and make a good thing out of old Georgie. It was funny the way her interest in him, any real painful interest, was sort of fading. "I've never had so much happen to me at one time," she said to herself. She sat on the floor beside George's chair and put her hand on the toe of his brown-and-white shoe.

Then George said, "Buddy, you've got to give us just one recitation." And Buddy's face turned as red as a traffic light. He was sitting on a footstool and looking down at his hands.

Jock reached over and touched him on the shoulder and said, "Come on, Buddy, the one about 'If love were like a rose.' " Buddy shook his head and kept his eyes on his hands.

Josie said to herself, "The kid's honestly kind-a shy." It gave her the shivers to see anybody so shy and ignorant of things. But then he began to say the poetry without looking up. It was something about a rose and a rose leaf, but nobody could hear him very good.

George said, "Louder! Louder!" The boy looked at him and said a verse about "sweet rain at noon." Next he stood up and moved his hands about as he spoke, and the blushing was all gone. He said the next one to Mrs. Roberts, and it began:

> *If you were life, my darling,*
> *And I, your love, were death . . .*

That verse ended with something silly about "fruitful breath." He went then to Billy Colton's wife, and the verse he said to her was sad. He *did* have a-way with him! His eyes were big and he could look sad and happy at the same time. "And I were page to joy," he said. He actually looked like one of the pages they have in stores at Christmas.

But now the kid was perfectly sure of himself, and he had acted timid at first. It was probably all a show. She could just hear him saying dirty limericks. She realized that he was bound to say a verse to her if he knew that many, and she listened carefully to the one he said to Mrs. Jackson:

> *If you were April's lady,*
> *And I were lord in May,*
> *We'd throw with leaves for hours*
> *And draw for days with flowers,*
> *Till day like night were shady*
> *And night were bright like day;*
> *If you were April's lady,*
> *And I were lord in May.*

He turned on Josie in his grandest manner:

> *If you were queen of pleasure,*
> *And I were king of pain,*
> *We'd hunt down love together,*
> *Pluck out his flying-feather*
> *And teach his feet a measure,*
> *And find his mouth a rein;*
> *If you were queen of pleasure,*
> *And I were king of pain.*

And Josie sat up straight and gave the brat the hardest look she knew how. It was too plain. "Queen of pleasure" sounded just as bad as whore! Especially coming right after the verse about "April's lady." The boy blushed again when she glared at him. No one made a noise for a minute. Josie looked at George, and he smiled and began clapping his hands, and everybody clapped. Buddy bowed and ran from the room.

"He's good, George. He's good," Jackson said, squinting his beady little eyes. Jackson was really a puny-looking little guy in the light of day! And he hadn't thought the boy was any better than anybody else did. It was just that he wanted to be the first to say something.

"He's really very good," Mrs. Jackson said.

George laughed. "He's a regular little actor," he said. "Gets it from Beatrice, I guess." Everybody laughed.

George's wife was an actress, then! She'd probably been the worst of the whole lot. There was no telling what this child was really like.

"How old is he, Jock?" Jackson asked. How that man liked to hear his own voice!

"Fourteen and a half," Jock said. "Have you seen him draw?" He talked about his kid brother like he was his own child. Josie watched him. He was talking about Buddy's drawings, about the likenesses. She watched him, and then he saw her watching. He dropped his eyes to his hands as Buddy had done. But in a minute he looked up; and as the talking and drinking went on he kept his eyes on Josephine.

It wasn't any of George's business. It wasn't any of his or anybody's how much she drank, and she knew very well that *he* didn't really give a damn! But it *was* smarter'n hell of him to take her upstairs, because the boys had stared at her all afternoon and all through supper. That was really why she had kept on taking the drinks when she had made up her mind to let up. She had said, "You're jealous. You're jealous, George." And he had put his hand over her mouth, saying, "Careful, Josie." But she was sort of celebrating so much's happening to her, and she felt good, and she was plain infuriated when George kissed her and went back downstairs. "He

was like his real self comin' up the steps," she said. He had
told her that she didn't have the gumption God gave a crab
apple.

Josie went off to sleep with her lips moving and awoke in
the middle of the night with them moving again. She was feeling just prime and yet rotten at the same time. She had a
headache and yet she had a happy feeling. She woke up saying,
"Thank your stars you're white!" It was something they used
to say around home when she was a kid. She had been dream-
ing about Jock. He was all right. She had dreamed that together she and Jock had watched a giant bear devouring a
bull, and Jock had laughed and for some reason she had said,
"Thank your stars you're white!" He was all right. She was
practically sure. His eyes were like George's, and he was as
stubborn.

It would have been perfectly plain to everybody if supper
hadn't been such an all-round mess. What with Jackson's
smutty jokes and his showing off (trying to get her to look at
him), and Mrs. Colton's flirting with her husband (holding his
hand on the table), nobody but George paid any attention to
Jock. And she was glad that she had smacked Jackson when
he tried to carry her up the stairs, for it made Jock smile his
crooked smile.

"They all must be in bed," she thought. The house was so
quiet that she could hear a screech owl, or something, down in
the woods.

She thought she heard a noise in her bathroom. She lay still,
and she was pretty sure she had heard it again. She supposed
it was a mouse, but it might be something else; she had never
before thought about where that door beside the bathtub
might lead. There was only one place it could go. She got up
and went in her stocking feet to the bathroom. She switched
on the light and watched the knob. She glanced at herself in
the mirror. Her new white silk dress was twisted and wrin-

kled. "Damn him," she whispered to herself. "He *could* have made me take off this dress." Then she thought she had seen the knob move, move as though someone had released it. She stood still, but there wasn't another sound that night.

In the morning when she turned off the bathroom light, she was still wondering. She looked out of the window; the high net was down. No one was in sight.

What they all did was to slip out on her before she woke up! And in the breakfast room that morning Amelia wanted to talk, but Josephine wasn't going to give the nigger the chance. There was no telling what they had let the niggers hear at breakfast. Amelia kept coming to the breakfast room door and asking if everything was all right, if Miss Josephine wanted this or wanted that, but Miss Josephine would only shake her head and say not a word after Amelia had once answered, "They've went back to Memphis." For all she knew, George and the kids had gone too. It would have been like him to leave and send after her, just because he had promised her she could stay a week, (He talked like it was such a great treat for her. She hadn't given a copper about the place at first. It had been *him*.) But he'd damned well better not have left her. She'd got a taste of this sort of thing for its own sake now, and she'd stay for good!

Buddy opened the outside door of the breakfast room.

"Good morning, Miss Carlson," he said.

"Hello," Josie said. She did wonder what Jock had told Buddy, what he had guessed to tell him. Buddy wasn't at dinner last night, or she couldn't remember him there.

He was wearing khaki riding pants and a short-sleeved shirt. He sat down across the table from her. "I guess we're all that's left," he said. He picked up the sugar bowl and smiled as he examined it. The corners of his mouth, turned up like in a picture kids draw on a blackboard.

"Did Jock and George go to Memphis? Did they?"

"Jock did."

"He did?"

"Yes, he did. And Henry told me he didn't much want to go. I was off riding when they all got up this morning. Daddy wanted me to go too, but I wasn't here." He smiled again, and Josie supposed he meant that he'd been hiding from them.

"Where's your dad?"

"He? Oh, he went to the village to see about some hams. What are you going to do now?"

Josie shrugged her shoulders and began to drink her coffee. Jock was gone. He might have just been scorning her with those looks all the time. She should have got that door open somehow and found out what was what. "Why didn't Jock want to go?" she asked Buddy.

"Our pleasant company, I suppose," he said. "Or yours."

She looked at him, and he laughed. She wondered could this brat be poking fun at her? "Queen of pleasure!" she said out loud, not meaning to at all.

"Did you like that poem?" he asked. It was certain that he wasn't timid when he was alone with somebody, not at least when alone with her.

"I don't know," she said. Then she looked at him. "I don't like the one you picked for me."

"That's not one of the best, is it?"

Neither of them spoke while Josie finished her coffee. She put in another spoonful of sugar before taking the last few swallows, and Buddy reddened when she motioned for him to give up the sugar bowl. Amelia came and removed the breakfast plate and the butter plate. She returned for Josie's coffee cup, and, finding it not quite ready, she stood behind Buddy's chair and put her hands on his shoulders. The scar was right beside his cheek. Buddy smiled and beat the back of his head against her ribs playfully. Finally Josie put her cup down and said, "That's all."

She went upstairs to her room. Jock had tried to get in through her bathroom last night, or had been so on her mind that her ears and eyes had made up the signs of it. Maybe Buddy had caught Jock trying to open the door and had told George. At any rate George had sent Jock away. If he sent him away, then Jock had definitely had notions. Josie smiled over that one. She was sitting on the side of her little canopied bed, smoking a red-tipped cigarette. There was the noise of an automobile motor in the yard. George was back! Josie went to her dressing table and drank the last of her whisky.

She sat on the stool before her dressing table, with her eyes on the hall door. She listened to George's footsteps on the stairs, and sat with her legs crossed, twitching the left foot, which dangled. George came in and closed the door behind him.

"I've bought you a ticket on the night train, Josie. You're goin' back tonight."

So he wasn't such a stickler for his word, after all! Not in this case. He was sending her home. Well, what did he expect her to say? Did he think she would beg to stay on? She would clear out, and she wasn't the one beaten. George was beaten. One of his kids that he was so mortally fond of, one for sure had had notions. "Almost for sure." George opened the door and left Josie staring after him. In a few minutes she heard his horse gallop past the house and out onto the dirt road.

She folded her white dress carefully and laid it on the bottom of her traveling bag. She heard Buddy somewhere in the house, singing. She wrapped her white shoes in toilet paper and stuck them at the ends of the bag. Buddy seemed to be wandering through the house, singing. His voice was high like a woman's, never breaking as she sometimes thought it did in conversation. It came from one part of the house and then another. Josie stopped her packing. "There's no such thing," she said.

She went down the steps like a child, stopping both feet on each step, then stepping to the next. One hand was on her hip, the other she ran along the banister. She walked through the front parlor with its bookcases and fancy chairs with the eagles worked in the needlepoint, and through the back parlor with the rocking chairs and the silly candle stand and the victrola. She stepped down into the breakfast room where the sunlight came through the blinds and put stripes on the brick wall. She went into the kitchen for the first time. Mammy, with a white dust cap on the back of her head, had already started supper. She stood by the big range, and Amelia sat in the corner chopping onions. Josie wasn't interested in the face of either. She went through the dark pantry and into the dining room. She looked through the windows there, but no one was in the yard. She went into the hall.

Buddy was near the top of the stairway which curved around the far end of the long hall, looking down at her. "Why don't you come up here?" He pronounced every word sharply and rolled his *r*'s. But his voice was flat, and his words seemed to remain in the hall for several minutes. His question seemed to float down from the ceiling, down through the air like a feather.

"How did he get up there without me hearing him?" Josie mumbled. She took the first two steps slowly, and Buddy hopped up to the top of the stair.

The door to the kids' room was open and Josie went in. Buddy shut the white paneled door and said, "Don't you think it's time you did something nice for me?"

Josie laughed, and she watched Buddy laugh. Queen of pleasure indeed!

"I want to draw you," he said.

"Clothes and all, Bud . . .?"

"No. That's not what I mean!"

Josie forced a smile. She suddenly felt afraid and thought she was going to be sick again but she couldn't take her eyes off him.

"That's not what I mean," she heard the kid say again,

without blinking an eye, without blushing. "I didn't know you were that sort of nasty thing here. I didn't believe you were a fancy woman. Go on out of here. Go away!" he ordered her.

As Josie went down the steps she kept puckering her lips and nodding her head. She was trying to talk to herself about how many times she had been up and down the steps, but she could still see the smooth brown color of his face and his yellow hair, and she could also see her hand trembling on the banister. It seemed like five years since she had come up the stairs with the matrons from Memphis.

In the breakfast room she tore open the frail door to George's little liquor cabinet and took a quart of bourbon from the shelf. Then she stepped up into the hall and went into the sitting room and took the portable victrola and that record. As she stomped back into the hall, Buddy came running down the steps. He opened the front door and ran out across the veranda and across the lawn. His yellow hair was like a ball of gold in the sunlight as he went through the white gate. But Josie went upstairs.

She locked her door and threw the big key across the room. She knocked the bottle of toilet water and the amber brush off her dressing table as she made room for the victrola. When she had started "Louisville Lady" playing she sat on the stool and began to wonder. "The kid's head was like a ball of gold, but I'm not gonna think about him ever once I get back to Memphis," she told herself. "No, by damn, but I wonder just what George'll do to me." She broke the blue seal of the whisky with her fingernail, and it didn't seem like more than twenty minutes or half an hour before George was beating and kicking on the door, and she was sitting on the stool and listening and just waiting for him to break the door, and wondering what he'd do to her.

A Spinster's Tale

My brother would often get drunk when I was a little girl, but that put a different sort of fear into me from what Mr. Speed did. With Brother it was a spiritual thing. And though it was frightening to know that he would have to burn for all that giggling and bouncing around on the stair at night, the truth was that he only seemed jollier to me when I would stick my head out of the hall door. It made him seem almost my age for him to act so silly, putting his white forefinger all over his flushed face and finally over his lips to say, "Sh-sh-sh-sh!" But the really frightening thing about seeing Brother drunk was what I always heard when I had slid back into bed. I could alway recall my mother's words to him when he was sixteen, the year before she died, spoken in her greatest sincerity, in her most religious tone:

"Son, I'd rather see you in your grave."

Yet those nights put a scaredness into me that was clearly distinguishable from the terror that Mr. Speed instilled by stumbling past our house two or three afternoons a week. The most that I knew about Mr. Speed was his name. And this I considered that I had somewhat fabricated—by allowing him the "Mr."—in my effort to humanize and soften the monster that was forever passing our house on Church Street. My father would point him out through the wide parlor window in soberness and severity to my brother with: "There goes Old Speed, again." Or on Saturdays when Brother was with the Benton boys and my two uncles were over having toddies with Father in the parlor, Father would refer to Mr. Speed's passing with a similar speech, but in a blustering tone of merry tolerance: "There goes Old Speed, again. The rascal!" These designations were equally awful, both spoken in tones that were foreign to my father's manner of addressing me; and not unconsciously I prepared the euphemism, Mister Speed, against the inevitable day when I should have to speak of him to someone.

I was named Elizabeth, for my mother. My mother had died in the spring before Mr. Speed first came to my notice on that late afternoon in October. I had bathed at four with the aid of Lucy, who had been my nurse and who was now the upstairs maid; and Lucy was upstairs turning back the covers of the beds in the rooms with their color schemes of blue and green and rose. I wandered into the shadowy parlor and sat first on one chair, then on another. I tried lying down on the settee that went with the parlor set, but my legs had got too long this summer to stretch out straight on the settee. And my feet looked long in their pumps against the wicker arm. I looked at the pictures around the room blankly and at the stained-glass windows on either side of the fireplace; and the winter light coming through them was hardly bright enough to show the colors. I struck a match on the mosaic hearth and lit the gas-logs.

Kneeling on the hearth, I watched the flames till my face felt hot. I stood up then and turned directly to one of the full-length mirror-panels that were on each side of the front window. This one was just to the right of the broad window and my reflection in it stood out strangely from the rest of the room in the dull light that did not penetrate beyond my figure. I leaned closer to the mirror trying to discover a resemblance between myself and the wondrous Alice who walked through a looking-glass. But that resemblance I was seeking I could not find in my sharp features, or in my heavy, dark curls hanging like fragments of hosepipe to my shoulders.

I propped my hands on the borders of the narrow mirror and put my face close to watch my lips say, "Away." I would hardly open them for the "a"; and then I would contort my face by the great opening I made for the "way." I whispered, "Away, away." I whispered it over and over, faster and faster, watching myself in the mirror: "A-way-a-way—away-away-awayaway." Suddenly I burst into tears and turned from the gloomy mirror to the daylight at the wide parlor window. Gazing tearfully through the expanse of plate glass there, I beheld Mr. Speed walking like a cripple with one foot on the curb and one in the street. And faintly I could hear him cursing the trees as he passed them, giving each a lick with his heavy walking cane.

Presently I was dry-eyed in my fright. My breath came short, and I clasped the black bow at the neck of my middy blouse.

When he had passed from view, I stumbled back from the window. I hadn't heard the houseboy enter the parlor, and he must not have noticed me there. I made no move of recognition as he drew the draperies across the wide front window for the night. I stood cold and silent before the gas-logs with a sudden inexplicable memory of my mother's cheek and a vision of her in her bedroom on a spring day.

That April day when spring had seemed to crowd itself through the windows into the bright upstairs rooms the old-fashioned mahogany sick-chair had been brought down from the attic to my mother's room. Three days before, a quiet service had been held there for the stillborn baby, and I had accompanied my father and brother to our lot in the gray cemetery to see the box (large for so tiny a parcel) lowered and covered with mud. But in the parlor now by the gas-logs I remembered the day that my mother had sent for the sick-chair and for me.

The practical nurse, sitting in a straight chair busy at her needlework, looked over her glasses to give me some little instruction in the arrangement of my mother's pillows in the chair. A few minutes before, this practical nurse had lifted my sick mother bodily from the bed, and I had had the privilege of rolling my mother to the big bay window that looked out ideally over the new foliage of small trees in our side yard.

I stood self-consciously straight, close by my mother, a maturing little girl awkward in my curls and long-waisted dress. My pale mother, in her silk bed-jacket, with a smile leaned her cheek against the cheek of her daughter. Outside it was spring. The furnishings of the great blue room seemed to partake for that one moment of nature's life. And my mother's cheek was warm on mine. This I remembered when I sat before the gas-logs trying to put Mr. Speed out of my mind; but that a few moments later my mother beckoned to the practical nurse and sent me suddenly from the room, my memory did not dwell upon. I remembered only the warmth of the cheek and the comfort of that other moment.

I sat near the blue burning logs and waited for my father and my brother to come in. When they came saying the same things about office and school that they said every day, turning on lights beside chairs that they liked to flop into, I realized not that I was ready or unready for them but that there had been, within me, an attempt at a preparation for such readiness.

They sat so customarily in their chairs at first and the talk ran so easily that I thought that Mr. Speed could be forgotten as quickly and painlessly as a doubting of Jesus or a fear of death from the measles. But the conversation took insinuating and malicious twists this afternoon. My father talked about the possibilities of a general war and recalled opinions that people had had just before the Spanish-American. He talked about the hundreds of men in the Union Depot. Thinking of all those men there, that close together, was something like meeting Mr. Speed in the front hall. I asked my father not to talk about war, which seemed to him a natural enough request for a young lady to make.

"How is your school, my dear?" he asked me. "How are Miss Hood and Miss Herron? Have they found who's stealing the boarder's things, my dear?"

All of those little girls safely in Belmont School being called for by gentle ladies or warm-breasted Negro women were a pitiable sight beside the beastly vision of Mr. Speed which even they somehow conjured.

At dinner, with Lucy serving and sometimes helping my plate (because she had done so for so many years), Brother teased me first one way and then another. My father joined in on each point until I began to take the teasing very seriously, and then he told Brother that he was forever carrying things too far.

Once at dinner I was convinced that my preposterous fears that Brother knew what had happened to me by the window in the afternoon were not at all preposterous. He had been talking quietly. It was something about the meeting that he and the Benton boys were going to attend after dinner. But quickly, without reason, he turned his eyes on me across the table and fairly shouted in his new deep voice: "I saw three horses running away out on Harding Road today! They were just like the mules we saw at the mines in the mountains! They were running to beat hell and with little girls riding them!"

The first week after I had the glimpse of Mr. Speed through the parlor window, I spent the afternoons dusting the bureau and mantel and bedside table in my room, arranging on the chaise longue the dolls which at this age I never played with and rarely even talked to; or I would absent-mindedly assist Lucy in turning down the beds and maybe watch the house-boy set the dinner table. I went to the parlor only when Father came or when Brother came earlier and called me in to show me a shin bruise or a box of cigarettes which a girl had given to him.

Finally I put my hand on the parlor doorknob just at four one afternoon and entered the parlor, walking stiffly as I might have done with my hands in a muff going into church. The big room with its heavy furniture and pictures showed no change since the last afternoon that I had spent there, unless possibly there were fresh antimacassars on the chairs. I confidently pushed an odd chair over to the window and took my seat and sat erect and waited.

My heart would beat hard when, from the corner of my eye, I caught sight of some figure moving up Church Street. And as it drew nearer, showing the form of some Negro or neighbor or drummer, I would sigh from relief and from regret. I was ready for Mr. Speed. And I knew that he would come again and again, that he had been passing our house for inconceivable numbers of years. I knew that if he did not appear today, he would pass tomorrow. Not because I had had accidental, unavoidable glimpses of him from upstairs windows during the past week, nor because there were in-distinct memories of such a figure, hardly noticed, seen on afternoons that preceded that day when I had seen him stum-bling like a cripple along the curb and beating and cursing the trees did I know that Mr. Speed was a permanent and formidable figure in my life which I would be called upon to deal with; my knowledge, I was certain, was purely in-tuitive.

I was ready now not to face him with his drunken rage directed at me, but to look at him far off in the street and to appraise him. He didn't come that afternoon, but he came the next. I sat prim and straight before the window. I turned my head neither to the right to anticipate the sight of him nor to the left to follow his figure when it had passed. But when he was passing before my window, I put my eyes full on him and looked though my teeth chattered in my head. And now I saw his face heavy, red, fierce like his body. He walked with an awkward, stomping sort of stagger, carrying his gray top coat over one arm; and with his other hand he kept poking his walnut cane into the soft sod along the sidewalk. When he was gone, I recalled my mother's cheek again, but the recollection this time, though more deliberate, was dwelt less upon; and I could only think of watching Mr. Speed again and again.

There was snow on the ground the third time that I watched Mr. Speed pass our house. Mr. Speed spat on the snow, and with his cane he aimed at the brown spot that his tobacco made there. And I could see that he missed his aim. The fourth time that I sat watching for him from the window, snow was actually falling outside; and I felt a sort of anxiety to know what would ever drive him into my own house. For a moment I doubted he would really come to my door; but I prodded myself with the thought of his coming and finding me unprepared. And I continued to keep my secret watch for him two or three times a week during the rest of the winter.

Meanwhile my life with my father and brother and the servants in the shadowy house went on from day to day. On week nights the evening meal usually ended with petulant arguing between the two men, the atlas or the encyclopedia usually drawing them from the table to read out the statistics. Often Brother was accused of having looked-them-up-previously and of maneuvering the conversation toward the particular subject, for topics were very easily introduced and dismissed by the two. Once I, sent to the library to fetch a cigar, returned to find the discourse shifted in two minutes' time from the Kentucky Derby winners to the languages in which the Bible was first written. Once I actually heard the conversation slip, in the course of a small dessert, from the comparative advantages of urban and agrarian life for boys between the ages of fifteen and twenty to the probable origin and age of the Icelandic parliament and then to the doctrines of the Campbellite church.

That night I followed them to the library and beheld them fingering the pages of the flimsy old atlas in the light from the beaded lampshade. They paid no attention to me and little to one another, each trying to turn the pages of the book and mumbling references to newspaper articles and to statements of persons of responsibility. I slipped from the library to the front parlor across the hall where I could hear the contentious hum. And I lit the gas-logs, trying to warm my long legs before them as I examined my own response to the unguided and remorseless bickering of the masculine voices.

It was, I thought, their indifferent shifting from topic to topic that most disturbed me. Then I decided that it was the tremendous gaps that there seemed to be between the subjects that was bewildering to me. Still again I thought that it was the equal interest which they displayed for each subject that was dismaying. All things in the world were equally at home in their arguments. They exhibited equal indifference to the horrors that each might suggest; and I wondered whether or not their imperturbability was a thing that they had achieved.

I knew that I had got myself so accustomed to the sight of Mr. Speed's peregrinations, persistent, yet, withal, seemingly without destination, that I could view his passing with perfect equanimity. And from this I knew that I must extend my preparation for the day when I should have to view him at closer range. When the day would come, I knew that it must

involve my father and my brother and that his existence therefore must not remain an unmentionable thing, the secrecy
of which to explode at the moment of crisis, only adding to its
confusion.

Now, the door to my room was the first at the top of the
long red-carpeted stairway. A wall light beside it was left
burning on nights when Brother was out, and, when he came
in, he turned it off. The light shining through my transom
was a comforting sight when I had gone to bed in the big
room; and in the summertime I could see the reflection of
light bugs on it, and often one would plop against it. Sometimes I would wake up in the night with a start and would
be frightened in the dark, not knowing what had awakened
me until I realized that Brother had just turned out the light.
On other nights, however, I would hear him close the front
door and hear him bouncing up the steps. When I then stuck
my head out the door, usually he would toss me a piece of
candy and he always signaled to me to be quiet.

I had never intentionally stayed awake till he came in until
one night toward the end of February of that year, and I
hadn't been certain then that I should be able to do it. Indeed, when finally the front door closed, I had dozed several
times sitting up in the dark bed. But I was standing with my
door half open before he had come a third of the way up the
stair. When he saw me, he stopped still on the stairway, resting his hand on the banister. I realized that purposefulness
must be showing on my face, and so I smiled at him and
beckoned. His red face broke into a fine grin, and he took
the next few steps two at a time. But he stumbled on the
carpeted steps. He was on his knees, yet with his hand still
on the banister. He was motionless there for a moment with
his head cocked to one side, listening. The house was quiet
and still. He smiled again, sheepishly this time, and kept
putting his white forefinger to his red face as he ascended on
tiptoe the last third of the flight of steps.

At the head of the stair he paused, breathing hard. He reached his hand into his coat pocket and smiled confidently as he shook his head at me. I stepped backward into my room.

"Oh," he whispered. "Your candy."

I stood straight in my white nightgown with my black hair hanging over my shoulders, knowing that he could see me only indistinctly. I beckoned to him again. He looked suspiciously about the hall, then stepped into the room and closed the door behind him.

"What's the matter, Betsy?" he said.

I turned and ran and climbed between the covers of my bed.

"What's the matter, Betsy?" he said. He crossed to my bed and sat down beside me on it.

I told him that I didn't know what was the matter.

"Have you been reading something you shouldn't, Betsy?" he asked.

I was silent.

"Are you lonely, Betsy?" he said. "Are you a lonely little girl?"

I sat upon the bed and threw my arms about his neck. And as I sobbed on his shoulder I smelled for the first time the fierce odor of his cheap whisky.

"Yes, I'm always lonely," I said with directness, and I was then silent with my eyes open and my cheek on the shoulder of his overcoat which was yet cold from the February night air.

He kept his face turned away from me and finally spoke, out of the other corner of his mouth, I thought, "I'll come home earlier some afternoons and we'll talk and play."

"Tomorrow."

When I had said this distinctly, I fell away from him back on the bed. He stood up and looked at me curiously, as though in some way repelled by my settling so comfortably in the covers. And I could see his eighteen-year-old head cocked to one side as though trying to see my face in the dark. He leaned over me, and I smelled his whisky breath. It was not repugnant to me. It was blended with the odor that he always had. I thought he was going to strike me. He didn't, however, and in a moment was opening the door to the lighted hall. Before he went out, again I said:

"Tomorrow."

The hall light dark and the sound of Brother's footsteps gone, I naturally repeated the whole scene in my mind and upon examination found strange elements present. One was something like a longing for my brother to strike me when he was leaning over me. Another was his bewilderment at my procedure. On the whole I was amazed at the way I had carried the thing off. Now I only wished that in the darkness when he was leaning over me I had said languidly, "Oh, Brother," had said it in a tone indicating that we had in common some unmentionable trouble. Then I should have been certain of his presence next day. As it was, though, I had little doubt of his coming home early.

I would not let myself reflect further on my feelings for my brother—my desire for him to strike me and my delight in his natural odor. I had got myself in the habit of postponing such elucidations until after I had completely settled with Mr. Speed. But, as after all such meetings with my brother, I reflected upon the posthumous punishments in store for him for his carousing and drinking and remembered my mother's saying that she had rather see him in his grave.

The next afternoon at four I had the chessboard on the tea table before the front parlor window. I waited for my brother, knowing pretty well that he would come and feeling certain that Mr. Speed would pass. (For this was a Thursday afternoon, and during the winter months I had found that there were two days of the week on which Mr. Speed never failed to pass our house. These were Thursday and Saturday.) I led my brother into that dismal parlor, chattering about the places where I had found the chessmen long in disuse. When I paused a minute, slipping into my seat by the chessboard, he picked up with talk of the senior class play and his chances for being chosen valedictorian. Apparently I no longer seemed an enigma to him. I thought that he must have concluded that I was just a lonely little girl named Betsy. But I doubted that his nature was so different from my own that he could sustain objective sympathy for another child, particularly a younger sister, from one day to another. And since I saw no favors that he could ask from me at this time, my conclusion was that he believed that he had never exhibited his drunkenness to me with all his bouncing about on the stair at night; but that he was not certain that talking from the other corner of his mouth had been precaution enough against his whisky breath.

We faced each other over the chessboard and set the men in order. There were only a few days before it would be March, and the light through the window was first bright and then dull. During my brother's moves I stared out the window at the clouds that passed before the sun and watched pieces of newspaper that blew about the yard. I was calm beyond my own credulity. I found myself responding to my brother's little jokes and showing real interest in the game. I tried to terrorize myself by imagining Mr. Speed's coming up to the very window this day. I even had him shaking his cane and his derby hat at us. But the frenzy which I expected at this step of my preparation did not come. And some part of Mr. Speed's formidability seemed to have vanished. I realized that by not hiding my face in my mother's bosom and by looking at him so regularly for so many months, I had come to accept his existence as a natural part of my life on Church Street, though something to be guarded against, or, as I had put it before, to be thoroughly prepared for when it came to my door.

The problem then, in relation to my brother, had suddenly resolved itself in something much simpler than the conquest of my fear of looking upon Mr. Speed alone had been. This would be only a matter of how I should act and of what words I should use. And from the incident of the night before, I had some notion that I'd find a suitable way of procedure in our household.

Mr. Speed appeared in the street without his overcoat but with one hand holding the turned-up lapels and collar of his gray suit coat. He followed his cane, stomping like an enraged blind man with his head bowed against the March wind. I squeezed from between my chair and the table and stood right at the great plate glass window, looking out. From the corner of my eye I saw that Brother was intent upon his play. Presently, in the wind, Mr. Speed's derby went back on his head, and his hand grabbed at it, pulled it back in place on his head, then returned to hold his lapels. I took a sharp breath, and Brother looked up. And just as he looked out the window, Mr. Speed's derby did blow off and across the sidewalk, over the lawn. Mr. Speed turned, shouting oaths that I could hear ever so faintly, and tried to stumble after his hat.

Then I realized that my brother was gone from the room; and he was outside the window with Mr. Speed chasing Mr. Speed's hat in the wind.

I sat back in my chair, breathless; one elbow went down on the chessboard disordering the black and white pawns and kings and castles. And through the window I watched Brother handing Mr. Speed his derby. I saw his apparent indifference to the drunk man's oaths and curses. I saw him coming back to the house while the old man yet stood railing at him. I pushed the table aside and ran to the front door lest Brother be locked outside. He met me in the hall smiling blandly.

I said, "That's Mr. Speed."

He sat down on the bottom step of the stairway, leaning backward and looking at me inquisitively.

"He's drunk, Brother," I said. "Always."

My brother looked frankly into the eyes of this half-grown sister of his but said nothing for a while.

I pushed myself up on the console table and sat swinging my legs and looking seriously about the walls of the cavernous hallway at the expanse of oak paneling, at the inset canvas of the sixteenth-century Frenchman making love to his lady, at the hat rack, and at the grandfather's clock in the darkest corner. I waited for Brother to speak.

"You don't like people who get drunk?" he said.

I saw that he was taking the whole thing as a thrust at his own behavior.

"I just think Mr. Speed is very ugly, Brother."

From the detached expression of his eyes I knew that he was not convinced.

"I wouldn't mind him less if he were sober," I said. "Mr. Speed's like—a loose horse."

This analogy convinced him. He knew then what I meant.

"You mustn't waste your time being afraid of such things," he said in great earnestness. "In two or three years there'll be things that you'll have to be afraid of. Things you really can't avoid."

"What did he say to you?" I asked.

"He cussed and threatened to hit me with that stick."

"For no reason?"

"Old Mr. Speed's burnt out his reason with whisky."

"Tell me about him." I was almost imploring him.

"Everybody knows about him. He just wanders around town, drunk. Sometimes downtown they take him off in the Black Maria."

I pictured him on the main streets that I knew downtown and in the big department stores. I could see him in that formal neighborhood where my grandmother used to live. In the neighborhood of Miss Hood and Miss Herron's school. Around the little houses out where my father's secretary lived. Even in nigger town.

"You'll get used to him, for all his ugliness," Brother said. Then we sat there till my father came in, talking gaily about things that were particularly ugly in Mr. Speed's clothes and face and in his way of walking.

Since the day that I watched myself say "away" in the mirror, I had spent painful hours trying to know once more that experience which I now regarded as something like mystical. But the stringent course that I, motherless and lonely in our big house, had brought myself to follow while only thirteen had given me certain mature habits of thought. Idle and unrestrained daydreaming I eliminated almost entirely from my experience, though I delighted myself with fantasies that I quite consciously worked out and which, when concluded, I usually considered carefully, trying to fix them with some sort of childish symbolism.

Even idleness in my nightly dreams disturbed me. And sometimes as I tossed half awake in my big bed I would try to piece together my dreams into at least a form of logic. Sometimes I would complete an unfinished dream and wouldn't know in the morning what part I had dreamed and what part pieced out. I would often smile over the ends that I had plotted in half wakeful moments but found pride in dreams that were complete in themselves and easy to fix with allegory, which I called "meaning." I found that a dream could start for no discoverable reason, with the sight of a printed page on which the first line was, "Once upon a time"; and soon could have me a character in a strange story. Once upon a time there was a little girl whose hands began to get very large. Grown men came for miles around to look at the giant hands and to shake them, but the little girl was ashamed of them and hid them under her skirt. It seemed that the little girl lived in the stable behind my grandmother's old house, and I watched her from the top of the loft ladder. Whenever there was the sound of footsteps, she trembled and wept; so I would beat on the floor above her and laugh uproariously at her fear. But presently I was the little girl listening to the noise. At first I trembled and called out for my father, but then I recollected that it was I who had made the noises and I felt that I had made a very considerable discovery for myself.

I awoke one Saturday morning in early March at the sound of my father's voice in the downstairs hall. He was talking to the servants, ordering the carriage I think. I believe that I awoke at the sound of the carriage horses' names. I went to my door and called "good-bye" to him. He was twisting his mustache before the hall mirror, and he looked up the stairway at me and smiled. He was always abashed to be caught before a looking-glass, and he called out self-consciously and affectionately that he would be home at noon.

I closed my door and went to the little dressing table that he had had put in my room on my birthday. The card with his handwriting on it was still stuck in the corner of the mirror: "For my young lady daughter." I was so thoroughly aware of the gentleness in his nature this morning that any childish timidity before him would, I thought, seem an injustice, and I determined that I should sit with him and my uncles in the parlor that afternoon and perhaps tell them all of my fear of the habitually drunken Mr. Speed and with them watch him pass before the parlor window. That morning I sat before the mirror of my dressing table and put up my hair in a knot on the back of my head for the first time.

Before Father came home at noon, however, I had taken my hair down, and I was not now certain that he would be unoffended by my mention of the neighborhood drunkard. But I was resolute in my purpose, and when my two uncles came after lunch, and the three men shut themselves up in the parlor for the afternoon, I took my seat across the hall in the little library, or den, as my mother had called it, and spent the first of the afternoon skimming over the familiar pages of *Tales of Ol' Virginny*, by Thomas Nelson Page.

My father had seemed tired at lunch. He talked very little and drank only half his cup of coffee. He asked Brother matter-of-fact questions about his plans for college in the fall and told me once to try cutting my meat instead of pulling it to pieces. And as I sat in the library afterward, I wondered if he had been thinking of my mother. Indeed, I wondered whether or not he ever thought of her. He never mentioned her to us; and in a year I had forgotten exactly how he treated her when she had been alive.

It was not only the fate of my brother's soul that I had given thought to since my mother's death. Father had always had his toddy on Saturday afternoon with his two bachelor brothers. But there was more than one round of toddies served in the parlor on Saturday now. Throughout the early part of this afternoon I could hear the tinkle of the bell in the kitchen, and presently the houseboy would appear at the door of the parlor with a tray of ice-filled glasses.

As he entered the parlor each time, I would catch a glimpse over my book of the three men. One was usually standing, whichever one was leading the conversation. Once they were laughing heartily; and as the Negro boy came out with the tray of empty glasses, there was a smile on his face.

As their voices grew louder and merrier, my courage slackened. It was then I first put into words the thought that in my brother and father I saw something of Mr. Speed. And I knew that it was more than a taste for whisky they had in common.

At four o'clock I heard Brother's voice mixed with those of the Benton boys outside the front door. They came into the hall, and their voices were high and excited. First one, then another would demand to be heard with: "No, listen now; let me tell you what." In a moment I heard Brother on the stairs. Then two of the Benton brothers appeared in the doorway of the library. Even the youngest, who was not a year older than I and whose name was Henry, wore long pants, and each carried a cap in hand and a linen duster over his arm. I stood up and smiled at them, and with my right forefinger I pushed the black locks which hung loosely about my shoulders behind my ears.

"We're going motoring in the Carltons' machine," Henry said.

I stammered my surprise and asked if Brother were going to ride in it. One of them said that he was upstairs getting his hunting cap, since he had no motoring cap. The older brother, Gary Benton, went back into the hall. I walked toward Henry, who was standing in the doorway.

"But does Father know you're going?" I asked.

As I tried to go through the doorway, Henry stretched his arm across it and looked at me with a critical frown on his face.

"Why don't you put up your hair?" he said.

I looked at him seriously, and I felt the heat of the blush that came over my face. I felt it on the back of my neck. I stooped with what I thought considerable grace and slid under his arm and passed into the hall. There were the other two Benton boys listening to the voices of my uncles and my father through the parlor door. I stepped between them and threw open the door. Just as I did so, Henry Benton commanded, "Elizabeth, don't do that!" And I, swinging the door open, turned and smiled at him.

I stood for a moment looking blandly at my father and my uncles. I was considering what had made me burst in upon them in this manner. It was not merely that I had perceived the opportunity of creating this little disturbance and slipping in under its noise, though I was not unaware of the advantage. I was frightened by the boys' impending adventure in the horseless carriage but surely not so much as I normally should have been at breaking into the parlor at this forbidden hour. The immediate cause could only be the attention which Henry Benton had shown me. His insinuation had been that I remained too much a little girl, and I had shown him that at any rate I was a bold, or at least a naughty, little girl.

My father was on his feet. He put his glass on the mantelpiece. And it seemed to me that from the three men came in rapid succession all possible arrangements of the words, boys-come-in. Come-in-boys. Well-boys-come-in. Come-on-in. Boys-come-in-the-parlor. The boys went in, rather showing off their breeding and poise, I thought. The three men moved and talked clumsily before them, as the three Benton brothers went each to each of the men carefully distinguishing between my uncles' titles: doctor and colonel. I thought how awkward all of the members of my own family appeared on occasions that called for grace. Brother strode into the room with his hunting cap sideways on his head, and he announced their plans, which the tactful Bentons, uncertain of our family's prejudices regarding machines, had not mentioned. Father and my uncles had a great deal to say about who was going-to-do-the-driving, and Henry Benton without giving an answer gave a polite invitation to the men to join them. To my chagrin both my uncles accepted with-the-greatest-of-pleasure what really had not been an invitation at all. And they persisted in accepting it even after Brother in his rudeness raised the question of room in the five-passenger vehicle.

Father said, "Sure. The more, the merrier." But he declined to go himself and declined for me Henry's invitation.

The plan was, then, as finally outlined by the oldest of the Benton brothers, that the boys should proceed to the Carltons' and that Brother should return with the driver to take our uncles out to the Carltons' house, which was one of the new residences across from Centennial Park, where the excursions in the machine were to be made.

The four slender youths took their leave from the heavy men with the gold watch chains across their stomachs, and I had to shake hands with each of the Benton brothers. To each I expressed my regret that Father would not let me ride with them, emulating their poise with all my art. Henry Benton was the last, and he smiled as though he knew what I was up to. In answer to his smile I said, "Games are *so* much fun."

I stood by the window watching the four boys in the street until they were out of sight. My father and his brothers had taken their seats in silence, and I was aware of just how unwelcome I was in the room. Finally my uncle who had been a colonel in the Spanish War and who wore bushy blond sideburns whistled under his breath and said, "Well, there's no doubt about it, no doubt about it."

He winked at my father, and my father looked at me and then at my uncle. Then quickly in a ridiculously over-serious tone he asked, "What, sir? No doubt about what, sir?"

"Why, there's no doubt that this daughter of yours was flirting with the youngest of the Messrs. Benton."

My father looked at me and twisted his mustache and said with the same pomp that he didn't know what he'd do with me if I started that sort of thing. My two uncles threw back their heads, each giving a short laugh. My uncle the doctor took off his pince-nez and shook them at me and spoke in the same mock-serious tone of his brothers:

"Young lady, if you spend your time in such pursuits you'll only bring upon yourself and upon the young men about Nashville the greatest unhappiness. I, as a bachelor, must plead the cause of the young Bentons!"

I turned to my father in indignation that approached rage.

"Father," I shouted, "there's Mr. Speed out there!"

Father sprang from his chair and quickly stepped up beside me at the window. Then, seeing the old man staggering harmlessly along the sidewalk, he said in, I thought, affected easiness:

"Yes. Yes, dear."

"He's drunk," I said. My lips quivered, and I think I must

have blushed at this first mention of the unmentionable to my father.

"Poor Old Speed," he said. I looked at my uncles, and they were shaking their heads, echoing my father's tone.

"What ever did happen to Speed's old maid sister?" my uncle the doctor said.

"She's still with him," Father said.

Mr. Speed appeared soberer today than I had ever seen him. He carried no overcoat to drag on the ground, and his stagger was barely noticeable. The movement of his lips and an occasional gesture were the only evidence of intoxication. I was enraged by the irony that his good behavior on this of all days presented. Had I been a little younger I might have suspected conspiracy on the part of all men against me, but I was old enough to suspect no person's being even interested enough in me to plot against my understanding, unless it be some vague personification of life itself.

The course which I took, I thought afterward, was the proper one. I do not think that it was because I was then really conscious that when one is determined to follow some course rigidly and is blockaded one must fire furiously, if blindly, into the blockade, but rather because I was frightened and in my fear forgot all logic of attack. At any rate, I fired furiously at the three immutable creatures.

"I'm afraid of him," I broke out tearfully. I shouted at them, "He's always drunk! He's always going by our house drunk!"

My father put his arms about me, but I continued talking as I wept on his shirt front. I heard the barking sound of the machine horn out in front, and I felt my father move one hand from my back to motion my uncles to go. And as they shut the parlor door after them, I felt that I had let them escape me.

I heard the sound of the motor fading out up Church Street, and Father led me to the settee. We sat there together for a long while, and neither of us spoke until my tears had dried.

I was eager to tell him just exactly how fearful I was of Mr. Speed's coming into our house. But he only allowed me to tell him that I *was* afraid; for when I had barely suggested that much, he said that I had no business watching Mr. Speed, that I must shut my eyes to some things. "After all," he said, nonsensically I thought, "you're a young lady now." And in several curiously twisted sentences he told me that I mustn't seek things to fear in this world. He said that it was most unlikely, besides, that Speed would ever have business at our house. He punched at his left side several times, gave a prolonged belch, settled a pillow behind his head, and soon was sprawled beside me on the settee, snoring.

But Mr. Speed did come to our house, and it was in less than two months after this dreary twilight. And he came as I had feared he might come, in his most extreme state of drunkenness and at a time when I was alone in the house with the maid Lucy. But I had done everything that a little girl, now fourteen, could do in preparation for such an eventuality. And the sort of preparation that I had been able to make, the clearance of all restraints and inhibitions regarding Mr. Speed in my own mind and in my relationship with my world, had necessarily, I think, given me a maturer view of my own limited experiences; though, too, my very age must be held to account for a natural step toward maturity.

In the two months following the day that I first faced Mr. Speed's existence with my father, I came to look at every phase of our household life with a more direct and more discerning eye. As I wandered about that shadowy and somehow brutally elegant house, sometimes now with a knot of hair on the back of my head, events and customs there that had repelled or frightened me I gave the closest scrutiny. In the daytime I ventured into such forbidden spots as the servants' and the men's bathrooms. The filth of the former became a matter of interest in the study of the servants' natures, instead of the object of ineffable disgust. The other became a fascinating place of wet shaving brushes and leather straps and red rubber bags.

There was an anonymous little Negro boy that I had seen many mornings hurrying away from our back door with a pail. I discovered that he was toting buttermilk from our icebox with the permission of our cook. And I sprang at him from behind a corner of the house one morning and scared him so that he spilled the buttermilk and never returned for more.

Another morning I heard the cook threatening to slash the houseboy with her butcher knife, and I made myself burst in upon them; and before Lucy and the houseboy I told her that if she didn't leave our house that day, I'd call my father and, hardly knowing what I was saying, I added, "And the police." She was gone, and Lucy had got a new cook before dinner time. In this way, from day to day, I began to take my place as mistress in our motherless household.

I could no longer be frightened by my brother with a mention of runaway horses. And instead of terrorized I felt only depressed by his long and curious arguments with my father. I was depressed by the number of the subjects to and from which they oscillated. The world as a whole still seemed unconscionably larger than anything I could comprehend. But I had learned not to concern myself with so general and so unreal a problem until I had cleared up more particular and real ones.

It was during these two months that I noticed the difference between the manner in which my father spoke before my uncles of Mr. Speed when he passed and that in which he spoke of him before my brother. To my brother it was the condemning, "There goes Old Speed again." But to my uncles it was, "There goes Old Speed," with the sympathetic addi-

tion, "the rascal." Though my father and his brothers obviously found me more agreeable because a pleasant spirit
had replaced my old timidity, they yet considered me a child;
and my father little dreamed that I discerned such traits in
his character, or that I understood, if I even listened to, their
anecdotes and their long funny stories, and it was an interest
in the peculiar choice of subject and in the way that the men
told their stories.

When Mr. Speed came, I was accustomed to thinking that
there was something in my brother's and in my father's natures that was fully in sympathy with the very brutality of
his drunkenness. And I knew that they would not consider
my hatred for him and for that part of him which I saw in
them. For that alone I was glad that it was on a Thursday
afternoon, when I was in the house alone with Lucy, that one
of the heavy sort of rains that come toward the end of May
drove Mr. Speed onto our porch for shelter.

Otherwise I wished for nothing more than the sound of my
father's strong voice when I stood trembling before the parlor
window and watched Mr. Speed stumbling across our lawn
in the flaying rain. I only knew to keep at the window and
make sure that he was actually coming into our house. I believe that he was drunker than I had ever before seen him,
and his usual ire seemed to be doubled by the raging weather.

Despite the aid of his cane, Mr. Speed fell to his knees once
in the muddy sod. He remained kneeling there for a time with
his face cast in resignation. Then once more he struggled to
his feet in the rain. Though I was ever conscious that I was
entering into young-womanhood at that age, I can only think
of myself as a child at that moment; for it was the helpless
fear of a child that I felt as I watched Mr. Speed approaching
our door. Perhaps it was the last time I ever experienced the
inconsolable desperation of childhood.

Next I could hear his cane beating on the boarding of the
little porch before our door. I knew that he must be walking

up and down in that little shelter. Then I heard Lucy's exasperated voice as she came down the steps. I knew immediately, what she confirmed afterward, that she thought it Brother, eager to get into the house, beating on the door.

I, aghast, opened the parlor door just as she pulled open the great front door. Her black skin ashened as she beheld Mr. Speed—his face crimson, his eyes bleary, and his gray clothes dripping water. He shuffled through the doorway and threw his stick on the hall floor. Between his oaths and profanities he shouted over and over in his broken, old man's voice, "Nigger, nigger." I could understand little of his rapid and slurred speech, but I knew his rage went round and round a man in the rain and the shelter of a neighbor's house.

Lucy fled up the long flight of steps and was on her knees at the head of the stair, in the dark upstairs hall, begging me to come up to her. I only stared, as though paralyzed and dumb, at him and then up the steps at her. The front door was still open; the hall was half in light; and I could hear the rain on the roof of the porch and the wind blowing the trees, which were in full green foliage.

At last I moved. I acted. I slid along the wall past the hat rack and the console table, my eyes on the drunken old man who was swearing up the steps at Lucy. I reached for the telephone; and when I had rung for central, I called for the police station. I knew what they did with Mr. Speed downtown, and I knew with what I had threatened the cook. There was a part of me that was crouching on the top step with Lucy, vaguely longing to hide my face from this in my own mother's bosom. But there was another part which was making me deal with Mr. Speed, however wrongly, myself. Innocently I asked the voice to send "the Black Maria" to our house number on Church Street.

Mr. Speed had heard me make the call. He was still and silent for just one moment. Then he broke into tears, and he seemed to be chanting his words. He repeated the word "child" so many times that I felt I had acted wrongly, with courage but without wisdom. I saw myself as a little beast adding to the injury that what was bestial in man had already done him. He picked up his cane and didn't seem to be talking either to Lucy or to me, but to the cane. He started out the doorway, and I heard Lucy come running down the stairs. She fairly glided around the newel post and past me to the telephone. She wasn't certain that I had made the call. She asked if I had called my father. I simply told her that I had not.

As she rang the telephone, I watched Mr. Speed cross the porch. He turned to us at the edge of the porch and shouted one more oath. But his foot touched the wet porch step, and he slid and fell unconscious on the steps.

He lay there with the rain beating upon him and with Lucy and myself watching him, motionless from our place by the telephone. I was frightened by the thought of the cruelty which I found I was capable of, a cruelty which seemed inextricably mixed with what I had called courage. I looked at him lying out there in the rain and despised and pitied him at the same time, and I was afraid to go minister to the helpless old Mr. Speed.

Lucy had her arms about me and kept them there until two gray horses pulling their black coach had galloped up in front of the house and two policemen had carried the limp body through the rain to the dreadful vehicle.

Just as the policemen closed the doors in the back of the coach, my father rode up in a closed cab. He jumped out and stood in the rain for several minutes arguing with the policemen. Lucy and I went to the door and waited for him to come in. When he came, he looked at neither of us. He walked past us saying only, "I regret the bluecoats were called." And he went into the parlor and closed the door.

I never discussed the events of that day with my father, and I never saw Mr. Speed again. But, despite the surge of pity

I felt for the old man on our porch that afternoon, my hatred and fear of what he had stood for in my eyes have never left me. And since the day that I watched myself say "away" in the mirror, not a week has passed but that he has been brought to my mind by one thing or another. It was only the other night that I dreamed I was a little girl on Church Street again and that there was a drunk horse in our yard.

Allegiance

———

"Come in." And: "Of course I remember you and knew I should the moment your voice came drawling on the wire."

The first one, two, three, four steps I take across the room are taken with trepidation. And, so to speak, in mid-air. I am afraid that I shall yield, for even at her age the old creature is still a great beauty. And there is about her, after all, that charm which has long been discredited in my mind.

As she rings for tea, I perceive that in her simplest gestures, in her smile, even in her old-lady dress there is that fascination about her which we, who knew her as children, have remembered as her "romantic quality." I discover in an instant that we have been mistaken to suppose her romantic quality was either vulgar ostentation or mere shallow vanity. And now that she is before me I know that I do not remember her, for herself, at all.

"I remember you so well, dear child, in your blue and red rompers and of course those fearful black stockings your mother would have you wear." Now I am in the air again,

treading air. I can feel myself recoil at the bare reference to
a woman whom she once grievously wronged, draw back at
her mention of a sister she cheated in a manner so subtle and
base that we have never known nor wished to know its nature,
and never shall.

Here in her little drawing room, the marble mantel lined
with her famous figurines, the Japanese screen shielding her
diminutive writing desk, and a lamp-shade dull gold stamped
with fleurs-de-lis, I feel myself withdraw momentarily to the
bosom of a family that has been nursed on hatred of the
mistress of this room. The tea is being served, but I feel that
there is less reality to the moment and to the noise of the
teacups than to many an hour I have sat with the others at
coffee pondering a heritage of resentment against this elegant
Londoner.

"I remember you better than the others, I should say. You
were all of you quiet children, like your mother, but there
were occasions when you alone were like my garrulous self.
I used to have at my fingertips bright things you had said to
me—impudent things about something I wore or something
I said . . . But, alas, alas, I've reached an age at which the
incidents of my own childhood and events of my young lady-
hood are a wee bit clearer than those of the dull years since."
(I smile to hear her say "dull years," but she thinks I smile
because I do not know her age.) "I suspect I'm a bit older
than you guess. Your mother and I were sisters, you might say,
in fact only. I was a young lady in Nashville the year she was
born. I was always more aunt than sister to her. I am more
of the generation of your Cousin Ellen Ballenger, who was a
sort of double first cousin of ours. To be exact, Ellen was
first cousin to Mama and first cousin once removed to your
grandfather."

· She is pouring the tea now, and this is absent-minded talk.
I listen but I am thinking all the while of how strange it is
to hear old familiar relationships rehearsed so easily in her

rather too broad English speech. She seems to have lapsed for a moment into the character of an uninteresting old Britisher recalling certain family ties of her people down in Devon or Dorset. But now she looks up to hand me my tea, saying, "Or do we still say 'first cousin once removed' in Tennessee?"

Her face colors a little as our eyes meet. Then she laughs and nervously she jingles the gold bracelets on her wrist. I observe that life has aged her more than I had at once perceived. For she has just now become utterly engrossed in the pleasurable reiteration of those old family ties.

But her laughter, which for one second has seemed as remote a sound as was the look in her eyes abstracted, is now present in the room again. Her eyes shine again with a light that is expressive and responsive. "How wicked of me to treat you so, to bore you with tedious things you know by heart. The longer you sit there the better I do remember you. It's a rather shocking transformation, you'll grant, from red rompers with a scalloped collar to the olive drab. It was not until I was addressing my note to you that I pictured you in uniform. Even with the war all about us here I had not connected events at all. I knew merely that you were in this country. (Dear old Mr. Gordon enclosed the address with my last American check.) And so, you see, it was not wartime sentiment that moved me to ask you here. Further, hadn't I put myself out on a limb, rather? I was not certain that you would bother to come." (Yet she had presumed to think I might. She has thought that one of us might have a change of heart after many years.) "I was not certain that you would bother to come, for very often young men haven't much interest in their kin. Perhaps you have given up something you would like to do this afternoon only to come here. . . . But there I go playing the old lady again."

And now I have the sense of being ignored, or of having my rudeness ignored. I feel an express shame, not of my rudeness, but of all the uncertainties of my mind as I sit in the presence of one so self-possessed. The direct and attentive gaze of her eyes is modest, even shy in a sense, yet she seems as conscious of the engaging qualities of her personality as of the pleasant effect of this little drawing room she has arranged with the light now falling from the west windows across the patterns of the carpet. While she talks I study the burgundy roosters in the patterns and once again the figurines of Louis Napoleon and Nell Gwynn and John Brown with their little china backs reflected in the mirror over the mantel. She is perceiving that I am "quiet" like my mother, and she is set now to support the conversation alone. I hear her. I raise my eyebrows. I nod agreement. I frown. Or I smile so genuinely that she is silent a moment to enjoy the satisfaction of her jest. I even remark on the irony of something, but my sentence is complete in itself and she has no illusion that I'm going to be a real talker after all. She doesn't try to draw me out. But while she speaks and while I listen I am also thinking that at some point I have betrayed, or at some point shall betray, someone or something.

I am remembering little notes that my mother used to read aloud, notes placed unanswered on the fire in the parlor at Nashville. Now I can visualize their being penned at this little desk shielded by the Japanese screen. I can picture her counting such notes among correspondence that she must take-care-of on a day when the weather isn't fine. Mere polite inquiries they were into the health of us all with a few chatty words at the end about how early a spring London was enjoying that year or some amusing and endearing household incident—something about her ancient, now dead, but once ever-ailing English husband or about her adored step-children. They were notes written in an even hand and there was never any rancor or remorse in them. And there was no reference, ever, to my mother's failure to reply. Their tone presumed it to be simply a matter of temperament. She was a person who *did* write letters, my mother a *quiet* person who didn't. But my mother used to say, "It's beautiful, beautiful. Her selfish ends are long since accomplished. Now she develops a sort of mystical, superhuman ignorance of what has been transpiring."

My aunt's figure is thin and erect, though her clothing is draped to conceal her thinness. Presently in the midst of her portrayal of three English types that are to be avoided (if one is to admire Englishmen) I realize that she is not ignoring me or my rudeness or even my innocent silence. These are things that she is coping with. It is only that I am suffering still from the shock of the greater ignorance she pretends to. I am no longer asking how did she dare to presume that I should not return her invitation unopened (as all the other notes since my mother's lifetime have been returned). I am no longer asking how or why; for her manner, her personal appearance, even her little drawing-room all bespeak her confidence in and her concern only for what is actual. What is more, they express as well her faith in the actual's being but the sum of a thousand accidents.

And that our meeting is a circumstance that she has ardently desired and wished to bring about there can be no doubt. I am certain, further, that she has known it could come about in just such a form as would allow all the privilege she is now exercising—namely, the privilege of assuming all such ignorance as should seem fitting—only by accident or by a series of accidents. In some corner of her mind there has ever been an awareness that these accidents might currently be casting themselves one upon the other. And so it must have appeared to her through the years that any little message which she could so easily scratch off might be the last, the efficient accident that the rest of the world would put down as the cause of our meeting.

"If these were normal times, nothing would please me more than to offer myself as your guide to England and the English. But how futile to speak of it even. You are in London on some terribly official business, no doubt, or on a leave so short that it will be over before you've got round to half the things you want to do. Likely you do not even want to understand this country. You want only to accomplish your mission and get yourself home again. I have been thinking as we sat here that you might be wondering how a person could bring herself to so completely quit her country as I seem to have done. Ah, I know . . . I know how you silent people are. You have more thoughts than the rest of us dare to suppose. I should hate to have to answer all the questions in the minds of people who have sat quietly while I talked on. And if I tried I could answer this one least well of all. My answer is, I do not know. But you must have observed that everyone has some aunt or other who has simply pulled out . . . pulled out on the family with not so much as a by-your-leave. I'm just another of those aunts that people have. The world's full of them."

I think: The degree of her long anxiety for the special accidental qualities which would make up the naturalness of our meeting is patent in the pleasure she takes from its realization.

"What of my own aunts! But you never knew—perhaps never heard of—the aunts I think of, did you? Yet I remember them so much better than so many people since their time. It is incredible how long people can be dead while their voices and even the moles on their necks are remembered by someone."

I think: The degree of her long anxiety for this meeting without *conditions,* for this easy manner of meeting and her clear vision of the necessity of this ease, now seems to me to have been hidden through all the years in the sensible, persistent irregularity of her notes to my mother and later to the individual children. I feel now how right were my mother's claims that this woman could endure anything to gain her ends. For it is as though in her anxiety she has known, too, how unpredictable were her chances.

But are her ends merely this in-person, this final, bold pretense at ignorance of her old wrong against my mother? If this is the depth of the interview's meaning for her, then I am tired of it already. If this is all, then I have satisfied my curiosity about her appearance and her apartments and I am ready to ask for my hat. Yet I do not even steal a glance in the direction of the small chair where my coat and cap are placed. And I ask myself, is it at this point that I betray?

Or was it when I opened her invitation (opened one of the notes our silent pact had forbidden us to do) that I betrayed? Or will it be later when I have listened? She has settled herself now in her chair. She has accepted a cigarette from my case. She is talking of those great-aunts of mine who long ago went off to Washington and St. Louis to live with their husbands, women whom even my mother could hardly have remembered. Her speech is casual, and she appears at first to be rambling through a mixture of recent events and old memories.

Yet, withal she now seems quite consciously allowing herself to become thus engrossed in things that she formerly asked my pardon for. She talks of London, and with a twinkle in her eye she speaks of the tediousness of being cut off from the Continent. Whatever are her ends I know that they are somewhere beyond a desire to play her role convincingly to the last. She seems hardly concerned with her role at all. I gasp a gasp that must be audible, because I recognize that she is still depending upon accidents, terrible accidents that are now possible within myself, in my own perceptions. She has the air of having given way to her woolgathering. *After all*, she is thinking, *the part that I can play in making him see is too small for consideration on any level.* As I read her conscious thoughts I am asking myself whether she, not subconsciously but in a consciousness too profound for such a stranger as I to read, can be attributing some magic potency to the mere actuality of this moment, to the actuality of any given moment, even to her faith in the solidness of the precious objects of her drawing room, to the sound of her own voice. If so, then, for her, each moment and indeed everything in the life and body of the world must have in itself a latent magic which might be exploited. I feel that I am in the presence of some newfangled sort of idolater and conjurer. As she speaks, I become increasingly aware that she believes it is no matter now what incident or what old wives' tale she may relate, that she considers that whatever words she uses or however her conversation may turn there is but one thing she *can* say and there is no predicting what turn of her mind or her speech might be the singular accident that would mean my comprehension.

But I hear only isolated sentences and snatches of sentences.

There are moments when I feel that I have dozed.

Yet I am in no sense drowsy.

Much less do I feel any boredom.

On the contrary it is a sort of literal enchantment I am caught in where all the past and all the future and all occurrences of the exterior world are of no consequence. Even the thing she has said a moment ago or the conclusion she will presently bring out are utterly lacking in any interest for me though her actual words in that split moment when they proceed from her lips consume my whole attention. Sometimes she is speaking of people who figure, or who have figured, in her life. "Mr. Williams always remembered Merle mercifully, I think." I wonder if I have smiled now when I should have frowned. She tells me that some other person she knows has always the air, with strangers, of himself being an angel-entertained-unawares. This gentleman will smile afterward, she says, and remark that the stranger was kind to him for-no-reason-at-all. It is, my aunt thinks, as if to say that he feels there is a perfectly good reason why the stranger should be kind to him if the stranger only knew *who* he is.

This man is probably someone here in London. But presently it seems to be of my own grandmother who has lain for forty years in a remote and neglected graveyard in Tennessee of whom she is speaking. "She was an extremely narrow and provincial woman, but this much must be said in her favor: If she never showed any originality in her housekeeping she was as well never guilty of any superficiality. Things were always easy. She knew what she was about. There was never any silly bustling when guests came, no matter how fine."

Finally her voice stops, and I wish that it had not stopped. It is as though some piece of furniture in the room had suddenly collapsed, even the chair I sit in. I come to my feet without knowing why I have risen. And immediately she rises with the same suddenness. "Perhaps, you would. . . ." She hesitates. But she has regained her composure almost before I recognize her loss of it. She turns with all ease, making a gesture toward the marble mantel, and this time I do steal a glance at my things on the fragile chair.

But the cap and the dull-colored coat have lose that quality which meant the probability of my departure. They mean no more than that I am actually here. Yet I realize that it is because I have entertained no thought of leaving just now that I dared turn my eyes to them! And I only wanted to see if there would be any temptation, or rather to see if I had lost all will to go. And so I am conscious again of betrayal and still do not know whether it is a possibility or a fact. My betrayal is like some boundless fear that has really had no beginning in me and can have no end. This room and this old woman and this woman's voice constitute the only certainty. I feel strangely that I must remain until I can identify my guilt or possible guilt with some moment of the visit if not with some object in the room or some trick of her behavior. And so now I say to myself that she has been right, that all experience can be translated into the terms of any one moment of life if one believes sufficiently in the reality of that moment. "Young man, would you be good enough to admire my figurines." Her smile is full of irony. "They are said to be world famous and of inestimable value."

I have hurried to join her before the mantel. I allow her to see that she has remembered correctly my having flashes of garrulousness like her own. I chatter about John Brown and remark endlessly upon the cunningness of the little nigger who stands at his side with John Brown's pink china hand on his coal-black head. I reveal my pedantry asking if it was not for Nell Gwynn that all flowers were pulled from some London park. I laugh at the face of Louis Napoleon.

I find suddenly that we are laughing together at the ridiculous sort of dignity which the artist has faithfully, if unknowingly, represented in the delicate figurine of the bourgeois emperor. Our eyes meet in the glass for an instant. Presently I see the whole room reflected there. I see the two of us looking over the heads of the world famous figurines. I catch the sound of our commingled laughter.

Then we are facing each other again and she is saying, "What if I should ask you to leave now, should ask you to go now and come again to finish our visit some other afternoon, would you think me too insufferably odd and rude? Would you?"

And before I have thought or considered what I am saying: "But I cannot come here again."

At first her countenance seems frozen in an austerity that is totally disarming to me after so much geniality. Her glance is set for a moment on some object in a far corner of the room. It might almost be my own cap and coat, yet I know it is not with an object that she is concerned. Rather, it is the thing I have just said. She is giving its meaning her most serious consideration.

While she does so, I realize the peculiar turn our intercourse has taken. In my voice there has been almost a plea to allow me to remain since I could not come here again. But it was to say: *I have come here and glimpsed the unique sort of power and truth you have discovered or created, but now I wish to remain to disprove its worth.* Perhaps that is how she is interpreting it. Or perhaps she thinks I have been un-affected by the interview and want only to cause her all pos-sible discomfort before I leave.

Yet of course she at last sees the thing as it is. She sees that I spoke before I thought, and laughing she shrouds herself again in her grand ignorance. "Of course you can come back, dear child, if you will. Let's say good-bye and plan on another afternoon."

Having once spoken plainly it is easy to speak plainly again. "Then I must ask you a question. I want to know why you suddenly desire me to go."

As each moment passes my departure seems to become more difficult for me. I turn with the same abruptness with which I have spoken and go to one of the long windows that overlook the quiet street and park.

There is no sound in the room, and I know that she is still standing there before the mantel. Finally her voice comes groping, yet with confidence in its effect, "Then you do think me rude."

"I don't understand, of course." But I imply that I should listen to explanation. I turn and face her. Our smiles are like smiles in photographs. "You asked your nephew to tea, my dear aunt. I suppose I am only surprised at what a very short tea-time you have. I thought you English lingered over tea things."

"See here," she says coming toward me, "there is no great mystery. To be very frank, I have an engagement I had for-gotten. I mixed my days. But it is one I intend keeping."

"Certainly it must be important."

"Yes, it's important as an old lady's social engagements go. But if I should describe it you would laugh."

"I should laugh. Yet it is important?"

She drops her eyes. And with her eyelids still closed—broad wrinkled, powdered lids—she says, "I promised someone I'd keep it, you see."

"Oh, it's your word and not the engagement that matters."

"You could understand that?" she asks with her eyes still closed, and I can imagine an echo to her last word "that."

I make my answer with a nod, as though not knowing that her closed eyes mean she cannot see me. But actually I do know that she has not yet my answer; and simultaneously I am filled with disgust for her and with a desire to tip-toe from her presence before she looks up again, for surely this is *it*. Once again I think I am free of the smell of this room. I can almost visualize a pure and self-righteous darkness in which I suspect she is holding herself behind those wrinkled lids. I feel that she has created a terrible war and brought me halfway round the world to prove that she, an old lady in a London apartment, can keep her word in some matter of etiquette. But the harm is not in its being only a small matter of decorum. The harm suddenly appears to be strangely in the altruism, the mere keeping of her word. It is as if her life which she has twisted and formed so wilfully has been but a vast circle by which route she has returned to the simple sort of truths that my mother possessed in the beginning. I shall leave now, believing what I wished to believe and what this room and this woman have for a time caused me to doubt: that my mother was good because she was simple and un-worldly, that my aunt is evil because she is complicated and worldly.

Then in an instant all of my victory is swept from me by the mere opening of her large, handsome, articulate blue eyes. Her last question is now translated and spoken by her eyes. But there is also the further question, "Could you understand more?" And whatever my dull eyes may reply, her lips part and she speaks with new indirectness.

"No. It is not my word. It is something much smaller." A

new earnestness has come over her countenance. It is she that has withdrawn from me now. The final accident did not occur. She is no longer hoping that I may see. I know that by "smaller" she means "larger," but beyond that I cannot conceive of what is in her mind. She gives me her hand. As we say good-bye I hear the jingling of her bracelets and observe the barely perceptible twitch at the corner of her mouth.

Now I am outside her door and on the stairs with my military coat over my arm. I wonder, with an insipid smile on my lips, at my own brutality. Have I been a soldier frightening an old lady at tea-time? But as I descend the stairs, her face is before me as it was by the window when she raised the wide, wrinkled lids and exposed the brilliant blue of her eyes. I hear again the jingling of her bracelets. And it is then, suddenly recalling now the hard circles of gold resting on the ancient skin drawn over the ungainly wrist bone, that I am filled with awe and with a sort of fear as of some fate I might have met at her hands. I feel that I have been in the presence of a withered savage tribeswoman, at the mercy of her absolute authority. But when finally I have passed through the vestibule and out onto the sidewalk and have inhaled gratefully the free air of the clean-swept city street there is no sense of freedom. As I wander in the half-light of evening through the wide thoroughfares and the broad squares of this foreign place it all seems suddenly as familiar as my mother's parlor; and though my mind is troubled by a doubt of the reality of all things and I am haunted for a while by an unthinkable distrust for the logic and the rarefied judgments of my dead mother, I feel myself still a prisoner in her parlor at Nashville with the great sliding doors closed and the jagged little flames darting from the grate.

The Death of a Kinsman

Cast of Characters
Robert Wade
Margie, his wife
Aunt Lida Wade
Miss Bluemeyer, their housekeeper
Myra Willis, family servant
Lennie, upstairs maid, Myra's niece
Paris, houseboy, Myra's nephew
The Wade children
   James
   Nancy
   Alfred
   Charles William
   Lida Sue

SCENE I

It is long before daybreak, but in the Wade house lights have been put on in the halls and in the pantry and in the upstairs sitting room and in nearly every room in the whole house and on the side porch as well. Nobody has been left sleeping. The curtain rises on the scene in the upstairs hall. It is a rectangular room running the entire width of the stage. A large stair well is in the center and back of the stage. On the wall beyond the balustrade which guards the descending stairs is an enormous mirror. Doors to the bedrooms are at either end of the hall. A door at the extreme right in the back wall opens into the service hall where there is presumably another stairway. The door at the head of the stairs (left, back) leads to the bedroom of Mr. and Mrs. Wade. The general effect is that all of the wall space, except that beyond the stair well, is taken up by the doorways. The elaborate door facings and the oak balustrade and the pilasters at the four corners of the stair well indicate that the house is one of those mansions put up in Midwestern cities during the early part of the present century. The floor is not carpeted, but it is partly covered by two large rugs. The one on the left is a handsome, though rather worn and faded, Oriental rug. On the right is an obviously new imitation of the same thing, with extremely bright colors and a general effect of silkiness. The end of the hall to the left (and front) is furnished as an upstairs sitting room. There are several upholstered chairs, a footstool, a small table and lamp. The only other furnishings are a table and chair at the right (front) corner of the balustrade. The table is an old-fashioned card table, the typical Southern antique, and the chair a ladder-back imitation antique with a cushion on the seat. On the table are an electric clock, a modern French-style telephone, and an ultra-modern desk lamp which, except for the dimly lit table lamp, is the only light burning as the curtain rises.

Simultaneously two Negro maids enter from doors at opposite ends of the hall. One is a tall, thin, stooped woman with a good deal of gray in her hair. The other is a somewhat more than plump young woman. Both are black. They advance hurriedly toward the middle of the room until simultaneously children's voices call from the rooms they have just quitted. "Myra, where are my good socks? What did you do with . . ." "Lennie, where's the brush I put . . ." The two women halt, exchange first exasperated grimaces and then indulgent smiles, and return to the children. Aunt Lida Wade appears from one of the doors at the left. Her thin white hair is in rollers and she is attired in a cinnamon-colored kimono. As she enters she is addressing her great-niece Nancy over her shoulder: "No, I don't know which dress you mean, Nancy, but it must be one of those in the back hall closet." Nancy's eleven-year-old whine can be heard from within: "You know the one, Aunt Lida; the one with the long sash." Aunt Lida answers in an impatient but conciliating voice: "I'll see. I'll see." She closes the door behind her and moves across the stage taking the small, practiced ladylike steps of a long-legged woman who would naturally move with great strides. She goes into the service hall, closing the door behind her. Now quick footsteps are heard on the dark stairway, and presently a Negro houseboy, wearing an unbuttoned white jacket, dashes up into the hall. He places a pair of highly polished brown shoes by the door at the head of the stairs and turns at once to descend the stairs. Seeing the dark stair well before him, he inadvertently reaches out and flicks the light switch on the wall beside him. The light does not come on, and grinning at himself he says, "Ah, shoot!" Meanwhile, the older Negro woman has entered from a door at the right; she addresses him contemptuously: "Ain't fix 'at even yit, have you, Paris?" His grin broadens into a big, silly smile, showing a mouth full of gleaming white teeth: "I cain't fix it, Aunt Myra." He puts his hand on the rail and disappears down the stairway. Now Aunt Lida enters from the service hall with three of Nancy's dresses over her arm. She passes Myra, who is moving slowly toward the head of the stairs.

AUNT LIDA: What an hour of the day to be gotten up, eh, Myra?

MYRA: Ain't it the truth, Miss Lida? An' him not on this place more'n three times in ten year.

AUNT LIDA: But he was the only relative any of us have in Detroit, Myra.

MYRA: Not much kin. An' getting all them chillun up.

AUNT LIDA: I don't see why the children should be gotten up, but you know Mr. Robert.

MYRA: I know white folks.

AUNT LIDA: Listen here, don't you talk about white folks to me, Myra Willis. If it were *your* Cousin Harry, you'd be off work for a week. *(She has now opened the door to Nancy's room.)*

MYRA *(at the head of the stairs, looking down into the darkness; still addressing Aunt Lida)*: Nobody ain't fix 'at light yit.

AUNT LIDA: Mr. Robert said he would do it today.

MYRA: He say.

AUNT LIDA: I know, I know. *(Closing the door behind her.)*
Mr. Wade opens the door of his room to fetch his shoes. Myra looks over her shoulder at him.

MR. WADE: Morning, Myra.

MYRA: It's still night to me. An' this here light ain't fix yit.

MR. WADE: By George, it's not. You tell Paris to bring the ladder up, and we'll fix it right now.

MYRA: Now? This now? At five o'clock in the mornin'? *(He picks up his shoes and closes the door.)*

MYRA: Lord God.

Miss Bluemeyer, the housekeeper, enters from the service hall. She is a large woman dressed in navy blue with tiny white ruffles at the collar. Her hair, cut like a man's, has obviously not been combed this morning, and she is still wearing her flat-heeled bedroom slippers. She is carrying a small tray with one cup of coffee and a silver sugar and cream set.

MISS BLUEMEYER: Are you in a great rush, Myra?

MYRA: Not me.

MISS BLUEMEYER: Then I would like to see you a minute, please. About something.

MYRA: Yassum.

Meanwhile, the housekeeper strides across the hall and knocks at the door at the head of the stairs.

MRS. WADE *(from within):* Just a minute! Who is it?

MISS BLUEMEYER: It is I.... Miss Bluemeyer.

Mrs. Wade opens the door. She is an extremely small woman of about forty. Her long brown hair falls about the shoulders of her negligee. She is pregnant.

MRS. WADE: Oh, I'm *so* much obliged to you, Miss Blue-meyer. You know that I'm not a bit of good till I've had my coffee. I'll just bet you had to make it yourself.

MISS BLUEMEYER: I did, Misses Wade. But that's all right; I made a cup for myself too.

MRS. WADE: Isn't it a hideous hour? *(Beginning to close the door.)*

MISS BLUEMEYER: Yes, it is, but I am awfully sorry about your cousin.

MRS. WADE: Yes, it is sad of course. He was very old, you know, and we knew him very little, really.

MISS BLUEMEYER: I see.

Mrs. Wade closes the door, and Miss Bluemeyer turns to Myra. With a movement of her head she indicates that Myra should follow her. Then she crosses the stage and seats herself at the telephone table. Myra follows and stands before Miss Bluemeyer, with her hands folded and resting against her white apron.

MISS BLUEMEYER *(smiling intimately and a little sadly):* Myra, tell me, did you ever know their Cousin Harry?—Mr. Wilson, that is.

MYRA: Yassum, oh, yassum. *(Casually.)* My sister Cora used to work for his own sister, Miss Jamie, in Nashville, way back yonder. Most of them Wilsons is dead though. He muss be the lass of 'em, I reckon.

MISS BLUEMEYER: That is not what I mean, Myra. I know that all of you knew one another back in Tennessee, but that is ten years or more—

MYRA: Yassum, we been in Deetroit ten year. Now, the two oldest chillun was born'd in Tennessee, but—

MISS BLUEMEYER: That is not what I mean, Myra. I mean —that is, I have been keeping house for Misses Wade nearly a year now and had never heard Cousin Harry's name—Mr. Wilson, that is to say—mentioned until his stroke a few weeks ago.

MYRA: No'm. He never come aroun' here much. He warn't congenial with 'em; that's all.

MISS BLUEMEYER: I . . . I did not mean to imply that there was more to it, Myra. I only mean that they are such wonderful people to feel so responsible for a person they hardly know.

MYRA (quickly): Yes'm, but he war kin to 'em.

MISS BLUEMEYER: Yet he never came to see them.

MYRA: It warn't because he warn't invited. (Resentfully.) He didn't care nothin' bout kinfolks. Stuck off to hisself and worked down in the depot up here. He was jess— (Breaks off suddenly, and begins again with an entirely different tone.) Well, anyhow, he 'uz kin to 'em, and the only one here kin to 'em. That's all.

MISS BLUEMEYER: I did not mean to be prying, you understand, Myra. It is only that it seems odd that they should make such to-do over a man they knew so slight.

MYRA: He didn't have no money, sho God.

MISS BLUEMEYER: That, Myra, is not what I meant.

MYRA: I don't know what you been meanin', Miss Bloomer, but he's daid an he war kin to 'em.

From the left the voice of Charles William, aged five and a half, is heard calling, "Myra! Myra!" A door is thrown open and a towheaded little boy rushes into the hall with his shoe-strings flopping about.

CHARLES WILLIAM: Myra, Alfred won't tie my bows!

MYRA (*who has turned around and advanced several steps in his direction*): I'll buss his back wide op'n.

CHARLES WILLIAM: You tie 'em, Myra.

MYRA (*already on her knees before him*): Come here, chile.

CHARLES WILLIAM: Is Cousin-Harry-Wilson dead, Myra.

MYRA: Sho.

CHARLES WILLIAM: Was he eighty-three years old?

MYRA: 'Course he was, C.W.

CHARLES WILLIAM: Still?

MYRA: He'll be eighty-three from here out, C.W.

CHARLES WILLIAM (*obviously comforted, he places his hand on the head bent over before him*): I love you, Myra.

Myra lifts her dark oval face and grins broadly at him. He whispers to her, "You haven't got your teeth in, Myra." She bends with laughter as Charles William runs back to his room. During the conversation Miss Bluemeyer examines her wristwatch and the electric clock very closely. She dials a number on the telephone and says after a moment, "Will you repeat that? Will you repeat that?" She dials the number again and then sets her watch and moves the hand of the clock a fraction of an inch. When Charles William is gone, she says:

MISS BLUEMEYER: Myra—

MYRA (*rising and moving toward the dark stairs*): I got go fetch Paris an the ladder for Mista Robert. This here light!

MISS BLUEMEYER: You *could* use the back stair, Myra.

MYRA: Not me. Not them straight-up-and-down steps. (*She goes down the steps.*)

Miss Bluemeyer rises and strides toward one of the doors at right. Aunt Lida Wade opens the door from Nancy's room, left, and the two women face each other in silence a moment. "Oh," says Aunt Lida, "I thought you were my nephew, Mr. Wade." Miss Bluemeyer makes her exit, and Aunt Lida remains a moment to giggle girlishly. Then she withdraws into Nancy's room again and closes the door. Lennie enters from door at right and moves sluggishly across the hall to head of stairs. Aunt Lida opens her door again and says, "Oh, I thought you were my nephew Mr. Robert." Lennie answers, "No'm, it's jess me." Aunt Lida closes her door again, but before Lennie has begun to descend the stairs Mr. Robert Wade, master of the house, opens the door to his room and steps into the hall. Mr. Wade is six feet, three inches in height. His hair and his small mustache are dark. The belt to his silk dressing robe is tied, but the robe is not brought together in front; and so his dark trousers and white shirt and his bow tie may be seen. He wears usually a pouty expression on his face and has little to say except when giving directions or explaining some matter to his family.

MR. WADE: Lennie, a full half hour ago I sent word for Paris to bring me the ladder.

Lennie makes no answer but fairly dives down the dark stair well. Her feet on the steps make a frightful racket. Aunt Lida opens her door again.

AUNT LIDA: Well, now, did you ever? No wonder the women in the house have been insulted when I mistook their steps for yours. How do you do it?

MR. WADE: That was Myra's little niece descending the stair. *(He walks around to the front balustrade and leans out over the stairs to peer up at the fixture.)*

AUNT LIDA: Ah! the dungeon stair. This is the moment I've been waiting for. Rumor has got around that my nephew has roused his family at five A.M. to watch him change light bulbs over the stairway.

MR. WADE: True . . . true. *(Still looking up at the fixture.)* And, incidentally, my wife's cousin is dead.

AUNT LIDA *(matter-of-factly)*: Poor Harry. You ought, in all conscience, to have made him come live with us years ago, Robert.

MR. WADE: He wouldn't live with his own sister, much less us. He had an allergy to the very idea of blood relations. *(Turning to Aunt Lida.)* You know, one of the few times I saw him he asked me how I could stand living under the same roof with you.

AUNT LIDA: I'm sure he did. And he told me that he left Tennessee to get away from his own flesh and blood, and that you and Margie and your younguns had to pursue him up here. *(They laugh merrily.)*

While they talk, the top of a ladder rises from the stair well.

AUNT LIDA: But we ought to have gotten him to come here and live, somehow.

MR. WADE: He'd have been miserable here, Aunt Lida. And he'd have made us more than miserable. He wouldn't have fitted in.

AUNT LIDA: Pooh! That's why it would have been all right. *(She whispers.)* When I selected Miss Bluemeyer for Margie's housekeeper I was careful to choose someone who wouldn't fit in. If she were congenial with us, her presence here would be an intrusion. That's why my presence is an intrusion, don't you see?

MR. WADE: Tut-tut, Auntie. *(Pronounced "ontee.")*

The head and shoulders of Paris have now appeared from the top landing where he is setting up the ladder. The ladder leans backward and forward, backward and forward, and Paris can be heard panting and grunting.

AUNT LIDA: Oh, but what I say about Miss Bluemeyer is really pretty true, Robert. She's always happy when we're sad, and sad when we're happy; and that's right convenient. This morning, for instance— Well, notice for yourself.

MR. WADE: Aunt Lida, you're just awful! The poor woman.

AUNT LIDA: Why, I'm crazy about her. She's perfect. And have you seen her this morning? She's mourning your Cousin Harry, as none of us would think of doing— Poor old codger's got his blessed relief at last—and, Robert *(rolling her eyes thoughtfully)*, she never even saw him once, did she? Once even? No! . . . But if she were showing the kind of relief that we feel for him, it *would* be kind of bad, now. You see!

MR. WADE: Oh, what difference does it make that she's—
(Breaking off.) What *in* the devil?

He whirls about. Paris, having steadied the ladder and hav-
ing climbed uneasily to the top of it, has been sitting there
tapping first his lip and then his forehead with his finger, try-
ing hard to think of something, then with a stupid but still
speculative expression on his face he has reached down and
brought up a long broom with the handle of which he has
now bent forward and poked (between the balusters) the back
of Mr. Wade's knee. Mr. Wade's knee bends slightly. He
whirls about, saying, "What in the devil." Paris jerks back the
broom, gives a short, hysterical laugh, and sputters out:

PARIS: Mista Robert!

MR. WADE: What in the name of sin do you mean by that,
boy!

PARIS *(solemnly)*: Somehow, I couldn't call yo name, Mista
Robert, why you reckon? Couldn't think of it till you whull
aroun an say, "Whut *in* de debil?" *(Catching Mr. Wade's*
exact intonation.)

MR. WADE *(leaving Aunt Lida, who stands in open-*
mouthed wonder and amazement at Paris's behavior, and
going round the balustrade to the head of the stair): Come
down off the ladder! Did you bring the screw driver and the
bulb?

PARIS: I brung the screw driber, Mista Robert.

MR. WADE: Well, go brung me a big bulb and a dust rag
from the pantry.

Paris disappears from the ladder and down the stairs. Mr.
Wade has now come down the stairs to the landing and
climbed to the top of the ladder. The ladder shakes violently,
and Aunt Lida cries out in a voice unlike her rather deep
speaking voice:

AUNT LIDA: Robert, mind; do be careful, honey!

MR. WADE: Careful, hell! *(He clambers down the ladder.)*
Paris! Paris, you come hold this ladder for me!

At the sound of Aunt Lida's voice doors from both right

and left and from the back are opened. Now the children come one by one to the head of the stairs and watch their father who is climbing the ladder again. The two older children come first and watch their father in silence; they are Nancy, from left, and James, from right—aged eleven and twelve respectively. Quick on James's heels come Charles William who is five and a half, and behind him Alfred, aged nine, still wearing the stocking cap he sleeps in. Then the fifth child, Lida Sue, the youngest of all, comes chattering. No one can understand what she says, for she has been slow learning to talk and now at four she stammers and lisps alternately. When the doors to the children's room opened, the door to their parents' room, at the head of the stairs, opened also; and Mrs. Wade, having glanced at her husband and smiled at Aunt Lida, has turned back into her room, leaving the door open. Her hair is now pinned up, and she wears a maternity dress. She can be seen moving about the room, making up the bed, etc. During the conversation that follows, Lida Sue, instead of watching her father, as she has sat down to do, allows her attention to be distracted by the glimpse she has had of her mother, and lying back on the floor and rolling on her left side she watches her mother's movements in the room. Aunt Lida, still wearing her cinnamon-colored kimono, has moved away from the balustrade on which the children are now leaning. She stands, arms akimbo, in the center of the hall with the back of her head of sparse, uncombed, gray hair to the audience.

AUNT LIDA *(to Mrs. Wade in a loud voice):* Margie, he's taking the whole business apart, screw by screw.

MRS. WADE *(from the bedroom):* It's the only way to do it, Aunt Lida.

AUNT LIDA: He has poor Paris holding the ladder, who ought to be down setting the table.

MRS. WADE: There's plenty of time. *(Still from the bedroom.)*

AUNT LIDA: I should say plenty of time. The greatest

plenty. There was no earthly reason in his getting the whole house up at this hour.

MRS. WADE: No sense, I admit. *(Only slight interest.)*

AUNT LIDA: And did you ever in your life hear of a man's choosing such a time for such a job?

MRS. WADE: Never in my life. *(Complete indifference.)*

AUNT LIDA: I've been after him for weeks to do it, myself, and I know you have. There's really no earthly reason why Paris shouldn't learn to take down a chandelier. Otherwise, let's take him back to Tennessee and bring Mamie's brother up here. Or let Paris learn to drive, and bring Sellars in the house. Sellars's too old to drive, anyway. *(She pauses. All of this is being delivered in a shaky but resonant voice that Mrs. Wade and possibly even the servants in the kitchen can hear.)* Sellars can do anything if you show him once. But the main thing, though, is the time for such a job, the unheard of hour of the morn . . .

MR. WADE *(interrupting with a booming voice, his early morning hoarseness adding to the onomatopoeic effect)*: Thunderation, Aunt Lida!

Aunt Lida seems only to have been waiting for this; immediately she dismisses from her mind the problem of the light fixture and all of this business in the hall. She raises her little right forefinger to her chin and frowns meditatively, trying to recollect for what she has originally come into the hall. Then of a sudden she turns and goes out the door leading to the service hall.

MR. WADE: Now, you see, children, this is not a very simple undertaking. Each of the glass sections must be removed separately, and for each there are three screws. Observe: one at the top and one on each side. Now, this protector must be broken down into its five component parts, and to do this you must understand the real structure of the fixture. Mind, now. *All* of the five pieces must be removed before the bulb—because of its large size—can be inserted. Once the bulb is in, each piece must be dusted and cleared of all dead bugs, lint, dust, trash, et cetera before being replaced.

Mr. Wade works in silence for several moments. Then suddenly the light shines brightly above the stair well. Mr. Wade, atop the ladder in a white shirt and a polka-dot bow tie with a sprinkling of dust on his black mustache, is a bright figure of enchantment for the five children who all fix a charmed gaze upon him, like five little green-eyed kittens. The spell is so absolute that they are momentarily blind and deaf to the sudden hilarious commotion on the part of Paris. This lantern-jawed houseboy, whose complexion is a dull copper color, who is supposed to be giving support to the unsteady ladder, has become so convulsed by laughter that he has thrown his whole weight against the ladder. One stern word of rebuke from Mr. Wade, however, makes Paris jump back from the quivering ladder.

Mr. WADE: Get away from this ladder, you idiot!

Paris runs up the steps until he is in plain view of the audience. He continues to cavort about, twisting and bending his body, completely unable to restrain himself, giggling and pointing to the mirror on the wall beyond the stairs. All the while he is sputtering, "Look-a-there! Look-a-there!" and pointing to the mirror. Mr. Wade sits uneasily atop the ladder, staring at Paris in exasperation. As Paris runs up the steps, the children by the balustrade all turn their faces toward him but move not a muscle in their bodies.

PARIS: Do y' see what I see, Mista Robert? Look-a-there, Mista Robert.

Slowly the five children move their eyes from the houseboy to the mirror opposite them. Then Mr. Wade, steadying himself on the ladder, looks in the mirror too. What he sees there are the eight brown-stockinged legs of the four older children and the row of brown balusters interspersed with the legs.

PARIS: I thought them posts was movin'! They's jest alike— all of them legs and all them little stair posts, Mista Robert.

In the mirror they all seem alike—posts and legs. Same size and same color. *(His words are interrupted now and again by his own giggling.)*

Mr. Wade's mustache twitches involuntarily, and his eyes narrow into little slits. Then he looks into the mirror for the first time. Recognizing the ridiculous likeness of the legs to the balusters, he tosses back his head and laughs aloud. And the children one by one, even down to Lida Sue, who has picked herself up from the floor, join in the laughter. Their mirth has just reached its peak when Miss Bluemeyer, the housekeeper, appears from left. Her short hair is now combed, and she has exchanged her slippers for a pair of oxfords. She advances toward the head of the stairs without showing any interest in the cause of their mirth. She passes the children with a tolerant smile, affecting to be absorbed in her own thoughts. When she reaches the head of the stairs, Lida Sue and Paris step to one side; and Lida Sue reaches for the Negro man's hand, which she holds until the housekeeper has passed. Miss Bluemeyer descends the first three or four steps and then stops as she addresses Mr. Wade.

Miss Bluemeyer: If you will pardon me, Mr. Wade, I would like to try and get by. I am going to run down and see how breakfast is going.

Mr. Wade: Good morning, Miss. Isn't that a sight up there in the mirror?

Miss Bluemeyer *(glancing briefly in the general direction of the glass)*: Oh, yes, isn't it? *(She takes another step as she speaks.)* I was going to say— *(She begins, but finding Mr. Wade's eyes fastened on her she hesitates.)* If you will pardon me, Mr. Wade, I must ask you to let me pass. *(Fearlessly, courageously.)*

Mr. Wade *(sternly)*: I suggest that you use the back stairs since we haven't quite finished operations here, Miss Bluemeyer.

Miss Bluemeyer gazes defiantly at Mr. Wade for a moment,

*then at Paris and Lida Sue, then at the four children who are
lined up along the balustrade and who, like sheep, have drawn
closer together, their slight movement having been almost
imperceptible to the audience.*

MISS BLUEMEYER *(utterly without expression, as though answering a question about the day of the week or the title of a
book)*: Good morning, kiddies. *(Presently she retreats to the
head of the stairs, at which point she stops to address Mr.
Wade again.)* I was going to say that when Paris has put away
the ladder, it will be time to set the table for breakfast. That
is, if you have an early breakfast in mind, Mr. Wade.

MR. WADE: I had an early breakfast in mind, Miss Bluemeyer, for there is a busy day ahead for us all.

MISS BLUEMEYER *(in a sympathetic stage whisper)*: The funeral won't be until tomorrow, I presume, Mr. Wade?

MR. WADE: Well . . . there'll be a little service in the undertaker's chapel today. I'm taking the body back to Tennessee
on the train tonight.

MISS BLUEMEYER: I see . . . I see. *(In a gentle voice, full of
sentimentality.)* He must have been a fine old man—Mr. Wilson. The few times I saw him he seemed very, very polite. I
imagine to ladies especially, being Southern.

MR. WADE: I suppose so. . . . Yes, I suppose he was. *(He
turns his attention back to the light fixture for a moment, and
then as though only now realizing what she has said he turns
again to her with a little jerk of his head.)* Did I understand
you to say you had seen him? But I didn't know you had ever
seen our cousin, Miss Bluemeyer.

MISS BLUEMEYER: Oh, really? *(Significantly, as though perceiving that there had been some conversation about her not
having seen Mr. Wilson.)*

MR. WADE: Yes, indeed . . . really. *(With parts of the fixture
in his hands he goes down several rungs of the ladder, then
jumping nimbly off onto the stairs and coming up into the
hall he hands these pieces to Paris. Miss Bluemeyer has mean-*

while moved past the children and as far as the telephone table in the direction of the door to the service hall.) I don't recall Mr. Wilson's having been to see us since you came, Miss Bluemeyer.

MISS BLUEMEYER: That is quite right.

MR. WADE *(his usually direct manner exaggerated somewhat)*: Miss Bluemeyer, I think you are behaving and speaking in a mighty strange manner.

MISS BLUEMEYER: I am sorry if that is your opinion, Mr. Wade.

MR. WADE: Well, I think . . .

MISS BLUEMEYER: Remember, I am not one of the servants, Mr. Wade, not one of your servants.

When Mr. Wade came up into the hall, all of the children turned about and faced him and Miss Bluemeyer; and now he turns and gives them a "look" which sends them off quietly but quickly to their rooms, the older ones leading the younger. Paris, who has until this time been standing on the stairs with the parts of the light fixture in his hands, now moves down toward the ladder, ascends it, and begins hurriedly and skillfully to reassemble the fixture.

MR. WADE: I am aware that you are not one of the servants, and I am not speaking to you as such. In fact, I don't mean to provoke any unpleasantness this morning.

MISS BLUEMEYER *(repentantly, mournfully)*: And *I* am truly sorry to have been any bother this morning, Mr. Wade —this morning of all mornings. The truth is I used to see Mr. Wilson elsewhere. I never met him, you understand.

MR. WADE: I see. But you never mentioned having seen him to my wife or my aunt?

MISS BLUEMEYER: I didn't know the family would be interested that I had seen him. You understand, he lived a door from a lady with whom I am great friends.

MR. WADE: I see, I see.

MISS BLUEMEYER: He was a solitary figure, Mr. Wade, and

this friend of mine had noticed him. She is an invalid, you understand, and when I was staying with her she would some-times look out the window and say, "There goes that old Mr. Wilson. He seems to be an independent sort like us, Madge." That is all there was to it, Mr. Wade, and I used to notice him quite of-ten.

MR. WADE: But this happened when you were staying with your invalid friend?

MISS BLUEMEYER: Yes. You will think it is odd, I know, but that was before I even came here, Mr. Wade.

MR. WADE: I was thinking just that. And when was it you first made the connection between your Mr. Wilson and our Cousin Harry Wilson? That is, when did you discover that the old man you watched from your friend's window was my wife's cousin?

MISS BLUEMEYER: Only the shortest time ago, Mr. Wade, only a few weeks. Only when I happened to mention to this friend of mine that Misses Wade's only relative in Detroit had had a stroke. "What is his name, Madge?" she asked me. I told her his name and she said, "Why, Madge, that must be the same old Mr. Wilson I have pointed out to you. They tell me *he's* had a stroke," she said. It quite struck me at the time, Mr. Wade, that it was quite a coincidence, but I didn't want to bother the family at the time of their grief with idle, outside talk.

MR. WADE: Of course not. I'm sure you didn't. And it was very considerate of you.

A pause, during which Mr. Wade straightens his tie and casts his eyes about the room as though trying to decide how this conversation should be concluded.

MISS BLUEMEYER: If you would not think it was too odd, Mr. Wade, would you mind telling me to what funeral home the remains will go?

MR. WADE: Why! *(Taken aback.)* Of course I wouldn't mind. To Lewis Brothers, I believe.

MISS BLUEMEYER: Lewis Brothers, you say? I don't believe I have heard of . . . ?

MR. WADE: No, it's a small, uh, shop, uh, concern on the other side of town. But the Lewises were from Tennessee, from my mother's county, and my aunt thought it would be— uh—nice.

MISS BLUEMEYER: I see . . . yes . . . Well I *do* thank you, Mr. Wade. (*Turning quickly to Paris, as though to change the subject.*) Paris, you can set the table now!

She walks rapidly toward the door to the service hall. As she reaches for the door knob, the door opens and Aunt Lida enters with still another dress for Nancy, a black one. Paris has meanwhile reassembled the light fixture. Mr. Wade turns toward him and exclaims in genuine surprise at Paris's achievement, "Say!" Simultaneously Mrs. Wade enters from the door to her room.

MR. WADE: Boy, how did you know how to put that thing together?

PARIS (*giving one glance at Mr. Wade*): I had to do somepn to make myself scass. I thought you gwine eat 'at woman alive, way you come down off 'at ladder.

AUNT LIDA: What in the world do you make of it, Margie?

MRS. WADE: What do you think, Aunt Lida?

The two women have met in the center of the stage, in front of Mr. Wade, and by first addressing each other, instead of Mr. Wade whose conversation has roused their interest, they reveal their mutual sympathy and understanding and their slight regard for any interpretation which Mr. Wade might put upon his own conversation.

MR. WADE (*having completely forgotten the episode with Miss Bluemeyer*): Margie! Aunt Lida! Look what Paris has learned! (*Paris sits beaming atop the ladder.*)

AUNT LIDA (*paying no attention to him*): Did you hear every word of what she said?

MRS. WADE: I think so.

AUNT LIDA: I could hear every word. She said she had watched him from her friend's window even before she came here. All through his sickness she has known he was the man she and her cripple friend watched. She *is* a weird one, now, I'll tell you.

MRS. WADE: It's a curious picture, isn't it—those two lonely women watching that lonely old man. Why hasn't she spoken of it, do you suppose?

MR. WADE: Margie! Aunt Lida! This is a great day. This is important. This is a turning point in Paris's life, in the life of us all. He has learned to put that fixture together. Now he can have a try at the chandelier downstairs. *(When the women continue to take no notice of him, Paris begins to descend the ladder.)*

AUNT LIDA: It's from sheer perversity that she hasn't mentioned it, poor creature. She seems to delight in the dreariness of her own life and in finding other dreary "solitary figures." And I suppose we mustn't begrudge her her greatest pleasure.

Paris has now disappeared down the ladder, and as the ladder is seen being slowly lowered from view, Mr. Wade begins to show interest in what the women are saying.

MR. WADE: Now, Auntie, awhile ago it was her sheer perversity that made Miss Blue so suitable for our household. You know, I think you are downright vicious about that "poor creature."

AUNT LIDA: Why, I'm not at all, Robert Wade!

MR. WADE: Indeed, you are. You seem to have developed a special voice, a special expression, a special vocabulary for talking about her.

MRS. WADE: That's nonsense, Robert. How could you accuse Aunt Lida of being vicious about *any*body, *ever?*

AUNT LIDA: There, you see.

MRS. WADE: A fine way your house would be in if it weren't for Aunt Lida. And your children, and your wife, and yourself!

MR. WADE *(waving his hands before his face)*: I didn't mean to start such a furor. I wasn't serious. That is, it's not a very serious crime of Aunt Lida's. That Bluemeyer is a strange duck. Anybody can see that.

AUNT LIDA: Now who's being cruel? I am interested in all people, Robert, and am not without sympathy for . . .

MR. WADE: But this seems a very special—. You have a wonderful interest in the ways and doings of all your friends and especially in your family, in us particularly *(indicating this household, by a gesture)*. A kindly, gentle, womanly interest. You have a real knowledge of people, too. You know us all better than we know each other. You are a wonderful, wonderful woman, Aunt Lida, and we couldn't live without you. But *(holding up one finger)* I still maintain that regarding Miss Blue—

AUNT LIDA: Her name is not . . .

MRS. WADE: Robert! What nonsense!

AUNT LIDA: And at such an hour. *(Unruffled.)*

When interrupted, Mr. Wade turned and began walking toward the door to his room. Now he hesitates at the doorway.

MR. WADE: Has my blue serge come back from the cleaner's, Aunt Lida?

AUNT LIDA: It'll be back today, Robert.

Mr. Wade goes into his room and closes the door. Mrs. Wade moves to the front of the stage and sits down in one of the upholstered chairs, at left.

MRS. WADE: Where are the children, Aunt Lida?

AUNT LIDA *(calling, in a voice almost as deep as Mr. Wade's)*: Chill-drun!

Doors on both sides of the stage open. The children peer out at their Aunt Lida.

AUNT LIDA: Come say good morning to your mama-dear.

The children run across the stage to Mrs. Wade, all hugging and kissing her at once, saying, "Good morning, Mamadear. Good morning, Mama-dear. How pretty you are, Mama."

Mrs. Wade kisses each of them, pushing the older ones slightly aside in order to lean over and kiss little Lida Sue who says, "P-p-puhty muhmuh." *Aunt Lida watches approvingly. Presently she says:*

AUNT LIDA: Not one of you has noticed how charmingly your mama-dear has done up her beautiful hair this morning.

MRS. WADE: Aunt Lida, I declare! *(Smiling and shaking her head.)*

All of the children go behind her chair and admire her coiffure, Nancy lifting Lida Sue up to where she can see.

JAMES: It's all plaited and fixed.

NANCY: It's fixed in a bun. It's charming, Mama-dear.

ALFRED: How long is it now, Mama-dear?

MRS. WADE: Too long, too long. I'm going to cut it again before . . .

CHILDREN: No, no, no.

AUNT LIDA *(coming forward)*: We won't let her cut that beautiful hair, will we, children? . . . Nancy, let me fix your sash. It's all twisted.

MRS. WADE: It's impractical. Especially now. It will be too much trouble.

AUNT LIDA: Nonsense. We'll take turns arranging it for you. We'll never let her cut this beautiful hair, will we, children?

CHILDREN: Never, never.

MRS. WADE: I'll do as I like about my hair, thank you, all. You'll some day all be sorry for spoiling me so. I'll be the spoiledest of spoiled women. I'll cut off all my hair and wear a ring in my nose, just to show you I can if I want to.

The children are delighted and they scream with laughter. "No, no, we won't let you, we won't let you."

MRS. WADE: I will. And I'll wear tow sacks for dresses and old tennis shoes with the toes cut out. I'll wear a stocking cap like Alfred's.

The children laugh again and chant, "No, never. No, never. No, never."

AUNT LIDA: Turn around, Charles William. I do believe you've managed to get your bottom rompers on backward again.

CHARLES WILLIAM: I like 'em.

AUNT LIDA: Stand still, child. *(She has got down on one knee and begun buttoning his little pants. Without more words about it, she makes him step out of his pants; she turns them around and puts them on properly. Meanwhile, Charles William continues to gaze at his mother.) (Addressing the children as she buttons-up Charles William.)* We're going to keep Mama-dear the ornament of this household, aren't we? She ought to let us get her a personal maid, instead of a housekeeper.

MRS. WADE: One day you'll all be sorry. And I can hear you mumbling behind my back about *she.*

AUNT LIDA: Take off that stocking cap, Alfred. You'll be bald before you're in long pants. *(Alfred hesitates, turns his face away and gazes at the wall, pouting.)* Take it off, Alfred, I said. *(He snatches off the cap, revealing a flat pompadour with every hair in place, and continues to stare at the wall, right.)* Look at him pouting, children. Stick a pin in his cheeks and they'd pop like a balloon. *(The children laugh; even Alfred gives up pouting and laughs with them.)* Margie, every one of your children has a different way of pouting while being reprimanded. Only a slightly different way, however, for they are all gazers. Alfred here gazes at a blank wall. James likes to gaze up at the ceiling. *(She mimics each as she describes his form of gazing. The children and Mrs. Wade laugh appreciatively after each piece of mimicry.)* Nancy is a window gazer. Charles William is a hand gazer, or a plate gazer, if we're at the table.

JAMES: What about Lida Sue, Aunt Lida?

AUNT LIDA *(still on one knee after buttoning Charles Wil-*

liam's pants, she turns to Lida Sue, who is nearby): Why, she's the fearless type who stares a hole right through you and makes you feel that you couldn't possibly be right. *(She places her hands on Lida Sue's shoulders and stares, with a ridiculous frown. Lida Sue and the other children laugh hysterically. But Mrs. Wade has become aware of the presence of Miss Bluemeyer, who has entered several moments before from the service hall with Mrs. Wade's breakfast on a tray. Mrs. Wade watches the housekeeper, whose eyes are fixed on Aunt Lida. During that moment Mr. Wade, now wearing his suit coat, enters from the bedroom.)*

MR. WADE *(observing all that is taking place)*: Is there breakfast for the rest of us downstairs, Miss Bluemeyer?

MISS BLUEMEYER: Yes, there is, Mr. Wade.

MR. WADE: Then let's break up this dog and pony show, what say? Breakfast, children! James! Nancy!

The children go frolicking to the head of the stairs and disappear down the steps. Aunt Lida has got to her feet and turned about so quickly that she catches Miss Bluemeyer's gaze still upon her.

AUNT LIDA: Is my petticoat showing, Miss Bluemeyer?

MISS BLUEMEYER: No, Miss Wade, not that I can see.

AUNT LIDA: Then, what is it, please? You were staring so, I thought something must be wrong. *(She pretends to examine her dress.)*

MISS BLUEMEYER: I beg your pardon.

MR. WADE *(coming forward; cordially)*: Ah, that's a mighty fine-looking breakfast a certain person's going to get this morning. *(Taking the tray from Miss Bluemeyer.)* Ah, look-a-here. I believe they've got you on double rations, Margie.

MRS. WADE *(clearing the coffee table that Aunt Lida has pushed before her)*: Well, I should think so.

Miss Bluemeyer, continuing to scrutinize the group until the very last, has finally retreated down the front stairs. Aunt

Lida goes and looks over the balustrade into the stair well.
Mr. and Mrs. Wade observe her action and exchange glances.

MR. WADE: Now, Aunt Lida! What is it? What's the matter? If that woman bothers you so, why don't you give her her
walking papers?

MRS. WADE: Don't talk so, Robert. Don't make a mountain
out of a molehill.

AUNT LIDA: No, dear. He's right. This is more than a molehill. When I looked over the bannister just now I could see
Miss Bluemeyer. She was running her hand through her hair,
like this, and clenching her other fist with all her might. *(She
comes to the front of the stage and speaks, as to herself, while
Mr. and Mrs. Wade look on in wide-eyed amazement.)* That
poor, embittered creature! My God, my God, when I looked
down that stair well I felt that I had been given a quick
glimpse of a soul suffering the tortures of hell. *(Turning to
Mrs. Wade.)* And it's our happiness that is her hell, mind
you, Margie. She can't abide the sight of our family happiness.
Particularly not this morning when one of her sort—a man
who reveled in his own bitterness and despised all those who
tried to make his life a less lonesome, a less dreary business
—lies dead in an undertaker's parlor. She cannot endure the
presence of our happiness. Particularly not mine. *(Now angrily.)* Can you tell me how the good Lord can endure the
existence of such a mean and jealous being in His world?
She watched me there on my knees fondling those children,
and it filled her with nothing but resentment and hatred.
(Quietly again.) No, you are right, Robert. She shall have her
proverbial walking papers the moment you and the corpse of
our Cousin Harry are safely on the night train to Tennessee.

MR. WADE: Aunt Lida, what a tirade! What a fit of temper!
And at such an hour of the morning! Who ever heard of making such an important decision before breakfast?

*Aunt Lida stares blankly at Mr. Wade for a moment; then
she turns her face slowly from him to the audience. She is*

*not smiling and she makes no answer. She doesn't seem to
have heard what he said.*

CURTAIN

SCENE II

*The curtain rises on a second scene in the upstairs hall. It is
the evening of the same day. One table lamp is lit, front and
left, and as the curtain rises Miss Bluemeyer switches on the
desk lamp, seats herself, and begins dialing a number on the
telephone. She is alone in the hall. The Wade family is still
at dinner. During the late afternoon a funeral service has been
held in the undertaker's chapel.*

MISS BLUEMEYER *(speaking into the telephone)*: Merton?
It's Bluemeyer speaking. Quite well, thank you. And you?
Oh, that's too bad. *(Pause.)* Well, let me tell you . . . *(Pause.)*
Ah, that's too bad, Merton. *(Pause.)* I want to tell you . . .
(Pause.) Well, have you taken something? *(Pause.)* Merton,
I want to tell you . . . *(Impatiently.)* Of course I am interested
in how you feel, but you said yourself for me to call you when
they got back. Yes, they have been back a couple of hours,
Merton. . . . No. . . . Why, I mean exactly this: When I talked
to you a few hours ago, when they had just left for the funeral
home—all but Misses Wade. She didn't go; she took her nap.
—I said to you then, you remember, they were sure to guess
whose flowers they were. Yes, I know you thought so too,
Merton, and that is not what I am calling to tell you. We both
knew they would, and I have already heard all about it, but
not the last of it, I am afraid. This is what I mean: I dreaded,
as you said you dreaded for me, that they would come home
all sentimentalized and would gush over me with their thanks.
The thing I was afraid of, Merton, was that they would think
I was playing up to them. . . . Don't rush me, Merton. I will
tell you the whole story right now if there is time. They are
all at dinner now, you see, and if I am interrupted I will call

you back from the kitchen phone when the Negroes have gone
to bed. . . . I *am* going to get on with it, Merton. Don't be
rude to your best friend. On the card I sent with the flowers,
you remember, I had the young man write, "From Two
Friends." Well, when *she* came back with the rest of the family, from the funeral, she had our card tucked in her little
gray glove. I was downstairs in the side hall, you understand,
when they came in, and she just stopped beside me for a
minute as though she were thinking of something. Then
she slips the card out, like she was a magician— She had that
air, Merton, that I should be surprised where she got it—and
says in a deep, businesslike voice, "Many thanks, Miss Bluemeyer, and thank the other friend for the family of the bereaved." Bereaved, indeed! They spent breakfast poking their
sly fun at the child Nancy for wanting to wear a black dress.
. . . No, that is all there was to it, Merton. No, not a question
about who the other friend was. No, not another word, not
from any of them. . . . No, I didn't want their thanks any
more than you. What I mean is they have hardly spoke another word to me since, except about the usual things. Dinner
was just awful, and I left just now without dessert. I couldn't
have eat *(pronounced eet)* it, and the children carrying on so
as if nobody had ever passed away, much less a poor lonesome
old man. But the grownups are all hopping mad, I can tell
you. *Mad,* you understand, because we had the presumption
to send flowers to somebody who was their relation. Wouldn't
you think *she* would understand, though, Merton, how it is.
. . . Of course, she does, and she is ashamed. If *he* had been
one of those who care to fawn over their relations, as *she* has!
Anybody who has so little pride and independence, indeed!
Of course, I know you know, but . . . *(Hearing someone on
the stairs.)* Well, that will be all. Thank you. Good-by, Merton. *(Sotto voce.)* Of course, I am not angry. Somebody's . . .
Yes. Good-by, Merton.

  Mr. and Mrs. Wade are ascending the stairs, arm in arm.

*Miss Bluemeyer moves toward her room, at right. Lennie
enters from door to service hall, right and back.*

MISS BLUEMEYER (*just before entering her room*): Lennie,
you need not turn down my bed tonight. I have some patterns
spread out.

LENNIE: Yehsm.

*Miss Bluemeyer closes the door behind her. Lennie enters
the boys' room through the other door, right. Mr. and Mrs.
Wade come forward and take seats in the sitting-room end
of the hall, extreme left. They have been talking quietly as
they came up the stairs and crossed the hall. Now their words
become audible.*

MR. WADE: The children couldn't have behaved better. I
think even Lida Sue would have behaved all right if I had
taken her.

MRS. WADE: I still feel a little as though I should have been
there. Mama always felt so sorry for Cousin Harry. She used
to say he was offish and surly even as a child. He never *was*
happy.

MR. WADE: God! Eighty-three years of it! . . . Well, did
you wire Cousin Lula what time I arrive with the body?

MRS. WADE: Oh, I wired her this morning. They'll want to
have a little service in Nashville, I'm sure.

MR. WADE: Oh, I'm *sure* they will. And I suppose I'll have
to attend that too?

MRS. WADE: Darling, I hope you will. It'll mean so much
to them.

MR. WADE: I know. I know. And it won't be nearly so bad
without Aunt Lida there.

MRS. WADE: Did she really behave badly?

MR. WADE: Well, I don't suppose the undertakers noticed,
and there was nobody else to notice it. But as soon as they
brought in that big wreath—it was a tremendous thing (*he
holds his hands out to indicate the size*)—she took herself up
to where they set it by the coffin and looked at the card.

MRS. WADE: And just what did the card say?

MR. WADE: "From Two Friends."

MRS. WADE *(smiling)*: Isn't that incredible?

MR. WADE: And a strange expression came over Aunt Lida's face that didn't leave it until after we were home. She sat through the whole service as stiff as a broom and didn't sing a word of either hymn.

MRS. WADE: She was obviously making her plans. I doubt if Miss Bluemeyer will still be on the place as late as noon tomorrow.

MR. WADE: Do you think she'll let her stay the night?

MRS. WADE: Aunt Lida ought to restrain herself. The woman is merely peculiar. I wish you would talk to Aunt Lida about it before you go, Robert.

MR. WADE: *You* will have to talk to her, Margie. She has never been known to take a man's advice on anything but money matters.

MRS. WADE: Aunt Lida's a mighty clever woman.

MR. WADE: Be serious, dear. There's more in this than meets the eye.

MRS. WADE: Speak for your own eye, Robert.

MR. WADE: Then, what is it? I know I am a mere unimaginative man, but . . .

MRS. WADE *(casually, as she settles herself in her chair)*: You make us out awfully ugly, honey—Aunt Lida and me.

MR. WADE: And how do you two make me out?

MRS. WADE: I really think you are coming to believe literally in our womanly contempt for mankind. I think you're good for lots more than breadwinning, my love. Our contempt is only skin deep. It's only a tiresome old joke that makes life easier for two women under the same roof.

MR. WADE: I wish it made it easier for three. . . . Tell me, then, what is it you see in this business that I don't see? What is it about Miss Bluemeyer's queerness that disturbs Aunt Lida so? Are we only detecting the first signs of old age in her?

MRS. WADE: It has nothing to do with old age. It is simply that someone has entered the field who won't play the game according to Aunt Lida's rules.

MR. WADE: What sort of nonsense is that? You and Aunt Lida are forever . . .

MRS. WADE: Robert Wade, stop linking me with your aunt as though there were no difference between us.

MR. WADE: Then her age . . .

MRS. WADE: I'm not speaking of the difference in our ages. Don't you really know that your wife and your maiden aunt are two quite different people? *(Hotly.)* If you haven't perceived *that* in thirteen years, how can you hope to comprehend the niceties of a problem between your maiden aunt and an old-maid housekeeper?

MR. WADE: What in the devil are you getting so worked up about?

MRS. WADE: Worked up! I say!

MR. WADE: Have you and Aunt Lida been quarreling, too?

MRS. WADE: Have we . . . ? *(Quietly.)* God in heaven, give me strength. For the ten years we have been in Detroit, Robert Wade, your Aunt Lida and I haven't had a cross word; and now you ask me calmly, have we been quarreling!

MR. WADE: And why is that such an outlandish question?

MRS. WADE: Don't you really know why it is? And don't you really know why Aunt Lida and I have such smooth sailing? It's because we have arranged our lives as we have. It's because Aunt Lida and I have played our roles so perfectly, as we've always seen them played in Tennessee: She, the maiden aunt, responsible and capable! I, the beautiful young wife, the bearer of children, the reigning queen! *(She laughs, and Mr. Wade jumps to his feet, obviously alarmed.)* Why, suh, sometimes ah can almos' heah the darkies a-croonin' in the quawtuhs! *(Her laughter is now definitely hysterical.)*

MR. WADE: Margie, I won't have you flying off like this!

MRS. WADE *(coming to her feet)*: I may fly off further than you think. *(Then she bursts into tears and throws her arms about his neck, weeping on his shirt front.)* Robert, forgive me. You know I adore Aunt Lida. *(But she continues to weep.)*

MR. WADE *(putting his arms around her)*: There, darling. Of course you do.

As he eases her into her chair again, Miss Bluemeyer throws open her door and hurries across the stage.

MISS BLUEMEYER: Oh, the dear thing! She has been such a brave lady up until now. It has been a very sad day for her, and I feel . . .

MR. WADE *(seated on Mrs. Wade's chair arm with his arms still around her; to Miss Bluemeyer)*: Hold on, ma'am. You're mistaken.

MISS BLUEMEYER: Indeed, I have been very much mistaken. Grief has strange ways, Mr. Wade. Let me get her a cup of coffee.

She turns and strides toward the door to the service hall. Suddenly she faces Lennie, who has been observing events from the door to the boys' room.

MISS BLUEMEYER: Lennie, bring Misses Wade a cup of coffee.

LENNIE: Yehsm, but she's jess having a nachal spell.

MISS BLUEMEYER: A natural spell?

LENNIE *(impatiently)*: She's six months gone, Miss Bloomer. *(She goes to fetch the coffee.)*

MISS BLUEMEYER: She's . . . ? Oh, of course.

The housekeeper glances quickly in the direction of Mr. and Mrs. Wade, and her glance is met by Mr. Wade's glare. She turns and makes a hurried exit into her own room. Aunt Lida's voice is heard on the stairs, and the three children come romping up the steps ahead of her.

MRS. WADE *(completely recovered)*: How silly of me.

MR. WADE: That Bluemeyer woman *is* morbid, Margie.

MRS. WADE: You mustn't worry yourself about her, Robert. What time does your train leave?

AUNT LIDA (*crossing from head of stairs to sitting room*): Robert, I told Paris to bring up your Gladstone. Isn't that what he should take, Margie?

MRS. WADE: I think so, Aunt Lida.

AUNT LIDA (*standing, hands clasped loosely before her*): You feel like packing for him, don't you, Margie?

MRS. WADE: There, you see, Robert!

AUNT LIDA: See what, Margie?

MR. WADE: Yes, what?

MRS. WADE: *He* knows very well what.

Charles William has now climbed on his mother's knees. Alfred is tugging at his father's hand. Lida Sue is walking round and round Aunt Lida.

AUNT LIDA: You children run and play.

ALFRED: Can we play in your room, Aunt Lida?

AUNT LIDA (*severely*): Yes, but don't touch one thing on my dresser. (*They scamper away to Aunt Lida's room, left.*)

MRS. WADE: I've made a little scene since we came upstairs, Aunt Lida. I've had a good cry and everything.

AUNT LIDA: Are you feeling right tired, honey?

MRS. WADE: I guess I am. I must be awfully tired, for I was protesting Robert's linking our names so eternally.

MR. WADE: Jealous of you, Aunt Lida!

AUNT LIDA: Pshaw! It *is* tiresome of you, Robert.

MRS. WADE: And what I was just now pointing out to him was an example of how well we know our roles and how clearly defined are our spheres of authority. (*Turning to Mr. Wade.*) Aunt Lida saw to it that your bag should be brought up, but she would leave the packing of it to me.

AUNT LIDA (*in good nature*): Now, if I am to be embarrassed by your referring to your private conversations about me, be good enough to explain what set you off on the subject.

There is a moment's silence.

MR. WADE: We were trying to fathom the reasons for your sudden strong feelings against the housekeeper.

There is another moment of silence. Aunt Lida puts her hand self-consciously to her string of pearls. Lennie enters from service hall with coffee.

AUNT LIDA: Oh, I see.

MRS. WADE *(uncertain of what she is going to say)*: Robert . . .

AUNT LIDA: Put the tray on the table here, Lennie. Are you right sure you want to drink coffee at this hour of the night, Margie?

MRS. WADE: Come to think of it, I guess I won't.

AUNT LIDA: Leave it there, Lennie, and I'll drink it.

LENNIE: Yehsm. *(She goes into the girls' room, left.)*

AUNT LIDA: What time is your train, Robert?

MR. WADE: I've got just about an hour. *(Looking at watch.)*

AUNT LIDA: Then you'd better set about packing. Margie's plainly not up to it.

MR. WADE *(rising from chair)*: You're dead right.

MRS. WADE: Do you mind?

MR. WADE: Not a bit, honey. *(He goes into his bedroom.)*

Aunt Lida sits down in the chair that Mr. Wade was occupying a few minutes before. With her foot she draws a footstool in front of her and rests her feet on it. She rests her head on the chair back and with her elbows raised she interlocks her fingers and places her hands over her eyes.

AUNT LIDA: Margie, I'm right tired, myself.

MRS. WADE: Poor dear, I know you are. It's been an awful strain on you, Aunt Lida.

AUNT LIDA: What has, Margie?

MRS. WADE: Oh, all of Cousin Harry's illness, with me in this condition, and the funeral today especially.

AUNT LIDA: Margie, I hope you don't ever think I underestimate you.

MRS. WADE: How so?

AUNT LIDA: I mean your powers of perception and understanding.

Mrs. Wade: I'm a simple, artless little mother-woman from upper Middle-Tennessee.

Aunt Lida: And I, I am a pore relation, a maiden aunt from the Cumberland Plateau. *(They laugh, and Aunt Lida removes her hands from before her eyes.)*

Aunt Lida: That's how your Cousin Harry saw us to the very end, you know.

Mrs. Wade: That's how we *are* to the very end, isn't it, Aunt Lida?

Aunt Lida: I don't know, Margie. It's sometimes hard, isn't it?

Mrs. Wade: Aunt Lida, it's great fun mostly. And what else is there better, with the given circumstances? When I was a girl I used to think . . .

Aunt Lida: Yes, and so did I, even I, even then. But what chance has a person? It's like throwing away money, the horrid stuff. Yet it's the coin of the realm, and you'd best use what you have of it.

Mrs. Wade: But I also thought . . .

Aunt Lida: Ah, and so did I. But that part was harder for me, not being the pretty little thing.

Mrs. Wade: Now, Aunt Lida, I was always told at home that you were a mighty attractive young girl.

Aunt Lida: Well, as your husband's great-aunt Rhody Baird from East Tennessee used to say of herself *(in the voice of a crone)*, "Like any other, I had my little lovyer. Hee-he-he—hee." And let me tell you I made them step and fetch for me; but I used to hate myself. Sometimes I hate myself now and think that your Cousin Harry was right about it all. People like him, and like her *(pointing with her thumb in the direction of Miss Bluemeyer's room)* make it hard. They point an accusing finger.

Mrs. Wade: I know what you mean.

Aunt Lida: Yes, I thought you did. And that's how we began this conversation.

Mr. Wade appears at the door of his room.

MR. WADE: Aunt Lida, does Paris think I'm not leaving till midnight?

AUNT LIDA *(rising from chair)*: I told that boy . . .

MR. WADE *(seeing Lennie as she comes out of the girls' room)*: Never mind, Aunt Lida. Lennie, you tell Paris to get up here with my Gladstone!

LENNIE *(stepping into the hall)*: Yehsuh, he's on the back stair, wipin' it. You wouldn't-a tetched it the way it wuz.

AUNT LIDA *(to Mrs. Wade)*: Lennie *always* has to add her nickel's worth.

LENNIE: Aw, Miss Lida, I got beds to tunn back.

AUNT LIDA: Girl, that sounded to me just this side of uppity. I'll have to speak to *your* Aunt Myra.

LENNIE: Wull, there's uppitier niggers than I be in this house.

MR. WADE *(coming forward)*: By George, this isn't getting me my Gladstone.

At this moment Paris enters from the service hall, and Lennie turns toward Aunt Lida's room. Simultaneously Myra appears on the stairway with a stack of clean, highly starched rompers and dresses for the smaller children piled high in her arms. She is mouthing over her shoulder at James and Nancy who are behind her: "Wull, make hase! Come ohn by me if y'aim to come, and mine these-here close." Nancy and James brush past her and gallop up the few remaining steps before her. Each carries a large walking cane with a crook handle. Meanwhile, Mr. Wade addresses Paris the length of the hall, "Paris, is that the bag Miss Lida told you to bring me?" Paris replies, "Yessuh, it the Glodstone." And Aunt Lida is saying to Lennie whom she has called back from her room, "You can leave my bed; the children are playing in there. And if you're going to change Miss Margie's sheets tonight, get Nancy to help you. I want her to learn to look after things."

MR. WADE *(still to Paris, who has stopped in his tracks at the far end of the hall):* It's *a* Glodstone, I'll grant you. It's the one Miss Margie's papa took to the Tennessee Centennial in 1896.

AUNT LIDA *(turning toward Paris):* What's this about the Gladstone?

MR. WADE *(to Aunt Lida):* Do you think I'm going to travel with that old carpetbag? Did you tell Paris . . . ?

AUNT LIDA: I *did* not!

MRS. WADE *(whose attention has been attracted by the noise of the children, James and Nancy, behind her—looking over her shoulder to Myra):* Myra, the clothes look lovely. Come let me see them.

MYRA: Yassum. 'At James come mighty nigh spillin' 'um "lovely close."

JAMES: I did not, Myra. It was Nancy.

AUNT LIDA: Don't contradict Myra, James.

LENNIE: Come ohn, Nancy.

AUNT LIDA: Paris, you march right back down there and get the new Gladstone.

MRS. WADE *(holding up one of Lida Sue's dresses):* They're positively lovely, Myra. Look, Aunt Lida! Of course, these ruffles here ought to be pressed over this way.

NANCY: Aunt Lida, I know how to turn back an old bed! Don't make me do it tonight, Aunt Lida. James and I want to roll back the big rug yonder and play slide-on-the-rag-rug.

MR. WADE: You *are not* going to play that game while I'm in this house. Do as your Aunt Lida says; and James, put that walking cane down and come help me pack.

PARIS: I don't know which-a-one you mean, Miss Lida.

AUNT LIDA *(stepping nearer to Mrs. Wade and examining the dress she holds up):* Of course, it should be over that way. I told you so, explicitly, Myra; and you knew how I wanted it. *(Suddenly laughing.)* Myra Willis, admit it! You just liked it better this way.

MYRA *(bending forward and laughing)*: Aw, Miss Lida, ain't you a sight.

PARIS: I don't know which-a-one you mean, Miss Lida.

NANCY: Aunt Lida, don't make me . . .

MR. WADE: For God's sake, tell him the right one, Auntie.

LENNIE: She ain't comin', Miss Lida.

MRS. WADE: Aunt Lida . . .

AUNT LIDA *(raising her voice)*: Now, see here, all of you . . .

At this moment Aunt Lida realizes that Miss Bluemeyer is standing in the open doorway to her room, right. Since Mr. Wade came from his room saying, "Does Paris think I'm not leaving till midnight?" she has been standing there, watching.

MISS BLUEMEYER: Mr. Wade.

MR. WADE *(furiously)*: Yes—ma'am!

MISS BLUEMEYER: I will see that you get the right luggage. *(Taking a step in the direction of door to service hall.)* Come with me, Paris.

AUNT LIDA: That won't be necessary, Miss Bluemeyer. Paris knows the suitcase we mean now.

PARIS *(quickly)*: Yessum, I suhtnly do.

He hurries through the service hall doorway, closing the door after him. At the same moment Lennie takes Nancy's hand and pulls her into her parents' room. "Come ohn, Nancy!" As they are closing the door, James rushes after them, pushing his way through the half-closed door and then closing it after him. Miss Bluemeyer begins walking slowly across the hall toward Aunt Lida, who watches her intently.

MRS. WADE *(pushing the child's dress at Myra and nodding her head significantly toward the girls' room)*: Here, Myra. *(Half-whispering.)* Robert, you will miss that train if you don't hurry.

MR. WADE: By George, yes! *(Looking at his watch.)*

Paris now runs up the stairs with a yellow-brown Gladstone bag. Myra goes into the girls' room.

PARIS: Here, Mista Robert. *(He sets the bag down at the head of the stairs.)*

MR. WADE *(striding in the direction of Paris)*: Tell Sellars to bring the car round.

PARIS: Sellars waitin' in the potecoshay.

Paris glances at Miss Bluemeyer, who has now reached the center of the hall, and runs down the stairs. Mr. Wade goes into his room and closes the door. Miss Bluemeyer suddenly turns about face and hastens to her room, leaving the door ajar.

MRS. WADE *(in alarm)*: Aunt Lida!

AUNT LIDA *(reassuringly, in her deepest voice)*: She's only going to fetch her hat and coat. She's quitting. She's not going to stay the night.

MISS BLUEMEYER *(enters with a light coat thrown over her left arm, a handbag in her left hand, and a soft felt hat in her right hand; with the latter she gesticulates rather wildly as she speaks in a loud masculine voice)*: No, not another hour in the house with such as you. *(Striding the length of the hall to face Aunt Lida.)* My conscience would burn me out before morning.

AUNT LIDA *(sternly, calmly)*: Just leave us your address, Miss Bluemeyer. We'll send your things tomorrow.

MISS BLUEMEYER: Send 'em or not, Miss Wade, as you like. Do I care if I never see them again? Not one thing that will remind me . . .

MRS. WADE *(rising from chair)*: Good night, Miss Bluemeyer! *(Miss Bluemeyer turns submissively and goes to the head of the stairs.)*

AUNT LIDA: Wait a moment.

MRS. WADE: No, Aunt Lida!

AUNT LIDA: Miss Bluemeyer, can't you calm yourself sufficiently to tell me what you have to say in a civilized manner? You and I will never see each other again, and you might be glad some day that you told me. *(Miss Bluemeyer laughs ironically.)*

MRS. WADE: Good *night,* Miss Bluemeyer.

MISS BLUEMEYER: No, Misses Wade, I will stay a bit. *(She returns to the group of chairs.)* I want to talk to you about your husband's aunt.

MRS. WADE *(turning her back and taking several steps in the direction of her room)*: I have no interest in what you may say. Good night.

MISS BLUEMEYER: Ah, shame, Misses Wade. You who are so kind to your husband's aunt ought to be kind to other lonesome beings in this world. *(Mrs. Wade stops and turns halfway round.)* Doesn't it seem maybe that's what is wrong with all the family falderal your sort go in for?

AUNT LIDA: It was not to hear your criticism of my niece that I called you back, Miss Bluemeyer.

MISS BLUEMEYER: It was not to criticize her I am staying. . . . *(Mr. Wade enters with his Gladstone. He pulls the door to behind him and stands listening.)* Misses Wade, I have a thing or two to say. . . .

MRS. WADE: If those things concern my aunt . . .

AUNT LIDA: Miss Bluemeyer, I asked you to stop a moment because I thought you had something to say about our late cousin, Mr. Wilson.

MISS BLUEMEYER *(suddenly, with emotion)*: Mr. Wilson! Mr. Wilson! Your *cousin,* Mr. Wilson! *(Then speaking in a hoarse monotone, obviously making a conscious effort at self-restraint.)* Can you not hear yourselves? Aunt! Niece! Nephew! Father! Son! Daughter! Cousin! *Cousin!* I can see the poor old fellow now tramping past Merton's window to the lunchroom or going up to the corner with a little package of laundry under his arm.

AUNT LIDA: Are you accusing us of unkindness to Cousin Harry?

MISS BLUEMEYER: Not to Cousin Harry, but to Mr. Wilson.

MR. WADE: I thought it had been definitely established that Cousin Harry *was* . . .

AUNT LIDA: Your distinction isn't quite clear, Miss Bluemeyer.

MISS BLUEMEYER: Oh, it is clear enough!

AUNT LIDA *(calmly)*: If only you could calm yourself. I do think you may have a point to make.

MRS. WADE: Aunt Lida, this whole interview is uncalled-for. . . . Even if you have no respect for our family, Miss Bluemeyer, remember that one near to us has died this day. We simply do not understand each other. Please say no more and go.

MISS BLUEMEYER: Do we not understand each other, Misses Wade? I understand a good deal of how this family business works. It makes a woman safe and sure being related this way and that way to everybody around her. And it keeps you from having to bother about anybody else, since they are not "kinfolks." I understand how it works, for I was one of nine, and I saw the women in my family making the most of it too. And I might have done the same, but I was a queer sort who couldn't make herself do it.

AUNT LIDA: Is that all, Miss Bluemeyer?

MISS BLUEMEYER: Not quite all. For a solid year I have watched you here giving directions and making this house your own. And I have seen it right along that you are really the same as I in lots of your feelings, Miss Wade, that you are really lost and alone in the world, but you would not have it so, you just wouldn't. All along I have seen you are really a brainy woman and yet to see you here saying the things you say and play-acting all the time! And then when the old man Wilson was dying, you, like the rest of 'em, talked of nothing but that he was kin, kin, kin. You have mocked and joked all this day and gave him a funeral only because he was a kinsman.

MR. WADE: Miss Bluemeyer.

MISS BLUEMEYER: I am going now, Mr. Wade. *(She goes to the head of the stairs where he is standing by the door.)* Good-by, Mr. Wade.

MR. WADE: Good-by, ma'am. And believe me, to us all our Cousin Harry was just a poor, lonely old man that we would have befriended if he had let us.

MISS BLUEMEYER: I know your feelings are good, Mr. Wade. But you are a man. For a man it is easier. *(She goes down the stairs. There is a moment's silence when each of the three persons present seems to be concerned with his own thoughts.)*

MRS. WADE: What could have so embittered a person?

MR. WADE: Why, the woman's crazy, and naturally Aunt Lida was the first to make it out. How long have you known she was insane, Aunt Lida?

AUNT LIDA: I don't know.

MR. WADE *(taking several steps forward, slowly)*: What do you mean?

MRS. WADE: She means that she doesn't know when she realized it.

MR. WADE: By the way she said it, I thought she meant she wasn't sure she was crazy.

MRS. WADE *(taking his arm)*: Oh, could a sane person possibly have been so critical and questioning of a happy family life?

AUNT LIDA: Robert, aren't you going to miss your train?

MR. WADE: By George! Well, aren't the children going to tell me good-by?

AUNT LIDA *(calling)*: Chill-drun!

Mr. Wade kisses Mrs. Wade.

MR. WADE: So long, Auntie.

AUNT LIDA *(casually)*: Toodle-loo. Hurry back, Robert.

The children have now appeared in the doorways from Aunt Lida's room and their parents' room. "Yes, ma'am!" "What, Aunt Lida?"

AUNT LIDA: Tell your daddy good-by. *(Slowly letting herself down into chair.)*

NANCY: Oh, of course!

JAMES: Sure!

All of the children rush toward their father to be kissed. As he bends and stoops to kiss each of them, he is saying, "Good-by, Alfred. Good-by, Nancy. Good-by, Lida Sue. Good-by, James. Good-by, Charles William." But Mrs. Wade is watching Aunt Lida, who, as the curtain falls, sits with her hands over her face, as before.

CURTAIN

Miss Leonora When Last Seen

————

Here in Thomasville we are all concerned over the whereabouts of Miss Leonora Logan. She has been missing for two
weeks, and though a half dozen postcards have been received
from her, stating that she is in good health and that no anxiety
should be felt for her safety, still the whole town can talk
of nothing else. She was last seen in Thomasville heading
south on Logan Lane, which is the narrow little street that
runs alongside her family property. At four-thirty on Wednesday afternoon—Wednesday before last, that is to say—she
turned out of the dirt driveway that comes down from her
house and drove south on the Lane toward its intersection
with the bypass of the Memphis-Chattanooga highway. She
has not been seen since. Officially, she is away from home on
a little trip. Unofficially, in the minds of the townspeople,
she is a missing person, and because of events leading up to
her departure none of us will rest easy until we know that the
old lady is safe at home again.

Miss Leonora's half dozen postcards have come to us from points in as many states: Alabama, Georgia, North Carolina, West Virginia, Kentucky—in that order. It is considered a fair guess that her next card will come from Missouri or Arkansas, and that the one after that will be from Mississippi or Louisiana. She seems to be orbiting her native state of Tennessee. But, on the other hand, there is no proof that she has not crossed the state, back and forth, a number of times during the past two weeks. She is quite an old lady, and is driving a 1942 Dodge convertible. Anyone traveling in the region indicated should watch out for two characteristics of her driving. First, she hates to be overtaken and passed by other vehicles—especially by trucks. The threat of such is apt to make her bear down on the accelerator and try to outdistance the would-be passer. Or, if passed, she can be counted on to try to overtake and pass the offender at first chance. The second characteristic is: When driving after dark, she invariably refuses to dim her lights unless an approaching car has dimmed its own while at least five hundred feet away. She is a good judge of distances, and she is not herself blinded by bright lights on the highway. And one ought to add that, out of long habit and for reasons best known to herself, Miss Leonora nearly always drives by night.

Some description will be due, presently, of this lady's person and of how she will be dressed while traveling. But that had better wait a while. It might seem prejudicial and even misleading with reference to her soundness of mind. And any question of that sort, no matter what the rest of the world may think, has no bearing upon the general consternation that her going away has created here.

Wherever Miss Leonora Logan is today, she knows in her heart that in the legal action recently taken against her in Thomasville there was no malice directed toward her personally. She knows this, and would say so. At this very moment she may be telling some new-found friend the history of the case—because I happen to know that when she is away from home she talks to people about herself and her forebears as she would never do to anyone here. And chances are she is giving a completely unbiased version of what has happened, since that is her way.

The cause of all our present tribulation is this: The Logan property, which Miss Leonora inherited from one of her paternal great-uncles and which normally upon her death would have gone to distant relatives of hers in Chicago, has been chosen as the site for our county's new consolidated high school. A year and a half ago, Miss Leonora was offered a fair price for the three-acre tract and the old house, and she refused it. This summer, condemnation proceedings were begun, and two weeks ago the county court granted the writ. This will seem to you a bad thing for the town to have done, especially in view of the fact that Miss Leonora has given long years of service to our school system. She retired ten years ago after teaching for twenty-five years in the old high school. To be sure, four of us who are known hereabouts as Miss Leonora Logan's favorites among the male citizenry refused to have any part in the action. Two of us even preferred to resign from the school board. But still, times do change, and the interests of one individual cannot be allowed to hinder the progress of a whole community. Miss Leonora understands that. And she knows that her going away can only delay matters for a few weeks at most. Nevertheless, she is making it look very bad for Thomasville, and we want Miss Leonora to come home.

The kind of jaunt that she has gone off on isn't anything new for the old lady. During the ten years since her retirement she has been setting out on similar excursions rather consistently every month or so, and never, I believe, with a specific itinerary or destination in mind. Until she went away this time, people had ceased to bother themselves with the question of her whereabouts while she was gone or to be concerned about any harm that might come to her. We have been more inclined to think of the practical value her trips have for us. In the past, you see, she was never away for more than a week or ten days, and on her return she would gladly give anyone a full and accurate account of places visited and of the condition of roads traveled. It has, in fact, become the custom when you are planning an automobile trip to address yourself to Miss Leonora on the public square one day and ask her advice on the best route to take. She is our authority not only on the main highways north, south, east, and west of here, in a radius of six or eight hundred miles, but even on the secondary and unimproved roads in places as remote as Brown County, Indiana, and the Outer Banks of North Carolina. Her advice is often very detailed, and will include warnings against "single-lane bridges" or "soft shoulders" or even "cops patrolling in unmarked cars."

It is only the facts she gives you, though. She doesn't express appreciation for the beauty of the countryside or her opinion of the character of towns she passes through. The most she is likely to say is that such-and-such a road is "regarded" as the scenic route, or that a certain town has a "well worked-out traffic system." No one can doubt that while driving, Miss Leonora keeps her eyes and mind on the road. And that may be the reason why we have never worried about her. But one asks oneself, What pleasure can she ever have derived from these excursions? She declares that she hates the actual driving. And when giving advice on the roads somewhere she will always say that it is a dull and tedious trip and that the traveler will wish himself home in Thomasville a thousand times before he gets to wherever he is going.

Miss Leonora's motivation for taking these trips was always, until the present instance, something that it seemed pointless even to speculate on. It just seemed that the mood came on her and she was off and away. But if anything happens to her now, all the world will blame *us* and say we *sent* her on this journey, sent her out alone and possibly in a dangerous frame of mind. In particular, the blame will fall on the four timid male citizens who were the last to see her in Thomasville (for I do not honestly believe we will ever see her alive here again) and who, as old friends and former pupils of hers at the high school, ought to have prevented her going away. As a matter of fact, I am the one who opened the car door for the old lady that afternoon and politely assisted her into the driver's seat—and without even saying I thought it unwise of her to go. I *thought* it unwise, but at the moment it was as if I were still her favorite pupil twenty years before, and as if I feared she might reprove me for any small failure of courtesy like not opening the car door.

That's how the old lady is—or was. Whatever your first relation to her might have been, she would never allow it to change, and some people even say that that is why she discourages us so about the trips we plan. She cannot bear to think of us away from Thomasville. She thinks this is where all of us belong. I remember one day at school when some boy said to her that he wished he lived in a place like Memphis or Chattanooga. She gave him the look she usually reserved for the people she caught cheating. I was seated in the first row of the class that day, and I saw the angry patches of red appear on her broad, flat cheeks and on her forehead. She paused a moment to rearrange the combs in her hair and to give the stern yank to her corset that was a sure sign she was awfully mad. (We used to say that, with her spare figure, she only wore a corset for the sake of that expressive gesture.) The class was silent, waiting. Miss Leonora looked out the window for a moment, squinting up her eyes as if she could actually make out the Memphis or even the Chattanooga skyline on the horizon. Then, turning back to the unfortunate boy, she said, grinding out her words to him through clenched teeth, "I wish I could *throw* you there!"

But it is ten years now since Miss Leonora retired, and,

strange as it may sound, the fact of her having once taught in our school system was never introduced into the deliberations of the school board last spring—their deliberations upon whether or not they ought to sue for condemnation of the Logan home place. No doubt it was right that they didn't let this influence their decision. But what really seems to have happened is that nobody even recalled that the old lady had once been a teacher—or nobody but a very few, who did not want to remind the others.

What they remembered, to the exclusion of everything else, and what they always remember is that Miss Leonora is the last of the Logan family in Thomasville, a family that for a hundred years and more did all it could to impede the growth and progress of our town. It was a Logan, for instance, who kept the railroad from coming through town; it was another Logan who prevented the cotton mill and the snuff factory from locating here. They even kept us from getting the county seat moved here, until after the Civil War, when finally it became clear that nobody was ever going to buy lots up at Logan City, where they had put the first courthouse. Their one idea was always to keep the town unspoilt, unspoilt by railroads or factories or even county politics. Perhaps they should not be blamed for wanting to keep the town unspoilt. Yet I am not quite sure about that. It is a question that even Miss Leonora doesn't feel sure about. Otherwise, why does she always go into that question with the people she meets away from home?

I must tell you about the kind of lodging Miss Leonora takes when she stops for rest, and about the kind of people she finds to talk to. She wouldn't talk to you or me, and she wouldn't put up at a hotel like mine, here on the square, or even at a first-class motel like one of those out on the Memphis-Chattanooga Bypass. I have asked her very direct questions about this, pleading a professional interest, and I have filled in with other material furnished by her friends of the road who have from time to time stopped in here at my place.

On a pretty autumn day like today, she will have picked a farmhouse that has one of those little home-lettered signs out by the mailbox saying "Clean Rooms for Tourists—Modern Conveniences." (She will, that is, unless she has changed her ways and taken to a different life, which is the possibility that I do not like to think of.) She stops only at places that are more or less in that category—old-fashioned tourist homes run by retired farm couples or, if the place is in town, by two old-maid sisters. Such an establishment usually takes its name from whatever kind of trees happen to grow in the yard— Maple Lawn or Elmwood or The Oaks. Or when there is a boxwood plant, it will be called Boxwood Manor. If the place is in the country, like the one today, it may be called Oak Crest.

You can just imagine how modern the modern conveniences at Oak Crest are. But it is cheap, which is a consideration for Miss Leonora. And the proprietors are probably good listeners, which is another consideration. She generally stops in the daytime, but since even in the daytime she can't sleep for long, she is apt to be found helping out with the chores. Underneath the Oak Crest "Clean Rooms for Tourists" sign there may be one that says "Sterile Day-Old Eggs" or, during the present season, "Delicious Apples and Ripe Tomatoes." It wouldn't surprise me if you found Miss Leonora today out by the roadside assisting with the sale of Oak Crest's garden produce. And if that's the case, she is happy in the knowledge that any passerby will mistake her for the proprietress's mother or old-maid sister, and never suppose she is a paying guest. In her carefully got-up costume she sits there talking to her new friend. Or else she is in the house or in the chicken yard, talking away while she helps out with the chores. . . . It is Miss Leonora's way of killing time—killing time until night falls and she can take to the road again.

Miss Leonora is an intellectual woman, and at the same time she is an extremely practical and simple kind of person. This makes it hard for any two people to agree on what she is really like. It is hard even for those of us who were her favorites when we went to school to her. For, in the end, we didn't really know her any better than anybody else did. Sometimes she would have one of us up to her house for coffee and cookies on a winter afternoon, but it was hardly a social occasion. We went up there strictly as her students. We never saw any of the house except the little front room that she called her "office" and that was furnished with a roller-top desk, oak bookcases, and three or four of the hardest chairs you ever sat in. It looked more like a schoolroom than her own classroom did, over at the high school. While you sat drinking coffee with her, she was still your English teacher or your history teacher or your Latin teacher, whichever she happened to be at the time, and you were supposed to make conversation with her about *Silas Marner* or Tom Paine or Cicero. If it was a good session and you had shown a little enthusiasm, then she would talk to you some about your future and say you ought to begin thinking about college— because she was always going to turn her favorites into professional men. That was how she was going to populate the town with the sort of people she thought it ought to have. She never got but one of us to college, however, and he came back home as a certified druggist instead of the doctor she had wanted him to be. (Our doctors are always men who have moved in here from somewhere else, and our lawyers are people Miss Leonora wouldn't pay any attention to when they were in school.) . . . I used to love to hear Miss Leonora talk, and I went along with her and did pretty well till toward the end of my last year, when I decided that college wasn't for me. I ought to have gone to college, and I had no better reason for deciding against it than any of the others did. It was just that during all the years when Miss Leonora was talking to you about making something of yourself and making Thomasville a more civilized place to live in, you were hearing at home and everywhere else about what the Logans had done to the town and how they held themselves above everybody else. I got to feeling ashamed of being known as her protégé.

As I said, Miss Leonora is an intellectual woman. She seldom comes out of the post office without a book under her arm that she has specially ordered or that has come to her from one of the national book clubs she belongs to; and she also reads all the cheapest kind of trash that's to be had at the drugstore. She is just a natural-born reader, and enjoys reading the way other people enjoy eating or sleeping. It used to be that she would bedevil all the preachers we got here, trying to talk theology with them, and worry the life out of the lawyers with talk about Hamilton and Jefferson and her theories about men like Henry Clay and John Marshall. But about the time she quit teaching she gave up all that, too.

Aside from the drugstore trash, nobody knows what she reads any more, though probably it is the same as always. We sometimes doubt that she knows herself what she reads nowadays. Her reading seems to mean no more to her than her driving about the country does, and one wonders why she goes on with it, and what she gets out of it. Every night, the light in her office burns almost all night, and when she comes out of the post office with a new book, she has the wrappings off before she is halfway across the square and is turning the pages and reading away—a mile a minute, so it seems—as she strolls through the square and then heads up High Street toward Logana, which is what the Logans have always called their old house. If someone speaks to her, she pretends not to hear the first time. If it is important, if you want some information about the roads somewhere, you have to call her name a second time. The first sign that she is going to give you her attention comes when she begins moving her lips, hurriedly finishing off a page or a paragraph. Then she slams the book closed, as though she is through with it for all time, and before you can phrase your question she begins asking you how you and all your family are. Nobody can give a warmer greeting and make you feel he is gladder to see you than she can. She stands there beating the new book against her thigh, as though the book were some worthless object that she would just as soon throw away, and when she has asked you about yourself and your family she is ready then to talk about any subject under the sun—anything, I ought to add, except herself. If she makes a reference to the book in her hand, it is only to comment on the binding or the print or the quality of the paper. Or she may say that the price of books had gotten all out of bounds and that the postal rate for books is too high. It's always something that any field hand could understand and is a far cry from the way she used to talk about books when we were in school.

I am reminded of one day six or eight years ago when I saw Miss Leonora stopped on the square by an old colored man named Hominy Atkinson. Or his name may really be Harmony Atkinson. I once asked him which it was, and at first he merely grinned and shrugged his shoulders. But then he said thoughtfully, as though it hadn't ever occurred to him before, "Some does call me the one, I s'pose, and some the other." He is a dirty old ignoramus, and the other Negroes say that in the summertime he has his own private swarm of flies that follows him around. His flies were with him that day when he stopped Miss Leonora. He was in his wagon, the way you always see him, and he managed to block the old lady's path when she stepped down off the curb and began to cross the street in front of the post office and had cut diagonally across the courthouse lawn. It was the street over there on the other side of the square that she was about to cross. I was standing nearby with a group of men, under the willow oak trees beside the goldfish pool. Twice before Miss Leonora looked up, Hominy Atkinson lifted a knobby hand to shoo the flies away from his head. In the wagon he was seated on a squat split-bottom chair; and on another chair beside him was his little son Albert. Albert was eight or nine years old at the time, a plump little fellow dressed up in an old-fashioned Buster Brown outfit as tidy and clean as his daddy's rags were dirty.

This Albert is the son of Hominy and the young wife that Hominy took after he was already an old man. The three of them live on a worn-out piece of land three or four miles from town. Albert is a half-grown boy now, and there is nothing very remarkable about him except that they say he still goes to school more regularly than some of the other colored children do. But when he was a little fellow his daddy and mama spoiled and pampered him till, sitting up there in the wagon that day, he had the look of a fat little priss. The fact is, from the time he could sit up in a chair Hominy used never to go anywhere without him—he was so proud of the little pickaninny, and he was so mortally afraid something might happen to him when he was out of his sight. Somebody once asked Hominy why he didn't leave the child home with his mama, and Hominy replied that her hands were kept busy just washing and ironing and sewing for the boy. "It's no easy matter to raise up a clean child," he pronounced. Somebody else asked Hominy one time if he thought it right to take the boy to the square on First Monday, where he would be exposed to some pretty rough talk, or to the Fairgrounds during Fair Week. Hominy replied, "What ain't fittin' for him to hear ain't fittin' for me." And it was true that you seldom saw Hominy on that corner of the square where the Negro men congregated or in the stable yard at the Fairgrounds.

Before Miss Leonora looked up at Hominy that morning, he sat with his old rag of a hat in his lap, smiling down at her. Finally she slammed her book shut and lifted her eyes. But Hominy didn't try to ask his question until she had satisfied herself that he, his young wife, and Albert there beside him were in good health, and several other of his relatives whose names she knew. Then he asked it.

"What does you need today, Miss Leonora?" he said. "Me, *I* needs a dollar bill."

She replied without hesitating, "I don't need anything I'd pay *you* a dollar for, Hominy." Hominy didn't bat an eye, only sat there gazing down at her while she spoke. "I have a full herd of your kind up at Logana, Hominy, who'll fetch and go for me without any dollar bill. You know that."

She was referring to the Negro families who live in the out-buildings up at her place. People say that some of them live right in the house with her, but when I used to go up there as a boy she kept them all out of sight. There was not even a sound of them on the place. She didn't even let her cook bring in the coffee things, and it gave you the queer feeling that either she was protecting you from them or them from you.

"What do you think you need a dollar for, Hominy?" she asked presently.

"I needs to buy the boy a book," he said.

"What book?" It was summertime, and she knew the boy wouldn't be in school.

"Why, most any book," said Hominy. "I jist can't seem to keep him in reading."

Miss Leonora peered around Hominy at Albert, who sat looking down at his own fat little washed-up hands, as if he might be ashamed of his daddy's begging. Then Miss Leonora glanced down at the book she had got in the mail. "Here, give him this," she said, handing the brand-new book up to that old tatterdemalion. It was as if she agreed with the old ignoramus that it didn't matter what kind of book the boy got so long as it was a book.

And now Albert himself couldn't resist raising his eyes to see the book that was coming his way. He gave Miss Leonora a big smile, showing a mouthful of teeth as white as his starched shirt collar. "Miss Leonora, you oughtn't to do—" he began in an airy little voice.

But his daddy put a stop to it. "Hush your mouth, honey.

Miss Leonora knows what she's doing. Don't worry about that none." He handed the book over to Albert, hardly looking at it himself. Those of us over by the goldfish pool were never able to make out what the book was.

"I certainly thank you, Miss Leonora," Albert piped.

And Hominy said solemnly, "Yes'm, we are much obliged to you."

"Then move this conveyance of yours and let me pass," said Miss Leonora.

Hominy flipped the reins sharply on the rump of his mule and said, "Giddap, Bridesmaid." The old mule flattened its ears back on its head and pulled away with an angry jerk.

But even when the wagon was out of her way Miss Leonora continued to stand there for a minute or so, watching the receding figure of Albert perched on his chair in the wagon bed and bent over his book examining it the way any ordinary child would have examined a new toy. As long as she stood there the old lady kept her eyes on the little black boy. And before she finally set out across the street, we heard her say aloud and almost as if for our benefit, "It may be. . . . It may be. . . . I suppose, yes, it may be."

II

School integration is not yet a burning issue in Thomasville. But some men in town were at first opposed to consolidation of our county high schools until it could be seen what kind of pressures are going to be put on us. In the past eighteen months, however, those men have more or less reversed their position. And they do not deny that their change of mind was influenced by the possibility that Logana might be acquired for the site of the new school. Nor do they pretend that it is because they think Logana such an ideal location. They have agreed to go along with the plan, so they say, because it is the only way of getting rid of the little colony of

Negroes who have always lived up there and who would make a serious problem for us if it became a question of zoning the town, in some way, as a last barrier against integration. What they say sounds very logical, and any stranger would be apt to accept the explanation at face value. But the truth of the matter is that there are people here who dislike the memory of the Logans even more than they do the prospect of integration. They are willing to risk integration in order to see that last Logan dispossessed of his last piece of real estate in Thomasville. With them it is a matter of superstition almost that until this happens Thomasville will not begin to realize its immemorial aspirations to grow and become a citified place.

So that you will better understand this dislike of the Logan name, I will give you a few more details of their history here. In the beginning, and for a long while, the Logan family didn't seem to want to spoil Thomasville with their own presence even. General Logan laid out the town in 1816, naming it after a little son of his who died in infancy. But during the first generation the Logan wives stayed mostly over in Middle Tennessee, where they felt there were more people of their own kind. And the men came and went only as their interest in the cotton crops required. In those years, Logana was occupied by a succession of slave-driving overseers, as was also the Logans' other house, which used to stand five miles below here at Logan's Landing.

Now, we might have done without the Logan women and without the county seat, which the women didn't want here, but when the Logans kept the railroad out everybody saw the handwriting on the wall. The General's grandson did that. He was Harwell Logan, for many years chief justice of the state, and a man so powerful that in one breath, so to speak, he could deny the railroad company a right of way through town and demand that it give the name Logan Station to our nearest flag stop. . . . And what was it the chief justice's son did? Why, it was he who prevented the cotton mill and snuff fac-

tory from locating here. The snuff factory would have pol-
luted the air. And the cotton mill would have drawn in the
riffraff from all over the county. . . . Along about the turn of
the century it looked as though we were going to get the insane asylum for West Tennessee, but one of the Logans was
governor of the state; he arranged for it to go to Bolivar instead. Even by then, none of the Logan men were coming
back here very much except to hunt birds in the fall. They
had already scattered out and were living in the big cities
where there was plenty of industry and railroads for them to
invest their money in; and they had already sold off most of
their land to get the money to invest. But they didn't forget
Thomasville. No matter how far up in the world a Logan may
advance, he seems to go on having sweet dreams about Thomasville. Even though he has never actually lived here himself,
Thomasville is the one place he doesn't want spoilt.

Just after the First World War, there was talk of our getting
the new veterans' hospital. During the depression, we heard
about a CCC camp. At the beginning of the Second World
War, people came down from Washington and took option
on big tracts of land for "Camp Logan." Very mysteriously
all of those projects failed to materialize. Like everything else,
they would have spoiled the town. But what else is there, I ask
you, for a town to have except the things that tend to spoil it?
What else is there to give it life? We used to have a boys' academy here, and a girls' institute, which is where Miss Leonora
did her first teaching. They were boarding schools, and boys
and girls came here from everywhere, and spent their money
on the public square. It wasn't much, but it was *something*.

The boys' academy closed down before I was born even, and
there isn't a trace left of it. The Thomasville Female Institute
burned in 1922, and nothing is left of it, either, except the
crumbling shells of the old brick buildings. All we have now
that you don't see on the square is the cotton gin and the flour
mill and the ice plant. We claim a population of eighteen
hundred, counting white and colored, which is about five

hundred short of what we claimed in the year 1880. It has been suggested that in the next census we count the trees in Thomasville instead of the people. They outnumber us considerably and they have more influence, too. It was to save the willow oaks on the public square and the giant sycamores along High Street that someone arranged to have the Memphis-Chattanooga Bypass built in 1952 instead of bringing the new highway through town. It was some Logan who arranged that, you may be sure, and no doubt it gladdens his heart to see the new motels that have gone up out there and to know that the old hotel on the square is never overcrowded by a lot of silly tourists.

To my mind, Miss Leonora Logan is a very beautiful woman. But to think she is beautiful nowadays perhaps you would have to have first seen her as I did when I was not yet five years old. And perhaps you would have to have seen her under the same circumstances exactly.

I don't remember what the occasion was. We were on a picnic of some kind at Bennett's Wood, and it seems to me that half the town was there. Probably it was the Fourth of July, though I don't remember any flags or speeches. A band was playing in the bandstand, and as I walked along between my mother and father I noticed that the trunks of the walnut trees had been freshly whitewashed. The bare earth at the roots of the trees was still dappled with the droppings from the lime buckets. My father pointed out a row of beehives on the far edge of the grove and said he hoped to God nobody would stir the bees up today as some bad boys had once done when there was an outing at Bennett's Wood. My father smiled at Mother when he said this, and my guess is that he had been amongst the boys who did it. My mother smiled, too, and we continued our walk.

It was just before dusk. My impression is that the actual picnicking and the main events of the day were already over. I was holding my mother's hand as we came out from under the trees and into the clearing where Bennett's Pond is. Several groups were out on the pond in rowboats, drifting about among the lily pads. One boat had just drawn up to the grassy bank on the side where we were. My mother leaned toward my father and said in a quiet voice, "Look at Miss Leonora Logan. Isn't she beautiful!"

She was dressed all in white. She had stood up in the boat the moment it touched shore, and it seemed to me that she had risen out of the water itself and were about to step from one of the lily pads onto the bank. I was aware of her being taller than most women whose beauty I had heard admired, and I knew that she was already spoken of as an old maid— that she was older than my mother even; but when she placed the pointed toe of her white shoe on the green sod beside the pond, it was as if that lovely white point had pierced my soul and awakened me to a beauty I had not dreamed of. Her every movement was all lightness and grace, and her head of yellow hair dazzled.

The last rays of the sun were at that moment coming directly toward me across the pond, and presently I had to turn my face away from its glare. But I had the feeling that it was Miss Leonora's eyes and the burning beauty of her countenance that had suddenly blinded me, and when my mother asked me fretfully what was the matter and why I hung back so, I was ashamed. I imagined that Mother could read the thoughts in my head. I imagined also that my mother, who was a plain woman and who as the wife of the hotel-keeper made no pretension to elegance—I imagined that she was now jealous of my admiration for Miss Leonora. With my face still averted, I silently reproached her for having herself suggested the thoughts to me by her remark to my father. I was very angry, and my anger and shame must have brought a deep blush to my whole face and neck. I felt my mother's two fingers thrust under the collar of my middy, and then I was soothed by her sympathetic voice saying "Why, child, you're feverish. We'd better get you home."

I must have had many a glimpse of Miss Leonora when I was a small boy playing on the hotel porch. But the next profound impression she made on me was when I was nine years old. One of the boarding students at the Institute had been stealing the other girls' things. It fell to Miss Leonora to apprehend the thief, who proved to be none other than a member of the Logan clan itself—a sad-faced, unattractive girl, according to all reports, but from a very rich branch of the family. She had been sent back to Thomasville to school all the way from Omaha, Nebraska.

Several hours after Miss Leonora had obtained unmistakable evidence of the girl's guilt and had told her she was to be sent home, it was discovered that the girl had disappeared. Word got out in the town that they were dragging the moat around the old windmill on the Institute grounds for the girl's body. Soon a crowd of townspeople gathered on the lawn before the Institute, near to where the windmill stood. This windmill was no longer used to pump the school's water—the school had town water by then—and there was not even a shaft or any vanes in evidence. But the old brick tower had been left standing. With its moat of stagnant, mossy water around it, it was thought to be picturesque.

The crowd assembled on the lawn some fifty or sixty feet away from the tower, and from there we watched the two Negro men at their work in the moat. The moat was fed by a sluggish wet-weather spring. It was about twenty feet wide and was estimated to be from ten to fifteen feet deep. And so the two men had had to bring in a boat to do their work from. On the very edge of the moat stood Miss Leonora, alongside Dr. Perkins, the chancellor of the Institute, and with them were several other teachers in their dark-blue uniforms. They all kept staring up at the windows of the old brick residence hall, as if to make sure that none of the girls were peering out at the distressing scene.

Presently we heard one of the Negro men say something to

the other and heard the other mumble something in reply. We couldn't make out what they said, but we knew that they had found the girl's body. In a matter of two or three minutes they were hauling it up, and all of the women teachers except Miss Leonora buried their faces in their hands. From where we were, the slimy object was hardly recognizable as anything human, but despite this, or because of it, the crowd sent up a chorus of gasps and groans.

Hearing our chorus, Miss Leonora whirled about. She glared at us across the stretch of lawn for a moment, and then she came striding toward us, waving both hands in the air and ordering us to leave. "Go away! Go away!" she called out. "What business have you coming here with your wailing and moaning? A lot you care about that dead girl!" As she drew nearer, I could see her glancing at the ground now and then as if looking for a stick to drive us away with. "Go away!" she cried. "Take your curious eyes away. What right have you to be curious about *our* dead?"

A general retreat began, down the lawn and through the open gateway in the spiked iron fence. I hurried along with the others, but I kept looking back at Miss Leonora, who now stood on the brow of the terraced lawn, watching the retreat with a proud, bemused expression, seeming for the moment to have forgotten the dead young woman in the moat.

How handsome she was standing there, with her high color and her thick yellow hair that seemed about to come loose on her head and fall down on the shoulders of her blue shirt-waist.

Beyond her I had glimpses of the two Negro men lifting the dead body out of the water. They moved slowly and cautiously, but after they had got the girl into the boat and were trying to move her out of the boat onto the lawn, I saw the girl's head fall back. Her wet hair hung down like Spanish moss beneath her, and when the winter sunlight struck it, all at once it looked as green as seaweed. It was very beautiful, and yet, of course, I didn't feel right in thinking it was. It is something I have never been able to forget.

One day when we were in high school, a girl in the class asked Miss Leonora to tell us about "the Institute girl who did away with herself"—because Miss Leonora did sometimes tell us about the old days at the Institute. She stood looking out the classroom window, and seemed to be going over the incident in her mind and trying to decide whether or not it was something we ought to know more about. Finally she said, "No, we'll go on with the lesson now."

But the class, having observed her moment of indecision, began to beg. "Please tell us, Miss Leonora. Please." I don't know how many of the others had been in the crowd that day when they pulled the girl out of the moat. I was not the only one, I'm sure. I think that everybody knew most of the details and only wanted to see if she would refer to the way it ended with her driving the crowd away. But Miss Leonora wouldn't have cared at all, even if she had thought that was our motive. She would have given us her version if she had wanted to.

"Open your books," she said.

But still we persisted, and I was bold enough to ask, "Why not?"

"I'll just tell you why not," she said, suddenly blazing out at me. "Because there is nothing instructive in the story for you."

After that day, I realized, as never before, that though she often seemed to wander from the subject in class, it was never really so. She was eternally instructing us. If only once she had let up on the instruction, we might have learned something— or I might have. I used to watch her for a sign—any sign—of her caring about what we thought of her, or of her *not* caring about her mission among us, if that's what it was. More and more it came to seem incredible to me that she was the same woman I had gone feverish over at Bennett's Wood that time, which was probably before Miss Leonora had perceived her mission. And yet I have the feeling she was the same woman still. Looking back on those high-school days, I know that all along she was watching me and others like me for some kind of sign from us—any sign—that would make us seem worthy of knowing what we wanted to know about her.

I suppose that what we wanted to know, beyond any doubt, was that the old lady had suffered for being just what she was —for being born with her cold, rigid, intellectual nature, and for being born to represent something that had never taken root in Thomasville and that would surely die with her. But not knowing that that was what we wanted to know, we looked for other, smaller things. She didn't, for instance, have lunch in the lunchroom with the other teachers, and she didn't go home for lunch. She had a Negro woman bring her lunch to her on a tray all the way from Logana, on the other side of town. Generally she ate alone in her classroom. Sometimes we made excuses to go back to the room during lunch hour, and when we came out we pretended to the others that we had had a great revelation—that we had caught Miss Leonora Logan eating peas with her knife or sopping her plate with a biscuit. We never caught her doing anything so improper, of course, but it gave us a wonderful pleasure to imagine it.

It was while I was in high school that Miss Leonora inherited Logana. She had already been living in the house most of her life—all of it except for the years when she taught and lived at the Institute—but the house had really belonged to her grandfather's brother in St. Louis. The morning we heard she had inherited the place, we thought surely she would be in high spirits about her good fortune, and before she came into the room that morning one of the girls said she was going to ask her how it felt to be an heiress. It was a question that never got asked, however, because when our teacher finally appeared before us she was dressed in black. She had inherited the house where she had lived most of her life as a poor relation, but she was also in mourning for the dead great-uncle away off in St. Louis. For us it was impossible to detect either the joy over the one event or grief over the other. Perhaps she felt neither, or perhaps she had to hide her feelings because she felt that it was really the great-uncle's death in St. Louis she had inherited and the house in Thomasville she had lost. Our lessons went on that day as though nothing at all had happened.

But before I ever started going to the high school, and before Miss Leonora went there to teach, I had seen her on yet another memorable occasion up at the Institute—the most memorable and dramatic of all, because it was the night that the place burned down. I remember the events of that night very clearly. It was a February night in 1922. The temperature was in the low twenties, and no doubt they had thrown open the drafts in every one of the coal-burning heaters up at the Institute.

The fire broke out in the refectory and spread very rapidly to the residence hall and the classrooms bulding. Like any big fire, it quickly drew the whole town to the scene. Before most of us got there it was already out of hand. All over town the sky looked like Judgment Day. On the way to the fire, we could hear the floors of the old buildings caving in, one after the other; and so from the beginning there was not much anybody could do. The town waterworks couldn't get enough pressure up there to be of any real use, and after that girl drowned herself they had filled in the old moat around the windmill.

The first thing that happened after I got in sight of the place was that the gingerbread porches, which were already on fire, began to fall away from the buildings. There were porches on the second and third floors of the residence hall, and suddenly they fell away like flaming ladders that somebody had given a kick to. The banisters and posts and rafters fell out into the evergreen shrubbery, and pretty soon the smell of burning hemlock and cedar filled the air. . . . The teachers had got all the girls out safely, and the first men to arrive even saved some of the furniture and the books, but beyond that there was nothing to be done except to stand and watch the flames devour the innards of the buildings. This was very fascinating to everybody, and the crowd shifted from one point to another, always trying to get a better view and to see into which room or down which corridor the flames would move next.

Miss Leonora was as fascinated as any of the rest of us, and it was this about her that impressed me that night. It was not till later that I heard about how she behaved during the first phase of the fire. She had dashed about from building to building screaming orders to everyone, even to the fire brigade when it arrived. She would not believe it when the firemen told her that the water pressure could not be increased. She threw a bucket of water in one man's face when he refused to take that bucket and climb up a second-story porch with it.

I didn't see any of that. When I arrived, Miss Leonora was already resigned to the total loss that was inevitable. On a little knob of earth on the north side of the lawn, which people used to call the Indian Mound, she had taken her position all alone and isolated from the general crowd. The other teachers had been sent off with the Institute girls to the hotel, where my mother was waiting to receive them. But wrapped in a black fur cape—it was bearskin, I think, and must have been a hand-me-down from some relative—Miss Leonora was seated on one of the iron benches that were grouped over there on the mound. Her only companions were two iron deer that stood nearby, one with its head lowered as if grazing, the other with its iron antlers lifted and its blank iron eyes fixed on the burning buildings.

She sat there very erect, looking straight ahead. It was hard to tell whether she was watching the flames or watching the people watch the flames. Perhaps she was fascinated equally by both. It was all over for her. She knew that practically nothing was going to be saved, but still she wanted to see how it would go. Now and then a shaft of flame would shoot up into the overcast sky, lighting up the mixture of cloud and smoke above us, and also lighting up the figure of Miss Leonora over on the mound. Some of the women whispered amongst themselves, "Poor Miss Leonora! The school was her life." But if you caught a glimpse of her in one of those moments when the brightest light was on her, it wasn't self-pity or despair you saw written on her face. You saw her, awareness of what was going on around her, and a kind of curiosity about it all that seemed almost inhuman and that even a child was bound to resent somewhat. She looked dead herself, but at the same time very much alive to what was going on around her.

III

When Miss Leonora's house was condemned two weeks ago, *somebody* had to break the news to her. They couldn't just send the clerk up there with the notice, or, worse still, let her read it in the newspaper. The old lady had to be warned of how matters had gone. . . . We left the courthouse at four o'clock that afternoon, and set out for the Logan place on foot. None of us wanted to go, but who else would go if we didn't? That was how Judge Potter had put it to us. I suppose we elected to go on foot merely because it would take longer to get up there that way.

It was while we walked along under the sycamores on High Street that I let the others talk me into doing the job alone. They said that I had, after all, been her very favorite—by which they meant only that I was her first favorite—and that if we went in a group she might take it as a sign of cowardice, might even tell us it was that to our faces. It was a funny business, and we laughed about it a little amongst ourselves, though not much. Finally I agreed that the other three men should wait behind the sumac and elderberry down in the Lane, while I went up to see Miss Leonora alone.

Once this was settled, the other three men turned to reminiscing about their experiences with Miss Leonora when they were in high school. But I couldn't concentrate on what they said. It may have been because I knew their stories so well. Or maybe it wasn't that. At any rate, when we had walked two blocks up High Street I realized that I was out of cigarettes, and I told the others to wait a minute while I stepped into the filling station, on the corner there, to buy a package. When I paid for the cigarettes, Buck Wallace, who operates the station, looked at me and said, "Well, how did it go? Do we condemn?"

I nodded and said, "We're on the way up there to tell her, Buck."

"I guessed you were," he said. He glanced out the window at the others, and I looked out at them, too. For a second it seemed that I was seeing them through Buck Wallace's eyes—them and myself. And the next second it seemed, for some reason, that I was seeing them through Miss Leonora's eyes—them and myself. We all had on our business suits, our light-weight topcoats, our gray fedoras; we were the innkeeper, the druggist, a bank clerk, and the rewrite man from the weekly paper. Our ages range from thirty to fifty—with me at the top —but we were every one of us decked out to look like the same kind of thing. We might have just that minute walked out of the Friday-noon meeting of the Exchange Club. In Buck Wallace's eyes, however, we were certainly not the cream of the Exchange Club crop—*not* the men who were going to get Thomasville its due. And in Miss Leonora's eyes we were a cut above the Exchange Club's ringleaders, though not enough above them to matter very much. To both her and Buck we were merely the go-betweens. It just happened that we were the last people left in town that the old lady would speak to, and so now we—or, rather, I—was going up to Logana and tell her she would have to accept the town's terms of unconditional surrender.

"You may be too late," Buck added as I was turning away. I looked back at him with lifted eyebrows. "She was in here a while ago," he went on to report, "getting her car gassed up. She said how she was about to take off on one of her trips. She said she might wait till she heard from the courthouse this afternoon and again she might not. . . . She was got up kind of peculiar."

When I rejoined the other men outside, I didn't tell them what Buck had said. Suddenly I mistrusted them, and I didn't trust myself. Or rather I knew I *could* trust myself to let *them* have their way if they thought Miss Leonora was about to leave town. I was pretty sure she wouldn't leave without hearing from us, and I was pretty sure they would want to head us back to the courthouse immediately and send official word up there before she could get away. It would have been the wise thing to do, but I didn't let it happen.

In the filling station Buck Wallace had said to me that she was "got up kind of peculiar," and that meant to my understanding, that Miss Leonora was dressed in one of two ways. Neither was a way that I had ever seen her dressed, and I wanted to see for myself. It meant either that she was got up in a lot of outmoded finery or she was wearing her dungarees! Because that is how, for ten years now, the old lady has been turning up at the tourist homes where she stops, and that is how, if you wanted to recognize her on the road, you would have to watch out for her. Either she would be in her finery—with the fox fur piece, and the diamond earrings, and the high-crowned velvet hat, and the kind of lace choker that even old ladies don't generally go in for any more and that Miss Leonora has never been seen to wear in Thomasville except by a very few—or she would be in her dungarees! The dungarees are the hardest to imagine, of course. With them she wears a home-knit, knee-length cardigan sweater. And for headgear she pulls on a big poke bonnet she has resurrected from somewhere, or sometimes she stuffs her long hair up under a man's hunting cap or an old broad-brimmed straw hat. A queer sight she must present riding about the countryside these autumn nights; and if she rides with the top of her convertible put back, as I've heard of her doing in the dead of winter even, why, it's enough to scare any children who may see her, and some grown people, too. . . . Here in Thomasville, only Buck Wallace and a few others have seen her so garbed, and they only rarely, only sometimes when she was setting out on a trip. They say she looks like some inmate who has broken out of the asylum over at Bolivar.

But that's how she turns up at the tourist homes. If she is with the two old maids at Boxwood Manor or Maple Lawn, she affects the choker and the diamond earrings. She sits down in their parlor and removes the high-crowned velvet, and she talks about how the traditions and institutions of our country have been corrupted and says that soon not one stone will be left upon another. And, still using such terms and phrases, she will at last get round to telling them the story of her life and the history of the Logan family in Thomasville. She tells it all in the third person, pretending it is some friend of hers she has in mind, and the family of that friend. But the old maids know right along that it is herself she is speaking of, and they say she seems to know they know it and seems not to care. . . . And if she is with the farm couple at Oak Crest, then she's in her dungarees. She at once sets about helping with the chores, if they will let her. She talks religion to them and says there is no religion left amongst the people in the towns, says that they have forsaken the fountain of living waters and hewed them out broken cisterns that can hold no water—and something like that. And finally she gets round to telling *them* her story, again pretending that it is some friend of hers she is speaking of, and again with her listeners knowing it is herself. The farm couple won't like seeing an old woman wearing dungarees, but they will catch the spirit of her getup, and they understand what it means. For they have known other old women there in the country who, thrown entirely on their own, living alone and in desperate circumstances, have gotten so they dress in some such outrageous way. And the two old maids probably still have some eye for fashion and they find Miss Leonora pretty ridiculous. But they remember other old ladies who did once dress like that, and it seems somehow credible that there might still be one somewhere.

When Miss Leonora is at home in Thomasville, it is hard to believe she ever dresses herself up so. Here we are used to seeing her always in the most schoolteacherish, ready-made-looking clothes. After the Institute burned, she changed from the uniform that the Institute teachers wore to what amounts to a uniform for what our high-school teachers—the drab kind of street dresses that can be got through the mail-order catalogues. Right up till two weeks ago, that's how we were still seeing the old lady dressed. It was hard to realize that in her old age she had had a change of heart and was wishing that either she had played the role of the spinster great lady the way it is usually played or that she had married some dirt farmer and spent her life working alongside him in the fields.

I even used to think that perhaps Miss Leonora didn't really want to go off masquerading around the country—that it was a kind of madness and meant something that would be much more difficult to explain, and that all the time she was at home she was dreading her next seizure. Recently, however, I've come to realize that that wasn't the case. For years her only satisfaction in life has been her periodic escapes into a reality that is scattered in bits and pieces along the highways and back roads of the country she travels. And what I hope above all else is that Miss Leonora *is* stopping today at Oak Crest or Boxwood Manor and *does* have on her dungarees or lace choker.

But now I must tell what makes me doubt that she is, after all, staying at one of those tourist homes she likes, and what makes me afraid that we may never see her here again.

I left the other men down at the corner of the Lane and went up the dirt driveway to Logana alone. Her car was parked at the foot of the porch steps, and so there was no question about her being there. I saw her first through one of the sidelights at the front door and wasn't sure it was she. Then she opened the door, saying, "Dear boy, come in." I laughed, it was so unlike her to call me that. That was not her line at all. She laughed, too, but it was a kind of laugh that was supposed to put me at my ease rather than to criticize or commend me, which would have been very much more in her line. . . . I saw at a glance that this wasn't the Miss Leonora I had known, and wasn't one that I had heard about from her tourist-home friends, either.

She had done an awful thing to her hair. Her splendid white mane, with its faded yellow streaks and its look of being kept up on her head only by the two tortoise-shell combs at the back, was no more. She had cut it off, thinned it, and set it in little waves close to her head, and, worse still, she must have washed it in a solution of indigo bluing. She had powdered the shine off her nose, seemed almost to have powdered its sharpness and longness away. She may have applied a little rouge and lipstick, though hardly enough to be noticeable, only enough to make you realize it wasn't the natural coloring of an old lady and enough to make you *think* how old she was. And the dress she had on was exactly right with the hair and the face, though at first I couldn't tell why.

As I walked beside her from the center hall into her "office," her skirt made an unpleasant swishing sound that seemed out of place in Miss Leonora's house and that made me observe more closely what the dress was really like. It was of a dark silk stuff, very stiff, with a sort of middy-blouse collar, and sleeves that stopped a couple of inches above the wrists, and a little piece of belt in back, fastened on with two big buttons,—very stylish, I think. For a minute I couldn't remember where it was I had seen this very woman before.

Then it came to me. All that was lacking was a pair of pixie glasses with rhinestone rims, and a half dozen bracelets on her wrists. She was one of those old women who come out here from Memphis looking for antiques and country hams and who tell you how delighted they are to find a southern town that is truly unchanged.

Even so, I half expected Miss Leonora to begin by asking me about my family and then about what kind of summer I had had. "Now, I know you have had a fine summer—all summers are fine to a boy your age," she would say. "So don't tell me what you have been doing. Tell me what you have been *thinking,* what you have been *reading.*" It was the room that made me imagine she would still go on that way. Because the room was the same as it used to be. Even the same coffee cups and blue china coffeepot were set out on the little octagonal oak table, beside the plate of butter cookies. And for a moment I had the same guilty feeling I used always to have; because, of course, I hadn't been reading anything and hadn't been thinking anything she would want to hear about.

What she actually said was much kinder and was what anybody might have said under the circumstances. "I've felt so bad about your having to come here like this. I knew they would put it off on you. Even you must have dreaded coming, and you must hate me for putting you in such a position."

"Why, no. I wanted to come, Miss Leonora," I lied. "And I hope you have understood that I had no part in the proceedings." It was what, for months, I had known I would say, and it came out very easily.

"I do understand that," she said. "And we don't even need to talk about any of it."

But I said, "The county court has granted the writ condemning your property. They will send a notice up to you tomorrow morning. You ought to have had a lawyer represent you, and you ought to have come yourself."

I had said what I had promised Judge Potter I would say;

she had her warning. And now I was on my own. She motioned me to sit down in a chair near the table where the
coffee things were. When she poured out the coffee into our
two cups, it was steaming hot. It smelled the way it used to
smell in that room on winter afternoons, as fresh as if it were
still brewing on the stove. I knew she hadn't made it herself,
but, as in the old days, too, the Negro woman who had made
it didn't appear or make a sound in the kitchen. You wouldn't
have thought there was one of them on the place. There didn't
seem to be another soul in the house but just herself and me.
But *I* knew that the house was full of them, really. And there
was still the feeling that either she was protecting me from
them or them from me. I experienced the old uneasiness in
addition to something new. And as for Miss Leonora, she
seemed to sense from the start that the other three men were
waiting down the Lane—the three who had been even less
willing than I to come, and who were that much nearer to the
rest of the town in their feelings. Several times she referred to
them, giving a little nod of her head in the direction of the
very spot where I had left them waiting.

"When I think of the old days, the days when I used to have
you up here—you and the others, too—I realize I was too hard
on you. I asked too much of my pupils. I know that now."

It was nothing like the things the real Miss Leonora used to
say. It was something anybody might have said.

And a little later: "I was unrealistic. I tried to be to you
children what I thought you needed to have somebody be.
That's a mistake, always. One has to try to be with people
what they want one to be. Each of *you* tried to be that for me,
to an admirable degree. Tim Hadley tried hardest—he went
to college—but he didn't have your natural endowments."
Then she took pains to say something good and something
forgiving about each of the four. And, unless I imagined it, for
each of those that hadn't come up with me she gave another

nod in the direction of the elderberry and sumac thicket down at the corner.

"We were a dumb bunch, all along the line," I said, not meaning it—or not meaning it about myself.

"Nonsense. You were all fine boys, and *you* were my brightest hope," she said, with an empty cheerfulness.

"But you can't make a silk purse out of—" I began.

"Nonsense," she said again. "It was neither you nor I that failed." But she didn't care enough to make any further denial or explanation. She set her cup down on the table and rose from her chair. "It's been like old times, hasn't it," she said with a vague smile.

I looked away from her and sat gazing about the office, still holding my empty cup in my hand. It hadn't been like old times at all, of course. The room and the silence of the house were the same, but Miss Leonora was already gone, and without her the house was nothing but a heap of junk. I thought to myself that the best thing that could happen would be for them to begin moving out the furniture and moving out the Negroes and tearing the place down as soon as possible. Suddenly, I spied her black leather traveling bag over beside the doorway, and she must have seen my eyes light upon it. "I'm about to get off on a little trip," she said.

I set my cup down on the table and looked up at her. I could see she was expecting me to protest. "Will it be long?" I asked, not protesting.

"I don't know, dear boy. You know how I am."

I glanced at the traveling bag again, and this time I noticed her new cloth coat lying on the straight chair beside the bag. I got up and went over and picked up the coat and held it for her.

On the way out to the car, I kept reminding myself that this was really Miss Leonora Logan and that she was going away before receiving any official notice of the jury's verdict. Finally, when we were standing beside her car and she was waiting for me to put the bag, which I was carrying, inside the car, I looked squarely into her eyes. And there is no denying it; the eyes were still the same as always, not just their hazel color but their expression, their look of awareness—awareness of you, the individual before her, a very flattering awareness until presently you realized it was merely of you as an individual in her scheme of things for Thomasville. She was still looking at me as though I were one of the village children that she would like so much to make something of. I opened the car door. I tossed the bag into the space behind the driver's seat. I even made sure I did the thing to her satisfaction by putting one hand out to her elbow as she slipped stiffly in under the steering wheel.

Neither of us made any pretense of saying good-bye. I stood there and watched the car as it bumped along down the driveway, raising a little cloud of dust in the autumn air. The last I saw of her was a glimpse of her bluinged head through the rear window of her convertible. When she turned out into the Lane and headed away from town toward the bypass, I knew that the other three men would be watching. But they wouldn't be able to see how she was got up, and I knew they would hardly believe me when I told them.

I have told nearly everybody in town about it, and I think nobody really believes me. I have almost come to doubt it myself. And, anyway, I like to think that in her traveling bag she had the lace-choker outfit that she could change into along the way, and the dungarees, too; and that she is stopping at her usual kind of place today and is talking to the proprietors about Thomasville. Otherwise, there is no use in anyone's keeping an eye out for her. She will look too much like a thousand others, and no doubt will be driving on the highway the way everybody else does, letting other people pass her, dimming her lights for everyone. Maybe she even drives in the daytime, and maybe when she stops for the night it is at a big, modern motel with air-conditioning and television in every room. The postcards she sends us indicate nothing about how she is dressed, of course, or about where and in what kind of places she is stopping. She says only that she is in good health, that it is wonderful weather for driving about the country, and that the roads have been improved everywhere. She says nothing about when we can expect her to come home.

A Wife of Nashville

The Lovells' old cook Sarah had quit to get married in the spring, and they didn't have anybody else for a long time—not for several months. It was during the Depression, and when a servant quit, people in Nashville (and even people out at Thornton, where the Lovells came from) tried to see how long they could go before they got another. All through the summer, there would be knocks on the Lovells' front door or on the wooden porch floor, by the steps. And when one of the children or their mother went to the door, some Negro man or woman would be standing there, smiling and holding out a piece of paper. A recommendation it was supposed to be, but the illegible note scribbled with a blunt lead pencil was something no white person could have written if he had tried. If Helen Ruth, the children's mother, went to the door, she always talked a while to whoever it was, but she hardly ever even looked at the note held out to her. She would give a piece of advice or say to meet her around at the back door for a handout. If one of the boys—there were three Lovell boys, and no girls—went to the door, he always brought the note in to Helen Ruth, unless John R., their father, was at home, sick with his back ailment. Helen Ruth would shake her head and say to tell whoever it was to go away! "Tell him to go back home," she said once to the oldest boy, who was standing in the sun-parlor doorway with a smudged scrap of paper in his hand. "Tell him if he had any sense, he never would have left the country."

"He's probably not from the country, Mother."

"They're all from the country," Helen Ruth said. "When they knock on the porch floor like that, they're bound to be from the country, and they're better off at home, where somebody cares something about them. I don't care anything about them any more than you do."

But one morning Helen Ruth hired a cheerful-looking and rather plump, light-complexioned young Negro girl named Jess McGehee, who had come knocking on the front-porch floor just as the others had. Helen Ruth talked to her at the front door for a while; then she told her to come around to the kitchen, and they talked there for nearly an hour. Jess stayed to fix lunch and supper, and after she had been there a few days, the family didn't know how they had ever got along without her.

In fact, Jess got on so well with the Lovells that Helen Ruth even decided to let her come and live on the place, a privilege she had never before allowed a servant of hers. Together, she and Jess moved all of John R.'s junk—a grass duck-hunting outfit, two mounted stags' heads, an outboard motor, and so on—from the little room above the garage into the attic of the house. John R. lent Jess the money for the down payment on a "suit" of furniture, and Jess moved in. "You would never know she was out there," Helen Ruth told her friends. "There is never any rumpus. And her room! It's as clean as yours or mine."

Jess worked for them for eight years. John R. got so one of

his favorite remarks was, "The honeymoon is over, but this is the real thing this time." Then he would go on about what he called Helen Ruth's "earlier affairs." The last one before Jess was Sarah, who quit to get married and go to Chicago at the age of sixty-eight. She had been with them for six years and was famous for her pies and her banana dishes.

Before Sarah, there was Carrie. Carrie had been with them when the two younger boys were born, and it was she who had once tried to persuade Helen Ruth not to go to the hospital but to let her act as midwife. She had quit them after five years, to become an undertaker. And before Carrie there was Jane Blakemore, the very first of them all, whom John R. and Helen Ruth had brought with them from Thornton to Nashville when they married. She lasted less than three years; she quit soon after John R., Jr., was born, because, she said, the baby made her nervous.

"It's an honorable record," John R. would say. "Each of them was better than the one before, and each one stayed with us longer. It proves that experience is the best teacher."

Jess's eight years were the years when the boys were growing up; the boys were children when she came, and when she left, the youngest, little Robbie, had learned to drive the car. In a sense, it was Jess who taught all three boys to drive. She didn't give them their first lessons, of course, because, like Helen Ruth, she had never sat at the wheel of an automobile in her life. She had not ridden in a car more than half a dozen times when she came to the Lovells, but just by chance, one day, she was in the car when John R. let John R., Jr., take the wheel. The car would jerk and lunge forward every time the boy shifted gears, and his father said, "Keep your mind on what you're doing."

"I am," John R., Jr., said, "but it just does that. What makes it do it?"

"Think!" John R. said. "Think! . . . *Think!*"

"I *am* thinking, but what makes it do it?"

Suddenly, Jess leaned forward from the back seat and said, "You letting the clutch out too fast, honey."

Both father and son were so surprised they could not help laughing. They laughed harder, of course, because what Jess said was true. And Jess laughed with them. When they had driven another block, they reached a boulevard stop, and in the process of putting on the brake John R., Jr., killed the engine and then flooded the motor. His father shouted, "Well, let it rest! We're just stuck here for about twenty minutes!"

Jess, who was seated with one arm around a big bag of groceries, began to laugh again. "Turn off the key," she said. "Press down on the starter a spell. Then torectly you turn on the key and she'll start."

John R. looked over his shoulder at her, not smiling, but not frowning, either. Presently, he gave the order, "Try it."

"Try what *Jess said?*" John R., Jr., asked.

"Try what Jess said."

The boy tried it, and in a moment he was racing the motor and grinning at his father. When they had got safely across the boulevard, John R. turned around to Jess again. He asked in a quiet, almost humble manner—the same manner he used when describing the pains in his back to Helen Ruth—where she had learned these things about an automobile. "Law," she said, "I learnt them listening to my brother-in-law that drives a truck talk. I don't reckon I really know'm, but I can say them."

John R. was so impressed by the incident that he did not make it one of his stories. He told Helen Ruth about it, of course, and he mentioned it sometimes to his close friends when they were discussing "the good things" about Negroes. With his sons, he used it as an example of how much you can learn by listening to other people talk, and after that day he would permit John R., Jr., to go for drives in the car without him provided Jess went along in his place. Later on, when the other boys got old enough to drive, there were periods when he turned their instruction over to Jess. Helen Ruth even talked of learning to drive, herself, with the aid of Jess. But it never came to more than talk with Helen Ruth, though John R. encouraged her, saying he thought driving was perhaps a serious strain on his back. She talked about it for several months, but in the end she said that the time had passed when she could learn new skills. When John R. tried to encourage her in the idea, she would sometimes look out one of the sun-parlor windows toward the street and think of how much she had once wanted to learn to drive. But that had been long ago, right after they were married, in the days when John R. had owned a little Ford coupé. John R. was on the road for the Standard Candy Company then, and during most of the week she was alone in their apartment at the old Vaux Hall. While he was away John R. kept the coupé stored in a garage only two blocks east, on Broad Street; in those days traveling men still used the railroads, because Governor Peay hadn't yet paved Tennessee's highways. At that time, John R. had not believed in women driving automobiles, and Helen Ruth had felt that he must be right about it; she had even made fun of women who went *whizzing* about town, blowing horns at every intersection. Yet in her heart she had longed to drive that coupé! Jane Blakemore was working for them then, and one day Jane had put Helen Ruth's longings into words. "Wouldn't it be dandy," she said, "if me and you clomb in that car one of these weekdays and toured out to Thornton to see all the folks—white and black?"

Without a moment's hesitation, however, Helen Ruth gave the answer that she knew John R. would have given. "Now, think what you're saying, Jane!" she said. "Wouldn't we be a fool-looking pair pulling into the Square at Thornton? *Think* about it. What if we should have a flat tire when we got out about as far as Nine Mile Hill? Who would change it? *You* certainly couldn't! Jane Blakemore, I don't think you use your head about anything!"

That was the way Helen Ruth had talked to Jane on more occasions than one. She was a plain-spoken woman, and she never spoke plainer to anyone than she did to Jane Blakemore during the days when they were shut up together in that apartment at the Vaux Hall. Since Jane was from Thornton and knew how plain-spoken all Helen Ruth's family were, she paid little attention to the way Helen Ruth talked to her. She would smile, or else sneer, and go on with her work of cooking and cleaning. Sometimes she would rebel and speak just as plainly as Helen Ruth did. When Helen Ruth decided to introduce butter plates to their table, Jane said, "I ain't never heard tell of no butter dishes."

Helen Ruth raised her eyebrow. "That's because you are an ignoramus from Thornton, Tennessee," she said.

"I'm ignoramus enough to know ain't no need in nastying up all them dishes for me to wash."

Helen Ruth had, however, made Jane Blakemore learn to use butter plates and had made her keep the kitchen scrubbed and the other rooms of the apartment dusted and polished and in such perfect order that even John R. had noticed it when he came on week ends. Sometimes he had said, "You drive yourself too hard, Helen Ruth."

Jess McGehee was as eager and quick to learn new things as Jane Blakemore had been unwilling and slow. She would even put finger bowls on the breakfast table when there was grapefruit. And how she did spoil the three boys about their food! There were mornings when she cooked the breakfast eggs differently for each one of them while John R. sat and shook his had in disgust at the way she was pampering his sons. John R.'s "condition" in his back kept him at home a lot of the time during the eight years Jess was with them. He had long since left off traveling for the candy company; soon after the first baby came, he had opened an insurance agency of his own.

When Jane Blakemore left them and Helen Ruth hired Carrie (after fifteen or twenty interviews with other appli-

cants), she had had to warn Carrie that John R.'s hours might
be very irregular, because he was in business for himself and
wasn't able merely to punch a time clock and quit when the
day ended. "He's an onsurance man, ain't he?" Carrie had
asked and had showed by the light in her eyes how favorably
impressed she was. "I know about him," she had said. "He's
a life-onsurance man, and that's the best kind to have."

At that moment, Helen Ruth thought perhaps she had
made a mistake in Carrie. "I don't like my servant to discuss
my husband's business," she said.

"No'm!" Carrie said with enthusiasm. "No, *ma'am!*" Helen
Ruth was satisfied, but afterward she had often to tell herself
that her first suspicion had been right. Carrie was nosy and
prying and morbid—and she gossiped with other people's
servants. Her curiosity and her gossiping were especially trying for Helen Ruth during her and John R.'s brief separation. They actually had separated for nearly two months right
after Kenneth, the middle boy, was born. Helen Ruth had
gone to her father's house at Thornton, taking the two babies
and Carrie with her. The boys never knew about the trouble
between their parents, of course, until Kenneth pried it out
of his mother after they were all grown, and, at the time,
people in Nashville and Thornton were not perfectly sure
that it was a real separation. Helen Ruth had tried to tell
herself that possibly Carrie didn't know it was a real separation. But she was never able to deny completely the significance of Carrie's behavior while they were at Thornton.
Carrie's whole disposition had seemed to change the afternoon
they left Nashville. Up until then, she had been a moody,
shifty, rather loud-mouthed brown woman, full of darky com-
pliments for white folks and of gratuitous promises of extra
services she seldom rendered. But at Thornton she had put
the old family servants to shame with her industriousness
and her respectful, unassuming manner. "You don't find them
like Carrie in Thornton any more," Helen Ruth's mother

said. "The good ones all go to Nashville or Memphis." But Helen Ruth, sitting by an upstairs window one afternoon, saw her mother's cook and Carrie sauntering toward the back gate to meet a caller. She saw Carrie being introduced and then she recognized the caller as Jane Blakemore. Presently the cook returned to the kitchen and Helen Ruth saw Carrie and Jane enter the servants' house in the corner of the yard. During the hour that they visited there, Helen Ruth sat quietly by the window in the room with her two babies. It seemed to her the most terrible hour of her separation from John R. When Carrie and Jane reappeared on the stoop of the servants' house and Carrie was walking with Jane to the gate, there was no longer any doubt in Helen Ruth's mind but that she would return to her husband, and return without any complaints or stipulations. During that hour she had tried to imagine exactly what things the black Jane and the brown Carrie were talking about, or, rather, *how* and in what terms they were talking about the things they must be talking about. In her mind, she reviewed the sort of difficulties she had had with Jane and the sort she had with Carrie and tried to imagine what defense they would make for themselves— Jane for her laziness and contrariness, Carrie for her usual shiftiness and negligence. Would they blame her for these failings of theirs? Or would they blandly pass over their own failings and find fault with her for things that she was not even aware of, or that she could not help and could not begin to set right? Had she really misused these women, either the black one or the brown one? It seemed to her then that she had so little in life that she was entitled to the satisfaction of keeping an orderly house and to the luxury of efficient help. There was too much else she had not had—an "else" nameless to her, yet sorely missed—for her to be denied these small satisfactions. As she sat alone with her two babies in the old nursery and thought of the two servants gossiping about her, she became an object of pity to herself. And presently John

R., wherever he might be at that moment—in his office or at
the club or, more likely, on a hunting or fishing trip somewhere—became an object of pity, too. And her two babies,
one in his crib and the other playing on the carpet with a
string of spools, were objects of pity. Even Carrie, standing
alone by the gate after Jane had gone, seemed a lone and
pitiful figure.

A few days later, Helen Ruth and Carrie and the two baby
boys returned to Nashville.

In Nashville, Carrie was herself again; everything was done
in her old slipshod fashion. Except during that interval at
Thornton, Carrie was never known to perform any task to
Helen Ruth's complete satisfaction. Hardly a meal came to
the table without the soup or the dessert or some important
sauce having been forgotten; almost every week something
important was left out of the laundry; during a general cleaning the upper sashes of two or three windows were invariably
left unwashed. Yet never in her entire five years did Carrie
answer back or admit an unwillingness to do the most menial
or the most nonessential piece of work. In fact, one of her
most exasperating pronouncements was, "You are exactly
right," which was often followed by a lengthy description of
how she would do the thing from then on, or an explanation
of how it happened that she had forgotten to do it. Not only
that, she would often undertake to explain to Helen Ruth
Helen Ruth's reason for wanting it done. "You are exactly
right and I know how you mean. You want them drapes shut
at night so it can seem like we're living in a house out in the
Belle Meade instead of this here Vox Hall flat, and some fool
might be able to look in from the yard."

"Never mind the reasons, Carrie" was Helen Ruth's usual
reply. But her answers were not always so gentle—not when
Carrie suggested that she have the second baby at home with
Carrie acting as midwife, not when Carrie spoke to her about

having the third baby circumcised. And the day that Helen Ruth began packing her things to go to Thornton, she was certain that Carrie would speak out of turn with some personal advice. That would have been more than she could bear, and she was prepared to dismiss Carrie from her service and make the trip alone. But neither then nor afterward did Carrie give any real evidence of understanding the reasons for the trip to Thornton.

In fact, it was not until long afterward, when Carrie had quit them to become an undertaker, that Helen Ruth felt that Carrie's gossip with other Nashville servants had, by accident, played a part in her separation from John R. She and John R. had talked of separation and divorce more than once during the first two years they were married, in the era of Jane Blakemore. It was not that any quarreling led to this talk but that each accused the other of being dissatisfied with their marriage. When John R. came in from traveling, on a week end or in the middle of the week—he was sometimes gone only two or three days at a time—he would find Helen Ruth sitting alone in the living room, without a book or even a deck of cards to amuse herself with, dressed perhaps in something new her mother had sent her, waiting for him. She would rise from her chair to greet him, and he would smile in frank admiration of the tall, graceful figure and of the countenance whose features seemed always composed, and softened by her hair, which was beginning to be gray even at the time of their marriage. But he had not come home many times before Helen Ruth was greeting him with tears instead of smiles. At first, he had been touched, but soon he began to complain that she was unhappy. He asked her why she did not see something of other people while he was away—the wives of his business and hunting friends, or some of the other Thornton girls who were married and living in Nashville. She replied that she did see them occasionally but that she was not the sort of woman who enjoyed having a lot of women friends. Besides, she was perfectly happy with her present life; it was only that she believed that he must be unhappy and that he no longer enjoyed her company. She understood that he had to be away most of the week, but even when he was in town, she saw very little of him. When he was not at his office, he was fishing out on Duck River or was off to a hunt up at Gallatin. And at night he either took her to parties with those hunting people, with whom she had little or nothing in common, or piled up on the bed after supper and slept. All of this indicated that he was not happy being married to her, she said, and so they talked a good deal about separating.

After the first baby came, there was no such talk for a long time—not until after the second baby. After the first baby came, Helen Ruth felt that their marriage must be made to last, regardless of hers or John R.'s happiness. Besides, it was at that time that one of John R.'s hunting friends—a rich man named Rufus Brantley—had secured the insurance agency for him; and almost before John R. opened his office, he had sold policies to other rich hunting friends that he had. For a while, he was at home more than he had ever been before. But soon, when his business was established, he began to attend more and more meets and trials, all over Tennessee and Alabama and Kentucky. He even acquired a few dogs and a horse of his own. With his friends he began to go on trips to distant parts of the country. It seemed that when he was not deer hunting in the State of Maine, he was deep-sea fishing in the Gulf. Helen Ruth did sometimes go with him to the local horse shows, but one night, at the Spring Horse Show, she had told Mrs. Brantley that she had a new machine, and Mrs. Brantley had thought she meant an automobile instead of a sewing machine. That, somehow, had been the last straw. She would never go out with "people like the Brantleys" after that. She was pregnant again before the first baby was a year old, and this soon became her excuse for going nowhere in the evening. The women she did visit with very occasionally in the daytime were those she had known as girls in Thornton, women whose husbands were bank tellers and office managers and were barely acquainted with John R. Lovell.

After the second baby came, Helen Ruth saw these women more frequently. She began to feel a restlessness that she could not explain in herself. There were days when she could not stay at home. With Carrie and the two babies, she would traipse about town, on foot or by streetcar, to points she had not visited since she was a little girl and was in Nashville with her parents to attend the State Fair or the Centennial. She went to the Capitol, to Centennial Park and the Parthenon, even out to the Glendale Zoo. Once, with Nancy Tolliver and Lucy Parkes, two of her old Thornton friends, she made an excursion to Cousin Mamie Lovell's farm, which was several miles beyond the town of Franklin. They went by the electric inter-urban to Franklin, and from there they took a taxi to the farm. Cousin Mamie's husband had been a second cousin of John R.'s father, and it was a connection the Thornton Lovells had once been very proud to claim. But for a generation this branch of the family had been in decline. Major Lovell had been a prominent lawyer in Franklin and had been in politics, but when he died, he left his family "almost penniless." His boys had not gone to college; since the farm was supposed to have been exhausted, they did not try to farm it but clerked in stores in Franklin. There was said to be a prosperous son-in-law in St. Louis, but the daughter was dead and Cousin Mamie was reported to have once called her son-in-law a parvenu to his face. Helen Ruth and her friends made the excursion because they wanted to see the house, which was one of the finest old places in the country and full of antiques.

But Cousin Mamie didn't even let them inside the house. It was a hot summer day, and she had all the blinds closed and the whole L-shaped house shut up tight, so that it would be bearable at night. She received them on the long ell porch. Later, they moved their chairs out under a tree in the yard, where Cousin Mamie's cook brought them a pitcher of iced tea. While they were chatting under the tree that afternoon, they covered all the usual topics that are dealt with when talking to an old lady one doesn't know very well—the old times, mutual friends and family connections, country living and city living, and always, of course, the lot of woman as it relates to each topic.

"Where are you and John R. living?" Cousin Mamie asked Helen Ruth.

"We're still at the Vaux Hall, Cousin Mamie."

"I'd suppose the trains would be pretty bad for noise there, that close to the depot."

"They're pretty bad in the summer."

"I'd suppose you had a place out from town, seeing how often John R.'s name's in the paper with the hound and hunt set."

"That's John R.'s life," Helen Ruth said, "not mine."

"He runs with a fine pack, I must say," said Cousin Mamie.

Nancy Tolliver and Lucy Parkes nodded and smiled. Lucy said, "The swells of Nashville, Miss Mamie."

But Cousin Mamie said, "There was a day when they weren't the swells. Forty years ago, people like Major Lovell didn't know people like the Brantleys. I think the Brantleys quarried limestone, to begin with. I guess it don't matter, though, for when I was a girl in upper East Tennessee, people said the Lovells started as land speculators hereabouts and at Memphis. But I don't blame you for not wanting to fool with Brantleys, Helen Ruth."

"John R. and I each live our own life, Cousin Mamie."

"Helen Ruth is a woman with a mind of her own, Miss Mamie," Nancy Tolliver said. "It's too bad more marriages can't be like theirs, each living their own life. Everyone admires it as a real achievement."

And Lucy Parks said, "Because a woman's husband hunts is no reason for her to hunt, any more than because a man's wife sews is any reason for him to sew."

"Indeed not," Cousin Mamie said, actually paying little attention to what Lucy and Nancy were saying. Presently, she continued her own train of thought. "Names like Brantley and Partee and Hines didn't mean a thing in this state even thirty years ago."

What Lucy and Nancy said about her marriage that day left Helen Ruth in a sort of daze and at the same time made her see her situation more clearly. She had never discussed her marriage with anybody, and hearing it described so matter-of-factly by these two women made her understand for the first time what a special sort of marriage it was and how unhappy she was in it. At the time, John R. was away on a fishing trip to Tellico Plains. She did not see him again before she took the babies and Carrie to Thornton. She sent a note to his office saying that she would return when he decided to devote his time to his wife and children instead of to his hounds and horses. While she was at Thornton her letters from John R. made no mention of her note. He wrote about his business, about his hounds and horses, about the weather, and he always urged her to hurry home as soon as she had seen everybody and had a good visit. Meanwhile, he had a room at the Hermitage Club.

When Helen Ruth returned to Nashville, their life went on as before. A year later, the third boy, Robbie, was born, and John R. bought a large bungalow on Sixteenth Avenue, not too far from the Tarbox School, where they planned to send the boys. Carrie was with them for three years after the separation, and though her work did not improve, Helen Ruth found herself making excuses for her. She began to attribute Carrie's garrulity to a "certain sort of bashfulness, or the Negro equivalent to bashfulness." And with the three small boys, and the yard to keep, too, there was so much more for Carrie to do than there had been before! Despite the excuses she made for her, Helen Ruth could see that Carrie was plainly getting worse about everything and that she now seemed to take pleasure in lying about the smallest, most un-important things. But Helen Ruth found it harder to con-front Carrie with her lies or to reprimand her in any way.

During the last months before Carrie quit, she would talk sometimes about the night work she did for a Negro under-taker. To make Helen Ruth smile, she would report things she had heard about the mourners. Her job, Carrie always said, was to sweep the parlors after the funeral and to fold up the chairs. It was only when she finally gave notice to Helen Ruth that she told her what she professed was the truth. She explained that during all those months she had been learning to embalm. "Before you can get a certificate," she said, "you has to handle a bad accident, a sickness, a case of old age, a drowning, a burning, and a half-grown child or less. I been waiting on the child till last night, but now I'll be getting my certificate."

Helen Ruth would not even let Carrie go to the basement to get her hat and coat. "You send somebody for them," she said. "But, *you,* you get off these premises, Carrie!" She was sincerely outraged by what Carrie had told her, and when she looked at Carrie's hands she was filled with new horror. Yet something kept her from saying all the things that one normally said to a worthless, lying servant who had been guilty of one final outrage. *"Leave,* Carrie!" she said, con-sciously restraining herself. *"Leave* this place!" Carrie went out the kitchen door and down the driveway to the street, bareheaded, coatless, and wearing her kitchen slippers.

After Carrie, there was old Sarah, who stayed with them for six years and then quit them to get married and go to Chicago. Sarah was too old to do heavy work even when she first came, and before she had been there a week, John R. had been asked to help move the sideboard and to bring the lad-

der up from the basement. He said it seemed that every minute he was in the house, he was lifting or moving something
that was too much for Sarah. Helen Ruth replied that perhaps
she should hire a Negro man to help in the house and look
after the yard. But John R. said no, he was only joking, he
thought Sarah far and away the best cook they had ever had,
and besides business conditions didn't look too good and it
was no time to be taking on more help. But he would always
add he did not understand why Helen Ruth babied Sarah so.
"From the first moment old Sarah set foot in this house, Helen
Ruth has babied her," he would say to people in Helen
Ruth's presence.

Sarah could neither read nor write. Even so, it took her
only a short while to learn all Helen Ruth's special recipes
and how to cook everything the way the Lovells liked it. For
two weeks, Helen Ruth stayed in the kitchen with Sarah, reading to her from *How We Cook in Tennessee* and giving detailed instructions for every meal. It was during that time
that her great sympathy for Sarah developed. Sarah was completely unashamed of her illiteracy, and it was this that first
impressed Helen Ruth. She admired Sarah for having no false
pride and for showing no resentment of her mistress's impatience. She observed Sarah's kindness with the children. And
she learned from Sarah about Sarah's religious convictions
and about her long, unhappy marriage to a Negro named
Morse Wilkins, who had finally left her and gone up North.

While Sarah was working for them, John R. and Helen
Ruth lived the life that Helen Ruth had heard her friends
describe to John R.'s Cousin Mamie. It was not until after
Sarah had come that Helen Ruth, recalling the afternoon at
Cousin Mamie's, identified Lucy Parkes's words about a wife's
sewing and a husband's hunting as the very answer she had
once given to some of Carrie's impertinent prying. That afternoon, the remark had certainly sounded familiar, but she had
been too concerned with her own decision to leave her hus-

band to concentrate upon anything so trivial. And after their reconciliation, she tried not to dwell on things that had led her to leave John R. Their reconciliation, whatever it meant to John R., meant to her the acceptance of certain mysteries— the mystery of his love of hunting, of his choice of friends, of his desire to maintain a family and home of which he saw so little, of his attachment to her, and of her own devotion to him. Her babies were now growing into little boys. She felt that there was much to be thankful for, not the least of which was a servant as fond of her and of her children as Sarah was. Sarah's affection for the three little boys often reminded Helen Ruth how lonely Sarah's life must be.

One day, when she had watched Sarah carefully wrapping up little Robbie in his winter play clothes before he went out to play in the snow, she said, "You love children so much, Sarah, didn't you ever have any of your own?"

Sarah, who was a yellow-skinned woman with face and arms covered with brown freckles, turned her gray eyes and fixed them solemnly on Helen Ruth. "Why, I had the cutest little baby you ever did see," she said, "and Morse went and killed it."

"Morse *killed* your baby?"

"He rolled over on it in his drunk sleep and smothered it in the bed."

After that, Helen Ruth would never even listen to Sarah when she talked about Morse, and she began to feel a hatred toward any and all of the men who came to take Sarah home at night. Generally, these men were the one subject Sarah did not discuss with Helen Ruth, and their presence in Sarah's life was the only serious complaint Helen Ruth made against her. They would come sometimes as early as four in the after-noon and wait on the back porch for Sarah to get through. She knew that Sarah was usually feeding one of them out of her kitchen, and she knew that Sarah was living with first one and then another of them, but when she told John R. she was going to put her foot down on it, he forbade her to do so. And so through nearly six years she tolerated this weakness of Sarah's. But one morning in the late spring Sarah told her that Morse Wilkins had returned from up North and that she had taken him back as her husband. Helen Ruth could not find anything to say for a moment, but after studying the large diamond on her engagement ring for awhile she said, "My servant's private life is her own affair, but I give you fair warning now, Sarah, I want to see no more of your men friends—Morse or *any other*—on this place again."

From that time, she saw no more men on the place until Morse himself came, in a drunken rage, in the middle of a summer's day. Helen Ruth had been expecting something of the sort to happen. Sarah had been late to work several times during the preceding three weeks. She had come one morning with a dark bruise on her cheek and said she had fallen getting off the streetcar. Twice, Helen Ruth had found Sarah on her knees, praying in the kitchen. The day Helen Ruth heard the racket at the back-porch door, she knew at once that it was Morse. She got up from her sewing machine and went directly to the kitchen. Sarah was on the back porch, and Morse was outside the screen door of the porch, which was hooked on the inside. He was a little man, shriveled up, baldheaded, not more than five feet tall, and of a complexion very much like Sarah's. Over his white shirt he wore a dark sleeveless sweater. "You come on home," he was saying as he shook the screen door.

Helen Ruth stepped to the kitchen door. "Is that her?" Morse asked Sarah, motioning his head toward Helen Ruth.

When Sarah turned her face around, her complexion seemed several shades lighter than Morse's. "I got to go," she said to Helen Ruth.

"No, Sarah, *he's* got to go. But *you* don't."

"He's gonna leave me again."

"That's the best thing that could happen to you, Sarah."

Sarah said nothing, and Morse began shaking the door again.

"Is he drunk, Sarah?" Helen Ruth asked.

"He's so drunk I don't know how he find his way here."

Helen Ruth went out onto the porch. "Now, you get off this place, and quick about it," she said to Morse.

He shook the screen door again. "You didn't make me come here, Mrs. Lovellel, and you can't make me leave, Mrs. Lovellel."

"I can't make you leave," Helen Ruth said at once, "but there's a bluecoat down on the corner who can."

Suddenly Sarah dropped to her knees and began praying. Her lips moved silently, and gradually she let her forehead come to rest on the top of the rickety vegetable bin. Morse looked at her through the screen, putting his face right against the wire. "Sarah," he said, "you come on home. You better come on now if you think I be there."

Sarah got up off her knees.

"I'm going to phone the police," Helen Ruth said, pretending to move toward the kitchen.

Morse left the door and staggered backward toward the driveway. "Come on, Sarah," he shouted.

"I got to go," Sarah said.

"I won't let you go, Sarah!"

"She can't make you stay!" Morse shouted. "You better come on if you coming!"

"It will be the worst thing you ever did in your life, Sarah," said Helen Ruth. "And if you go with him, you can't ever come back here. He'll kill you someday, too—the way he did your baby."

Sarah was on her knees again, and Morse was out of sight but still shouting as he went down the driveway. Suddenly, Sarah was on her feet. She ran into the kitchen and on through the house to the front porch.

Helen Ruth followed, calling her back. She found Sarah on

the front porch waving to Morse, who was halfway down the block, running in a zigzag down the middle of the street, still shouting at the top of his voice. Sarah cried out to him, "Morse! Morse!"

"Sarah!" Helen Ruth said.

"Morse!" Sarah cried again, and then she began mumbling words that Helen Ruth could not quite understand at the time. Afterward, going over it in her mind, Helen Ruth realized that what Sarah had been mumbling was, "If I don't see you no more on this earth, Morse, I'll see you in Glory."

Sarah was with the Lovells for four more months, and then one night she called up on the telephone and asked John R., Jr., to tell his mother that she was going to get married to a man named Racecar and they were leaving for Chicago in the morning.

Jess McGehee came to them during the Depression. Even before Sarah left the Lovells, John R. had had to give up all of his "activities" and devote his entire time to selling insurance. Rufus Brantley had shot himself through the head while cleaning a gun at his hunting lodge, and most of John R.'s other hunting friends had suffered the same financial reverses that John R. had. The changes in the Lovells' life had come so swiftly that Helen Ruth did not realize for awhile what the changes meant in her relationship with John R. It seemed as though she woke up one day and discovered that she was not married to the same man. She found herself spending all her evenings playing Russian bank with a man who had no interest in anything but his home, his wife, and his three boys. Every night, he would give a brief summary of the things that had happened at his office or on his calls, and then he would ask her and the boys for an account of everything they had done that day. He took an interest in the house and the yard, and he and the boys made a lily pool in the back yard, and singlehanded he screened in the entire front porch. Sometimes he took the whole family to Thornton for a week end, and he and Helen Ruth never missed the family reunions there in September.

In a sense, these were the happiest years of their married life. John R.'s business got worse and worse, of course, but since part of their savings was in the bank at Thornton that did not fail, they never had any serious money worries. Regardless of their savings, however, John R.'s loss of income and his having to give up his friends and his hunting wrought very real, if only temporary changes in him. There were occasions when he would sit quietly and listen to his family's talk without correcting them or pointing out how foolish they were. He gave up saying "Think!" to the boys, and instead would say, "Now, let's see if we can't reason this thing out." He could never bring himself to ask for any sympathy from Helen Ruth for his various losses, but as it was during this time that he suffered so from the ailment in his back (he and Helen Ruth slept with boards under their mattress for ten years), the sympathy he got for his physical pain was more than sufficient. All in all, it was a happy period in their life, and in addition to their general family happiness they had Jess.

Jess not only cooked and cleaned, she planned the meals, did the marketing, and washed everything, from handkerchiefs and socks to heavy woolen blankets. When the boys began to go to dances, she even learned to launder their dress shirts. There was nothing she would not do for the boys or for John R. or for Helen Ruth. The way she idealized the family became the basis for most of the "Negro jokes" told by the Lovells during those years. In her room she had a picture of the family, in a group beside the lily pool, taken with her own box Brownie; she had tacked it and also a picture of each of them on the wall above her washstand. In her scrapbook she had pasted every old snapshot and photograph that Helen Ruth would part with, as well as old newspaper pictures of

John R. on horseback or with a record-breaking fish he had caught. She had even begged from Helen Ruth an extra copy of the newspaper notice of their wedding.

Jess talked to the family a good deal at mealtime, but only when they had addressed her first and had shown that they wanted her to talk. Her remarks were mostly about things that related to the Lovells. She told a sad story about a "very loving white couple" from Brownsville, her home town, who had been drowned in each other's arms when their car rolled off the end of a river ferry. The point of the story was that those two people were the same, fine, loving sort of couple that John R. and Helen Ruth were. All three of the boys made good grades in school, and every month Jess would copy their grades in her scrapbook, which she periodically passed around for the family to appreciate. When Kenneth began to write stories and articles for his high-school paper, she would always borrow the paper overnight; soon it came out that she was copying everything he wrote onto the big yellow pages of her scrapbook.

After three or four years, John R. began to say that he thought Jess would be with them always and that they would see the day when the boys' children would call her "Mammy." Helen Ruth said she would like to agree with him about that, but actually she worried, because Jess seemed to have no life of her own, which wasn't at all natural. John R. agreed that they should make her take a holiday now and then. Every summer, they would pack Jess off to Brownsville for a week's visit with her kinfolks, but she was always back in her room over the garage within two or three days; she said that her people fought and quarreled so much that she didn't care for them. Outside her life with the Lovells, she had only one friend. Her interest was the movies, and her friend was "the Mary who works for Mrs. Dunbar." Jess and Mary went to the movies together as often as three or four times a week, and on Sunday afternoons Mary came to see Jess or Jess went to see Mary, who lived over the Dunbar's garage. Jess always took along her scrapbook and her most recent movie magazines. She and Mary swapped movie magazines, and it was apparent from Jess's talk on Monday mornings that they also swapped eulogies of their white families.

Sometimes Helen Ruth would see Mrs. Dunbar downtown or at a P.-T.A. meeting; they would discuss their cooks and smile over the reports that each had received of the other's family. "I understand that your boys are all growing into very handsome men," Mrs. Dunbar said once, and she told Helen Ruth that Jess was currently comparing one of the boys— Mrs. Dunbar didn't know which one—to Neil Hamilton, and that she was comparing Helen Ruth to Irene Rich, and John R. to Edmund Lowe. As the boys got older, they began to resent the amount of authority over them—though it was small—that Jess had been allowed by their parents and were embarrassed if anyone said Jess had taught them to drive the car. When John R., Jr., began at the university, he made his mother promise not to let Jess know what grades he received, and none of the boys would let Jess take snapshots of them any more. Their mother tried to comfort Jess by saying that the boys were only going through a phase and that it would pass in time. One day, she even said this in the presence of Robbie, who promptly reported it to the older boys, and it ended with John R., Jr.'s, complaining to his father that their mother ought not to make fun of them to Jess. His father laughed at him but later told Helen Ruth that he thought she was making a mistake, that the boys were getting big enough to think about their manly dignity, and that she would have to take that into consideration.

She didn't make the same mistake again, but although Jess never gave any real sign of her feelings being hurt, Helen Ruth was always conscious of how the boys were growing away from their good-natured servant. By the time Robbie was sixteen, they had long since ceased to have any personal conversation with Jess, and nothing would have induced Robbie to submit to taking drives with her but the knowledge that his father would not allow him to use the car on dates until he had had months of driving practice. Once, when Robbie and Jess returned from a drive, Jess reported, with a grin, that not a word had passed between them during the entire hour and a half. Helen Ruth only shook her head sadly. The next day she bought Jess a new bedside radio.

The radio was the subject of much banter among the boys and their father. John R. said Helen Ruth had chosen the period of hard times and the Depression to become more generous with her servant than she had ever been before in her life. They recalled other presents she had given Jess recently, and from that time on they teased her regularly about how she spoiled Jess. John R. said that if Jess had had his back trouble, Helen Ruth would have retired her at double pay and nursed her with twice the care that he received. The boys teased her by saying that at Christmas time she reversed the custom of shopping for the servant at the ten-cent stores and for the family at the department stores.

Yet as long as Jess was with them, they all agreed that she was the best help they had ever had. In fact, even afterward, during the war years, when John R.'s business prospered again and his back trouble left him entirely and the boys were lucky enough to be stationed near home and, later, continue their education at government expense, even then John R. and the boys would say that the years when Jess was with them were the happiest time of their life and that Jess was the best servant Helen Ruth had ever had. They said that, and then there would be a silence, during which they were probably thinking about the summer morning just before the war when Jess received a telephone call.

When the telephone rang that morning, Helen Ruth and John R. and the boys had just sat down to breakfast. As was usual in the summertime, they were eating at the big drop-leaf table in the sun parlor. Jess had set the coffee urn by Helen Ruth's place and was starting from the room when the telephone rang. Helen Ruth, supposing the call was for a member of the family, and seeing that Jess lingered in the doorway, said for her to answer it there in the sun parlor instead of running to the telephone in the back hall.

Jess answered it, announcing whose residence it was in a voice so like Helen Ruth's that it made the boys grin. For a moment, everyone at the table kept silent. They waited for Jess's eyes to single out one of them. John R., Jr., and Kenneth even put down their grapefruit spoons. But the moment Jess picked up the instrument, she fixed her eyes on the potted fern on the window seat across the room. At once her nostrils began to twitch, her lower lip fell down, and it seemed only an act of will that she was twice able to say, "Yes, ma'am," in answer to the small, unreal, metallic voice.

When she had replaced the telephone on its cradle, she turned quickly away and started into the dining room. But Helen Ruth stopped her. "Jess," she asked, her voice full of courtesy, "was the call for you?"

Jess stopped, and they all watched her hands go up to her face. Without turning around, she leaned against the door jamb and began sobbing aloud. Helen Ruth sprang up from the table, saying, "Jess, honey, what *is* the matter?" John R. and the boys stood up, too.

"It was a telegram for me—from Brownsville."

Helen Ruth took her in her arms. "Is someone dead?"

Between sobs, Jess answered, "My little brother—our baby brother—the only one of 'em I cared for." Then her sobs became more violent.

Helen Ruth motioned for John R. to move the morning paper from the big wicker chair, and she led Jess in that direction. But Jess would not sit down, and she could not be pulled away from Helen Ruth. She held fast to her, and

Helen Ruth continued to pat her gently on the back and to try to console her with gentle words. Finally, she said, "Jess, you must go to Brownsville. Maybe there's been some mistake. Maybe he's not dead. But you must go, anyway."

Presently, Jess did sit in the chair, and dried her eyes on Helen Ruth's napkin. The boys shook their heads sympathetically and John R. said she certainly must go to Brownsville. She agreed, and said she believed there was a bus at ten that she would try to catch. Helen Ruth patted her hand, telling her to go along to her room when she felt like it, and said that *she* would finish getting breakfast.

"I want to go by to see Mary first," Jess said, "so I better make haste." She stood up, forcing a grateful smile. Then she burst into tears again and threw her arms about Helen Ruth, mumbling, "Oh, God! Oh, God!" The three boys and their father saw tears come into Helen Ruth's eyes, and through her tears Helen Ruth saw a change come over their faces. It was not exactly a change of expression. It couldn't be that, she felt, because it was exactly the same on each of the four faces. It hardly seemed possible that so similar a change could reflect four men's individual feelings. She concluded that her own emotion, and probably the actual tears in her eyes, had made her imagine the change, and when Jess now pulled away and hurried off to her room, Helen Ruth's tears had dried and she could see no evidence of the change she had imagined in her husband's and her sons' faces.

While Jess was in her room preparing to leave, they finished breakfast. Then Helen Ruth began clearing the table, putting the dishes on the teacart. She had said little while they were eating, but in her mind she was all the while going over something that she knew she must tell her family. As she absent-mindedly stacked the dishes, her lips moved silently over the simple words she would use in telling them. She knew that they were watching her, and when Robbie offered to take Jess to the bus station, she knew that the change she had seen in all their faces had been an expression of sympathy for *her as* well as of an eagerness to put this whole episode behind them. "I'll take Jess to her bus," he said.

But Helen Ruth answered, in the casual tone she had been preparing to use, that she thought it probably wouldn't be the thing to do.

"Why, what do you mean, Helen Ruth?" John R. asked her.

"It was very touching, mother," Kenneth said in his new, manly voice, "the way she clung to you." He, too, wanted to express sympathy, but he also seemed to want to distract his mother from answering his father's question.

At that moment, Jess passed under the sun-parlor windows, walking down the driveway, carrying two large suitcases. Helen Ruth watched her until she reached the sidewalk. Then, very quietly, she told her family that Jess McGehee had no baby brother and had never had one. "Jess and Mary are leaving for California. They think they're going to find themselves jobs out there."

"You knew that right along?" John R. asked.

"I knew it right along."

"Did she know you did, Helen Ruth?" he asked. His voice had in it the sternness he used when questioning the boys about something.

"No, John R., she did not. I didn't learn it from her."

"Well, I don't believe it's so," he said. "Why, I don't believe that for a minute. Her carrying on was too real."

"They're going to California. They've already got their two tickets. Mrs. Dunbar got wind of it somehow, by accident, from Mrs. Lon Thompson's cook, and she called me on Monday. They've saved their money and they're going."

"And you let Jess get away with all that crying stuff just now?" John R. said.

Helen Ruth put her hands on the handle bar of the teacart. She pushed the cart a little way over the tile floor but stopped when he repeated his question. It wasn't to answer his question that she stopped, however. "Oh, my dears!" she said, addressing her whole family. Then it was a long time before she said anything more. John R. and the three boys remained seated at the table, and while Helen Ruth gazed past them and toward the front window of the sun parlor, they sat silent and still, as though they were in a picture. What could she say to them, she kept asking herself. And each time she asked the question, she received for answer some different memory of seemingly unrelated things out of the past twenty years of her life. These things presented themselves as answers to her question, and each of them seemed satisfactory to her. But how little sense it would make to her husband and her grown sons, she reflected, if she should suddenly begin telling them about the long hours she had spent waiting in that apartment at the Vaux Hall while John R. was on the road for the Standard Candy Company, and in the same breath should tell them about how plainly she used to talk to Jane Blakemore and how Jane pretended that the baby made her nervous and went back to Thornton. Or suppose she should abruptly remind John R. of how ill at ease the wives of his hunting friends used to make her feel and how she had later driven Sarah's worthless husband out of the yard, threatening to call a bluecoat. What if she should suddenly say that because a woman's husband hunts, there is no reason for *her* to hunt, any more than because a man's wife sews, there is reason for him to sew. She felt that she would be willing to say anything at all, no matter how cruel or absurd it was, if it would make them understand that everything that happened in life only demonstrated in some way the lonesomeness that people felt. She was ready to tell them about sitting in the old nursery at Thornton and waiting for Carrie and Jane Blakemore to come out of the cabin in the yard. If it would make them see what she had been so long in learning to see, she would even talk at last about the "so much else" that had been missing from her life and that she had not been able to name, and about the foolish mysteries she had so nobly accepted upon her reconciliation with John R. To her, these things were all one now; they were her loneliness, the loneliness from which everybody, knowingly or unknowingly, suffered. But she knew that her husband and her sons did not recognize her loneliness or Jess McGehee's or their own. She turned her eyes from the window to look at their faces around the table, and it was strange to see that they were still thinking in the most personal and particular terms of how they had been deceived by a servant, the ignorant granddaughter of an ignorant slave, a Negro woman from Brownsville who was crazy about the movies and who would soon be riding a bus, mile after mile, on her way to Hollywood, where she might find the friendly faces of the real Neil Hamilton and the real Irene Rich. It was with effort that Helen Ruth thought again of Jess McGehee's departure and the problem of offering an explanation to her family. At last, she said patiently, "My dears, don't you see how it was for Jess? How else can they tell us anything when there is such a gulf?" After a moment she said, "How can I make you understand this?"

Her husband and her three sons sat staring at her, their big hands, all so alike, resting on the breakfast table, their faces stamped with identical expressions, not of wonder but of incredulity. Helen Ruth was still holding firmly to the handle of the teacart. She pushed it slowly and carefully over the doorsill and into the dining room, dark and cool as an underground cavern, and spotlessly clean, the way Jess McGehee had left it.

What You Hear From 'Em?

———

Sometimes people misunderstood Aunt Munsie's question, but she wouldn't bother to clarify it. She might repeat it two or three times, in order to drown out some fool answer she was getting from some fool white woman, or man, either. "What you hear from 'em?" she would ask. And, then, louder and louder: "What you hear from 'em? *What you hear from em?*" She was so deaf that anyone whom she thoroughly drowned out only laughed and said Aunt Munsie had got so deaf she couldn't hear it thunder.

It was, of course, only the most utterly fool answers that ever received Aunt Munsie's drowning-out treatment. She was, for a number of years at least, willing to listen to those who mistook her "'em" to mean any and all of the Dr. Tolliver children. And for more years than that she was willing to listen to those who thought she wanted just *any* news of her two favorites among the Tolliver children—Thad and Will. But later on she stopped putting the question to all insensitive and frivolous souls who didn't understand that what she was interested in hearing—and *all* she was interested in hearing—was when Mr. Thad Tolliver and Mr. Will Tolliver were going to pack up their families and come back to Thornton for good.

They had always promised her to come back—to come back sure enough, once and for all. On separate occasions, both Thad and Will had actually given her their word. She had not seen them together for ten years, but each of them had made visits to Thornton now and then with his own family. She would see a big car stopping in front of her house on a Sunday afternoon and see either Will or Thad with his wife and children piling out into the dusty street—it was nearly always summer when they came—and then see them filing across the street, jumping the ditch, and unlatching the gate to her yard. She always met them in that pen of a yard, but long before they had jumped the ditch she was clapping her hands and calling out "Hai-ee! Hai-ee, now! Look-a-here! Whee! Whee! Look-a-here!" She had got so blind that she was never sure whether it was Mr. Thad or Mr. Will until she had her arms around his waist. They had always looked a good deal alike, and their city clothes made them look even more alike nowadays. Aunt Munsie's eyes were so bad, besides being so full of moisture on those occasions, that she really recognized them by their girth. Will had grown a regular wash pot of a stomach and Thad was still thin as a rail. They would sit on her porch for twenty or thirty minutes—whichever one it was and his family—and then they would be gone again.

Aunt Munsie would never try to detain them—not seriously. Those short little old visits didn't mean a thing to her. He—Thad or Will—would lean against the banister rail and tell her how well his children were doing in school or college, and she would make each child in turn come and sit beside her on the swing for a minute and receive a hug around the waist or shoulders. They were timid with her, not seeing her any more than they did, but she could tell from their big Tolliver smiles that they liked her to hug them and make over them. Usually, she would lead them all out to her back yard and show them her pigs and dogs and chickens. (She always had at least one frizzly chicken to show the children.) They would traipse through her house to the back yard and then traipse through again to the front porch. It would be time for them to go when they came back, and Aunt Munsie would look up at *him*—Mr. Thad or Mr. Will (she had begun calling them "Mr." the day they married) —and say, "Now, look-a-here. When you comin' back?"

Both Thad and Will knew what she meant, of course, and whichever it was would tell her he was making definite plans to wind up his business and that he was going to buy a certain piece of property, "a mile north of town" or "on the old River Road," and build a jim-dandy house there. He would say, too, how good Aunt Munsie's own house was looking, and his wife would say how grand the zinnias and cannas looked in the yard. (The yard was all flowers—not a blade of grass, and the ground packed hard in little paths between the flower beds.) The visit was almost over then. There remained only the exchange of presents. One of the children would hand Aunt Munsie a paper bag containing a pint of whisky or a carton of cigarettes. Aunt Munsie would go to her back porch or to the pit in the yard and get a fern or a wandering Jew, potted in a rusty lard bucket, and make Mrs. Thad or Mrs. Will take it along. Then the visit was over, and they would leave. From the porch Aunt Munsie would wave good-by with one hand and lay the other hand, trembling slightly, on the banister rail. And sometimes her departing guests, looking back from the yard, would observe that the banisters themselves were trembling under her hand—so insecurely were those knobby banisters attached to the knobby porch pillars. Often as not Thad or Will, observing this, would remind his wife that Aunt Munsie's porch banisters and pillars had come off a porch of the house where he had grown up. (Their father, Dr. Tolliver, had been one of the first to widen his porches and remove the gingerbread from his house.) The children and their mother would wave to Aunt Munsie from the street. Their father would close the gate, resting his hand a moment on its familiar wrought-iron frame, and wave to her before he jumped the ditch. If the children had not gone too far ahead, he might even draw their attention to the iron fence which, with its iron gate, had been around the yard at the Tolliver place till Dr. Tolliver took it down and set out a hedge, just a few weeks before he died.

But such paltry little visits meant nothing to Aunt Munsie. No more did the letters that came with "her things" at Christmas. She was supposed to get her daughter, Lucrecie, who lived next door, to read the letters, but in late years she had taken to putting them away unopened, and some of the presents, too. All she wanted to hear from *them* was when they were coming back for good, and she had learned that the Christmas letters never told her that. On her daily route with her slop wagon through the Square, up Jackson Street, and down Jefferson, there were only four or five houses left where she asked her question. These were houses where the amount of pig slop was not worth stopping for, houses where one old maid, or maybe two, lived, or a widow with one old bachelor son who had never amounted to anything and ate no more than a woman. And so—in the summertime, anyway—she took to calling out at the top of her lungs, when she approached the house of one of the elect, "What you hear from 'em?" Sometimes a Miss Patty or a Miss Lucille or a Mr. Ralph would get up out of a porch chair and come down the brick walk to converse with Aunt Munsie. Or sometimes one of them would just lean out over the shrubbery planted around the porch and call, "Not a thing, Munsie. Not a thing lately."

She would shake her head and call back, "Naw. Naw. Not a thing. Nobody don't hear from 'em. Too busy, they be."

Aunt Munsie's skin was the color of a faded tow sack. She was hardly four feet tall. She was generally believed to be totally bald, and on her head she always wore a white dust cap with an elastic band. She wore an apron, too, while making her rounds with her slop wagon. Even when the weather got bad and she tied a wool scarf about her head and wore an overcoat, she put on an apron over the coat. Her hands and feet were delicately small, which made the old-timers sure she was of Guinea stock that had come to Tennessee out of South Carolina. What most touched the hearts of old ladies on Jackson and Jefferson Streets were her little feet. The sight of her feet "took them back to the old days," they said, because Aunt Munsie still wore flat-heeled, high button shoes. Where ever did Munsie find such shoes any more?

She walked down the street, down the very center of the street, with a spry step, and she was continually turning her head from side to side, as though looking at the old houses and trees for the first time. If her sight was as bad as she sometimes let on it was, she probably recognized the houses only by their roof lines against the Thornton sky. Since this was nearly thirty years ago, most of the big Victorian and ante-bellum houses were still standing, though with their lovely ginger-bread work beginning to go. (It went first from houses where there was someone, like Dr. Tolliver, with a special eye for style and for keeping up with the times.) The streets hadn't yet been broadened—or only Nashville Street had—and the maples and elms met above the streets. In the autumn, their leaves covered the high banks and filled the deep ditches on either side. The dark macadam surfacing itself was barely wide enough for two automobiles to pass. Aunt Munsie, pulling her slop wagon, which was a long, low, four-wheeled vehicle about the size and shape of a coffin, paraded down the center of the street without any regard for, if with any awareness of, the traffic problems she sometimes made. Seizing the wagon's heavy, sawed-off-looking tongue, she hauled it after her with a series of impatient jerks, just as though that tongue were the arm of some very stubborn, overgrown white child she had to nurse in her old age. Strangers in town or trifling high-school boys would blow their horns at her, but she was never known to so much as glance over her shoulder at the sound of a horn. Now and then a pedestrian on the sidewalk would call out to the driver of an automobile, "She's so deaf she can't hear it thunder."

It wouldn't have occurred to anyone in Thornton—not in those days—that something ought to be done about Aunt Munsie and her wagon for the sake of the public good. In those days, everyone had equal rights on the streets of Thornton. A vehicle was a vehicle, and a person was a person, each with the right to move as slowly as he pleased and to stop where and as often as he pleased. In the Thornton mind, there was no imaginary line down the middle of the street, and, indeed, no one there at that time had heard of drawing a real line on *any* street. It was merely out of politeness that you made room for others to pass. Nobody would have blown a horn at an old colored woman with her slop wagon—nobody but some Yankee stranger or a trifling high-school boy or maybe old Mr. Ralph Hadley in a special fit of temper. When citizens of Thornton were in a particular hurry and got caught behind Aunt Munsie, they leaned out their car windows and shouted: "Aunt Munsie, can you make a little room?" And Aunt Munsie didn't fail to hear *them*. She would holler, "Hai-ee, now! Whee! Look-a-here!" and jerk her wagon to one side. As they passed her, she would wave her little hand and grin a toothless, pink-gummed grin.

Yet, without any concern for the public good, Aunt Munsie's friends and connections among the white women began to worry more and more about the danger of her being run down by an automobile. They talked among themselves and

they talked to her about it. They wanted her to give up collecting slop, now she had got so blind and deaf. "Pshaw," said
Aunt Munsie, closing her eyes contemptuously. "Not me."
She meant by that that no one would dare run into her or her
wagon. Sometimes when she crossed the Square on a busy
Saturday morning or on a first Monday, she would hold up
one hand with the palm turned outward and stop all traffic
until she was safely across and in the alley beside the hotel.

Thornton wasn't even then what it had been before the
Great World War. In every other house there was a stranger
or a mill hand who had moved up from Factory Town. Some
of the biggest old places stood empty, the way Dr. Tolliver's
had until it burned. They stood empty not because nobody
wanted to rent them or buy them but because the heirs who
had gone off somewhere making money could never be got to
part with "the home place." The story was that Thad Tolliver
nearly went crazy when he heard their old house had burned,
and wanted to sue the town, and even said he was going to
help get the Republicans into office. Yet Thad had hardly put
foot in the house since the day his daddy died. It was said the
Tolliver house had caught fire from the Major Pettigru
house, which had burned two nights before. And no doubt it
had. Sparks could have smoldered in that roof of rotten
shingles for a long time before bursting into flame. Some even
said the Pettigru house might have caught from the Johnston
house, which had burned earlier that same fall. But Thad
knew and Will knew and everybody knew the town wasn't to
blame, and knew there was no firebug. Why, those old houses
stood there empty year after year, and in the fall the leaves
fell from the trees and settled around the porches and stoops,
and who was there to rake the leaves? Maybe it was a good
thing those houses burned, and maybe it would have been as
well if some of the houses that still had people in them
burned, too. There were houses in Thornton the heirs had

never left that looked far worse than the Tolliver or the Pettigru or the Johnston house ever had. The people who lived in them were the ones who gave Aunt Munsie the biggest fool answers to her question, the people whom she soon quit asking her question of or even passing the time of day with, except when she couldn't help it, out of politeness. For, truly, to Aunt Munsie there were things under the sun worse than going off and getting rich in Nashville or in Memphis or even in Washington, D.C. It was a subject she and her daughter Lucrecie sometimes mouthed at each other about across their back fence. Lucrecie was shiftless, and she liked shiftless white people like the ones who didn't have the ambition to leave Thornton. She thought their shiftlessness showed they were *quality*. "Quality?" Aunt Munsie would echo, her voice full of sarcasm. "Whee! Hai-ee! You talk like *you* was *my* mammy, Crecie. Well, if there be quality, there be quality *and* quality. There's quality and there's *has-been* quality, Crecie." There was no end to that argument Aunt Munsie had with Crecie, and it wasn't at all important to Aunt Munsie. The people who still lived in those houses—the ones she called has-been quality—meant little more to her than the mill hands, or the strangers from up North who ran the Piggly Wiggly, the five-and-ten-cent store, and the roller-skating rink.

There was this to be said, though, for the has-been quality: They knew *who* Aunt Munsie was, and in a limited, literal way they understood what she said. But those *others*—why, they thought Aunt Munsie a beggar, and she knew they did. They spoke of her as Old What You Have for Mom, because that's what they thought she was saying when she called out, "What you hear from 'em?" Their ears were not attuned to that soft "r" she put in "from" or the elision that made "from 'em" sound to them like "for Mom." Many's the time Aunt Munsie had seen or sensed the presence of one of those *other* people, watching from next door, when Miss Florence Lovell, say, came down her front walk and handed her a little parcel of scraps across the ditch. Aunt Munsie knew what they thought of her—how they laughed at her and felt sorry for her and despised her all at once. But, like the has-been quality, they didn't matter, never had, never would. Not ever.

Oh, they mattered in a way to Lucrecie. Lucrecie thought about them and talked about them a lot. She called them "white trash" and even "radical Republicans." It made Aunt Munsie grin to hear Crecie go on, because she knew Crecie got all her notions from her own has-been-quality people. And so it didn't matter, except that Aunt Munsie knew that Crecie truly had all sorts of good sense and had only been carried away and spoiled by such folks as she had worked for, such folks as had really raised Crecie from the time she was big enough to run errands for them, fifty years back. In her heart, Aunt Munsie knew that even Lucrecie didn't matter to her the way a daughter might. It was because while Aunt Munsie had been raising a family of white children, a different sort of white people from hers had been raising her own child, Crecie. Sometimes, if Aunt Munsie was in her chicken yard or out in her little patch of cotton when Mr. Thad or Mr. Will arrived, Crecie would come out to the fence and say, "Mama, some of your chillun's out front."

Miss Florence Lovell and Miss Patty Bean, and especially Miss Lucille Satterfield, were all the time after Aunt Munsie to give up collecting slop. "You're going to get run over by one of those crazy drivers, Munsie," they said. Miss Lucille was the widow of old Judge Satterfield. "If the Judge were alive, Munsie," she said, "I'd make him find a way to stop you. But the men down at the courthouse don't listen to the women in this town any more. Not since we got the vote. And I think they'd be most too scared of you to do what I want them to do." Aunt Munsie wouldn't listen to any of that. She knew that if Miss Lucille had come out there to her gate, she must have *something* she was going to say about Mr. Thad or

Mr. Will. Miss Lucille had two brothers and a son of her own who were lawyers in Memphis, and who lived in style down there and kept Lucille in style here in Thornton. Memphis was where Thad Tolliver had his Ford and Lincoln agency, and so Miss Lucille always had news about Thad, and indirectly about Will, too.

"Is they doin' any good? What you hear from 'em?" Aunt Munsie asked Miss Lucille one afternoon in early spring. She had come along just when Miss Lucille was out picking some of the jonquils that grew in profusion on the steep bank between the sidewalk and the ditch in front of her house.

"Mr. Thad and his folks will be up one day in April, Munsie," Miss Lucille said in her pleasantly hoarse voice. "I understand Mr. Will and his crowd may come for Easter Sunday."

"One day, and gone again!" said Aunt Munsie.

"We always try to get them to stay at least one night, but they're busy folks, Munsie."

"When they comin' back sure enough, Miss Lucille?"

"Goodness knows, Munsie. Goodness knows. Goodness knows when any of them are coming back to stay." Miss Lucille took three quick little steps down the bank and hopped lightly across the ditch. "They're prospering so, Munsie," she said, throwing her chin up and smiling proudly. This fragile lady, this daughter, wife, sister, mother of lawyers (and, of course, the darling of all their hearts), stood there in the street with her pretty little feet and shapely ankles close together, and holding a handful of jonquils before her as if it were her bridal bouquet. "They're *all* prospering so, Munsie. Mine *and* yours. You ought to go down to Memphis to see them now and then, the way I do. Or go up to Nashville to see Mr. Will. I understand he's got an even finer establishment than Thad. They've done well, Munsie—yours *and* mine—and we can be proud of them. You owe it to yourself to go and see how well they're fixed. They're rich men by our standards in Thornton, and they're going farther—*all* of them."

Aunt Munsie dropped the tongue of her wagon noisily on the pavement. "What I want to go see 'em for?" she said angrily and with a lowering brow. Then she stooped and, picking up the wagon tongue again, she wheeled her vehicle toward the middle of the street, to get by Miss Lucille, and started off toward the Square. As she turned out into the street, the brakes of a car, as so often, screeched behind her. Presently everyone in the neighborhood could hear Mr. Ralph Hadley tooting the insignificant little horn on his mama's coupé and shouting at Aunt Munsie in his own tooty voice, above the sound of the horn. Aunt Munsie pulled over, making just enough room to let poor old Mr. Ralph get by but without once looking back at him. Then, before Mr. Ralph could get his car started again, Miss Lucille was running along beside Aunt Munsie, saying, "Munsie, you be careful! You're going to meet your death on the streets of Thornton, Tennessee!"

"Let 'em," said Aunt Munsie.

Miss Lucille didn't know whether Munsie meant "Let 'em run over me; I don't care" or meant "Let 'em just dare!" Miss Lucille soon turned back, without Aunt Munsie's ever looking at her. And when Mr. Ralph Hadley did get his motor started, and sailed past in his mama's coupé, Aunt Munsie didn't give him a look, either. Nor did Mr. Ralph bother to turn his face to look at Aunt Munsie. He was on his way to the drugstore, to pick up his mama's prescriptions, and he was too entirely put out, peeved, and upset to endure even the briefest exchange with that ugly, uppity old Munsie of the Tollivers.

Aunt Munsie continued to tug her slop wagon on toward the Square. There was a more animated expression on her face than usual, and every so often her lips would move rapidly and emphatically over a phrase or sentence. Why should she go to Memphis and Nashville and see how rich they were? No matter how rich they were, what difference did it make; they didn't own any land, did they? Or at least none in Cameron County. She had heard the old Doctor tell them—tell his boys and tell his girls, and tell the old lady, too, in her day—that nobody was rich who didn't own land, and nobody stayed rich who didn't see after his land firsthand. But of course Aunt Munsie had herself mocked the old Doctor to his face for going on about land so much. She knew it was only something he had heard his own daddy go on about. She would say right to his face that she hadn't ever seen *him* behind a plow. And was there ever anybody more scared of a mule than Dr. Tolliver was? Mules or horses, either? Aunt Munsie had heard him say that the happiest day of his life was the day he first learned that the horseless carriage was a reality.

No, it was not really to own land that Thad and Will ought to come back to Thornton. It was more that if they were going to be rich, they ought to come home, where their granddaddy had owned land and where their money counted for something. How could they ever be rich anywhere else? They could have a lot of money in the bank and a fine house, that was all—like that mill manager from Chi. The mill manager could have a yard full of big cars and a stucco house as big as you like, but who would ever take him for rich? Aunt Munsie would sometimes say all these things to Crecie, or something as nearly like them as she could find words for. Crecie might nod her head in agreement or she might be in a mood to say being rich wasn't any good for anybody and didn't matter, and that you could live on just being quality better than on being rich in Thornton. "Quality's better than land or better than money in the bank here," Crecie would say.

Aunt Munsie would sneer at her and say, "It never were."

Lucrecie could talk all she wanted about the old times! Aunt Munsie knew too much about what they were like, for both the richest white folks and the blackest field hands. Nothing about the old times was as good as these days, and there were going to be better times yet when Mr. Thad and Mr. Will Tolliver came back. Everybody lived easier now than they used to, and were better off. She could never be got to reminisce about her childhood in slavery, or her life with her husband, or even about those halcyon days after the old Mizziz had died and Aunt Munsie's word had become law in the Tolliver household. Without being able to book-read or even to make numbers, she had finished raising the whole pack of towheaded Tollivers just as the Mizziz would have wanted it done. The Doctor told her that she *had* to—he didn't ever once think about getting another wife, or taking in some cousin, not after his "Molly darling"—and Aunt Munsie *did*. But, as Crecie said, when a time was past in her mama's life, it seemed to be gone and done with in her head, too.

Lucrécie would say frankly she thought her mama was "hard about people and things in the world." She talked about her mama not only to the Blalocks, for whom she had worked all her life, but to anybody else who gave her an opening. It wasn't just about her mama, though, that she would talk to anybody. She liked to talk, and she talked about Aunt Munsie not in any ugly, resentful way but as she would about when the sheep-rains would begin or where the fire was last night. (Crecie was twice the size of her mama, and black the way her old daddy had been, and loud and good-natured the way he was—or at least the way Aunt Munsie wasn't. You wouldn't have known they were mother and daughter, and not many of the young people in town did realize it. Only by accident did they live next door to each other; Mr. Thad and Mr. Will had bought Munsie her house, and Crecie had heired hers from her second husband.) *That* was how she talked about her mama—as she would have about any lonely, eccentric, harmless neighbor. "I may be dead wrong, but I think Mama's kind of hardhearted," she would say. "Mama's a good old soul, I reckon, but when something's past, it's gone and done with

for Mama. She don't think about day before yestiddy—yestiddy, either. I don't know, maybe that's the way to be. Maybe
that's why the old soul's gonna outlive us all." Then, obviously thinking about what a picture of health she herself was
at sixty, Crecie would toss her head about and laugh so loud
you might hear her all the way out to the fair grounds.

Crecie, however, knew her mama was not honest-to-God
mean and hadn't ever been mean to the Tolliver children, the
way the Blalocks liked to make out she had. All the Tolliver
children but Mr. Thad and Mr. Will had quarreled with her
for good by the time they were grown, but they had quarreled
with the old Doctor, too (and as if they were the only ones who
shook off their old folks this day and time). When Crecie
talked about her mama, she didn't spare her anything, but she
was fair to her, too. And it was in no hateful or disloyal spirit
that she took part in the conspiracy that finally got Aunt
Munsie and her slop wagon off the streets of Thornton. Crecie
would have done the same for any neighbor. She had small
part enough, actually, in that conspiracy. Her part was merely
to break the news to Aunt Munsie that there was now a law
against keeping pigs within the city limits. It was a small part
but one that no one else quite dared to take.

"They ain't no such law!" Aunt Munsie roared back at
Crecie. She was slopping her pigs when Crecie came to the
fence and told her about the law. It had seemed the most appropriate time to Lucrecie. "They ain't never been such a law,
Crecie," Aunt Munsie said. "Every house on Jackson and Jefferson used to keep pigs."

"It's a brand-new law, Mama."

Aunt Munsie finished bailing out the last of the slop from
her wagon. It was just before twilight. The last, weak rays of
the sun colored the clouds behind the mock orange tree in
Crecie's yard. When Aunt Munsie turned around from the
sty, she pretended that that little bit of light in the clouds hurt
her eyes, and turned away her head. And when Lucrecie said

that everybody had until the first of the year to get rid of their
pigs, Aunt Munsie was in a spell of deafness. She headed out
toward the crib to get some corn for the chickens. She was
trying to think whether anybody else inside the town still kept
pigs. Herb Mallory did—two doors beyond Crecie. Then
Aunt Munsie remembered Herb didn't pay town taxes. The
town line ran between him and Shad Willis.

That was sometime in June, and before July came, Aunt
Munsie knew all there was worth knowing about the conspiracy. Mr. Thad and Mr. Will had each been in town for a
day during the spring. They and their families had been to
her house and sat on the porch; the children had gone back to
look at her half-grown collie dog and the two hounds, at the
old sow and her farrow of new pigs, and at the frizzliest frizzly
chicken Aunt Munsie had ever had. And on those visits to
Thornton, Mr. Thad and Mr. Will had also made their usual
round among their distant kin and close friends. Everywhere
they went, they had heard of the near-accidents Aunt Munsie
was causing with her slop wagon and the real danger there was
of her being run over. Miss Lucille Satterfield and Miss Patty
Bean had both been to the mayor's office and also to see Judge
Lawrence to try to get Aunt Munsie "ruled" off the streets,
but the men in the courthouse and in the mayor's office didn't
listen to the women in Thornton any more. And so either Mr.
Thad or Mr. Will—how would which one of them it was matter to Munsie?—had been prevailed upon to stop by Mayor
Lunt's office, and in a few seconds' time had set the wheels of
conspiracy in motion. Soon a general inquiry had been made
in the town as to how many citizens still kept pigs. Only two
property owners besides Aunt Munsie had been found to have
pigs on their premises, and they, being men, had been docile
and reasonable enough to sell what they had on hand to Mr.
Will or Mr. Thad Tolliver. Immediately afterward—within
a matter of weeks, that is—a town ordinance had been passed

forbidding the possession of swine within the corporate limits of Thornton. Aunt Munsie had got the story bit by bit from Miss Florence and Miss Patty and Miss Lucille and others, including the constable himself, whom she did not hesitate to stop right in the middle of the Square on a Saturday noon. Whether it was Mr. Thad or Mr. Will who had been prevailed upon by the ladies she never ferreted out, but that was only because she did not wish to do so.

The constable's word was the last word for her. The constable said yes, it was the law, and he admitted yes, he had sold his own pigs—for the constable was one of those two reasonable souls—to Mr. Thad or Mr. Will. He didn't say which of them it was, or if he did, Aunt Munsie didn't bother to remember it. And after her interview with the constable, Aunt Munsie never again exchanged words with any human being about the ordinance against pigs. That afternoon, she took a fishing pole from under her house and drove the old sow and the nine shoats down to Herb Mallory's, on the outside of town. They were his, she said, if he wanted them, and he could pay her at killing time.

It was literally true that Aunt Munsie never again exchanged words with anyone about the ordinance against pigs or about the conspiracy she had discovered against herself. But her daughter Lucrecie had a tale to tell about what Aunt Munsie did that afternoon after she had seen the constable and before she drove the pigs over to Herb Mallory's. It was mostly a tale of what Aunt Munsie said to her pigs and to her dogs and her chickens.

Crecie was in her own back yard washing her hair when her mama came down the rickety porch steps and into the yard next door. Crecie had her head in the pot of suds, and so she couldn't look up, but she knew by the way Mama flew down the steps that there was trouble. "She come down them steps like she was wasp-nest bit, or like some youngon who's got hisself wasp-nest bit—and her all of eighty, I reckon!" Then, as

Crecie told it, her mama scurried around in the yard for a minute or so like she thought Judgment was about to catch up with her, and pretty soon she commenced slamming at something. Crecie wrapped a towel about her soapy head, squatted low, and edged over toward the plank fence. She peered between the planks and saw what her mama was up to. Since there never had been a gate to the fence around the pigsty, Mama had taken the wood ax and was knocking a hole in it. But directly, just after Crecie had taken her place by the plank fence, her mama had left off her slamming at the sty and turned about so quickly and so exactly toward Crecie that Crecie thought the poor, blind old soul had managed to spy her squatting there. Right away, though, Crecie realized it was not *her* that Mama was staring at. She saw that all Aunt Munsie's chickens and those three dogs of hers had come up behind her, and were all clucking and whining to know why she didn't stop that infernal racket and put out some feed for them.

Crecie's mama set one hand on her hip and rested the ax on the ground. "Just look at yuh!" she said, and then she let the chickens and the dogs—and the pigs, too—have it. She told them what a miserable bunch of creatures they were, and asked them what right they had to always be looking for handouts from her. She sounded like the boss-man who's caught all his pickets laying off before sundown, and she sounded, too, like the preacher giving his sinners Hail Columbia at camp meeting. Finally, shouting at the top of her voice and swinging the ax wide and broad above their heads, she sent the dogs howling under the house and the chickens scattering in every direction. "Now, g'wine! G'wine widja!" she shouted after them. Only the collie pup, of the three dogs, didn't scamper to the farthest corner underneath the house. He stopped under the porch steps, and not two seconds later he was poking his long head out again and showing the whites of his doleful brown eyes. Crecie's mama took a step toward him and then she halted. "You want to know what's the commotion about?

I reckoned you would," she said with profound contempt, as though the collie were a more reasonable soul than the other animals, and as though there were nothing she held in such thorough disrespect as reason. "I tell you what the commotion's about," she said. "They *ain't* comin' back. They ain't never comin' back. They ain't never had no notion of comin' back." She turned her head to one side, and the only explanation Crecie could find for her mama's next words was that that collie pup did look so much like Miss Lucille Satterfield.

"Why don't I go down to Memphis or up to Nashville and see 'em sometime, like *you* does?" Aunt Munsie asked the collie. "I tell you why. Becaze I ain't nothin' to 'em in Memphis, and they ain't nothin' to me in Nashville. *You* can go!" she said, advancing and shaking the big ax at the dog. "A collie dog's a collie dog anywhar. But Aunt Munsie, she's just their Aunt Munsie here in Thornton. I got mind enough to see *that*." The collie slowly pulled his head back under the steps, and Aunt Munsie watched for a minute to see if he would show himself again. When he didn't, she went and jerked the fishing pole out from under the house and headed toward the pigsty. Crecie remained squatting beside the fence until her mama and the pigs were out in the street and on their way to Herb Mallory's.

That was the end of Aunt Munsie's keeping pigs and the end of her daily rounds with her slop wagon, but it was not the end of Aunt Munsie. She lived on for nearly twenty years after that, till long after Lucrecie had been put away, in fine style, by the Blalocks. Ever afterward, though, Aunt Munsie seemed different to people. They said she softened, and everybody said it was a change for the better. She would take paper money from under her carpet, or out of the chinks in her walls, and buy things for up at the church, or buy her own whisky when she got sick, instead of making somebody bring her a nip. On the Square she would laugh and holler with the white folks the way they liked her to and the way Crecie and all the other old-timers did, and she even took to tying a bandanna about her head—took to talking old-nigger foolishness, too, about the Bell Witch, and claiming she remembered the day General N. B. Forrest rode into town and saved all the cotton from the Yankees at the depot. When Mr. Will and Mr. Thad came to see her with their families, she got so she would reminisce with them about their daddy and tease them about all the silly little things they had done when they were growing up: "Mr. Thad—him still in kilts, too—he says, 'Aunt Munsie, reach down in yo' stockin' and git me a copper cent. I want some store candy.'" She told them about how Miss Yola Ewing, the sewing woman, heard her threatening to bust Will's back wide open when he broke the lamp chimney, and how Miss Yola went to the Doctor and told him he ought to run Aunt Munsie off. Then Aunt Munsie and the Doctor had had a big laugh about it out in the kitchen, and Miss Yola must have eavesdropped on them, because she left without finishing the girls' Easter dresses.

Indeed, these visits from Mr. Thad and Mr. Will continued as long as Aunt Munsie lived, but she never asked them any more about when they were sure enough coming back. And the children, though she hugged them more than ever—and, toward the last, there were the children's children to be hugged—never again set foot in her back yard. Aunt Munsie lived on for nearly twenty years, and when they finally buried her, they put on her tombstone that she was aged one hundred years, though nobody knew how old she was. There was no record of when she was born. All anyone knew was that in her last years she had said she was a girl helping about the big house when freedom came. That would have made her probably about twelve years old in 1865, according to her statements and depictions. But all agreed that in her extreme old age Aunt Munsie, like other old darkies, was not very reliable about dates and such things. Her spirit softened, even her voice lost some of the rasping quality that it had always had, and in general she became not very reliable about facts.

Two Pilgrims

_____

We were on our way from Memphis to a small town in north-
ern Alabama, where my uncle, who was a cotton broker, had a
lawsuit that he hoped could be settled out of court. Mr.
Lowder, my uncle's old friend and lawyer, was traveling with
him. I had just turned seventeen, and I had been engaged to
come along in the capacity of chauffeur. I sat alone in the
front seat of the car. The two men didn't discuss the lawsuit
along the way, as I would have expected them to do. I don't
know to this day exactly what was involved, or even whether
or not Mr. Lowder managed to settle the matter on that trip.
From the time we left the outskirts of Memphis, the two men
talked instead about how good the bird hunting used to be
there in our section of the country. During the two hours
while we were riding through the big cotton counties of West
Tennessee, they talked of almost nothing but bird dogs and
field trials, interrupting themselves only when we passed
through some little town or settlement to speak of the fine
people they knew who had once lived there. We went through

Collierville, La Grange, Grand Junction, Saulsbury. At La Grange, my uncle pointed out a house with a neo-classic portico and said he had once had a breakfast there that lasted three hours. At Saulsbury, Mr. Lowder commented that it somehow did his soul good to see the name spelled that way. Though it was November, not all the trees had lost their leaves yet. There was even some color still—dull pinks and yellows mixed with reddish browns—and under a bright, limitless sky the trees and the broad fields of grayish cotton stalks, looking almost lavender in places, gave a kind of faded-tapestry effect.

After we crossed the Tennessee River at Savannah, the country changed. And it was as if the new kind of country we had got into depressed the two men. But it may have been only the weather, because the weather changed, too, after we crossed the river. The sky became overcast, and everything seemed rather closed in. Soon there was intermittent rain of a light, misty sort. I kept switching my windshield wiper on and off, until presently my uncle asked me in a querulous tone why I didn't just let the thing run. For thirty or forty miles, the two men had little to say to each other. Finally, as we were passing through a place called Waynesboro—a hard-looking hill town with a cement-block jailhouse dominating the public square—my uncle said that this town was where General Winfield Scott had made one of his halts on the notorious Trail of Tears, when he was rounding up the Cherokees to move them west, in 1838. The two men spoke of what a cruel thing that had been, but they agreed that one must not judge the persons responsible too harshly, that one must judge them by the light of their times and remember what the early settlers had suffered at the hands of the Indians.

Not very long after we had left Waynesboro, Mr. Lowder remarked that we were approaching the old Natchez Trace section and that the original settlers there had been a mighty rough lot of people. My uncle added that from the very earli-

est days the whole area had been infested with outlaws and
robbers and that even now it was said to be a pretty tough section. They sounded as though they were off to a good start; I
thought the subject might last them at least until lunchtime.
But just as this thought occurred to me, they were interrupted.

We came over the brow of one of the low-lying hills in that
country of scrub oaks and pinewoods, and there before us—in
a clearing down in the hollow ahead—was a house with smoke
issuing from one window toward the rear and with little gray
geysers rising at a half-dozen points on the black-shingled
roof. It was an unpainted, one-story house set close to the
ground and with two big stone end chimneys. All across the
front was a kind of lean-to porch. There was a old log barn beyond the house. Despite my uncle's criticism, I had switched
off the windshield wiper a mile or so up the road, and then I
had had to switch it on again just as we came over the hill.
Even with the wiper going, visibility was not very good, and
my first thought was that only the misty rain in the air was
keeping the roof of that house from blazing up. Mr. Lowder
and my uncle were so engrossed in their talk that I think it
was my switching the wiper on again that first attracted their
attention. But instantly upon seeing the smoke, my uncle said,
"Turn in down there!"

"But be careful how you slow down," Mr. Lowder warned.
"This blacktop's slick." Already he and my uncle were
perched on the edge of the back seat, and one of them had put
a hand on my shoulder as if to steady me.

The little house was in such a clearing as must have been
familiar to travellers in pioneer days. There were stumps
everywhere, even in the barn lot and among the cabbages in
the garden. I suppose I particularly noticed the stumps because a good number were themselves smoldering and sending
up occasional wisps of smoke. Apparently, the farmer had
been trying to rid himself of the stumps in the old-fashioned

way. There was no connection between these fires and the one
at the house, but the infernal effect of the whole scene was in-
escapable. One felt that the entire area within the dark ring of
pinewoods might at any moment burst into flame.

I turned the car off the macadam pavement, and we bumped
along some two hundred feet, following wagon ruts that led
more toward the barn than toward the house. The wide barn
door stood open, and I could see the figure of a man inside
herding a couple of animals through a door at the other end,
where the barn lot was. Then I heard Mr. Lowder and my
uncle open the back doors of the car. While the car was still
moving, they leaped out onto the ground. They both were big
men, more than six feet tall and with sizable stomachs that began just below the breastbone, but they sprinted off in the
direction of the house like two boys. As they ran, I saw them
hurriedly putting on their black gloves. Next, they began strip-
ping off their topcoats. By the time I had stopped the car and
got out, they had pulled their coats over their heads, and I
realized then that each had tossed his hat onto the back seat
before leaping from the car. Looking like a couple of hooded
night riders, they were now mounting the shallow porch
steps. It was just as they gained the porch that I saw the
woman appear from around the far side of the house. At the
sight of the hooded and begloved men on her porch—the
porch of her burning house—the woman threw one hand to
her forehead and gave such an alarmed and alarming cry that
I felt something turn over inside me. Even the two intruders
halted for an instant on the porch and looked at her.

I thought at first glance that she was an old woman, she was
so stooped. Then something told me—I think it was the plain-
tive sounds she was making—that she was more young than
old. After her first outcry, she continued a kind of girlish wailing, which, it seemed to me, expressed a good deal more than
mere emotional shock. The noises she made seemed to say
that all this *couldn't* be happening to *her*. Not hooded bandits

added to a house-burning! It wasn't right; life *couldn't* be so hard, *couldn't* be as evil as this; it was more than she should be asked to bear!

"Anybody inside, Miss?" my uncle called out to the girl.

She began shaking her head frantically.

"Well, we'll fetch out whatever we can!" he called. Glancing back at me—I was trying to make a hood of my own topcoat and preparing to join them—my uncle shouted, "Don't you come inside! Stay with that girl! And calm her down!" With that, he followed Mr. Lowder through the doorway and into the house.

Presently, they were hurling bedclothes and homemade-looking stools and chairs through the side windows. Then one or the other of them would come dashing out across the porch and into the yard, deposit on the ground a big pitcher and washbasin or a blurry old mirror with a carved wooden frame, and then dash back inside again. Now and then when one of them brought something out, he would pause for just the briefest moment, not to rest but to examine the rescued object before he put it down. It was comical to see the interest they took in the old things they brought out of that burning house.

When I came up to where the woman was standing, she seemed to have recovered completely from her first fright. She looked at me a little shame-facedly, I thought. Her deep-socketed eyes were almost freakishly large. And I noticed at once that they were of two different colors. One was a mottled brown, the other a gray green. When finally she spoke, she turned her eyes away and toward the house. "Who are you-all?" she asked.

"We were just passing by," I said.

She looked at me and then turned away again. I felt she was skeptical, that she suspected we had been sent by someone. Each time she directed her eyes at me, I read deceit or guilt or suspicion in them.

"Where you coming from?" she asked in an idle tone, cran-

ing her neck to see what some object was that had come flying
out the window. She seemed abundantly calm now. Without
answering her question, I yanked my coat over my head and
ran off toward the house. My uncle met me on the porch steps.
He handed me a dresser drawer he was carrying, not failing to
give the contents a quick inventory. Then he gave me a rather
heavy punch on the chest. "*You* stay out there and keep that
girl calm," he said. "You hear what I say! She's apt to go to
pieces any minute."

The woman was taking a livelier interest in matters now. I
set the drawer on a stump, and when I looked up, she peered
over me to see which drawer it was I had brought and what
extra odds and ends my uncle might have swept into it. On
top lay a rusty fire poker and a couple of small picture frames
with the glass so smashed up you couldn't make out the pictures. Underneath, there was a jumble of old cloth scraps and
paper dress patterns and packages of garden seeds. Seeing all
this, the woman opened her mouth and smiled vacantly, perhaps a little contemptuously. She was so close to me that I became aware of the sweetness of her breath! I could not have
imagined that her breath would be sweet. Though the skin on
her forehead and on her high cheekbones was clear and very
fair, there were ugly pimples on her chin and at the corners of
her mouth. Her dark hair was wet from the drizzle of rain
and was pushed behind her ears and hung in clumps over the
collar of her soiled denim jacket. She was breathing heavily
through her parted lips. Presently, when our eyes met, I
thought I detected a certain momentary gleefulness in her expression. But her glance darted back toward the house at once.

The two men had pressed on beyond the front rooms and
into the ell of the house. Now the woman took a couple of
steps in order to look through one of the front windows and
perhaps catch a glimpse of them back there.

"We were coming from Memphis," I said. "We're *from*

Memphis." But she seemed no longer interested in that subject.

"It's no use what they're doing," she said. "Unless they like it."

"It's all right," I said, still hoping to distract her. "We're on our way to a place in Alabama."

"They your bosses?" she asked. She couldn't take her eyes off the window.

"No, it's my uncle and his lawyer."

"Well, they're right active," she commented. "But there ain't nothing in there worth their bustle and bother. Yet some folks like to take chances. It's just the worst lot of junk in there. We heired this place from my grandma when she passed on last spring; the junk was all hern."

Just then, Mr. Lowder and my uncle came running from the house. Each of them was carrying a coal-oil lamp, his right hand supporting the base of the lamp and his left clamped protectively on the fragile chimney. I almost burst out laughing.

"It's gotten too hot in there," Mr. Lowder said. "We'll have to stop."

When they had set down their lamps, they began examining each other's coats, making sure they weren't on fire. Next, they tossed their coats on the bare ground and set about pulling some of the rescued articles farther from the house. I went forward to help, and the woman followed. She didn't follow to help, however. Apparently, she was only curious to see which of her possessions these men had deemed worth saving. She looked at everything she came to with almost a disappointed expression. Then Mr. Lowder picked up an enamelled object, and I noticed that as he inspected it a deep frown appeared on his brow. He held the thing up for my uncle to see, and I imagined for a moment that he was trying to draw laughter from all of us. It was a child's chamber pot, not much larger than a beer mug. "Did you bring this out?" Mr. Lowder asked my uncle.

My uncle nodded, and, still bending over, he studied the pot for a second, showing that he had not really identified it before. Then he looked at the woman. "Where's your child, Ma'am?" he asked in a quiet voice.

The woman gaped at him as though she didn't understand what he was talking about. She shifted her eyes to the tiny pot that Mr. Lowder was still holding aloft. Now her mouth dropped wide open, and at the same time her lips drew back in such a way that her bad teeth were exposed for the first time. It was impossible not to think of a death's-head. At that instant, the whole surface of the shingled roof on the side of the house where we were standing burst into flames.

A few minutes before this, the rain had ceased altogether, and now it was as though someone had suddenly doused the roof with kerosene. My back was to the house, but I heard a loud "swoosh" and I spun around in that direction. Then I heard the woman cry out and I spun back again. Mr. Lowder set the chamber pot on the ground and began moving rather cautiously toward her. My uncle stood motionless, watching her as though she were an animal that might bolt. As Mr. Lowder came toward her, she took a step backward, and then she wailed, "My baby! Oh, Lord, my baby! He's in thar!" Mr. Lowder seized her by the wrist and simultaneously gave us a quick glance over his shoulder.

My uncle snatched up a ragged homespun blanket from the ground and threw it over his head. I seized a patchwork quilt that had been underneath the blanket, and this time I followed him inside the house. Even in the two front rooms it was like a blast furnace, and I felt I might faint. The smoke was so dense that you couldn't see anything an arm's length away. But my uncle had been in those two front rooms and he knew there was no baby there. With me at his heels, he ran right on through and into the first room in the ell, where there wasn't so much smoke—only raw flames eating away at the wall toward the rear. The windowlights had burst from the heat in there, and there was a hole in the ceiling, so that you could look right up through the flames to the sky. But my eyes were smarting so that I couldn't really see anything in the room, and I was coughing so hard that I couldn't stand up straight. My uncle was coughing, too, but he could still manage to look about. He made two complete turns around the room and then he headed us on into the kitchen. There wasn't anything recognizable to me in the kitchen except the black range. One of the two window frames fell in as we ran through. The next instant, after we had leaped across the burning floor boards and had jumped off the back stoop of the house, the rafters and the whole roof above the kitchen came down.

There must have been a tremendous crash, though I hardly heard it. Even before my uncle and I could shed our smoldering blankets, we saw the man coming toward us from the barn. "You're afire!" he called out to us. But we had already dropped the blankets before I understood what he was saying. He was jogging along toward us. One of his legs was shorter than the other, and he couldn't move very fast. Under one arm he was carrying a little towheaded child of not more than two years. He held it exactly as though it might be a sack of corn meal he was bringing up from the barn.

"Do you have another baby?" my uncle shouted at him.

"No, narry other," the man replied.

My uncle looked at me. He was coughing still, but at the same time he was smiling and shaking his head. "You all right?" he asked me. He gave my clothes a quick once-over, and I did the same for him. We had somehow got through the house without any damage, even to our shoes or our trouser legs.

By the time the man came up to the house, my uncle had dashed off to tell the woman her baby was safe. I tried to explain to the man about the mistake his wife had made. "Your wife thought your baby was in the house," I said.

He was a stocky, black-haired man, wearing overalls and a long-sleeved undershirt. "She *whut?*" he said, looking at me darkly. He glanced up briefly at the flames, which were now leaping twenty or thirty feet above the framework of the kitchen. Then he set out again, in the same jogging pace, toward the front of the house. I caught a glimpse of the baby's intense blue eyes gazing up at the smoke and flames.

"She thought the baby was inside the house," I said, following the man at a trot.

"Like hell she did!" he said under his breath but loud enough for me to hear.

As we rounded the corner of the house, I heard my uncle call out to the woman that her baby was safe. She was seated on a stump with her face hidden in her hands. My uncle and Mr. Lowder once again began pulling rescued objects farther away from the house. As the man passed him, Mr. Lowder looked up and said, "Did you get all the stock out?"

"Yup," said the man.

"I guess you're lucky there's no wind," Mr. Lowder said.

And my uncle said, "It must have started in the kitchen and spread through the attic. You didn't have any water drawn?"

The man stopped for a second and looked at my uncle. He shifted the baby from one hip to the other. "The pump's broke," he said. "It was about wore out, and *she* broke it for good this morning."

"Isn't that the way it goes," my uncle said sympathetically, shaking his head.

Then, still carrying the baby, the man shuffled on toward his wife. The woman kept her face hidden in her hands, but I think she heard him coming. Neither of them seemed to have any awareness that their house and most of their possessions were at that moment going up in flames. I was watching the man when he got to her. He still had the baby under his arm. I saw him draw back his free hand, and saw the hand come down in a resounding slap on the back of her head. It knocked her right off the stump. She hit the ground in a sitting position and still she didn't look up at her husband. "J'you aim to git them fellows burnt alive?" he thundered.

Mr. Lowder and my uncle must have been watching, too, because we all three ran forward at the same moment. "Lay off that!" Mr. Lowder bellowed. "Just lay off, now!"

"She knowed this here young'un warn't in no house!" the man said, twisting the baby to his shoulder. "I reckoned she'd like as not lose her head. That's how come I carried him with me, and I told her plain as daylight I was a-goin' to."

"Now, you look here, Mister," my uncle said, "the girl was just scared. She didn't know what she was saying."

"Probably she couldn't remember, in her fright," Mr. Lowder said.

The man stood staring down at his wife. "She's feared of her own shadow, and that's how come I carried him to the barn."

"Well, you're not going to beat her with us here," Mr. Lowder said firmly. "She was scared out of her wits, that's all."

"Who sent y' all out here?" the man asked my uncle, turning his back on Mr. Lowder. "Ain't they goan send no fire engine?"

It was as he spoke the word that we heard the fire truck coming. The whine of the siren must have first reached us from a point three or four miles distant, because at least five minutes elapsed before the fire truck and the two carloads of volunteers arrived. It turned out that somebody else had stopped by before we did and had hurried on to the next town to give the alarm. I thought it strange that the woman hadn't told us earlier that they were expecting help from town. But, of course, there was little about the woman's behavior that didn't seem passing strange to me.

As soon as we heard the siren, she began pushing herself up from the ground. Without a glance at any of the rest of us, she went directly to her husband and snatched the baby from him. The baby's little face was dirty, and there were wide streaks on it, where some while earlier there must have been a flow of tears. But his eyes were dry now and wore a glazed look. He seemed to stare up at the flaming house with total indifference. Almost as soon as he was in his mother's arms, he placed his chin on the shoulder of her denim jacket and quietly closed his eyes. He seemed to have fallen asleep at once. With her baby in her arms, the woman strode away into the adjoining field, among the smoking stumps and toward the edge of the pinewoods. There she stopped, at the edge of the woods, and there she remained standing, with her back turned toward the house and toward us and toward all the activity that ensued after the fire truck and the other cars arrived. She was still standing there, with the baby on her shoulder, when we left the scene.

We stayed on for only a few minutes after the local fire brigade arrived. Mr. Lowder and my uncle could see that their work here was done and they were mindful of the pressing business that they hoped to transact in Alabama that afternoon. We lingered just long enough to see most of the articles they had rescued from the flames thoroughly soaked with water. The sight must have been disheartening to them, but they didn't speak of it. The inexpert firemen couldn't control the pressure from their tank, and whenever there came a great spurt of water they lost their grip on the hose. They seemed bound to spray everything but the burning house. We withdrew a little way in the direction of our car and joined a small group of spectators who had now come on the scene.

I didn't tell my uncle or Mr. Lowder what I was thinking during the time that we stood there with the local people who had gathered. I could still see the woman down in the field, and I wondered if my uncle or Mr. Lowder were not going to tell some local person how suspicious her behavior had been —and her husband's, too, for that matter. Surely there was some mystery, I said to myself, some questions that ought to be answered or asked. But no question of any kind seemed to arise in the minds of my two companions. It was as if such a fire were an everyday occurrence in their lives and as if they lived always among such queer people as that afflicted poor-white farmer and his simple wife.

Once we had got back into the car and were on our way again, I was baffled by the quiet good humor—and even seren-ity—of those two men I was traveling with. The moment they had resettled themselves on the back seat of the car, after giving their overcoats a few final brushings and after placing their wide-brimmed fedoras firmly on their heads again, they began chatting together with the greatest ease and noncha-lance. I could not see their faces; I had to keep my eyes on the road. But I listened and presently I heard my uncle launch upon a reminiscence. "I did the damndest thing once," he said. "It was when I was a boy of just eight or nine. The family have kidded me about it all my life. One morning after I had been up to mischief of some kind, Father took me into the kitchen and gave me a switching on my legs with a little shoot he had broken off the privet hedge. When I came outside again, I was still yowling, and the other children who were playing there in the house lot commenced guying me about it. All at once, I burst out at them: 'You'd cry, too, if he beat *you* with the shovel handle!' I hadn't aimed to say it; I just said it. My brothers kid me about it to this day."

"Yes," said Mr. Lowder. "It's like that—the things a person will say." He liked my uncle's story immensely. He said it sounded so true. As he spoke, I could hear one of them strik-ing a match. It wasn't long before I caught the first whiff of cigar smoke. Then another match was struck. They were both smoking now. Pretty soon their conversation moved on to other random topics.

Within the next half hour, we got out of that hill country along the Tennessee River and entered the rich and beautiful section to the east of it, near the fine old towns of Pulaski and

Fayetteville. I could not help remarking on the change to my uncle. "Seems good to have finally got out of that godfor-saken-looking stretch back there," I said over my shoulder.

"How do you mean 'godforsaken'?" my uncle replied. I recognized a testiness in his tone, and his reply had come so quickly that I felt he had been waiting for me to say exactly what I had said.

"It's just ugly, that's all," I mumbled, hoping that would be the end of it.

But Mr. Lowder joined in the attack, using my uncle's tone. "I wouldn't say one kind of country's any better-looking than another—not really."

And then my uncle again: "To someone *your* age, it just depends on what kind of country—if any—you happen to be used to."

"Maybe so," said I, not wanting to say more but unable to stop myself. "Maybe so, but I could live for a hundred years in that scrubby-looking country without ever getting used to it."

No doubt the rolling pasture land on both sides of the high-way now—still green in November, and looking especially green after recent rain—caused me to put more feeling into my statement than I might otherwise have done. And it may also have had its effect on the two men in the back seat.

There was a brief pause, and then my uncle fired away again. "Every countryside has its own kind of beauty. It's up to you to learn to see it, that's all."

Then Mr. Lowder: "And if you don't see it, it's just your loss. Because it's *there*."

"Besides, a lot you know about that country," my uncle went on, in what seemed to me an even more captious spirit than before. "And how could you? How could you judge, fly-ing along the highway at fifty miles an hour, flapping that damned wiper off and on?"

"More than that," said Mr. Lowder with renewed energy,

"you would have to have seen that country thirty years ago to understand why it looks the way it does now. That was when they cut out the last of the old timber. I've heard it said that when the first white men came through that section it had the prettiest stand of timber on the continent!"

Suddenly I blurted out, "But what's that got to do with it?" I was so irritated that I could feel the blood rising in my cheeks and I knew that the back of my neck was already crimson. "It's how the country looks now I'm talking about. Anyway, I'm only here as your driver. I don't *have* to like the scenery, do I?"

Both men broke into laughter. It was a kind of laughter that expressed both apology and relief. My uncle bent forward, thumped me on the shoulder with his knuckle, and said, "Don't be so touchy, boy." Almost at once, they resumed their earlier dialogue. One of them lowered a window a little way to let out some of the smoke, but the aroma of their cigars continued to fill the car, and they spoke in the same slow cadences as before and in the same tranquil tone.

We reached the town in Alabama toward the middle of the afternoon and we spent the night in an old clapboard hotel on the courthouse square. After dinner that night, the two men sat in the lobby and talked to other men who were staying there in the hotel. I found myself a place near the stove and sat there with my feet on the fender, sometimes dozing off. But even when I was half asleep I was still listening to see whether, in their talk, either Mr. Lowder or my uncle would make any reference to our adventure that morning. Neither did. Instead, as the evening wore on and they got separated and were sitting with two different groups of men, I heard them both repeating the very stories they had told in the car before we crossed the Tennessee River—stories about bird hunting and field trials and about my uncle's three-hour breakfast in the old house with the neo-classic portico.

Their Losses

_____

At Grand Junction, the train slowed down for its last stop
before getting into the outskirts of Memphis. Just when it
had jerked to a standstill, Miss Patty Bean came out of the
drawing room. She had not slept there but had hurried into
the drawing room the minute she'd waked up to see how her
aunt, who was gravely ill and who occupied the room with
a trained nurse, had borne the last hours of the trip. Miss
Patty had been in there with her aunt for nearly an hour.
As she came out the nurse was whispering to her, but Miss
Patty pulled the door closed with apparent indifference to
what the nurse might be saying. The train, which had rocked
mercilessly all night long, now stood motionless. For a moment Miss Patty, clad in a dark dressing gown and with her
graying auburn hair contained in a sort of mesh cap, faced
the other passengers in the Pullman car with an expression
of alarm.

The other passengers, several of whom, already dressed,
were standing in the aisle while the porter made up their

berths, glanced at Miss Patty, then returned their attention immediately to their luggage or to their morning papers, which had been brought aboard at Corinth. They were mostly businessmen, and the scattering of women appeared to be businesswomen. In the silence and stillness of the train stop, not even those who were traveling together spoke to each other. At least half the berths had already been converted into seats, but the passengers did not look out the windows. They were fifty miles from Memphis, and they knew that nothing outside the windows would interest them until the train slowed down again, for the suburban stop of Buntyn.

After a moment Miss Patty's expression faded from one of absolute alarm to one of suspicion. Then, as though finally gathering her wits, she leaned over abruptly and peered out a window of the first section on her left. What she saw was only a deserted-looking cotton shed and, far beyond it, past winter fields of cotton stalks and dead grass, a two-story clapboard house with a sagging double gallery. The depot and the town were on the other side of the train, but Miss Patty knew this scene and she gave a sigh of relief. "Oh, uh-huh," she muttered to herself. "Grand Junction."

"Yes, sweet old Grand Junction," came a soft whisper.

For an instant Miss Patty could not locate the speaker. Then she became aware of a very tiny lady, dressed in black, seated right beside where she stood; indeed, she was leaning almost directly across the lady's lap. Miss Patty brought herself up straight, throwing her shoulders back and her heavy, square chin into the air, and said, "I was not aware that this section was occupied."

"Why, now, of course you weren't—of course you weren't, my dear," said the tiny lady. She was such an inconspicuous little soul that her presence could not alter the impression that there were only Memphis business-people in the car.

"I didn't know you were there," Miss Patty explained again.

"Why, of course you didn't."

"It was very rude of me," Miss Patty said solemnly, blink-ing her eyes.

"Oh, no," the tiny lady protested gently.

"Oh, but indeed it was," Miss Patty assured her.

"Why, it was all right."

"I didn't see you there. I beg your pardon."

The tiny lady was smiling up at Miss Patty with eyes that seemed as green as the Pullman upholstery. "I came aboard at Sweetwater during the night," she said. She nodded toward the curtains of Miss Patty's berth, across the aisle. "I guess you were as snug as a bug in a rug when I got on."

Miss Patty lowered his chin and scowled.

"You're traveling with your sick aunt, aren't you?" the lady went on. "I saw you go in there awhile ago, and I in-quired of the porter." The smile faded from her eyes but remained on her lips. "You see, I haven't been to bed. I'm bringing my mother to Brownsville for burial." She nodded in the direction of the baggage car ahead.

"I see," Miss Patty replied. She had now fixed this dimin-utive person with a stare of appraisal. She was someone from her own world. If she heard the name, she would undoubt-edly know the family. Without the name, she already *knew* the life history of the lady, and she could almost have guessed the name, or made up one that would have done as well. Her impulse was to turn away, but the green eyes of Miss Ellen Watkins prevented her. They were too full of unmis-takable sweetness and charity. Miss Patty remained a mo-ment, observing the telltale paraphernalia: the black gloves and purse on the seat beside Miss Ellen; the unobtrusive hat, with its wisp of a veil turned back; the fresh powder on the wrinkled neck.

"I'm Ellen Louise Watkins," the tiny lady said. "I believe you're Miss Bean, from Thornton."

Miss Patty gave a formal little bow—a Watkins from Brownsville, a daughter of the late Judge Davy Watkins.

They were kin to the Crocketts. Davy Crockett's blood had come to this end: a whispering old maid in a Pullman car.

"How *is* your aunt this morning?" Miss Ellen whispered, leaning forward.

But Miss Patty had turned her back. She put her head and shoulders inside the curtains of her berth, and as Miss Ellen waited for an answer, all to be seen of Miss Patty was the dark watered silk of her dressing gown, drawn tightly about her narrow hips and falling straight to a hemline just above her very white and very thin and bony ankles.

When Miss Patty pushed herself into the aisle again and faced Miss Ellen, she held, thrown over her arms, a navy-blue dress, various white and pink particulars of underwear, and a pair of extremely long and rumpled silk stockings, and in her hands she had bunched together her black pumps, an ivory comb and brush, and other articles she would need in the dressing room. The train began to move as she spoke. "I believe," she said, as though she were taking an oath, "that there has been no change in my aunt's condition during the night."

Miss Ellen nodded. The display of clothing over Miss Patty's arms brought a smile to her lips, and she was plainly making an effort to keep her eyes off the clothing and on Miss Patty's face. This uninhibited and even unladylike display reminded her of what she had always heard about the Bean family at Thornton. They were eccentric people, and bigoted. But quickly she reproached herself for retaining such gossip in her mind. Some of the Beans used to be in politics, and unfair things are always said about people in public life. Further, Miss Ellen reminded herself, the first instant she had set eyes on Miss Patty, she had *known* the sort of person she was. Even if the porter had not been able to tell her the name, she could almost have guessed it. She knew how Miss Patty would look when she had got into those garments—as though she had dressed in the dark and were proud of it. And there would be a hat—a sort of brown fedora—that she would pull on at the last minute before she got off the train. She had known many a Miss Patty Bean in her time, and their gruffness and their mannish ways didn't frighten her. Indeed, she felt sorry for such women. "Are you going to have breakfast in the diner?" she asked.

"I am," Miss Patty replied.

"Then I'll save you a seat. I'll go ahead and get a table. There's not too much time, Miss Bean."

"As you will, Miss Watkins." Miss Patty turned toward the narrow passage that led to the ladies' dressing room. Suddenly she stopped and backed into Miss Ellen's section. She was making way for the conductor and a passenger who had evidently come aboard at Grand Junction. A porter followed, carrying a large piece of airplane luggage. The Pullman conductor came first, and the passenger, a lady, was addressing him over his shoulder. "But why could not they stop the *Pullman* at the platform, instead of the *coaches?*" It was a remarkably loud voice, and it paused after every word, obviously trying for a humorous effect.

The conductor was smiling grimly. "Here you are, ma'am," he said. "You can sit here till I find space for you—if this lady don't mind. She has the whole section." He indicated Miss Ellen's section and continued down the aisle, followed by the porter, without once looking back.

"But suppose she *does* mind?" the new passenger called after him, and she laughed heartily. Some of the other passengers looked up briefly and smiled. The lady turned to Miss Patty, who was still there holding her possessions. "*Do* you mind?" And then, "Why, Patty Bean! How very nice!"

"It is not my section." Miss Patty thrust herself into the aisle. "It is not my section, Cornelia."

"Then it must be— Why, will wonders never cease? Ellen Louise Watkins!"

Miss Ellen and Miss Patty exchanged surprised glances.

"Why, of course you shall sit here with me," Miss Ellen said. "How good to see you, Cornelia!"

Cornelia Weatherby Werner had already seated herself, facing Miss Ellen. She was a large woman in all her dimensions, but a good-looking woman still. She wore a smart three-cornered hat, which drew attention to her handsome profile, and a cloth coat trimmed with Persian lamb. "I declare it's like old times," she said breathlessly. "Riding the Southern from Grand Junction to Memphis and seeing everybody you know! Nowadays it's mostly *that* sort you see on the Southern." She gestured openly toward the other passengers. "I'll bet you two have been gadding off to Washington. Are you traveling together?"

Miss Ellen and Miss Patty shook their heads.

"Ellen and I are old schoolmates, too, Patty," Cornelia continued. "We were at Ward's together after I was dismissed from Belmont. By the way," she said, smiling roguishly and digging into her purse for cigarettes, "I still have that infernal habit. It's old-fashioned now, but I still call them my coffin nails. Which reminds me—" She hesitated, a package of cigarettes in one hand, a silver lighter in the other. "Oh, do either of you smoke? Well, not before breakfast anyhow. And not on a Pullman, even when the conductor isn't looking, I'll bet. I was saying it reminds me I have just been to Grand Junction to put my old mother to her last rest." As she lit her cigarette, she watched their faces, eager for the signs of shock.

Miss Ellen gave a sympathetic "Oh." Miss Patty stared.

"You mustn't look so lugubrious," Cornelia went on. "The old dear hadn't spoken to me in thirty-one years—not since I got married and went to Memphis. I married a Jew, you know. You've both met Jake? He's a bank examiner and a good husband. Let's see, Patty, when was it I came down to Thornton with Jake? During the Depression sometime—but we saw Ellen only last May."

Miss Ellen leaned forward and stopped her, resting a tiny

hand on her knee. "Cornelia, dear," she whispered, "we're all making sad trips these days. I'm taking Mother to Brownsville for burial. She died while we were visiting her invalid cousin at Sweetwater."

Cornelia said nothing. Presently she raised her eyes questioningly to Miss Patty.

"My aged aunt," Miss Patty said. "She is not dead. She is in the drawing room with an Irish nurse. I'm bringing her from Washington to spend her last days at Thornton, where she is greatly loved."

Miss Ellen looked up at Miss Patty and said, "I'm sure she is."

"She is," Miss Patty affirmed. There was a civility in her tone that had not been there when she had last addressed Miss Ellen, and the two exchanged a rather long glance.

Cornelia gazed out the window at the passing fields. Her features in repose looked tired. It was with obvious effort that she faced her two friends again. Miss Patty was still standing there, with her lips slightly parted, and Miss Ellen still rested a hand on Cornelia's knee. Cornelia shuddered visibly. She blushed and said, "A rabbit ran over my grave, I guess." Then she blushed again, but now she had regained her spirit. "Oh, just listen to me." She smiled. "I've never said the right thing once in my life. Is there a diner? Can we get any breakfast? You used to get the *best* breakfast on the Southern."

At the word "breakfast," Miss Patty did an about-face and disappeared down the passage to the ladies' room. Miss Ellen seized her purse and gloves. "Of course, my dear," she said. "Come along. We'll all have breakfast together."

There were no other passengers in the diner when Cornelia and Miss Ellen went in. The steward was eating at a small table at the rear of the car. Two Negro waiters were standing by the table talking to him, but he jumped to his feet and came toward the ladies. He stopped at the third table on the right, as though all the others might be reserved, and after wiping his mouth with a large white napkin, he asked if there would be anyone else in their party.

"Why, yes, as a matter of fact," Miss Ellen answered politely, "there will be one other."

"Do you think you can squeeze one more in?" Cornelia asked, narrowing her eyes and laughing. The steward did not reply. He helped them into chairs opposite each other and by the broad window, and darted away to get menus from his desk at the front of the car. A smiling Negro waiter set three goblets upright, filled them with water, and removed a fourth goblet and a setting of silver. "Sometime during the past thirty years," Cornelia remarked when the waiter had gone, "conductors and stewards lost their sense of humor. It makes you thank God for porters and waiters, doesn't it? Next thing you know— Why, merciful heavens, here's Patty already!"

Miss Ellen glanced over her shoulder. There was Miss Patty, looking as though she had dressed in the dark and were proud of it. She was hatless, her hair apparently without benefit of the ivory comb and brush. The steward was leading her toward their table. Without smiling, Cornelia said, "He didn't have to ask her if she were the other member of this party." Miss Ellen raised her eyebrows slightly. "Most passengers don't eat in the diner any more," Cornelia clarified. "They feel they're too near to Memphis to bother." When Miss Patty sat down beside Miss Ellen, Cornelia said, "Gosh a'might, Patty, we left you only two seconds ago and here you are dressed and in your right mind. How do you do it?"

They received their menus, and when they had ordered, Miss Patty smiled airily. "I'm always in my right mind, Cornelia, and I don't reckon I've ever been 'dressed' in my life." As she said "dressed," her eyes traveled from the three-cornered hat to the brocaded bosom of Cornelia's rust-colored dress.

Cornelia looked out the window, silently vowing not to speak again during the meal, or, since speaking was for her the most irresistible of all life's temptations, at least not to let herself speak sharply to either of these crotchety old maids. She sat looking out the window, thanking her stars for the great good luck of being Mrs. Jake Werner, of Memphis, instead of an embittered old maid from Grand Junction.

Miss Ellen was also looking out the window. "Doesn't it look bleak?" she said, referring to the brown-and-gray fields under an overcast sky.

"Oh, doesn't it!" Cornelia agreed at once, revealing that Miss Ellen had guessed her very thoughts.

"It *is* bleak," Miss Patty said. "See how it's washed. This land along here didn't use to look like that." The two others nodded agreement, each remembering how it had used to look. "This used to be fine land," she continued, "but it seems to me that all West Tennessee is washing away. Look at those gullies! And not a piece of brush piled in them." Miss Ellen and Cornelia shook their heads vaguely; they were not really certain why there should be brush in the gullies. Cornelia discovered that a glass of tomato juice had been set before her and she began pouring salt into it. Miss Ellen was eating her oatmeal. Miss Patty took a sip from her first cup of coffee. She had specified that it be brought in a cup instead of a pot. It was black and a little cool, the way she liked it. She peered out the window again and pursued her discourse warmly. "And the towns! Look! We're going through Moscow. It's a shambles. Why, half the square's been torn away, and the rest ought to be. Mind you, we went through La Grange without even noticing it. They used to be good towns, fine towns."

"Lovely towns!" responded Miss Ellen. The thought of the vanishing towns touched her.

"There was something about them," Cornelia said, groping. "An atmosphere, I think."

Miss Patty cleared her throat and defined it: "The atmosphere of a prosperous and civilized existence."

Miss Ellen looked bewildered, and Cornelia frowned thoughtfully and pursed her lips. Presently Cornelia said profoundly, "All the business has gone to Memphis."

"Yes," Miss Patty said. "Indeed it has!"

They were being served their main course now. Cornelia looked at her trout and said to the waiter, "It looks delicious. Did you cook this, boy?"

"No, ma'am," the waiter said cheerfully.

"Well, it looks delicious. The same old Southern Railway cooking.

Miss Patty and Miss Ellen had scrambled eggs and ham. Miss Patty eyed hers critically. "The Southern Railway didn't use to cook eggs this way," she said. "And it's no improvement."

Miss Ellen leaned forward and bent her neck in order to look directly up into Miss Pattys' face. "Why, now, you probably like them country style, with some white showing," she said. "*These* are what my niece calls Toddle House style. They cook them with milk, of course. They're a little like an omelet." The subject held great interest for her, and she was happy to be able to inform Miss Patty. "And you don't break them into such a hot pan. You don't really break them in the pan, that is." Miss Patty was reaching across Miss Ellen's plate for the pepper. Miss Ellen said no more about the eggs. She busied herself with a small silver box of saccharin, prying the lid open with her fingernail. She saw Cornelia looking at the box and said, "It was my grandmother's snuffbox. For years it was just a keepsake, but now I carry my tablets in it."

The old box, which Miss Patty was now examining admiringly, somehow made Cornelia return to the subject they had left off. "In my grandmother's day, there was a lot of life in this section—entertainment and social life. My own mother used to say, 'In Mama's day, there were people in the country; in my day, there were people in town; now there's nobody.' "

Miss Patty gazed at Cornelia with astonishment. "Your mother was a very wise woman, Cornelia," she said.

"That's a moot question," Cornelia answered. Now they were on a subject that she was sure she knew something about, and she threw caution to the wind. She spoke excitedly and seemed to begin every sentence without knowing how it would end. "My mother is dead now, and I don't mean to ever say another word against her, but just because she is dead, I don't intend to start deceiving myself. The fact remains that she was opinionated and narrow and mentally cruel to her children and her husband and was tied to things that were over and done with before she was born. She's dead now, but I shall make no pretense of mourning someone I did not love. We don't mourn people we don't love. It's not honest."

"No, we don't, do we?" Miss Ellen said sympathetically.

"I beg to differ with you," Miss Patty said with the merest suggestion of a smile. She, too, felt on firm ground. She had already mourned the deaths of all her immediate family and of most of her near kin. She addressed her remarks to Miss Ellen. "Mourning is an obligation. We only mourn those with whom we have some real connection, people who have represented something important and fundamental in our lives."

Miss Ellen was determined to find agreement. "Of course, of course—you are speaking of wearing black."

"I am not speaking of the symbol. I am speaking of the mourning itself. I shall mourn the loss of my aunt when she goes, because she is my aunt, because she is the last of my

aunts, and particularly because she is an aunt who has maintained a worthwhile position in the world."

Miss Ellen gasped. "Oh, no, Miss Bean! Not because of her
position in the world!"

"Don't mistake me, Miss Watkins."

"I beg you to reconsider. Why, why—" She fumbled, and
Miss Patty waited. "Now that Mother's gone, I've lost nearly
everybody, and it has always been my part and my privilege
to look after the sick in our family. My two older brothers
never married; they were quiet, simple, home-loving men,
who made little stir in the world, content to live there in the
house with Mother and Nora and me after Father was gone.
And Nora, my only sister, developed melancholia. One morning, she could just not finish lacing her high shoes, and after
that she seldom left the house or saw anybody. What I want
to say is that we also had a younger brother, who was a distinguished professor at Knoxville, with four beautiful children. You see, I've lost them all, one by one, and it's been no
different whether they were distinguished or not. I can't conceive—" She stopped suddenly, in real confusion.

"Don't mistake me," Miss Patty said calmly. "I am speaking of my aunt's moral position in the world."

"Why, of course you are," said Miss Ellen, still out of
breath.

"My aunt has been an indomitable character," Miss Patty
continued. "Her husband died during his first term in Con-
gress, forty years ago, and she has felt it her duty to remain
in Washington ever since. With very slight means, she has
maintained herself there in the right manner through all the
years, returning to Thornton every summer, enduring the
heat and the inconvenience, with no definite place of abode,
visiting the kin, subjecting herself to the role of the indigent
relation, so that she could afford to return to Washington in
the fall. Her passing will be a loss to us all, for through her
wit and charm she was an influence on Capitol Hill. In a

sense, she represented our district in Washington as none of
our elected officials has done since the days of"—bowing her
head deferentially toward Miss Ellen—"of David Crockett."

"What a marvelous woman!" exclaimed Miss Ellen.

Cornelia looked at Miss Ellen to see whether she meant
Miss Patty's aunt or Miss Patty. She had been marveling privately at Miss Patty's flow of speech, and reflected that she
could already see it in print in the county paper's obituary
column. "If my mother had been a person of such wit and
charm," she said, "I would mourn her, too."

"I never knew your mother," Miss Patty replied, "but
from what you say I can easily guess the sort of woman she
was. I would mourn her passing if I were in your shoes, Cornelia. She wanted to retain the standards of a past era, a better era for all of us. A person can't do that and be a pleasant,
charming personality and the darling of a family."

"All I know," said Cornelia, taking the last bite of her
trout, "is that my young-ladyhood was a misery under that
woman's roof and in that town." She glanced dreamily out
the window. The train was speeding through the same sort
of country as before, perhaps a little more hilly, a little more
eroded. It sped through small towns and past solitary stations
where only the tiresome afternoon local stopped—Rossville,
Collierville, Bailey, Forest Hill. Cornelia saw a two-story
farmhouse that was painted up only to the level of the second
story. "That house has been that way as long as I can remember," she said, and smiled. "Why do you suppose they don't
make them a ladder, or lean out the upstairs windows?"
Then, still looking out at the dismal landscape—the unculti-
vated land growing up in sweet gum and old field pine, with
a gutted mud road crossing and recrossing the railroad track
every half mile or so—Cornelia said, "I only got away by the
skin of my teeth! I came back from Ward's with a scrapbook
full of names, but they were nothing but 'cute Vanderbilt
boys.' I would have been stuck in Grand Junction for life,

nursing Mama and all the hypochondriac kin, if I hadn't met Jake. I met him in Memphis doing Christmas shopping. He was a bank teller at Union Planters." She laughed heartily for the first time since she had come into the diner. "It was an out-and-out pickup. Jake still tells everybody it was an out-and-out pickup."

"I don't like Memphis," said Miss Patty. "I never have."

"I've never felt that Memphis liked me," said Miss Ellen.

"It's a wretched place!" Cornelia said suddenly. And now she saw that she had unwittingly shocked her two friends. The train had passed through Germantown; big suburban estates and scattered subdivisions began to appear in the countryside. There was even a bulldozer at work on the horizon, grading the land for new suburban sites. "It's the most completely snobbish place in the world," she went on. "They can't forgive you for being from the country—they hate the country so, and they can't forgive your being a Jew. They dare not. If you're either one of those, it's rough going. If you're both, you're just out! I mean *socially,* of course. Oh, Jake's done *well,* and we have our friends. But as Mama would have said—and, God knows, probably did say about us many a time—*we're* nobody." Then, for no reason at all, she added, "And we don't have any children."

"What a shame," Miss Ellen said, hastening to explain, "that you have no children, I mean. I've always thought that if—"

"Oh, no, Ellen. They might have liked me about the way I liked Mama. I'm glad that when I die, there'll be no question of to mourn or not to mourn."

"In truly happy families, Cornelia, there is no question," Miss Ellen said softly. She stole a glance at Miss Patty. "I'm just certain that Miss Bean had a very congenial and happy family, and that she loved them all dearly, in addition to being naturally proud of the things they stood for."

Miss Patty had produced a wallet from somewhere on her

person and was examining her check. She slammed the wallet on the table, turned her head, and glared at the dimunitive Miss Ellen. "How I regarded the members of my family as individuals is neither here nor there, Miss Watkins."

But Miss Ellen raised her rather receding chin and gazed directly up at Miss Patty. "To me, it seems of the greatest consequence." Her voice trembled, yet there was a firmness in it. "I am mourning my mother today. I spent last night remembering every endearing trait she had. Some of them were faults and some were virtues, but they were nonetheless endearing. And so I feel strongly about what you say, Miss Bean. We must love people as people, not for what they are, or were, in the world."

"My people happened to be very much *of* the world, Miss Watkins," said Miss Patty. "Not of *this* world but of *a* world that we have seen disappear. In mourning my family, I mourn that world's disappearance. How could I know whether or not we were really happy? There wasn't ever time for asking that. We were all like Aunt Lottie, in yonder, and there was surely never any love or happiness in the end of it. When I went to Washington last week to fetch Aunt Lottie home, I found her living in a hateful little hole at the Stoneleigh Court. All the furniture from larger apartments she had once had was jammed together in two rooms. The tables were covered with framed photographs of the wives of Presidents, Vice-Presidents, Senators, inscribed to Lottie Hathcock. But there was not a friend in sight. During the five days I was there, not one person called." Miss Patty stood up and waved her check and two one-dollar bills at the waiter.

Miss Ellen sat watching the check and the two bills with a stunned expression. But Cornelia twisted about in her chair excitedly. "Your aunt was Mrs. Hathcock!" she fairly screamed. "Oh, Patty, of course! She was *famous* in her day. And don't you remember? I met her once with you at the Maxwell House, when we were at Belmont. You took me along, and after supper my true love from Vandy turned up in the lobby. You were so furious, and Mrs. Hathcock was so cute about it. She was the cleverest talker I've ever listened to, Patty. She was interested in spiritualism and offered to take us to a séance at Mr. Ben Allen's house."

Miss Patty looked at Cornelia absent-mindedly. Her antagonism toward the two women seemed suddenly to have left her, and she spoke without any restraint at all. "Aunt Lottie has long since become a Roman Catholic. Her will leaves her little pittance of money and her furniture to the Catholic Church, and her religious oil paintings to me. The nurse we brought along has turned out to be an Irish Catholic." She glanced in the direction of their Pullman car and said, "The nurse has conceived the notion that Aunt Lottie is worse this morning, and she wanted to wire ahead for a Memphis priest to meet us at the Union Station. She knows there won't be any priests at Thornton."

Cornelia, carried away by incorrigible gregariousness, began, "Ah, Patty, might I see her? It would be such fun to see her again, just for old times' sake. It might even cheer her a little."

Miss Patty stared at Cornelia in silence. Finally she said, "My aunt is a mental patient. She doesn't even remember me, Cornelia." She snatched a piece of change from the waiter's tray and hurried past the steward and out of the car.

Miss Ellen was almost staggering as she rose from the table. She fumbled in her purse, trying to find the correct change for the waiter. She was shaking her head from side to side, and opening and closing her eyes with the same rhythm.

Cornelia made no move toward rising. "Depend upon *me*," she said. "Did you *know?*"

Miss Ellen only increased the speed of her head-shaking. When she saw Cornelia still sitting there, casually lighting a cigarette, she said, "We're approaching Buntyn. I imagine you're getting off there."

"No, that's the country-club stop. I don't get off at the country-club stop."

"There's not much time," Miss Ellen said.

Presently Cornelia pulled a bill from her purse and summoned the waiter. "Well, Ellen," she said, still not getting up. "I guess there's no way I could be of help to you at the station, is there?"

"No, there's nothing, dear."

In her lethargy Cornelia seemed unable to rise and even unable to tell Miss Ellen to go ahead without her. "I suppose you'll be met by a hearse," she said, "and Patty will be met by an ambulance, and—and I'll be met by Jake." For a moment, she sat behind a cloud of cigarette smoke. There was a puzzled expression in her eyes, and she was laughing quietly at what she had said. It was one of those sentences that Cornelia began without knowing how it would end.

Bad Dreams

———

The old Negro man had come from somewhere in West
Tennessee, though certainly not from the Tollivers' home
town. Mr. James Tolliver had simply run across him in downtown St. Louis and had become obligated or attached to him
somehow. For two or three years, Mr. James had kept him as
a hand around his office there, no doubt believing every day
he would discover some real use for him. Then one evening,
without a word to his wife or to anybody else, he brought the
old fellow home with him and installed him in an empty room
above the garage.

Actually, this was likely to make little difference to Mrs.
James Tolliver, whom everybody called Miss Amy. It would
concern Miss Amy hardly at all, since the old fellow was
clearly not the house-servant type. He might do for a janitor
(which was Mr. James's plan) or even a yardman (under Mr.
James's close supervision), and he could undoubtedly pick up
odd jobs in the neighborhood. But his tenure of the room
above the garage was bound to go almost unnoticed by Miss

Amy and by her three half-grown sons and two elderly female relatives. They would hardly know he was on the place. They hardly knew the room he would occupy was on the place. Yet during the first few minutes after his arrival the old Negro must have supposed that Miss Amy was a nervous and exacting fussbudget and that every member of the family had a claim on that unoccupied servant's room above the garage.

The Tollivers' garage, having been designed originally as a carriage house and stable, was of remarkable amplitude. When the Tollivers' two Lincolns were in their places at night, there was space enough for two more cars of the same wonderful length and breadth. And on the second floor, under the high mansard roof, the stairway opened onto an enormous room, or area, known as the loft room, in one end of which there was still a gaping hay chute, and from the opposite end of which opened three servant's rooms. The Tollivers' housemaid, Emmaline, and her husband, Bert, shared with their infant daughter a suite of two rooms and bath. The third room had been unoccupied for several years and was furnished only with an iron bedstead and a three-legged chest of drawers.

It happened that Emmaline was in her quarters on that late afternoon in October when Mr. James arrived with the old Negro. Her husband, who was houseboy and butler, was in the house setting the table for dinner, and she herself had just hurried out for one reassuring glance at their four-month-old baby, for whom they had not yet agreed upon a name. When the sounds of Mr. James's car reached her ears, Emmaline was in the room with the sleeping baby. She had no idea that anything unusual was astir, but at the first sound of the Lincoln motor she began moving away from the baby bed and toward the door to the loft room. It was almost dark, but, craning her neck and squinting her eyes, she gave a last loving and protective look toward the dark little object in its cagelike bed. Then she went out, closing the door behind her. She had taken only two steps across the rough flooring of the wide, unlighted loft room when she saw Mr. James ascending the stairs, followed by an old Negro man whom she had never seen before.

The Negro man halted at the top of the steps to get his breath, and, catching sight of Emmaline, he abruptly jerked the tattered felt hat from his head. Emmaline, at the same moment commenced striding with quickened step toward him and Mr. James.

"Is that somebody you aim to put up out here, Mr. James?" she asked in a loud and contentious whisper as she approached the two men.

"Is there no electric light in this room?" Mr. James said sternly.

He had heard Emmaline's question distinctly enough, and she knew that he was not pretending he had not. Mr. James was, after all, Emmaline's and Bert's landlord, the master of the house where they worked, and a Tolliver of the pre-eminent Tolliver family of Thornton, Tennessee, where she and Bert were born; and this was merely his way of saying that he did not desire to have any conversation with her about the old fellow. But why didn't he? Why could it be, Emmaline asked herself. Then the truth about the whole situation came to her, and as she recognized the true picture of what was happening now and of what, indeed, had been happening for several months past, she began uttering a volley of objections that had no relation to any truth: Why, now, Mr. James ought to have given Miss Amy some warning of this, oughtn't he? Miss Amy was going to be right upset, wasn't she, being taken by surprise, with Mr. James's moving somebody or other into her good storeroom where she was planning to put the porch furniture any week now? And besides, weren't the two old aunts expecting some of their antiques sent up from Tennessee? And where else *could* the aunts store their antiques? And wasn't it a shame, too, how crazy about playing in that room James, Jr., and little Landon always had been? Why, the room was half-full of basketballs and bows and arrows and bowie knives this minute unless the boys had moved them this very day!

She was addressing this collection of untruths not to Mr. James but frankly to the old Negro, who stood with his hat in one hand and a knotty bundle of clothes under the other arm. The old man gave no sign either that he recognized Emmaline's hostility or that he really believed his moving in would cause a great stir in the family. He stood at the top of the steps gazing with respect at the great, dark, unceiled loft room, as though it might be a chapel of some kind. So little, his manner seemed to say, such a one as he knew about even the loft rooms of the rich.

Mr. James, in the meantime, was walking heavily across the floor in the direction of the empty servant's room. Suddenly Emmaline turned and ran on tiptoe after him. "Mr. James!" she whispered rather frantically.

Mr. James stopped and did a soldierly about-face. "Emmaline," he said, "I want some light in this place."

In a single moment, total darkness seemed to have overcome the loft room. And at that same moment came the waking cry of Bert's and Emmaline's baby. With her next step Emmaline abandoned her tiptoeing and began stabbing the floor with her high heels. As she passed Mr. James, she reached one arm into the empty room to switch on a light and said, "Now that's what I been afraid of—that we would go and wake that baby of mine before I help Bert serve supper."

"In here," Mr. James said to the old Negro, and gestured toward the room. "And we'll have you a stove of some sort before winter sets in."

The weak light from inside the bedroom doorway only made the wide loft room seem darker. Mr. James remained completely beyond the reach of the light. "Is there no electrical outlet in this loft room, Emmaline?" he said.

The baby had set up a steady, angry wailing now. "No, sir," Emmaline replied softly.

"In here," Mr. Jame's voice repeated. This time the words came plainly as an order for the old man to advance. At once there was the sound of the old man's shambling across the rough flooring, and presently there was the sound of Mr. James's heavy footsteps as he went off toward the stairs. Somewhere in the darkness the two men passed each other, but Emmaline knew they made no communication as they passed. She heard Mr. James's firm footsteps as he descended the dark stairs, but still she didn't go to the baby, who was crying now in a less resentful manner. She waited by the open door until the old man came into the light.

"Who are you, old fellow?" she asked when he shuffled past her into the room. "Who are you?" As though who he was were not the thing Emmaline knew best in the world at this moment! As though guessing who the old fellow was hadn't been what gave her, a few minutes before, the full, true picture of what was now happening and of what had been happening for several months past. Ever since the baby came, and before too, she had been trying to guess how the Tollivers felt about her and Bert's living here on the place with a baby. Did they want them to get rooms somewhere else? Did they want her to take the baby down to her mama's, in Tennessee, and leave her there? She had talked to Miss Amy about the first plan and then the second, hoping thus to find out just what the Tollivers thought. But Miss Amy had always put her off. "We'll talk about it later, Emmaline, after Mr. James decides what he thinks is best," she would say, or, "I'll have to discuss it with Mr. James some more." Day after day Emmaline had wondered how much talk there had already been about it and what had been said. For some reason it had all seemed to depend on Mr. James.

And now she knew why. Mr. James had been waiting to spring *this* on them. It would be all right about the baby if she and Bert would take on this old granddaddy to look after for as long as he lived. Ah, she and Bert hadn't thought of that! They had known about the old fellow ever since Mr. James first found him, and Bert had seen him a good many times, had even talked to him on various occasions at Mr. James's office. But he was such a dirty, ignorant old fellow that Bert had sheered away from much conversation or friendliness with him. Both Bert and Emmaline had even sheered away from any talk with Mr. James *about* him. They didn't like to have Mr. James connecting them in his mind with such a dirty old ignoramus just because they happened to be colored people.

But here the dirty, ignorant old fellow was, standing in the very room that Emmaline had come to think of as her baby's future nursery. Here he had come—himself to be nursed and someday, no doubt, to die on her hands. She studied the room for a moment, mocking her earlier appraisals of it as a possible nursery. What mere trash all her thoughts about it had been. When she had not even *known* that she could keep the two rooms she had, she had been counting on a third. She had been going to make the room that the baby slept in now into a sort of living room. Oh, the window-shopping she had already done for living-room furniture! For some reason, the piece she had had her heart most set on was a drop-leaf table. And how she had pictured the new baby's room, as it would have been—painted the same pink as the old nursery in the Tollivers' house!

Emmaline looked at the room more realistically now than she ever had done before. There was no door connecting it with hers and Bert's room, as there was between their room and the baby's. There was but the one door and one small window, and it really wasn't finished nearly so well as the two other servant's rooms. The walls were of rough sheathing, not plaster, and it would be harder to heat. In the neighborhood, there was a German washwoman who had been washing for people hereabouts since long before the Tollivers bought their place, and she had told Emmaline how the coach- man used to sleep in this room and how the very finest car- riage harness had always hung on the walls there under his protection. The massive hooks, which evidently had held the harness, were still on the walls and they caught Emmaline's eye momentarily. They were the hardware of a barn.

She and Bert were still living, after all, in a barn. And yet she had named this room a nursery. It was the plaster on the walls of her own two rooms that had deceived her. She real- ized that now, and realized that those rooms might never look the same to her again, just as her life here with Bert and the baby would hardly be the same while this old Tennessee hobo was present to be a part of it—to eat with them in the house (it was bad enough eating with the grouchy, complaining, overpaid cook, Nora Belle) and to share their bathroom (he would have to pass through her very own bedroom to reach the bathroom; she resolved that instant to make him use a chamber and to permit him to empty it only once a day). The ill-furnished bedroom and the old man standing in the center of it, now dropping his bundle on the lumpy mattress, brought back to her all the poverty and nigger life she had known as a girl in Tennessee, before the Tollivers had sent back for her. And this unwashed and ragged old man was like the old uncles and cousins whom she had been taught to respect as a little girl but whom she had learned to despise before she ever left home. While she stared at him, the old man replaced and then removed his hat at least three or four times. Finally, he hung the hat over one of the big harness hooks.

The hat hanging on the wall there seemed an all too familiar sight to Emmaline, and the uncovered head and the whole figure of the old man seemed just as infuriatingly familiar. Perhaps she had thought she would never set eyes again on such a shiftless and lousy-looking creature. Certainly she had thought she would never again have to associate such a one with herself and with the place she lived in. His uncut and unkempt white hair was precisely like a filthy dust mop that ought to be thrown out. Even the whites of his eyes looked soiled. His skin was neither brown nor black but, rather (in this light, at least), the same worn-out gray as his overcoat. Though the evening was one in early autumn, and warm for the season, the old fellow wore a heavy overcoat that reached almost to his ankles. One of the coat's patch pockets was gone; the other was torn but was held in place with safety pins and was crammed full of something—probably his spare socks, and maybe his razor wrapped in a newspaper, or a piece of a filthy old towel. God knew what all. The coat was buttonless and hung open, showing the even more disreputable rags he wore underneath. For a moment Emmaline wondered if it was really likely that Mr. James had let the old fellow hang around his office for two or three years looking like that. And then she reflected that it was a fact, and characteristic of Mr. James.

But now the old Negro was hers, hers and Bert's. Miss Amy wouldn't so much as know he was on the place. It was Miss Amy's policy not to know janitors and yardmen existed. And Mr. James—he, too, was out of it now. The final sound of Mr. James's footsteps on the stairs seemed to echo in her ears. The old fellow was nobody's but hers and Bert's.

The baby continued to wail monotonously, and rather dispassionately now, as though only to exercise her lungs. Suddenly, Emmaline said to the old man, "That's my baby you hear crying in there." The old man still had not spoken a word. Emmaline turned away from him abruptly. She went first to the door of the room where she and Bert slept, and then to that of the baby's room. She opened each door slightly, fumblingly took the key from the inside, and then closed and locked the door from the loft side. When she had locked both doors and tried them noisily and removed the keys, and while the baby cried on, Emmaline took her leave. She went down the steps, through the garage, and across the yard toward the house. Just before she reached the back porch, she began hurrying her steps. Bert would be wondering what had kept her so long, and she could hardly wait to tell him.

It was nine o'clock. Emmaline had made a half-dozen trips back to see about the baby. At seven-thirty she had offered her breast, and the baby had fed eagerly for several minutes and then dozed off. It was not unusual that Emmaline should make so many trips when the baby was fretful, except that she could usually persuade Bert to go for her at least once or twice to the foot of the steps and listen. Tonight, however, Bert had seemed incapable of even listening to her reports on how the baby was crying—whether "whining sort of puppy-like" or "bawling its lungs out." When she first came in from the garage, he had asked her in his usual carefree, good-natured way if "that little old sweet baby was cutting up." But when she told him about the old fellow's being out there, all the good cheer and animation habitual to Bert seemed to go out of him for a while. In the dining room, he was as lively and foolish-talking as ever when one of the boys said something to him, but in the pantry he listened only absent-mindedly to what she said about the old fellow and not at all to her reports on the baby. Then, as soon as dinner was over and the dishes were brought out, he took off his white coat and, without stopping to eat any supper, lit into washing the table dishes in the pantry sink.

At nine o'clock, the two of them went up the steps into the loft room. There was no sound from the baby. They crossed in the darkness to the door of the room where they slept. Emmaline was turning the key in the lock when the door to the old man's room opened. In his undershirt and galluses, and barefoot, he showed himself in the doorway. Presently, he made a noise like "pst" and beckoned with one hand. Bert went over to him. There was a brief, whispered exchange between them, and Bert returned to where Emmaline was waiting. He told her that the old fellow wanted to use the toilet. Emmaline stepped inside the room and switched on the light. With her finger still on the switch she looked searchingly into Bert's eyes. But his eyes told her nothing. She would have to wait a little longer to learn exactly what was going on in his head.

Then, upon hearing the old man's bare feet padding over the floor of the loft, Emmaline stepped to the door that joined her room to the baby's room, opened it softly, and went in there and waited in the dark, listening to the baby's breathing. She did this not out of any delicacy of feeling but because she felt she could not bear another sight of the dirty old man tonight. When he had been to the toilet and she had heard him go away again, Emmaline went back into their bedroom. She found Bert seated on the bed with one shoe already removed and his fingers casually unlacing the string of the other.

"Is *that* all you care?" she said belligerently. He seemed to be preparing for bed as though nothing extraordinary had happened.

"Just what you mean 'care'?" Bert answered in a whisper.

Emmaline's eyes widened. When Bert whispered, it wasn't for the baby's sake or for anybody else's but because he was resenting something some white person had said or done. It was a satisfaction to her to know he was mad, yet at the same time it always roiled her that he whispered at times when her impulse would be to shout. Bert would whisper even if the nearest white person was ten blocks away, and in his mind he always set about trying to weasel out of being mad. She regarded him thoughtfully for a moment. Then she pretended to shift the subject. "Didn't the old fellow ask you for nothing to eat?" she asked. "I thought he would be looking for you to bring him something." She had made herself sound quite casual. Now she moved to the door to the loft room, opened it, took the key from the outside, and fitted it into the lock from the inside.

"No use locking that door," Bert said, still in a whisper.

"The old fellow says he's got to go to the toilet two or three times before morning, and he don't have any chamber."

Emmaline turned around slowly. "You sound right mad about things, Bert," she said with affected calm.

"What you mean 'mad'?" Bert said, clearing his throat.

He began to smile, but well before he smiled, Emmaline could see that he was no longer mad, that he really hadn't been mad since before they left the house, that his whispering was only a sort of left-over frog in his throat from his having been mad when she first told him.

He proceeded now to pull off his other shoe. He arranged the two highly polished black shoes side by side and then, with the heel of his right foot, pushed them carefully under the bed. And now, since Bert was pigeon-toed, he sat there with the heels of his sock feet nearly a foot apart and his big toes almost touching. Before leaving the house, he had slipped on his white coat again, as protection against the mildly cool night air, because Bert was ever mindful of dangers to his health from the cold. He was perhaps even more mindful of dangers from uncleanliness. The socks on his feet, the sharply creased whipcord trousers, the starched shirt underneath the white coat, all bespoke a personal cleanliness that the symbolic whiteness of the butler's coat could never suggest. "Well, I'll tell you," he said presently, in his naturally loud and cheerful voice. "I *was* mad about it, Emmaline, but I'm not no more."

"*Was* mad about it?" she said, taking a step toward him. The emphasis of his "no more" was somehow irksome to her. "I tell you I *am* mad about it," she said. "And I aim to stay mad about it, Bert. I'm not going to have it."

"Why, no use being mad about it," Bert said. He dropped his eyes to his feet and then looked up again. "No use my being mad about it and no use your getting that crazy-woman look in your eyes about it. Ever since you came over in the house for supper, Emmaline, you been acting your crazy-woman worst." He began laughing deep in his throat. Then he got up from the bed. In his sock feet, he began walking about the room. "Like this," he said. He trotted clownishly about the room, bent forward at the waist, with his eyes sort of popped out. "You been walking around like this." He could nearly always make Emmaline laugh by mimicking her and saying she was a crazy woman. "You been walking around like 'Stracted Mag."

But Emmaline refused to laugh. "It's not so, Bert," she said. "You know it ain't." She didn't want to give in to his resolute cheerfulness. At a time like this, she found his cheerfulness a trial to her soul.

"Why, you been your 'Stracted Mag worse tonight," he said. He went up to her and pretended to jabber wildly in her face. The 'Stracted Mag to whom he referred had been a poor, demented old Negro woman wandering the streets of their home town when Bert and Emmaline were children, jabbering to everyone, understood by no one, but credited by all with a fierce hatred of the white race.

"Not me," Emmaline said very seriously, backing away from him. "You're the 'Stracted Mag here." It seemed downright perverse of him to be making jokes at such a time, but it was like him. Whenever he was put out of humor, whenever he quarreled with her—usually about her occasional failure to keep their rooms in order, or to keep his clothes in order and clean—or when he complained about some particularly dirty piece of work Miss Amy had set him to, he was always bound and compelled to get around at last to some happy, self-mollifying view of the matter. He could no more tolerate protracted gloom on any subject, from himself or from anyone else, than he could go for more than an hour without washing his hands. Not, that is, except when he was awakened in the middle of the night. Then Bert wasn't himself. Right now, Emmaline could tell from the way he was acting that he either considered the situation too hopeless to be taken seriously or had already decided what was to be done. Anyhow, he had cooked up some way of looking at it cheerfully.

But Emmaline was not yet ready to accept a cheerful view. She pretended to resent his calling her 'Stracted Mag. "Who *you* to be calling anybody 'Stracted Mag. In *my* day she was giddy and foolish like you, not pop-eyed wild." Emmaline was nearly six years older than Bert and actually they had known each other only slightly in Thornton, their courtship and marriage having taken place after they had come here to work for the Tollivers. "In *my* day," Emmaline said, "she was simple foolish, not wild-eyed crazy."

"Naw! Naw!" Bert said in utter astonishment. "How can you say so?" Her contradiction of the picture he carried of that old Negro woman left Bert absurdly shaken. "How can you say so, Emmaline, when I seen her one time fighting a dog in the street?"

"Oh, I don't reckon you did, sure enough," Emmaline said in a tone she would have used with a child.

"You know I did!" Bert said. "Down on her all fours, in the horse manure, fighting and scrapping with that old spotted dog of Miss Patty Bean's. And it was just because she hated Miss Patty and all them Beans so."

"Well, not in my day," Emmaline insisted, stubbornly and purposefully. She stared straight into Bert's eyes. "In my day, she didn't mix with man nor dog. She muttered and mumbled and kept all to herself." Emmaline evidently knew the exact effect her contradiction was having upon Bert. Like the names of other characters in Thornton, 'Stracted Mag's name was on their lips almost daily and had ceased to be a mere proper noun for her and Bert. It had become a word whose meaning neither of them could have defined, though it was well-established between them—a meaning that no other words in their vocabulary could express.

Bert looked at Emmaline reproachfully. He could hardly

believe that she would thus tamper with the meaning of a single one of their stock of Thornton words, or even pretend to do so. He felt as he would have felt if she had threatened to deprive him of his sight or hearing by some sort of magic. She could so easily snatch this word from his vocabulary and render him even less able than he was to express his feelings about things in the world. He saw that in order to stop her, he must tell her at once how easy it was going to be to get rid of the old man. Still sitting on the bed, he reached forth and took Emmaline by the arm, just above the wrist. "Come sit down on the bed," he said urgently. "I aim to tell you about the old fellow."

Emmaline took two steps and sat down beside him. With his hand still on her forearm, he felt the tension of her muscles. She *was* her 'Stracted Mag worst tonight! He often told her in a joking way that she was like that old Mag, but it was really no joke at all. He knew that many a time Emmaline would have left the Tollivers' service or said something out of the way to one of the old aunts if it had not been for him. Emmaline was a good, hard-working, smart sort of a woman—smarter than most anyone gave her credit for, but at a moment's notice she could get a look so bughouse-wild in her face that you felt you had to talk fast if you were going to keep her calm. Bert's mother had been that sort of woman, too. In fact, he felt that most of the women he had ever had much to do with had been that sort; he felt that he had spent no small part of his life keeping Negro women from blurting out their resentment at white people. Emmaline was more easily handled than some, but it was because, after all, she used more sense about what she expected to get out of life than most of her sort did. Like him, she had no illusions about someday leaving domestic service. She accepted as good enough for her the prospect of spending her life in the service of such a family as the Tollivers, provided she did not have to live in the leaking, lean-to kind of shack she had been brought up in, and provided that in her comfortable quarters she might at the same time be raising a family of her own. She and Bert saw eye to eye on that. Emmaline was smart and she was not an unhandsome woman. She was tall and, though she was a little stooped, her figure was slender and well formed, and the proportions of her head and her rather long neck were decidedly graceful. Yet when excited, as she had been tonight, her eyes seemed actually to swell from their sockets, her nostrils would spread until her nose seemed completely flattened, and her heavy lower lip would protrude above her upper lip; at those times her shoulders appeared more stooped than usual, her arms longer, her brown skin darker.

"Look here," Bert was saying. "We going to get shed of that old man. You know that, don't you?"

"What you mean get shed of him?" she asked. There was contention in her voice, but already her eyes showed her satisfaction with what he said.

"I mean he can't stay here with us."

"Who says he can't, Bert?"

"You and me won't let him."

"What we got to do with it, Bert? All I know is we ain't going to stay if he does. Is that what you mean?"

"No!" Bert exclaimed—so loud that the baby stirred in her bed in the next room. "That aint' what I mean. You think we going to vacate here for *him*? Quit the best me or you either has ever had or is like to have?"

Emmaline said, "There's other people in this here very block we could work for—mighty good places, Bert."

"And bring Baby with us?" Because they had not given the baby a name, Bert used "Baby" as a name. "And you know it wouldn't be like working with folks from Thornton."

Emmaline's eyes seemed to swell again. She asked, almost begged, him to tell her. "What we going to do, Bert? He's nasty and ignorant, and living so close. I tell you this—just as sure as Mr. James is a Thornton white man, that old fellow is a Thornton sort of nigger. Maybe where one is there's got to be the other."

"We going to run him off!" Bert said. He had released her arm, but he took it again, and at the same time he began grinning at her. "We going to run him off." He said it with a carefree kind of enthusiasm, as though he were playing a game, said it in a loud voice, as though he were trying to wake the baby or trying to make the old man hear. "Why, we going to run him off just by telling him we don't want him. He'll know what we mean. He'll think we mean worser than we do, and he'll git. And nobody will care."

"Mr. James will care," Emmaline warned.

"Nobody will care enough to stop us. I studied it out while I was washing dishes," he said. "Mr. James has done done all he's about to do for that old man. He allows he's fixed things so we'll be afraid *not* to look after the old man and keep him. But Mr. James's not going to do no more than that. I can tell by the way you said he walked off across the floor of the loft room. Mr. James is through and done with the old fellow. He can say to hisself now that he done what he could. But both him and Miss Amy thinks heaps more of us and having us wait on them than to be letting us go because we run off such as him. Oh, Lord, we'll run him off all right."

Emmaline felt fully reassured, and her eyes seemed to have sunk back into their sockets. But she asked quietly, "How?" She could hear the old man snoring in his room and she could hear the baby beginning to whimper. But before she got up to go to the baby, she repeated, "How?"

Bert laughed under his breath. "We'll just tell him to git, and he'll git."

"When, Bert?"

"Well, tomorrow," Bert said thoughtfully. "And not the day after, either. We'll scare him off while we're new to him, and he'll think we're worser than we know how to be. He's

lived hard, and with harder folks than you and me, Emmaline."

When Emmaline brought the baby in on her shoulder a
few minutes later, her features were composed again, and
Bert was humming softly to himself. He had removed his
white coat and his shirt and had hung them on hangers in
the big wardrobe beside the bed. At the sight of the baby, he
commenced talking a baby talk that was incomprehensible
even to Emmaline. But Emmaline beamed and let him snatch
the baby from her in mock roughness. Uttering a steady stream
of almost consonantless baby talk, he first threw the baby a
few inches in the air, and then danced about the room with
her—he in his sock feet, whipcord trousers, and gleaming-
white undershirt. Finally, the baby's dark, screwed-up little
face relaxed into the sweetest of smiles.

"Don't wake her up no more than need be, Bert," Emmaline protested feebly. "She ain't slept half her due all day."

Bert let himself fall across the bed on his back, holding
the baby at arm's length above him. Now with his muscular
brown arms he was bringing the baby down to his face and
then raising her again like a weight. Each time her laughing
little face touched his own, Bert would say, "Timmy-wye-ea!
Timmy-wye-ea!" And the meaning of this Emmaline, for sufficient reason, did understand. It was Bert's baby talk for "Kiss
me right here."

Later on, after the baby had fed at Emmaline's breast and
had been sung to sleep on her shoulder, she was put down in
her own bed in the dark room. Then Bert and Emmaline
were not long in retiring. After their light was out, they lay
in bed talking for a while, though not once mentioning the
old man, whose intermittent snoring they heard from the next
room. As they so often did, they went to sleep debating what
name they should give the baby. They could never agree
(probably the baby would be called Baby all her life), but
neither did they ever fully disagree about the appropriateness

of the various possible names. They went off to sleep pronouncing softly to one another some of the possibilities: Amy Amelia, Shirley Elizabeth, Easter May, Rebecca Jane.

They were awakened by a terrible shrieking—a noise wild enough to be inhuman, and yet unmistakably human. Emmaline sprang from her bed and ran through the darkness to the baby's crib. So swift and unfaltering were her steps that as she reached her hands into the crib, she imagined that Bert mightn't yet be fully awake. She even muttered to herself, "I pray God he ain't." Yet in the next awful moment, when she would have caught up the baby—except that she found no baby there—the thought that Bert might be still asleep seemed the worst, last terror her heart could ever know. Searching the empty crib with her hands, she screamed Bert's name. Her voice came so shrill and loud it caused a painful sensation in her own ears.

And Bert, who all the while stood in the darkness only a few inches from her, and with the baby in his arms, raged forth at her out of the darkness, "God, woman! God damn, woman! You want to make your baby deaf? You yell at me like that again, woman, and I'll knock you flat on the floor." It was Bert in his worst midnight temper.

His own movements had been swifter than Emmaline's. He had even had to open the door between the rooms, yet had arrived so far ahead of Emmaline that he was holding the baby in his arms by the time her hands began searching the crib. Perhaps he had awakened a moment before she had. It seemed to both of them that they were already awake when the baby cried out, and at first neither had believed it could be *their* baby making such a noise. The two of them had come, as on one impulse, simply to make sure about the baby. All of this, of course, they revealed to each other much later; at the moment they stood in the dark cursing each other.

"You'll knock *who* flat on the floor" Emmaline cried in a

voice only a trifle less shrill and less loud than that in which she had called Bert's name. "Give me that baby of mine!" she demanded. She felt about for the light switch. When she found it, she was asking, "You'll knock who flat on the floor, you bastardy, black son of Ham?" But when the light came on, her voice and her words changed, and so, no doubt, did her whole face. She saw Bert, clad in his immaculately white pajamas, holding on his shoulder the tiny, wooly-headed baby, clad in its white cotton nightgown. Beads of sweat shone on the brown skin of Bert's forehead. His wide, brown hands held firmly to the little body that was squirming incessantly on his shoulder. And in the first moment of light, Emmaline saw Bert throwing his head back in order to look into the baby's face.

Emmaline moved toward Bert with outstretched arms. "Honey," she said in a new voice, "hand me m'baby. Let me have her, Bert."

Bert let her take the baby from him. He, too, seemed to have been changed by the light. "Something's wrong with her," he said. "She ain't made a sound since I picked her up." His eyes were now fixed on the little face. "Look at her eyes, Emmaline!" The baby's dark eyes were fairly bulging from her head, and she was gasping tearfully for breath. "I think your baby's dying, Emmaline," Bert said.

Emmaline seized the baby and began patting her gently up and down the spine. This soon restored the baby's breath somewhat and allowed her to begin shrieking again. Emmaline walked from one room to the other, and then back again. Back and forth she walked, talking quietly to the baby, patting her between the shoulder blades or sometimes gently stroking her little body. Meanwhile, Bert followed at Emmaline's heels, trying to peer over her shoulder into the baby's face. At last the baby left off shrieking, and began crying in a more normal way.

At this change, Bert went to the bathroom and washed

his face and hands in cold water. When he returned, he said impatiently, "What's got in her?"

"She's sick somehow, Bert," Emmaline said. Though the baby had stopped shrieking, still she was crying passionately and with no hint of abatement.

"Maybe she's hungry," Bert suggested in a voice of growing impatience.

"I just tried her while you was in the bathroom and she wouldn't take it," Emmaline said. Then she said, "Oh, Lord," and by this she meant to say it was bad enough worrying over the baby without Bert's having one of his real fits of midnight anger. She thought of stories she had heard, as a girl, of men whipping their little babies when they cried at night, whipping them to death sometimes. "Let him try!" she said to herself, but it didn't quiet her fears. Also, she now thought she heard sounds coming from the old man's room. She had forgotten his presence there until now. What if he should take this time to go to the toilet? . . . Bert would kill him.

All at once she knew for a certainty that the old man *would* come in. Oh, Bert would kill him when he came! Or there would be such an awful fight somebody would hear them in the house and Mr. James would come out and maybe shoot Bert with that little pistol he kept on his closet shelf. All she could see before her eyes was blood. And all the time she was pacing the floor, from the baby's room, where the light was on, to hers and Bert's room, where there was no light except that which came through the open doorway.

"Someway you've got to stop her," Bert said, putting his hands over his ears. He nearly always woke when the baby cried at night, but the crying had never been like this before, had never begun so suddenly or with such piercing shrieks.

"I *is* trying to stop her, Bert, but I can't," Emmaline said excitedly. "You go on back to bed, Bert."

He sat down on the side of the bed and watched Emmaline walking and listened to the baby's crying. Once he got up and

went to the dresser to peer at the face of the alarm clock. It
was a quarter to one. "Aw, she's hungry and don't know it,"
he said after a while. "You *make* her take something. It's
time she fed."

Emmaline sat down in the big wicker rocking chair in the
baby's room, slipped off the strap of her nightgown, and tried
to settle the baby to her breast. But the baby pushed away and
commenced thrashing about, throwing her head back and
rolling her eyes in a frightening way. Now Emmaline began
to sob. "The baby's sick, Bert," she said. "She's afire with
fever, she is."

"Let me walk her some," Bert said, coming into the lighted
room.

"Oh, don't hurt her, Bert," Emmaline pleaded. "Don't
hurt her."

"Why, I ain't going to hurt no little baby," Bert said,
frowning. "I ain't going to hurt Baby. You know that, Emmaline." As he took the baby, his wife saw the look of concern
in his eyes. He was no longer in his midnight temper—not for
the time being at least. Or, anyway, he was out of the depths
of it.

But Emmaline sat in the rocking chair sobbing while Bert
walked with the baby from one room to the other. Finally, he
stopped before her and said, "You cut out your crying—she
ain't got much fever I can feel. Something's ailing her, and
she's sick all right, but your carrying on don't help none."

In the far room Emmaline could hear the old man knocking about, as though he were in the dark. He was looking
for the light, she thought. And she thought, Bert can hear
him too. Suddenly she wailed, "If the baby's sick, Bert, then
why ain't you gone to the house to get somebody to—"

"To get somebody?" Bert shouted back at her. "What in
hell you mean?"

"To get some of them to call a doctor, Bert."

"Go wake Mr. James to call a doctor?" Now the baby began

shrieking as at the outset, but Bert shouted above the shrieking. "On top of him sending that old fellow—"

"Then go out and find a doctor. Get dressed and go out
and find us a doctor somewheres." She was on her feet and
wresting the baby from Bert.

Bert stood nodding his head, almost smiling, in a sudden
bewilderment. Then he went into the other room and took
his shirt off the coat hanger. He was leaning over the dresser
drawer to get out clean underwear when Emmaline heard
the unmistakable sound of their door from the loft room
opening. The sound came at a moment when the baby had
completely lost her breath again. Emmaline commenced
shaking the baby violently. "Oh, Lord! Oh, Lord God!" she
cried out. She was standing in the doorway between the two
rooms. Bert looked over his shoulder. She thought at first he
was looking at her, but then she saw he was looking at the
shadowy figure in the other doorway.

Now the baby's gasping for breath claimed Emmaline's attention again. But even so, the shadow of a question fell across
her mind: Did Bert keep his knife in the drawer with his
underwear? It was a needless question she asked herself, however.

She could not see that Bert was smiling at the old man.
Afterward, she did remember hearing him saying politely,
"Our baby's sick." But at the moment the words meant nothing to her. There, in her arms, the baby seemed to be gagging.
And then Emmaline felt her baby being jerked away from
her. It happened so quickly that she could not even try to
resist. She saw Bert springing to his feet. Then she beheld the
dirty old man holding the baby upside down by her feet, as
he would have held a chicken. Among the shadows of the
room he was somehow like another shadow. Barefoot and
shirtless, he gave the effect of being totally naked except for
some rather new-looking galluses that held up his dark
trousers. A naked-looking, gray figure, he stood holding the

baby upside down and shaking her until her nightgown fell almost over her head, exposing her white diaper and her black, heaving little stomach.

Emmaline felt all the strength go out of her body, and it seemed to her that she was staggering blindly about, or falling. Indistinctly, as though from a great distance, she heard the voices of the two men. The old man's voice was very deep and —she resisted such a thought—was a voice fraught with kindliness. Presently, Emmaline realized that Bert was standing by her with his arm about her waist, and the baby was crying softly in the old man's arms.

"But something *sure* must be ailing her," Bert was saying quietly. He was talking about the baby and didn't seem to realize that though Emmaline had remained on her feet, she had lost consciousness for a moment. "She don't yell like that, and she *woke up* yelling bloody murder," Bert said.

The old man smiled. He was gap-toothed, and the few teeth he had were yellow-brown. "Bad dreams," he said. "Bad dreams is all. I reckon he thought the boogyman after him."

Bert laughed good-naturedly. "I reckon so," he said, looking at Emmaline. He asked her if she was all right, and she nodded. "How come we didn't suppose it was bad dreams?" he asked, smiling. "It just didn't come to us, I reckon. But what could that little old baby have to dream about?" He laughed again, trying to imagine what the baby could have to dream about.

Emmaline stared at Bert. At some point, he had waked up all the way and had become himself as he was in the daytime. She had a feeling of terrible loss for a moment, and the next moment was one of fear.

What if Bert *had* straightened up and turned away from the dresser drawer with his knife in his hand? Yet it wasn't that question that frightened her. It was another. Why had she tried to start Bert on his way to get a doctor? She wasn't sure, and she knew she would never be sure, whether it was really to get a doctor, or to get him away before the old man came into the room, or to get him to that drawer where he kept his knife before the old man came in. Now, in a trembling voice, she said, "Let me have the baby."

The baby had stopped crying altogether. All signs of hysteria were gone. She sniffled now and then and caught her breath, but she had forgotten her nightmare and forgotten how frightened and quarrelsome her parents' voices had sounded a short while before. In the half-darkness of the room, her eyes were focused on the buckle of one of the old man's galluses.

Emmaline came forward and took the baby, who, though she seemed sorry to leave the old man, was now in such a happy frame of mind that she made not a whimper of objection. On Emmaline's shoulder, she even made soft little pigeon-like speeches.

It was during this time, while the baby cooed in her mother's arms, that Bert and Emmaline and the old man stood staring at one another in silence, all three of them plainly absorbed in thoughts of their own. It was only for a moment, because soon the old man asked to be allowed to hold the baby again. Emmaline felt that she could not refuse him. She told him that the baby was not a boy but a girl, that they had not yet named her, but that Bert usually just called her plain Baby; and then she let the baby go to the old man. Whatever other thoughts she and Bert were having, they both were so happy to have found the baby wasn't the least bit sick, after all, that they were content to stand there a while contemplating the good spirits the old man had put her in. The baby changed hands several times, being passed to Bert, then to Emmaline, and then back to the old man. Finally, she began to fret.

"Now she's hongry," the old man said with authority.

There could be no doubt that that was what this sort of fretting meant. Emmaline automatically stepped up and took the baby from him. She went into the lighted room where the crib was and closed the door. As she sat down in the wicker rocking chair and gave the baby her breast, she could hear the old fellow still talking to Bert in the next room. It occurred to her then that all the while they had stood there passing the baby back and forth and delighting in the baby's good spirits, the old man had been talking on and on, as though he didn't know how to stop once he had begun. Emmaline hadn't listened to him, but as she now heard his bass voice droning on beyond the closed door, she began to recollect the sort of thing he had been saying. Off his tongue had rolled all the obvious things, all the unnecessary things, all the dull things—every last thing that might have been left unsaid: He guessed he had a way with children; they flocked to him in any neighborhood where he lived and he looked after them and did for them. Along with the quality of kindliness in his voice was a quality that could finally make you forget kindliness, no matter how genuine. Why, he didn't mind doing for children when their folks wanted to go out and have a good time. Young folks ought to go out and have their good time of it before they got like him, "a decrepited and lonesome old wreck on time's beach." What Bert and Emmaline needed was some of their old folks from Tennessee —or the likes of them—to show them something about raising children, so they wouldn't go scaring themselves to death and worrying where they needn't. Tears of pity came into Emmaline's eyes—pity for herself. It would be like that from now on. She heard the old man's voice going on and on in the next room even after she had heard Bert letting himself down on the bed. She even thought she heard the old man saying that if they didn't want him to stay, he would leave tomorrow. That's what he *would* say, anyhow. He would be saying it again and again for years and years because he knew that Bert would not have the heart, any more than she would, to run him off after tonight.

She got up and turned off the light, and then, with the
baby in her arms, found her way back to the rocking chair.
She continued to sit there rocking long after the old man had
talked himself out for this time and had, without shutting the
bathroom door, used the toilet and finally gone off to his own
room. She went on rocking even long after she knew the baby
was asleep and would be dead to the world until morning.
During the time she and Bert and the old man had stood in
the shadowy room in silence, each absorbed in his own
thoughts, she had been remembering that the baby's shrieking had awakened her from a nightmare of her own. She had
not been able to remember at the time what the nightmare
was, but now she did. There wasn't much to the dream. She
was on the Square in Thornton. Across the courthouse yard
she spied old 'Stracted Mag coming toward her. The old
woman had three or four cur dogs on leash, and she was walking between two Thornton white ladies whom Emmaline
recognized. As the group drew near to Emmaline, she had the
impulse to run forward and throw her arms about old Mag
and tell her how she admired her serene and calm manner.
But when she began to run she saw old Mag unleash the dogs,
and the dogs rushed upon her growling and turning back
their lips to show their yellow, tobacco-stained teeth. Emmaline tried to scream and could not. And then she did manage
to scream. But it was the baby shrieking, of course, and she
had waked from her nightmare.

As she rocked in the dark with her sleeping baby, she shook
her head, trying to forget the dream she had just remembered.
Life seemed bad enough without fool dreams to make it worse.
She would think, instead, about the old man and how she
would have to make him clean himself up and how she would
have to train him to keep out of the way except when she
wanted him to do for the baby when the baby got older. She
even tried to think kindly of him and managed to recall
moments of tenderness with her old granddaddy and her un-

cles in Thornton, but as she did so, tears of bitterness stung
her eyes—bitterness that out of the past, as it seemed, this old
fellow had come to disrupt and spoil her happy life in St.
Louis.

In the next room, Bert, in his white pajamas, lay on their
bed listening to the noise that the rocking chair made. It went
"quat-plat, quat-plat," like any old country rocking chair. He
knew that the baby must be asleep by now, but he didn't want
Emmaline to come back to bed yet. For while he and Emmaline and the old man had stood together in the brief silence,
Bert, too, had realized that the baby had awakened *him* from
a nightmare. He had thought he was a little boy in school
again, in the old one-room Negro grade school at Thornton.
He was seated at the back of the room, far away from the
stove, and he was cold. It seemed he had forgotten to go to the
privy before he left home, as he so often used to forget, but
he could not bring himself to raise his hand and ask to go
now. On top of all this, the teacher was asking him to read,
and he could not find the place on the page. This was a dream
that Bert often had. It could take one of several endings—
all of them equally terrible to him. Sometimes the teacher
said, "Why can't you learn, boy?" and commenced beating
him. Sometimes he ran past the teacher (who sometimes was
a white man) to the door and found the door locked. Sometimes he got away and ran down to the school privy, to find
indescribable horrors awaiting him there.

As he lay in bed tonight, he could not or would not remember how the dream had ended this time. And he would
not let himself go back to sleep, for fear of having the dream
again. There had been nights when he had had the dream
over and over in all its variations. Why should he go back to
sleep now and have that dreadful dream when he could stay
awake and think of pleasant things?—of the pleasanter duties
ahead of him tomorrow, of polishing the silver, of scouring
the tile floor in the pantry, perhaps of washing Miss Amy's

car if she didn't go out in the afternoon. He stayed awake for a long time, but without thinking of the old man at all, without even thinking of what could be keeping Emmaline in the next room.

And while Bert lay there carefully not thinking of his bad dream and not thinking of the old man, and while Emmaline thought of the old man and wept bitterly because of him, wasn't it likely that the old man himself was still awake— in the dark room with the three-legged chest of drawers, the unplastered walls, and the old harness hooks? If so, was it possible that he, too, had been awakened from a bad dream tonight? Who would ever know? Bert and Emmaline would tell each other in the morning about their dreams—their loneliness was only of the moment—and when Baby grew up, they would tell her about themselves and about their bad dreams. But who was there to know about *his?* Who is there that can imagine the things that such a dirty, ignorant, old tramp of a Negro thinks about when he is alone at night, or dreams about while he sleeps? Such pathetic old tramps seem, somehow, to have moved beyond the reach of human imagination. They are too unlike us, in their loneliness and ignorance and age and dirt, for us even to guess about them as people. It may be necessary for us, when we meet them in life or when we encounter them in a story, to treat them not as people but as symbols of something we like or dislike. Or is it possible to suppose, for instance, that their bad dreams, after all—to the very end of life, and in the most hopeless circumstances—are only like Bert's and Emmaline's. Is it possible that this old fellow had been awakened tonight from a miserable dream of his own childhood in some little town or on some farm in that vague region which the Tollivers called West Tennessee? Perhaps, when he returned from the toilet, he sat up in bed, knowing that at his age he wasn't likely to get back to sleep soon, and thought about a nightmare he had remembered while standing in that shadowy room with Bert and Emmaline. It might even be that the old fellow smiled to himself and took comfort from the thought that anyway there were not for him so many nightmares ahead as there were for Bert and for Emmaline, and certainly not so many as for their little wooly-headed baby who didn't yet have a name.

Cookie

Two nights a week, he *had* to be home for supper, and some weeks, when his conscience was especially uneasy, he turned up three or four times. Tonight, she had a dish of string beans, cooked with cured side meat, on the table when he came in. The smoky odor of the fat struck him when he opened the front door, but he couldn't believe it until he went back to the dining room and saw the dish on the table. "Good God!" he said to himself. "That's fine. Where did she get fresh beans at this time of year?"

Presently his wife, who was, like himself, past fifty, came through the swinging door from the pantry.

"Ah," she said, "my husband is right on time tonight." She came to him and undid the buttons of his overcoat, as she used to undo the children's. It was his lightweight "fall coat," which she had brought down from the attic only two weeks before. She took it and folded it over the back of a dining-room chair, as she would have a visitor's. She knew that he would be leaving right after coffee.

He leaned over the dish and smelled it, and then sat down at the place that was set for him. It was directly across the round dining-room table from her place. She stepped to the pantry door and called: "Cookie, we're ready when you are." She pulled out her chair and sat down.

"Shall we have the blessing tonight?" she said, with some small hope in her smile.

"Oh, let's not." He smiled back. It was a cajoling smile.

"All right, then." She smoothed the tablecloth with her fingers.

He served himself from the dish of beans and selected a piece of the side meat. He bent his head over and got one whiff of the steaming dish. "You're too good to me," he said evenly. He pushed the dish across the table to within her reach.

"Nothing's too good for one's husband."

"You're much too good to me," he said, now lowering his eyes to his plate.

Cookie came through the swinging door with a vegetable dish in each hand. She was a brown, buxom Negro woman, perhaps a few years older than her mistress. She set the dishes on the table near her mistress's plate.

"Good evenin', Cookie," he said to her as she started back to the kitchen.

"Yessuh," she said, and went on through the doorway.

His wife was serving herself from a dish. "Here are some of your baked potatoes," she said.

"Ah!" he said. "You *are* too good . . ." This time he left the sentence unfinished.

She passed him the dish. "And here are simply some cold beets."

"Fine . . . fine . . . fine."

"Do you think we would like a little more light?" she said. She pushed herself back from the table.

"We might. We might."

She went to the row of switches by the doorway that led to the hall. She pushed the second switch, and the light overhead was increased. She pushed the third, and the wall lights by the sideboard came on. With each increase of light in the room her husband said, "Ah . . . fine . . . ah . . . fine." It was a small dining room—at least, it seemed so in the bright light, for the house was old and high-ceilinged. The woodwork was a natural pine, with heavy door facings and a narrow chair rail. The paper above the chair rail was a pale yellow, and no pictures were on the walls. There were two silver candlesticks and a punch bowl on the sideboard. Through the glass doors of the press the cut-glassware showed. The large light fixture, a frosted glass bowl, hung from a heavy "antiqued" chain low over the table, and the bright light brought out a spot here and there on the cloth.

She was taking her seat again when Cookie pushed through the door with the meat and the bread.

"What's this? A roast? You're outdoing yourself tonight, Cookie," he said.

"Y'all want all iss light?" Cookie said, blinking, and she set the meat down before him.

"Well, it's—well, it's cold-water cornbread!" He took two pieces of bread from the plate that Cookie held to him.

"Y'all want all iss light?" Cookie said to her mistress, who was selecting a small piece of bread and smiling ingenuously at her husband.

"Yes, Cookie," she said, "I think so. I thought I'd turn 'em up some."

"Wull, I could a done it, Mizz."

"It's all right, Cookie. I didn't want the bread burned."

"Wull, it ain't Judgment Day, Mizz. Y'all could a waited. I'd a done it, stead of you havin' to do it." She put the bread on the table and covered it with the napkin that she had held the plate with.

"It's all right, Cookie."

Cookie opened the door to go back to the kitchen. As she went through, she said, "Lawd a *mercy!*"

His wife pushed her plate across the table, and he put on it a slice of roast that he had carved—an outside piece, because it was more done. He cut several slices, until he came to one that seemed rare enough for himself. "Any news from the chillun?" he said.

"Yes," she said. "Post cards from all three."

"Only post cards?"

She began to taste her food, taking so little on her fork that it was hardly visible.

"Now, that's just rotten!" he said. He brought a frown to his face. "They ought to write you letters. They ought to write you at least once a week! I'm going to write the boys tomorrow and tell 'em."

"Now, please, honey! Please don't! They're well. They said so, and that's all I need to know. They're just busy. Young people don't have time for letters." She eased her knife and fork down on her plate. "They're young!"

"What's that got to do with it?" he said. "They ought always to have time for *you.*" He went on eating and talking at the same time. "These beets are fine," he said. Then, after swallowing, "I won't have that! They ought to write their mother once a week. When I was in med school, you know how much I wrote Mama. Father would have beaten me, I believe, and taken me out, if I hadn't. I ought to take them out just once." He stopped eating for a moment, and shaking his fork at her, he spoke even more earnestly: "And just one month I should forget to send *her* that check."

His wife sat, somewhat paled, making no pretense of eating. "Now, please, honey," she said. "She has two little children and a husband who is far from well. I had a letter from her last week, written while the children were taking a little nap. Remember that she has two little children to look after."

Her lips trembled. "There's nothing for the boys to write. They say on every single card they miss being home."

He saw that her lips were quivering, and he began eating again. He frowned. Then he smiled suddenly and said, as if with relief, "I'll tell you. Yes. You ought to go up and see 'em. You haven't been to Nashville since they were *both* in med."

She wiped her mouth with her napkin and smiled. "No, there's no need in my going," she said. And she began to eat her dinner again.

Cookie came in with a small pan of hot bread, holding it with a kitchen towel. She uncovered the plate of bread on the table and stacked the hot bread of top of what was there. With her free hand, she reached in front of her mistress and felt the untouched piece of bread on her plate. " 'S got cole on ya," she said. She picked it up in her brown hand and threw it on the cooking pan. She placed a piece of hot bread on her mistress's plate, saying, "Now, gwine butter't while 't's hot."

Her mistress pushed the bread plate across the table toward her husband. She said to him, "Cookie and I are going to get a box of food off to 'em next week, like we used to send 'em in military school. Aren't we, Cookie?"

"Fine . . . fine . . . fine," he said. He took a piece of the cornbread and began to butter it.

Cookie nodded her head toward him and said to her mistress, *"He* hear from 'em?" Then she took several steps around the table, picked up the bread plate, and returned it to its former place. She was tucking the napkin about its edges again.

"No, I have *not!*" He brought the frown to his face again. "They ought to write their mammy, oughtn't they, Cookie?"

"Sho-God ought. 'S a shame," Cookie said. She looked at her mistress. And her mistress put her knife and fork down

again. Her lips began to quiver. She gazed tearfully at her
husband.

He looked away and spoke out in a loud voice that seemed
almost to echo in the high-ceilinged room: "What are you
goin' to send 'em? What are you going to send them young-
ons, Cookie?"

Cookie looked at him blankly and then at the butter plate,
which was in the center of the table. "Whatever she say."

"Well, what do you say, Mother?"

She cleared her throat and ran her hand in a series of pats
over her thick and slightly graying hair that went in soft
waves back over her ears. "I had thought that we might get
hold of two fat guinea hens," she said.

"Fine . . . fine."

"I thought we might get some smoked sausage, not too
new and—"

"Ah . . . fine."

"And we might spare one of the fruitcakes we've got
soaking."

"How does that suit you, Cookie?" he said.

Cookie was on her way toward the kitchen again. "Yessuh,"
she said.

He ate in silence for several minutes, took a second helping
of string beans, and another piece of bread. She nibbled at a
piece of bread. She put more salt and pepper on her meat
and ate a few bites. And then she arranged her knife and
fork on her plate. Finally, he put his knife and fork down on
his empty plate and, with his mouth still full, said, "There's
not more, surely?"

She smiled, nodding her head. "Pie."

"No! What kind!"

"I cooked it myself." She picked up a little glass call bell
beside her plate and tinkled it. He sat chewing his last bite,
and presently Cookie appeared in the doorway with two plates
of yellow lemon pie topped with an inch of white meringue.

"This is where she can beat you, Cookie," he said as the cook set the piece of pie before him.

Cookie made a noise that was somewhat like "Psss." She looked at her mistress and gave her a gold-toothed smile. She started to leave with the dinner plates.

"Wait a minute, Cookie," he said. She stopped and looked at him, with her lower lip hanging open. He was taking big bites of the pie. "Cookie, I've been wantin' to ask you how your 'corporosity' is."

"M'whut, Boss-Man?"

"And, furthermore, I understand from what various people are saying around that you have ancestors." He winked at his wife. She dropped her eyes to her plate.

"Whut's he mean, Mizz?" Cookie asked, standing with the two dinner plates in hand.

"Just some of his foolishness, Cookie," she said, with her eyes still on her plate.

He thought to himself that his wife was too good to tease even Cookie. He said to himself, "She doesn't realize that they really eat it up."

"M' coffee's bilin'," Cookie said, and she went through the swinging door.

His wife looked up from her plate. "You know Cookie never has liked to joke. Now, please, honey, don't tease her. She's getting along in her years now. Her temper's quicker than it used to be."

He had finished his pie when Cookie brought in the coffee. She brought it on a tray—two cups and a kitchen pot. She set a cup at each place, filled them, and set the pot on the table-cloth.

"How's that church of yours comin', Cookie?" he said.

"It's makin' out, Boss-Man."

"Haven't you-all churched nobody lately?"

"No, suh, not us."

"How about Dr. Palmer's cook, Cookie? Is she a member in standing?"

"Sho. Mean 'at gal Hattie?" She looked at her mistress and smiled.

He looked at his wife, who he thought was shaking her head at Cookie. Then he looked at Cookie. "Yes," he said, almost absent-mindedly. "He brought her in from the country. That's it—Hattie! That's her name."

"Yessuh. She's from out on Pea Ridge."

"She's givin' 'im some trouble. Drinkin', ain't she, Cookie?"

" 'Cep' *he* didn't get her from Pea Ridge."

"No, Cookie?"

"She put in a year for some ladies he know out near the sand banks, and—"

"She's a drinker, ain't she, Cookie?"

"Yessuh. I *reckon* she is." She tilted her head back and gave him her gold-toothed laugh, which ended in a sort of sneer this time. "She uz dancin' roun' outside chuch las' night an' say to me she want to teach me how to do dat stuff. I tell huh she's drunk, an' she say, 'Sho I is. I teach you how to hit de bottle, too!' "

He pushed his chair away from the table, still holding his coffee, and laughed aloud. He saw that his wife was looking threateningly at Cookie. "What else did she say, Cookie?" he pressed her.

"Oh, dat gal's a big talker. She's full of lies. De way she lies 'bout huh boss-man's terble. She lie 'bout anybody an' everybody in Thornton. She call names up an' down de street."

"What sort of lies?" He leaned forward, smiling, and winked at his wife.

"Them ladies from the sand banks—she say they's in an' out his place mos' any night. Doc Palmer's a bachlorman, sho, but Hattie say hit ain't jus' Doc Palmer! They comes there to meet the ladies—all sorts of menfolks, married or not. She say she see 'em *all* 'bout his place sooner later."

His wife had quit sipping her coffee and was staring at Cookie.

"Who, for instance, Cookie? Let us in on it," he said.

The cook turned to him and looked at him blankly. "You, Boss-Man."

His wife stood up at her place, her napkin in her hand. Her eyes filled with tears. "After all these years!" she said. "Cookie, you've forgotten your place for the first time, after all these years."

Cookie put her hands under her apron, looked at her feet a moment, and then looked up at him, her own eyes wet. Her words came almost like screams. "Hattie say she *seen* ya! But she's a liar, ain't she, Boss-Man?"

Her mistress sat down, put one elbow on the table, and, brought her napkin up to cover her face. "I'm disappointed in you, Cookie. Go to the kitchen."

Cookie went through the swinging door without looking at her mistress.

In a moment, his wife looked up at him and said, "I'm sorry. I'd not thought she was capable of a thing like that."

"Why, it's all right—for what she said. Doctors will get talked about. Even Cookie knows the girl's a liar."

His wife seemed, he thought, not to have heard him. She was saying, "A servant of mine talking to my husband like that!"

"It's only old-nigger uppitiness," he reassured her.

"I shall speak to her tonight," she said. "I promise you."

"Oh, I suppose you'll think you have to fire her."

She looked at him, her features composed again. She ran her hand over her hair in a series of pats. "No, no," she said. "I can't fire Cookie. I'll speak to her tonight. It'll never happen again."

"Now I think of it, perhaps she ought to be sent on her way after talking like that."

"I'll look after the matter."

He poured himself a second cup of coffee and, as he drank it, he watched his wife closely. He frowned again and said, "Why, she might talk to *you* that way someday. That's all I thought."

She smiled at him. "There's no danger. I'll have a talk with her tonight."

She helped him on with his overcoat. He said, "Got to see some country people tonight. Might even have to drive over to Huntsboro." She was buttoning his coat. "There's a lot of red throat over there."

"I can't have her talking that way to my husband," she said aloud, yet to herself. "But I won't fire her," she told him. "She's too much one of us—too much one of the family, and I know she'll be full of remorse for speaking out of turn like that."

He looked directly into her eyes, and she smiled confidently. She told him she would leave the back light on, because lately the nights had been cloudy and dark. As he stopped in the hall to pick up his hat and his case, he heard Cookie come through the swinging door.

"Now, Cookie, I want to have a little talk with you," his wife said, and Cookie said, "Yes'm, Mizz."

He went out, closing the door softly behind him, and as he crossed the porch, he could still hear their voices inside—the righteousness and disillusion of Cookie's, the pride and discipline of his wife's. He passed down the flight of wooden steps and stepped from the brick wall onto the lawn. He hesitated a moment; he could still hear their voices indistinctly—their senseless voices. He began walking with light, sure steps over the grass—their ugly, old voices. In the driveway, his car, bright and new and luxurious, was waiting for him.

Miss Leonora When Last Seen and Fifteen Other Stories

by Peter Taylor

Peter Taylor is one of the rare masters of the short-story form. His works have appeared in such leading magazines as *The New Yorker, The Sewanee Review* and *Encounter,* and one of them has taken first prize in the O'Henry Memorial Awards. His flawless technique makes every phrase a pleasure and his combination of perceptiveness and irony give the reader an amazing mixture of humor, wonder and shudders. The stories are subtle, at times outrageous, and they always create a wonderfully (and tragically) recognizable experience. One concerns the surprising changes of character of a rather unusual school teacher; another, the odd behaviour of a bride. He presents an assortment of intriguing people — they are touching, peculiar, attractive and unpredictable — in stories which make fascinating and highly enjoyable reading.